Germanicus

SCEPTRE

Also by David Wishart

I, Virgil
Ovid
Nero

Germanicus

DAVID WISHART

SCEPTRE

First published in 1997 by Hodder and Stoughton
A division of Hodder Headline PLC
A Sceptre book

10 9 8 7 6 5 4 3 2 1

British Library Cataloguing in Publication Data

Wishart, David
  Germanicus
  1. Germanicus – Fiction 2. Biographical fiction
  I. Title
  823.9'14 [F]

  ISBN 0 340 68282 5

Typeset by Palimpsest Book Production Limited,
Polmont, Stirlingshire
Printed and bound in Great Britain by
Mackays of Chatham PLC, Chatham, Kent

Hodder and Stoughton
A division of Hodder Headline PLC
338 Euston Road
London NW1 3BH

For my wife Rona,
who suggested another Corvinus book.

AUTHOR'S NOTE ∫

'So ended the avenging of Germanicus's death. The subject has been a vexed one, not only for his contemporaries but also for succeeding generations. Some report rumours as established facts, others twist the truth into its opposite; and the passing years augment both distortions' (Tacitus, *Annals*, III, 19).

Leaving aside the question of Tacitus's own shortcomings in this area, the quote is a salutary reminder of the difference between the historian and the historical novelist. Both have an obligation to be accurate where actual events are concerned, but thereafter they part company. To the historian subjectivity, speculation and the attribution of motive are anathema; to the novelist they form the basics of his stock-in-trade. I would therefore plead guilty with reservations to committing Tacitus's first crime, although I am (I hope!) totally innocent of his second. My explanation of Germanicus's death is possible and plausible, yes; I hope it is convincing and it may even be true; but it is by no means established fact.

Readers of Tacitus will notice one minor piece of fudging. Rome had two consuls, and I have been careful to mention only one, Corvinus's Uncle Cotta. Cotta was indeed consul for AD 20, but his colleague was Corvinus himself. This I had to ignore: first because for 'my' Corvinus to hold Rome's top magistracy would not fit the character I have tried to create; second because being in his early twenties he would have been far too young. An even more minor point, but one I feel guilty over, is that Cotta's family name was Aurelius, not Valerius. By common Roman practice he had been adopted into the Aurelii, probably to perpetuate a failing line. This, too,

• David Wishart

I ignored because I needed him to have strong connections with Corvinus.

My thanks to Roy Pinkerton; to my wife Rona and the staff of the St Andrews University and Carnoustie libraries for finding me books; and to Anne Buchanan, ex-RNR, for her help with ships and sailing. Any faults or errors remaining are of course completely mine.

Dramatis Personae ∫

Purely fictional characters appear in lower case.

THE IMPERIALS

TIBERIUS (otherwise the Wart; so called on account of his skin problems): the current emperor.

LIVIA: 'the empress'; Tiberius's mother and Germanicus's grandmother.

GERMANICUS: Tiberius's stepson, lately dead in Syria.

AGRIPPINA: his wife.

DRUSUS: Tiberius's son; currently commanding in Pannonia.

LIVILLA: his wife.

ROME

Agron: an Illyrian metalsmith; friend and client of Corvinus.

Bathyllus: Corvinus's head slave.

Capax: Daphnis's cousin, Piso's former coachman; now a freelance litterman.

CARILLUS: Piso's freedman; now a Suburan butcher.

CORVINUS (Marcus Valerius Messalla Corvinus): a rich young noble with no interest in politics.

COTTA (Marcus Valerius Cotta Maximus Messalinus): Corvinus's uncle; one of the two current consuls.

Crispus, Caelius: a dealer in scandal, loosely attached to the Treasury.

Daphnis: Scylax's slave assistant.

Lippillus, Flavonius: an officer of the Aventine Watch.

MESSALINUS (Marcus Valerius Messalla Messalinus): Corvinus's father.

Meton: Corvinus's chef.

PERILLA, Rufia: stepdaughter of the poet Ovid; now Corvinus's wife.

PISO, Gnaeus Calpurnius: ex-governor of Syria, accused with his wife PLANCINA of murdering Germanicus.

Priscus, Titus Helvius: Corvinus's mother's husband.

REGULUS, Livineius: one of the defence lawyers in Piso's trial.

Scylax: Corvinus's client; owner/manager of a training gym.

Secundus, Gaius: a friend of Corvinus; formerly on Drusus's staff in Pannonia.

TRIO, Lucius Fulcinius: one of the prosecutors in Piso's trial.

Vipsania: Corvinus's mother; now married to Priscus.

ANTIOCH

ACUTIA: Vitellius's wife.

ARTABANUS: current king of Parthia.

Baucis: Martina's sister.

CELER, Domitius: formerly on Piso's staff; now second-in-command to Rufus.

Critias: Corvinus and Perilla's temporary head slave.

Giton: Vonones's former coachman.

LAMIA, Aelius: the current Syrian governor.

MARSUS, Publius Vibius: the Syrian deputy governor under Piso and Lamia.

MARTINA: a Syrian suspected of poisoning Germanicus.

Orosius: a clerk in the records' office; friend of Giton.

Philotimus: owner of the Two Cedars guest house; Corvinus and Perilla's landlord.

RUFUS, Publius Suillius: Perilla's ex-husband; now commanding the Third Gallic Legion.

Sulpicia: Marsus's wife.

TAURUS, Statilius: Corvinus's friend, currently serving as tribune with the Sixth Legion.

Theon: captain of the *Artemis*.

VITELLIUS, Publius: a senior member of Lamia's staff; friend and colleague of Germanicus who helped prepare and present the case against Piso in Rome.

VONONES: an exiled king of Parthia, now dead.

N

CAPPADOCIA

ARMENIA

Taurus Mts.

COMMAGENE

R. Euphrates

PARTHIAN
EMPIRE

CILICIA

AMANUS

• Cyrrhus

• Celenderis

ANTIOCH

Seleucia•

SYRIA

R. Orontes

Laodicea•

• Apamea

CYPRUS

Raphaneae

• Palmyra

0   100

Miles

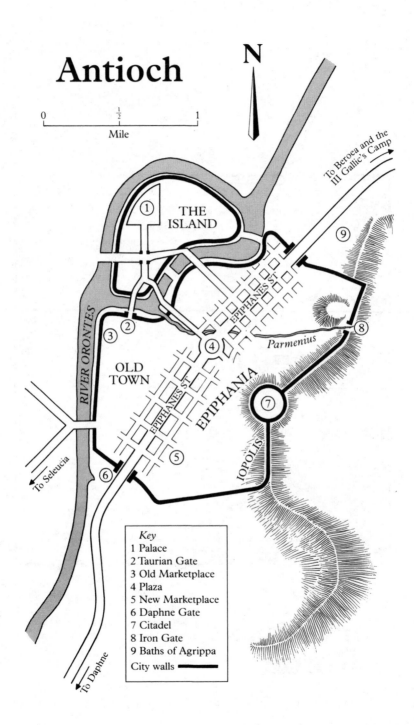

Antioch

0 · ½ · 1
Mile

N

To Beroea and the
III Gallic's Camp

① THE
ISLAND

⑨

EPIPHANES ST

②
③

Parmenius

⑧

RIVER ORONTES

OLD
TOWN

④

EPIPHANES ST

EPIPHANIA

To Seleucia

⑦

⑤

IOPOLIS

⑥

To Daphne

Key
1 Palace
2 Taurian Gate
3 Old Marketplace
4 Plaza
5 New Marketplace
6 Daphne Gate
7 Citadel
8 Iron Gate
9 Baths of Agrippa
City walls ▬▬▬

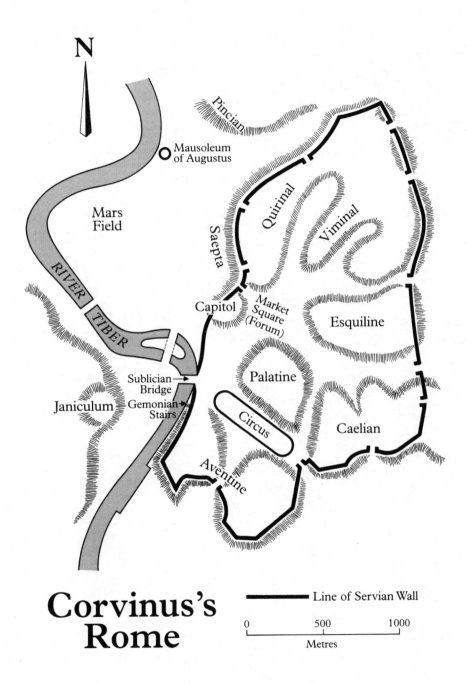

N

Pincian

Mausoleum
of Augustus

Mars
Field

RIVER

TIBER

Saepta

Quirinal

Viminal

Capitol

Market
Square
(Forum)

Esquiline

Sublician
Bridge

Janiculum

Gemonian
Stairs

Palatine

Circus

Caelian

Aventine

Corvinus's
Rome

—— Line of Servian Wall

| 0 | 500 | 1000 |

Metres

So there I was, joy of joys unlooked for, back at the palace for another private talk with the empress. Hermes, the messenger-ape who led me through the maze of corridors to her office, hadn't changed in the eighteen months since I'd seen him last; not even his underwear, judging by the mouldy cheese smell that drifted back and up my nostrils. I didn't make any smartass comments, mind; there're some things even I won't risk, and sassing palace slaves is one of them. Besides, you don't cross gorillas. Not when they can lead you up dark dead-ends where they can work their evil will in peace and shove your head where you won't find it until the next census.

The secretary in the lemon tunic behind the desk hadn't changed either. He gave me a look like I'd stepped in dog puke somewhere along the way and the fact was still painfully obvious, then carried on tidying his already immaculate nails with a slip of pumice, waiting for an introduction.

The gorilla spoke. 'Marcus Valerius Messalla Corvinus, to see Her Excellency the Empress.'

Amazing what you can teach these things, with patience and a bit of fruit. The secretary never batted an elegant eyelash. He consulted his appointments list and made a firm tick.

'You're late, Corvinus,' he said.

'Yeah, well, I . . .'

'Never mind. We're here now, and that's all that matters, isn't it?' He stood up with a flash of insincere teeth and a whiff of hair oil. 'Her Excellency will see you immediately. That's all, Hermes.'

The ape nodded and loped off without a backward glance. Feeding time at the canteen, no doubt.

'This way, sir.' The secretary knocked gently on the double doors, pushed them open and stepped aside.

I recognised the smell at once. Camphor. It brought me out in a sweat. After the last time I'd been in this room I'd sworn never to let Bathyllus buy another mothball again. Old age, old crimes. Livia.

She was sitting behind her desk, as if she'd never moved. The same lifeless cosmetic mask, the same dead eyes. I wiped my sweaty hands on my mantle.

'Come in, Corvinus,' she said. 'How nice to see you again. Do have a seat.'

I pulled up the ancient Egyptian chair. That was familiar, too.

'Your Excellency.'

Her dead eyes focused behind my left shoulder.

'Make absolutely sure that we're not disturbed, Phormio,' she said.

'Yes, Excellency,' the secretary murmured. I heard the doors close with a solid *thunk* and tried not to think of tombs. Shit. She might at least have told the guy to bring us some wine. I could've murdered a cup of Setinian.

The eyes swung back to me.

'And how is the lovely Rufia Perilla?' The mask cracked and I realised that Livia was smiling. Or trying to. 'Well, I hope?'

'Uh, she's okay. Excellency.'

'No problems with the divorce or the wedding?'

'No.' My palms were sweating again. I wiped them surreptitiously.

'That's good. I'm glad I was able to help there. Her ex-husband Suillius Rufus really was quite unsuitable. He's still serving in Syria, as I understand.'

'Yeah. He commands the Third Gallic.' I crossed my legs, leaned back and tried to look calm. The chair creaked dangerously.

'He wasn't too upset, then? About losing his wife?'

'I wouldn't know, Excellency.' Like hell I didn't. Rufus, by all accounts, had been fit to be tied when he got the news that Perilla was divorcing him and marrying me. Getting his Eagle had been no compensation. I swallowed and wiped my palms a third time. At that precise moment given the choice between a fist-fight with an arena leopard and swapping social chit-chat with Livia I'd've gladly picked the cat, no contest. 'Uh, I'm sorry, but might I ask why you sent for me? Please?'

She held up a hand. 'Corvinus, you really must have patience. It's a most valuable virtue and one well worth cultivating.' Not from where I'm sitting, lady, I thought. The sooner I was out of here and on the lee side of a wine jug getting quietly smashed the better. 'I promise you we'll come round to my reasons in due course. Meanwhile let me assure you that I bear you no ill-will with regard to our past meeting. None at all. Quite the reverse, in fact.'

Oh, sure! The last time I'd sat in this chair Livia had made it clear she'd dance on my grave wearing her best clogs, and I doubted that she'd sweetened up any since. I trusted her just as much as I would a snake with a migraine.

'The Third Gallic, you say.' Her eyes were on the desk, and she was toying with the writing-tablet in front of her. 'They're based in Antioch, are they not?'

'Yeah. Yeah, that's right. So far as I know.' I cleared my throat.

'Then that would make sense. Rufus was a protégé of my grandson Germanicus, of course. No doubt the appointment was made before he died.' Her eyes came up and looked directly into mine, and I felt my balls freeze. 'So unfortunate, my grandson's death, was it not? Such a loss to Rome. And to our family.'

The silence lengthened. Oh, Jupiter! Jupiter Best and Greatest! I still didn't know what the empress wanted from me, but I did know I wanted nothing to do with it. There was complicity in those eyes, and knowing what I did about Livia and her involvement with past 'unfortunate' deaths the last thing I needed was a shared secret. And of course there'd been the rumours. She'd know about these. Sure she would.

'If you think so, Excellency,' I said at last.

Livia laughed suddenly. The sound was like an ungreased gate swinging.

'Oh, Corvinus, I like you,' she said. 'I like you very much. You're so terribly transparent.'

'Uh, yeah.' I was sweating worse than ever. Baiae must be

nice this time of year. Or maybe somewhere further off. Like Alexandria. 'Yeah, well . . .'

The empress stood up and groped for her stick. I'd forgotten how old she was. And how tiny. Seated, I was almost her standing height.

'I know exactly what you're thinking,' she said. 'You think I arranged Germanicus's death myself.'

She'd hit it smack on the button, of course. Sure I thought that, along with half of Rome; but I wasn't going to admit it, not to her face, despite the candid invitation. Not with less than a five-hundred-mile start on a racing yacht and a Parthian passport in my fist. Instead I said nothing, which was an answer in itself. I must've looked shifty as hell, and I knew it.

She was still smiling at me. I've seen cats at the Games smile like that just before they overtake their lunch.

'You see?' she said. 'Transparent as glass. Of course that's what you think. I could argue the case myself. First of all, Germanicus was married to Agrippina who is a Julian and whom, as you know, I cannot stand. Their children, although part Claudian, naturally carry the Julian blood. Secondly, Germanicus was poisoned; and again as you know I'm no stranger to poisons. Thirdly, his death is popularly attributed to the Syrian governor Calpurnius Piso and his wife Plancina, and Plancina is one of my oldest and closest friends. I thus have motive, means and – through Plancina – opportunity. I am therefore guilty. A simple solution. QED.'

'Lady, please! I really don't . . .' I swallowed and clammed up: I was sweating buckets now. Jupiter! What the hell did the woman want from me? Blood? Sympathy? A round of applause, maybe?

Her smile faded.

'I'm sorry, Corvinus,' she said. 'I'm teasing you, and I really shouldn't do that, especially since I want to ask a favour of you. Forgive me. Now watch what happens next and listen very carefully, because I don't want you leaving here with the feeling that I've somehow cheated.' Leaning on her stick she hobbled over to the portable altar in the corner of the room and laid her hand on the top. 'Are you ready?'

Ready for what? 'Uh, yeah. Yeah, go ahead.'

'I swear,' she said slowly, 'by all the gods above and below, by my hope of escaping torment in the next world for the murders I have committed in this and by my hope for my own eventual deification, that I was neither directly nor indirectly responsible for the death of my grandson Germanicus Caesar.' I was staring at her. She took her hand away. 'There. Close your mouth, now, please, you look ridiculous. Does that satisfy you, or would you like to dictate the words yourself?'

'No, that about covers it.' My head was spinning. 'You mind explaining why, now?'

She lowered herself painfully back into her chair. It must've been built up because we were on the level again.

'Why the oath?' she said. 'Or why I brought you here in the first place?'

'Both, Excellency. They're the same thing anyway, aren't they?'

'Naturally. But if you've realised that then the answer to your question should be obvious.'

'Let's pretend it isn't. Tell me anyway.'

'Oh, Corvinus! You disappoint me!' Her thin lips turned down. 'Of course, now you know that I wasn't responsible for Germanicus's death I want you to find out who was.'

We stared at each other. She wasn't smiling any more, and the dead eyes were expressionless. I swallowed painfully.

'Excellency, this wouldn't be, uh, official, would it?' I said at last.

She tutted with impatience. 'Don't be a fool, boy! Of course it isn't! Officially my grandson died of a fever. You know that.'

I nodded. 'Okay. Just asking. So why me?'

'Because you've already shown certain . . . talents in that direction.' Was that a smile again? I doubted it. 'And I'm betting on your curiosity.'

She had me there. Ever since the business with the altar I'd stopped sweating. Instead I could feel the little tingle at the nape of my neck that I'd been missing these past eighteen months. Not regretting, just missing.

'Fair enough,' I said. 'You have any ideas yourself?'

This time I detected a definite smile; but it was like the smile you sometimes get on the face of an old Greek statue; the smug sort I always feel like wiping off with a hammer.

'Naturally I do,' she said. 'But that's all they are. Ideas. I would hate to prejudice your investigation by sharing them.'

'Yeah. Sure.' I hoped that didn't sound as sour as I thought it did; I hadn't missed the irony there. 'So no help at all, right?'

'No help at all, Corvinus. But then, no hindrance, either.' She paused. 'Well? Was I right? About your curiosity? I need a definite answer.'

Shit. I'd hate to play her at dice, not with these eyes staring across the table at me. She had me hooked, and she knew it. Nevertheless I hesitated for form's sake. 'No help and no hindrance, right, lady?'

'You have my word.'

Uh uh. Whatever that was worth. But then, I didn't have any choice. 'Yeah. Yeah, okay,' I said. 'I'll settle for that.'

The smile widened. 'Good. I thought you might. And now if you'll excuse me I have work to do.'

She turned back to the writing-tablet in front of her. It was like she'd forgotten me already. I stood up. Then a thought struck me. It wasn't a pleasant one, but I couldn't leave without putting it into words. I cleared my throat, and the mask raised itself.

'Yes, Corvinus? What is it now?' Testy as hell. You'd've thought I'd been the one asking the favour.

'Uh . . . one last thing, Excellency.' I hesitated. 'The rumours in the Market Square. They don't just concern you. Maybe you'd like to add something to that oath you took after all.'

She didn't blink. 'You mean in respect of my son.'

'The emperor. Yeah.'

'Young man.' She placed her hands flat on the desk. 'I cannot and will not answer for Tiberius. We are no longer close, and I refuse to perjure myself where I have no definite knowledge.' She waited. I waited longer. 'However I will say that I find the attempts to link him with Germanicus's death both malicious and . . . ill informed. My son, unlike myself' – that smile again – 'is not by nature a murderer. Will that serve?'

It'll have to, lady, I thought. For the moment, anyway. But I didn't say anything. I just nodded.

'Good. Thank you, Corvinus. Come back when you've solved our little mystery, won't you? That's all.'

This time Oily Phormio wasn't poised at the door to let me out. With a brief bow to the top of her head and a few parting politenesses that she ignored, I left.

Hermes wasn't in evidence outside either, but I couldn't wait to get shot of the place and back to the real life of the city. Outside the gates I just stood and breathed for a while. After the atmosphere of the palace, Rome had never smelled so sweet.

2

I thought things over in the litter on the way home. The facts of the case were pretty straightforward. Germanicus had been the nephew and adopted son of the Emperor Tiberius (aka the Wart). At his death the previous year he'd been thirty-four, two years older than his stepbrother Drusus, and Rome's blue-eyed darling. After his campaigns in Germany the Wart had sent him east to dicker with the Parthians over Armenia and generally make sure the bastards knew their place and kept to it. Which was where Piso came in.

Calpurnius Piso was the Syrian governor. Syria borders on the Parthian Empire, Armenia and our screen of client kingdoms, so the two were bound to see a lot of each other; which was a pity, because they hated each other's guts. The wives didn't get along either. Piso's Plancina was an arrogant, snobbish bitch with imperial connections who had no intention of playing second fiddle even to a granddaughter of Augustus, while Agrippina could've given even old Cato lessons in character building and made him thank her for the privilege. A situation like that was bound to lead to trouble. Finally Piso had yelled obstruction, thrown his hands in the air and left the province.

Meanwhile Germanicus had fallen ill. He got worse – both he himself and his friends suspecting poisoning and witchcraft – and died accusing Piso and Plancina. After his death Piso made the mistake of trying to shove his way back into power. The attempt didn't come off and he was captured by Germanicus's appointee governor and sent back for trial. Agrippina was on her way back, too, with her husband's ashes.

I remembered the next part myself. The funeral party had

arrived in Rome in November. The whole city was in mourning, except, so it seemed, the Wart and his mother who carried on as normal. There'd been no state funeral and no special games; in fact, the Imperials had hardly bothered to go the length of seeing the guy buried. Curious, right? Curious enough for even their biggest supporters' noses to start twitching. Sure I'd thought Livia was guilty, with Tiberius covering for her. If it hadn't been for that business with the altar I'd still think so. Even now I wouldn't've risked a heavy bet.

We'd reached the Septizonium, which is a real bugger to get along eight hours out of the daylight ten, and the road was jam-packed up ahead. The litter slowed to a crawl, and five minutes later we came to a dead stop. Litters aren't really my bag. They're de rigueur when you go visiting and want to arrive with a clean mantle, but generally I can do without them. I had the lads set me down and went the rest of the way on foot. It'd been a long hard winter and a cold spring, but the weather had broken at last and the slopes of the Palatine were beginning to look interesting again. Good walking weather, in other words, if you don't mind the disapproving stares of the fat guys with beefsteak faces who pass you in litters of their own.

So. Piso and Plancina got back just after the Spring Festival to find themselves charged with murder and treason. Not by the Wart: Tiberius was careful to stay neutral. The trial was held privately in the Senate House, with the mob baying for blood at the doors: like I say, Germanicus was everyone's hero and they wanted his murderer's head. They got it. When they couldn't make the poisoning charge stick, Germanicus's pals went all out for a conviction for treason based on Piso's armed revolt after the Caesar's death, which would come to the same thing. As a result, Plancina slipped through the net, but Piso was caught. The bastard committed suicide before the verdict came in. Case closed.

Only it wasn't, seemingly. Not unofficially, not any more. These might be the facts, but even as facts they stank like fish sauce in a heatwave. Whether Piso was guilty or not, whether the Imperials were involved or not, Germanicus had been murdered. It wasn't just the rumours. Livia had said so, and as an expert on murder they don't come better than the empress. So who had done it, and why?

I turned up Poplicolan Street, heading for my own gate. There was a flower-seller on the corner and I bought a bunch of late narcissi for Perilla. Call it a prospective peace offering. A sweet girl, Perilla, but the news that Livia wanted me for a sunbeam was going to go down with her like a slug in a salad. I wished I'd thought of a quick trip to the Argiletum for the latest tome on speculative philosophy, but that would've really made her suspicious. Besides, she'd've read it in bed. Out loud. In preference to anything else.

Crumbs in the mattress I can take. Speculative philosophy at bedtime is a complete bummer.

My head slave Bathyllus had the door open for me before I knocked. He always did, Jupiter knew how; the little bastard could've cleaned up in the prediction business without even breaking sweat. He also had a flask of Setinian and a wine cup waiting in the lobby, as per standing orders. This time the wine was neat, because Bathyllus had known where I was going that morning. I hadn't told Perilla, though. She'd only have worried.

'You have a visitor, sir,' he murmured.

'Hmm?' I let the nectar slip past my tonsils and sing its way down towards my sandal straps. Not just neat Setinian, this, but the Special, the strongest I'd got. Bathyllus's prognosticative faculties were shit hot that day. 'What visitor?'

'Your uncle the consul Marcus Valerius Cotta Maximus Messallinus, sir.' He rolled the five names off his tongue. That explained the perfect butler act: Bathyllus was the biggest snob in Rome. 'He's with the Lady Perilla. In the atrium.'

I grinned. 'You lock the spoons up, little guy?'

Bathyllus didn't answer, of course. He just sniffed as he took my mantle and folded it neatly. Sniffing's about all he allows himself to express his disapproval. Mind you, a sniff from Bathyllus hits most people like a clout from a knuckleduster. Not me, I'm immune. And he doesn't even try with Perilla.

I took my flowers, empty cup and wine jug through the hall. Perilla was sitting by the pool. Even in her plain white mantle she looked sexy as hell. Forget the spoons. Anyone with my uncle's tastes and experience wouldn't've given them a second thought. Maybe I should've got back earlier.

'Hi, lady.' I gave her the bunch of narcissi and planted a smacker on top of her smile. 'Uncle Cotta.'

'You carrying that jug around for show, boy, or can anyone join in?' Cotta held up an empty wine cup of his own.

I poured. Perilla was looking at the flowers. Hard.

'Corvinus,' she said. 'What are these, exactly?'

'Uh, they're called flowers. They grow in parks and gardens, you know?' I poured myself another whopper of the Special and drank it down. 'Big open spaces with earth and walls round them. They're a present.'

'Why?'

Oh, Jupiter! I looked at Uncle Cotta. The bastard was grinning like a drain. Perilla wasn't.

'Marcus, dear,' she said, 'I can count the number of times you've brought me flowers on the fingers of one hand. Jewellery, yes. Books, yes. But not flowers. You don't think of them unless you're feeling especially guilty or want something out of the ordinary. So tell me why the flowers, please. Now.'

There was no escape. I sent Uncle Cotta out to look at the garden and told her. Not everything. Just where I'd been. And that I was glad as hell to get back.

'But why didn't you say? Before you went, I mean?' Perilla blew her nose while I tried to get the mascara stains off the front of my best tunic. Bathyllus would have a fit when he saw them. 'Livia could've done anything to you.'

'At her age? Come on, lady!'

'Don't joke.' Another sniffle, but this time cut short: Perilla's got her own pride. 'What did she want?'

So I told her that as well. All of it. I reckoned I was safe enough now to let her have the whole nasty truth.

'Why you?' Her beautiful eyes were wide. 'If she really wants to find out who was responsible for her grandson's death there are dozens of better ways to go about it.'

'Hey, thanks.' I sat down and poured myself a third cup of the Special. 'Confidence in my powers of deduction always was one of your strong points, lady.'

She kissed me. 'You know perfectly well that's not what I meant.'

I grinned. 'Yeah, sure. So maybe I've got more going for

me than you think. Or maybe the old girl's finally hocked her marbles.'

'But you agreed?'

'Sure I agreed. You don't say no to the empress. Not when she's in that mood. Not when she's in any mood.'

Perilla sat down. 'Very well,' she said at last. 'It can't be helped, I suppose. Where do we start?'

I stared at her. ' "We"? There's no "we", Perilla. Livia gave me the job. She didn't mention sharing it with sassy divorcees with a down on flowers. Besides, things could get difficult.'

'That's nonsense.'

'Believe it!'

'All right, Corvinus, if you say so.' Her brow creased. 'But if you're going to be brought back on a board one night with your throat cut or sent off to exile in Spain then I'd like to know the reason. Now don't argue, please. We'll discuss it later if we must.'

At that point Cotta came sidling back thirsting for wine and I had to leave it and play the genial host.

Livia, yeah. I can understand what makes her tick, or I can begin to, anyway. But not Perilla. Her I'll never understand. Not if I live to be ninety.

3 ∫

Having Cotta round at that moment was a plus, which didn't
happen all that often because likeable though the guy was (at
least I liked him) nine times out of ten he'd get the vote for the
Most Dispensable Member of the Group. This was the tenth time.
Cotta scored because as consul he'd been one of the presiding
officers at the Piso trial, which like I said was held behind closed
doors. The drawback was that smart though the guy might be in
his way he couldn't put two and two together without using an
abacus, and all we'd get from him was the authorised version;
which on reflection might not be a bad thing because Cotta
was also a blabbermouth and with Germanicus's death officially
written off as natural and the case closed the Wart wouldn't
take kindly if word got around that Corvinus was ripping the
scabs off.

Prising information out of a witness without letting on why
you're interested is an art calling for delicacy, finesse and a good
sense of timing. Or alternatively, in Cotta's case, a good dinner
and two flasks of Falernian. Luckily Meton the chef had done us
proud: calf's brain and almond sausage, wild duck braised with
dates, puréed greens in a lovage savoury sauce and a honey
and pine kernel omelette to finish. By the time we'd reached
the nuts the guy was purring. It wasn't too hard to introduce
the subject either. Piso had been dead less than a month, and
the Senate were still feeling their oats. It isn't every day you get
to preside over a case of high treason, and Cotta had loved every
minute of it.

'They murdered him, all right,' he said. 'They were guilty as
hell, the pair of them.'

'Is that right?' I signalled to Bathyllus to pour more wine. 'Tell us.'

'Okay.' Cotta settled back. 'Take motive. Syria's the plum imperial province, top of the tree, and the Syrian governor's practically vice-regent of the whole eastern sector. If you're into power you can't go much higher unless your last name's Caesar. And it's a good place for making money.'

'Yeah?'

'Yeah.' He held up his cup and watched Bathyllus pour in the Falernian. 'It needs to be. The Syrian governorship's the end of the line. After that you're out to grass and all you have to look forward to is having your arse licked in the Senate. Any governor who doesn't use Syria to put aside for his old age needs his head examined. Piso was no fool. He was salting it away like there was no tomorrow.'

'He'd already been accused of peculation in Spain, hadn't he?' That was Perilla. She was doing her Roman matron act, sitting in a chair with her eyes demurely cast down.

Cotta gave her a speculative glance before answering. 'That's right,' he said. 'In Tarraco. Trio made a point of it at the trial.'

'Trio?'

'The guy who brought the case.'

'Wouldn't Piso consider it too dangerous to risk fraud a second time?'

'The Spanish charge was old history, Perilla. No one paid it any attention. Still, I'd be interested to know where you picked up the information.'

I shot Perilla a warning look. Demure Roman matron, hell. Jupiter knew where she'd got that nugget from, but smartass comments we could do without at this stage. I wanted Cotta kept sweet.

Perilla ignored me. 'I knew someone once who was on the Spanish staff,' she said. 'It is true, isn't it?'

'Sure it's true. The fact of the accusation, anyway. Whether the guy was actually guilty or not was never proved because the case never got the length of the court.' Cotta cracked a nut. 'Anyway, there's Piso sitting pretty at Antioch, fresh out from Rome and good for at least a couple of years' hard graft. And what does the Wart do?'

'He sends out his adopted son and heir.' I slit an apple.

'Right, Marcus. And the last thing any governor with his way to make wants is a ranking Caesar with a special commission breathing down his neck and checking the invoices. Especially a stiff-backed stickler for the proprieties like Germanicus.'

Uhuh. That made sense. 'You think Tiberius sent him on purpose? To keep an eye on Piso?'

'No.' Cotta sipped his wine. 'No, Piso was a friend of the Wart's, as much as the boil-ridden bastard has friends. He wouldn't've made him governor in the first place if he hadn't been sure of him. Anyway, Tiberius is a realist. He knows a certain amount of graft's inevitable. The provincials expect it, and an absolutely straight governor would worry them like hell. So long as Piso didn't get too greedy Tiberius would leave him alone. It was just an unfortunate coincidence.' He grinned. 'Unfortunate for Piso.'

'And for Germanicus. If Piso did kill him.'

'Yeah.' Another grin. 'You could say that. You ever meet the guy, Marcus?'

'Germanicus? No, never. I don't move in your exalted circles.'

'Count yourself lucky, boy. He was a self-righteous prig, honest and open as the day is long. A squeaky-clean marvel with hero written large all over him. No wonder everyone loved him and Piso hated his guts. And Agrippina's worse.'

'I have always,' Perilla said, 'had a high regard for the character of Julia Agrippina.'

'Is that right?' Cotta glanced at her over the rim of his wine cup. 'Personally the lady makes my balls shrink.'

Perilla's lips drew themselves into a hard, thin line. I recognised the signs. Leaning over I picked an apple from the fruit bowl and hefted it. She gave me a quick half smile and ducked her head.

'Yes, Valerius Cotta,' she said. 'I can quite see that Agrippina would make your balls shrink. You can put that down now, please, Marcus. It won't be necessary.'

Cotta was still grinning. 'I'm sorry if I offended you, lady.' Like hell he was! He'd done it deliberately. 'Tastes differ, after all.'

I gave Perilla another warning look as I steered my uncle back on course.

'So the wives didn't exactly hit it off either?' I said.

'Fought like cat and dog.' Cotta drained his cup and held it out to Bathyllus. The little guy filled it – not, I noticed, all the way up; Bathyllus may not say much but he's smart. And he can judge a situation to the inch: we wanted Cotta to talk, not pass out on us. 'If you can call it fighting. Women's stuff, mostly. Snide remarks in public. Monkeying around with the seating plans at dinner parties. Power dressing. You know the sort of thing the little darlings get up to. Eh, Perilla?'

Shit, Cotta was pushing his luck this evening. I was thankful I had Perilla on my side or she'd've handed him his head long since; but this was really tempting fate. Even Bathyllus winced as the temperature suddenly dropped to below freezing. Over on the far wall I spotted a spider making a frantic dash for cover. Dumb animals sense these things.

'Yes, of course, Uncle Cotta,' Perilla said sweetly. You could've used the tone to pickle mummies. 'But then we don't know any better, do we?'

I glared at her. Cotta didn't seem to notice.

'Plancina couldn't take treatment like that,' he went on. 'She was First Lady of Syria, and Jupiter help anyone who forgot it. Not only that, she was a crony of the empress's, and Agrippina and Livia hate each other like poison. So she could expect a lot of sympathy in imperial quarters.'

I nodded. Yeah. Right. Livia had said as much herself, and Agrippina wasn't exactly flavour of the month with the Wart, either, from all accounts. It all added up. 'So what we've got,' I said, 'are four big fish in a small pond who cramp each other's style and hate each other's guts. You think that's reason enough for murder?'

'What more do you want, boy?'

I didn't answer. Sure, Cotta was right, within his limits. Even although I'd never met any of the people involved, from his description it made a lot of sense. Six months of that sort of life, in that sort of closed society, and the two couples would be at one another's throats. That, plus the circumstantial evidence, and Germanicus's own suspicions, was pretty damning. No wonder Piso and Plancina had had a hanging jury. I might've convicted them myself and never thought twice about it.

'They had the motive, then,' Perilla was saying. 'But what about the means and the opportunity?'

Cotta helped himself to a peach and carefully removed the stone.

'Them too,' he said. 'That was where Martina came in.'

4 ∫

'Who?' I said.

'Martina. One of the locals.'

'A freedwoman?' I held up my cup for Bathyllus to fill. I wasn't drinking much (you've probably noticed); at this stage in the investigation I needed a clear head.

'No. She was freeborn, so far as I know.' Cotta flicked the loosened peach stone on to his plate. 'Local girl, like I said. Syrian, despite the Roman name. She laundered the imperial drawers. Something like that, anyway.'

'One of the house servants,' Perilla interpreted. I smiled.

'Right. Anyway, Martina and Plancina were thick as eels in a stewpot. And our lovely laundress had a reputation for dealing in what you might call noxious substances.'

'Poisons?'

'You bet your bootlaces, lady.' Cotta quartered the peach and bit messily into one of the sections. 'Plus certain equally nasty literary efforts. The sort you see scratched on lead tablets and buried at midnight.'

Germanicus had accused Piso and Plancina of killing him by poison and witchcraft. I was beginning to get the picture sharp and clear; too clear. It couldn't be this obvious, surely?

'So what happened to Martina?' I said, passing him a napkin. 'After Germanicus's death?'

He wiped his chin. 'Oh, they got her. Picked her up easy as pie and shipped her over to Italy as the prime prosecution witness. Only she managed to swallow one of her own concoctions at Brindisi, so that was that.'

Something cold touched my spine. *That was that.* Sure it was.

'But why should—' Perilla began. I reached across under cover of the table and put a hand on her thigh. She shut up tight as a clam. Yeah, she'd seen the implications too, but I didn't want her going into them now. Obvious, hell! I should've had more faith in Livia. Or maybe less.

'What's that, Perilla?' Cotta was busy with his second slice of peach.

'Nothing.' She gave him a brilliant smile. 'Just a muddle-headed observation. Go on, Uncle Cotta.'

He grunted. 'Right. So exit the star witness. They found an empty ampoule tied up in the woman's pigtail. Pity. If she'd had her day in court we'd really have had the bastards cold. As it was Vitellius and Veranius had to drop the murder charge and get the pair for treason instead. Or Piso, anyway.' Vitellius and Veranius, I knew, were the friends of Germanicus who'd put the case itself carefully together in Syria and brought it to Rome. With Martina dead they must've been left spitting blood. 'Once the poisoning charge went down the tube, of course, they'd no call to hold Plancina.'

'Especially since she was such a good friend of Livia's,' I said. The bitch! The scheming old bitch! 'Are they still in Rome, by the way? Vitellius and Veranius?'

'No.' Cotta frowned at his last two pieces of fruit and dug out a blemish from one of them with the point of his knife. 'Vitellius went back out to Antioch. Veranius is on his estate in Sicily. What's that to you anyway, boy?'

'Nothing. Just curious.' The guy was beginning to twitch. Pity. I'd've liked to ask a few more questions about Martina the Witchy Laundress, but he would really've begun to smell a rat, and that I didn't want. 'So Plancina was off the hook?'

'She reserved her defence. We went through the motions, sure, but in the end the Wart begged as a personal favour to him and Livia that the charges be quashed.'

'Tiberius used his veto?' I couldn't help myself. The question slipped out sharper than I'd meant it to. Perilla's head went up.

'No.' Luckily Cotta was still busy with the peach. 'Not as such. Of course not; he's got no legal rights in a criminal trial. But you know how it is. He stood there embarrassed as hell with his boils glowing like a fifty-lamp candelabrum asking us to let the woman go and we had to tug our forelocks and do it. Right?'

'Right.' Yeah, that figured. You don't buck the emperor, whatever the legal ins and outs. But it smelled, and no mistake. 'So Tiberius protected Plancina. How about Piso? You said they were friends. Personal friends.'

'Sure. But with friends like the Wart you don't need enemies. Tiberius had made it clear right from the start that the guy was on his own, Marcus. No umbrella, no safety net.' Cotta popped the last slice of peach into his mouth and chewed. 'No nothing. We had to decide two things, and two things only: whether there was a murder rap to answer and whether Piso had tried to subvert the legions and retake the province by force. The first was easy. With Martina dead there was no case, however much we might want to think otherwise. And the second was what my smart lawyer pals call incontrovertible fact.' He reached over for another filbert and cracked it. 'If we'd been given access to the letters, mind, it might've been another matter.'

My stomach went cold; and beside me I felt Perilla stiffen.

'And what letters are these, Uncle Cotta?' she said.

Cotta held up his cup. I motioned wearily to Bathyllus. Shit. I didn't want the guy drunk now. He'd as hard a head as mine, but another cup was pushing it.

'The ones between Piso and the Wart, of course.' Bathyllus was splashing wine into the cup: it'd look more than it was. I made a mental vow to up the little guy's perquisites. 'We asked to see them but they turned us down flat.'

'"They"? Tiberius *and* Piso? Both of them?'

'Sure. Odd, right?' Jupiter! If Cotta said it was odd you could bet your last copper penny it was downright weird. 'They must've had some reason, but they weren't saying.'

'They didn't give a reason?'

'Zero. Zilch. Pan-faced and poker-arsed, the pair of them. Like I said, all we got was the flat refusal.' He drank. 'Then there was the business of the note.'

'What note was this?' You could've cut the tension now with a knife. I was amazed Cotta didn't seem to feel it, but then he's more self-centred than I am.

'If it existed.' His hand scrabbled in the nut bowl and came up with a stuffed date. He stared at it pop-eyed for a while like he'd never seen one before in his life. That, and the non sequitur, told me his last swallow of wine had taken him over the limit. 'If it existed,' he said again.

'Go on, Uncle,' Perilla prompted. 'This is fascinating.' How the woman could be so calm and patient beat me, but she was. Personally I had a dozen ice-cold centipedes doing clog dances all up my backbone, and I was having difficulty stopping myself from grabbing the bastard by the throat and shaking the information out the hard way.

'Yeah.' Cotta gave her a fatuous grin, nodded and bit the date in half. 'If it existed.' The wine had definitely got to the guy. He'd always had an irritating habit of sticking with a phrase when he was drunk, like a non-swimmer hanging on to an inflated bladder. It was the one way you could tell he'd had enough, before he actually passed out. 'Maybe it didn't. Jupiter knows we never saw hide nor hair of the bugger.'

'Let's pretend,' I said carefully, 'that it did. Okay?'

'Okay.' Cotta was frowning. 'Okay, Marcus. The day Plancina reserved her defence Piso went home, wrote a note for his lawyer and gave it to his freedman.'

'His freedman?'

I got the full bland pop-eyed look. 'You want the guy's name?'

'*Yes*, I want his name!'

'Carus? Carillus? Something like that.'

'You like to pick one, maybe?'

'Corvinus!' Perilla laid a hand on my arm.

'Okay.' I backed down. 'Never mind.'

'Anyway,' Cotta went on, 'Piso wrote a note and handed it to this freedman guy—'

'Sealed?'

'Marcus!'

Cotta gave me his bug-eyed stare again. 'Sealed. Then he went to bed as usual. Or so everybody thought at the time.'

I knew what was coming next. I just knew it. 'And that was the night he killed himself, right?'

'Right.' He nodded. 'Right. They found him in the morning with his throat cut. Best thing he could've done, of course. It would've come to the same thing anyway. At least this way he didn't pull his family down the tube as well.'

'I shouldn't have thought he'd be too concerned about Plancina,' Perilla said drily.

'Yeah.' Cotta grinned. 'By that stage he couldn't've given a toss about her. His sons were different, they'd been involved in the treason. Or the elder one had, anyway. Tiberius included him in the amnesty, buggered if I know why. Personally I'd've nailed Piso's foreskin to the Speakers' Platform.'

I settled back and held up my cup for Bathyllus to fill. My brain was spinning. Jupiter! What was going on here? Cotta's story had as many holes in it as a maggoty Raetian cheese, and it stank even worse. Maybe Piso had been guilty, maybe he and Plancina had murdered Germanicus. But if so how did the Wart fit in? How much, now, could I afford to believe that bitch Livia? And if the Imperials were involved, did I want any part of it, promise to the empress or not?

The answer to that last one was no. And yes. That was the real bummer.

I was suddenly aware that someone was saying something. Nothing very important, but it meant I had to pay attention.

'Hey, this is good Falernian, Marcus.' Cotta was swirling the last inch or so round in his cup. 'Better than I get at your father's. Messallinus has a palate like a camel's scrotum.'

Hint, hint. What the hell. It didn't matter any more. Let the guy get plastered, he'd earned it and so had I. The thinking could wait. I signalled to Bathyllus to go all the way and turned my attention to the postprandial chit-chat.

'Uh . . . you seen Dad lately, Uncle Cotta?'

'Every day, boy.' He took a mouthful of wine, held it and swallowed. 'It's the drawback to the job. One of the many. He's on the grain supply commission I'm heading. Along with old what's-his-name. Sejanus's uncle.'

'Blaesus?'

'Blaesus. Your father hasn't lost his talent for arselicking, boy. He knows how to pick his friends. And the Sejanus tribe will be telling us when we can scratch our balls soon, you mark my words. You're better off out of it, the way you are.'

Perilla shifted in her seat. Uh-oh. I could've cheerfully stran-gled Cotta. My refusal to stand for public office is the only real no-go area I've got with Perilla (yeah, well, maybe there are one or two others. Like the late-night squid and pickle snacks or not letting the barber pull the hairs out of my nostrils. But these are minor). She sees it as a shirked duty, which is true enough, I suppose. I see it as on a par with not wishing a set of impacted anal glands on yourself. Anyway, knowing how highly she valued Uncle Cotta's opinions in general bringing out that particular gem was like tossing a pork chop to a wolverine.

'Like yourself, I suppose, Valerius Cotta,' she said sweetly. 'You didn't have to run for consul, did you?'

I knew that tone. It meant that whoever she was talking to had about ten seconds to find a deep hole somewhere, pile the dirt on top of them and stay put till spring. It didn't faze Cotta, though. Maybe the guy was going deaf in his old age. Or maybe he was just drunk and didn't care. No prizes for guessing which.

'No. I didn't have to run for consul.' He beamed at her. 'But then rank has its rewards, lady. You'd be amazed how many prim and proper matrons want to be screwed by one of Rome's serving senior magistrates. To coin a phrase. Isn't that right, Marcus?'

I had to laugh. Even if I knew, from the expression on Perilla's face, that I'd pay for it later. Uncle Cotta may've been no great shakes as a politician or a criminologist, but he could certainly handle himself. Even against Perilla.

We finished the flask cup for cup, while Perilla looked on in resigned disapproval. Ah, well. I had an excuse, apart from the simple fact that the wine deserved it. Starting from tomorrow, whether I liked it or not, I'd be up to my eyes in the politi-cal trash-heap again. And that wasn't a thought I wanted to face sober.

5

My Falernian is pretty smooth stuff, mind, unlike the Special that after a few cups will suddenly sneak up from behind and give you a belt like a blackjack. Besides, I was a good half-flask shy of Cotta, which didn't happen all that often. The result was that when we finally got rid of the guy long after the lamps were lit I was still this side of capable, while Rome's current consul was pissed as a newt and repeating every second word. Backwards.

We left Bathyllus and his minions clearing away. Perilla offered me her shoulder to lean on with a disapproving little sniff. I played along as far as the bedroom door. Then I stopped pretending and grabbed her in earnest.

'Corvinus, don't swallow my earring, please,' she said. 'You'll give yourself indigestion.'

'Mmm.' I pushed the door open with my foot. Why the hell did I have the architect build me such a big bedroom? The bed was miles away.

'Marcus, please. Give me a chance to . . .'

I didn't. It's more fun that way. Perilla enjoys it too, although she'd never admit it. We made it to the bed, just. After which any matronly protests were academic and not taken seriously by either party.

'We should've had Meton lay us on a few oysters,' I said after the first time around.

'They're out of season,' Perilla said. At least that's what I think she said. The words got a bit muffled because her face was pressed to the hollow between my shoulder and throat.

'Onions, then. Or is that for wind?'

'Corvinus . . .'

'Mmm?'

'Just be quiet.'

So I lay there listening to the carts outside and being very grateful to have Perilla wrapped round me until she started nuzzling my earlobe again and we moved on to the main course. That took some time, luckily. With Perilla slow is definitely best.

'Marcus,' she said when we'd finished and cooled down far enough to talk.

'Yeah?'

'Could I possibly let down my hair now? I mean, if you don't mind, of course.'

I grinned down at her. 'I imagined you already had, lady.'

'Oh, ha ha.' She threw me off and slipped out of bed. I watched while she took off her earrings, pulled the pins out of her hair and let the beautiful tawny mane do what it felt like . . .

Hold on. Something was wrong here. No self-respecting Roman matron pulls out her own pins. Pulling pins is the maid's job.

'Hey!' I said. 'Where's Phryne?'

Phryne was the cross-eyed niece of old Harpale's that she'd taken on when we'd got married. A sort of peace offering to the dead Davus.

'I gave her the evening off.' Perilla shrugged herself out of her tunic; the mantle, of course, hadn't made it the length of the bed.

Jupiter! Legs like that shouldn't be allowed short of an original Praxiteles bronze. 'Yeah? Why?'

'No reason.'

I smiled to myself. Sure there wasn't. If Perilla would insist on keeping up this ice-maiden pose even when we both knew it was phoney as a woollen toupee then it was fine with me. Without the ice and prickles she just wouldn't be the same girl.

'You tired yet?' I said.

'That depends what you have in mind.' What could've been Praxiteles's best had disappeared under a baggy linen sleeping tunic. Ah, well.

'Just a talk this time.' I patted the mattress beside me. 'Unless you've got a dozen bootleg oysters and an onion or two squirrelled away for emergencies.'

She came back over and slipped under the blanket on her side of the bed. Or almost on her side.

'You want to discuss Piso and Plancina, I suppose,' she said.

A marvellous body, bagged at present though it was, and intuition as well. Who says you can't have everything?

'Yeah. You mind?'

'Of course I mind. But I'd prefer it to having you mumbling away to yourself into my back half the night.'

'Would I do that to you, lady?'

'You would. You have.' She kissed me. 'So I'd like the mumbling now, please. While I'm not trying to sleep. That way I don't miss breakfast.'

'Yeah. Well. Okay.' I sat up with my back to the headboard while she snuggled against me under the blanket. 'First thing. The laundry lady with the evil eye and the penchant for poisons.'

'Martina. You think the empress had her killed.' A statement, not a question.

'Don't you?'

'It would seem logical. Somebody certainly did. Suicides don't usually hide empty poison bottles in their hair when they've finished with them.'

'You noticed that?'

'I'm not stupid, Corvinus. Stop acting like your Uncle Cotta. Whoever tied that bottle into the woman's bun wanted to make sure people assumed she'd smuggled it in that way in the first place. In other words, that it was straight suicide. And Livia and poison are practically synonyms.'

'Livia swore she wasn't involved in Germanicus's murder.'

'Not *directly* involved. Do you believe her?'

I considered. 'Yeah, I believe her, though I wouldn't go to the wall over it because that old fraud's more devious than an Ostian landlord. Still, she didn't have to send for me, she didn't have to do the business with the altar, and she sure as hell didn't have to ask me to dig the dirt.'

'But the empress doesn't have to be responsible for Germanicus's death to have murdered Martina. She'd only be protecting her friend.'

'Yeah, right.' I eased my arm out from under her and rested

it along the back of the headboard. 'That's something else that worried me. You think they really knew each other?'

'Plancina and the empress?' She grinned. 'Of course they did.'

'Cut it out. You know who I mean. Martina and Plancina. Cotta said they were thick as eels in a stewpot.'

'So?'

I sighed. 'Perilla, Plancina was the wife of the governor. Also she was a bigger snob than our Bathyllus, which is putting her straight at the top of the tree. You think she'd trade pickle recipes with a Syrian laundress?'

'If the laundress also happened to be a professional poisoner and she needed her services, yes.'

'Okay. So Plancina invites this well-known local poisoner round to Government House for a spot of honeyed wine, introduces her to her friends and generally lets everyone know they're bosom pals. Then she takes her aside one day and says, "Oh, by the way, Martina, while you're washing the crown prince's smalls tomorrow the governor and I would like you to poison him. Only when you've done it don't say we were involved, will you? There's a dear."'

Perilla was frowning. 'Put like that it does sound fishy.'

'Damn right it sounds fishy! If Plancina were using the woman she wouldn't go within a mile of her. And I'll tell you another thing that's queer as a five-legged cat and that's whatever game the Wart's playing.'

'Why he should put himself out to protect Plancina, you mean.'

'No.' I shook my head. 'That had to be Livia's doing. The two may not get on but she's still the guy's mother. She knows things about him that would make your hair curl, and you can be sure as hell she can still twist his arm when it matters. Also if the Wart has the guts to tell the empress to get lost when she tells him she wants a favour then he's a braver man than I am.'

'So what do you find odd, then?' Perilla was sitting up too, now. I had her hooked.

'Cotta said Piso and the Wart were pals. Yet Tiberius makes it very plain right from the start that the guy's on his own. No loaded hints to the jury, no files in the cake. Right?'

'But naturally, Corvinus! The emperor had to show himself impartial. Piso may have been a personal friend, but he was on trial for an offence against the state.'

'Is that all?'

'Oh, and murder, of course. But as your Uncle Cotta said that charge wouldn't stand.'

I was grinning. 'You've just made my point, lady. To anybody with an ounce of curiosity – even to Uncle Cotta who didn't like the guy, for Jupiter's sake – the murder was the most important thing in this whole business. Germanicus is a five-star gold-plated national hero. He's Cincinnatus, Scaevola and any other blue-eyed wonder-boy you like to name rolled into one, and he's been chopped. The mob's banging on the Senate House doors screaming for Piso to be handed out to them in cubes. Yet suddenly the actual death is shelved. Tiberius fixes it so's the Senate has to concentrate on the treason charge, whereas what they're busting a gut to know is who hung their darling's clogs up for him. You get me?'

Perilla was quiet for a long time.

'Yes, of course,' she said at last. 'You're saying that Tiberius ensured Piso's conviction, but on his own terms and for his own reasons.'

'Right. Terms that affected events postdating his son's death and which had nothing directly to do with it, and the proof for which according to that old bastard Cotta is incontrovertible. No need to dig any further. Full stop, end of paragraph, end of trial.'

'That does sound rather odd.'

'You bet your pants it sounds odd! Then there's the letters.'

'Yes. That was odd too.' Perilla's brow furrowed. 'Why should Tiberius refuse to produce the official provincial correspondence?'

'*Private* official correspondence. Personal to governor and vice versa. Forget gripes about taxes or notifications of repairs to the public toilets. We're talking super-secret here. The stuff that goes out under the sphinx seal and back in the diplomatic bag.'

'Then there's your answer, Corvinus. The emperor wouldn't want sensitive material bandied about in open court. And Piso would appreciate that.'

'But the trial wasn't held in open court. It was held behind closed doors, broad-stripers only, no riff-raff allowed. And the Wart only had to give his word that none of the information in the letters was pertinent. He didn't do that. He just told the Senate they couldn't play. So what does that suggest?'

'That some of it was pertinent, of course.'

'Yeah. And the Wart knew it. And there's something even weirder than that.'

'Really?' Perilla stifled a yawn.

I thumped her lightly in the ribs. 'Come on, we're getting somewhere! Don't quit on me now!'

'I'm sorry, Marcus. It slipped out. Don't mind me, please, I'm only exhausted.'

'Cut the sarcasm, lady.' I grinned. 'You asked for it, you got it. The Wart's position I can understand, just, although what he had on the burner's another question. Piso's different. His life's on the line and he knows it. So why does *he* clam up? From what Cotta told us the guy didn't even lodge a token protest or say, 'Gosh, fellows, I really wish I could help but my hands're tied.' Conclusion: he was as keen to keep their straight patrician noses out of the mail bag as the emperor was.'

Perilla groaned. 'Corvinus, be sensible! How could Piso agree to hand his letters over to the Senate when the emperor had already refused? If he did that he'd be finished whatever happened.'

'Things couldn't be any worse. What could the Wart have done to him that his senatorial pals weren't about to do anyway?'

'He could have set aside his sons' inheritance.'

That brought me up sharp. Yeah. Sure. She was right. Tiberius could've done that, and guys like Cotta would've supported him with both hands. But he hadn't. He'd done exactly the opposite and included them in the special plea for amnesty. Even though the elder had committed active treason. And *that* could mean . . .

'They had a deal!' I said. 'The Wart and Piso had a deal! Or at least Piso thought they had.'

Perilla shifted against me impatiently. 'What do you mean, "thought they had"? The only member of the family to suffer was Piso himself, and quite rightly so. He left his province illegally while still its official governor and then tried to incite the Syrian legions to mutiny. Now I'm willing to accept that your deal idea is possible and that Piso agreed to co-operate in exchange for a family indemnity, but if so the emperor fulfilled his side of the bargain.'

'Yeah, but what if the deal went further back than that? What if the Wart and Piso refused to produce their love letters because they were evidence of a conspiracy to murder?'

That hit home. Perilla's eyes widened.

'You think Piso murdered Germanicus on the emperor's instructions? Oh, Corvinus, that's crazy!'

'Crazy, hell!' I was getting really excited now. 'It's what everyone believes, and why shouldn't they be right for once? Why else would Tiberius want the murder charge played down? Why else would Piso co-operate over the letters, unless he knew he was finished either way? The Wart probably had Martina put underground as well. Or at least connived with his mother to have it done.'

'All right. Then tell me why.'

I frowned. 'Why what?'

'Why should the emperor arrange to have his own son and heir murdered?'

'How should I know, lady? We're only talking theoretical possibilities here.'

'Very well.' She sat up. 'Let's consider the possibilities. First. Do you think Tiberius is by nature a poisoner?'

I opened my mouth to say yes. Then I closed it. She had me, of course. The Wart might be six different kinds of bastard but poison wasn't his style. We'd been through that one before.

'Germanicus was poisoned,' she went on. 'Or so his friends claim. So was Martina. That does show a certain consistency of method, don't you think? Livia I would believe, but not the emperor. Not even by connivance.'

'Plancina arranged the first death. She may've arranged the second too, for all we know. Or maybe it was Livia and her together, with Tiberius's blessing.'

'Don't quibble, Marcus. It doesn't matter who arranged the actual killings. Not in that sense. But if you're asking me to believe that the Emperor Tiberius connived at two crimes involving poison, the first through a woman and the second with a woman as victim with perhaps another female intermediary, then I'm sorry but I can't accept it.'

Yeah. Put that way I couldn't accept it either, and it was my theory.

'Okay.' I fell back on my last line of defence. 'So what about the note? The one Cotta wasn't sure existed.'

'Perhaps it didn't.'

'Oh, come on, Perilla! Who'd make a story like that up?'

'Lots of people, mostly ones with nasty minds like yours. You were going to tell me Piso thought the matter over and decided to tell his lawyers about the arrangement with Tiberius after all, and that Tiberius had him murdered. Weren't you?'

'Uh, yeah.' I shifted uncomfortably. 'Yeah. Something like that.'

'Very well. So answer me four questions first. One. What made Piso change his mind and decide that telling the whole truth would do him any good? Two. Was the note ever delivered, and if so who to and what were its contents? Three. How did Tiberius know Piso had taken an independent line in time to arrange a fake suicide? And four. If Piso was in his own home surrounded by his own slaves how did the emperor manage the murder?'

Oh, bugger. I wasn't up to this at two in the morning, not without some liquid encouragement. I suddenly felt tired. She was right. Again. This was getting monotonous.

'Yeah, okay, Perilla,' I said. 'And you can add a fifth for good measure. If the Wart found out Piso was thinking of welching on the deal then why should he go ahead and save the guy's sons? Tiberius may be straight but he isn't soft. He wouldn't give a convicted traitor anything but the rope to hang himself with.'

'Exactly.' Perilla kissed me on the cheek and snuggled back down under the blanket. 'Never mind, Corvinus. We'll get there eventually.'

'Sure,' I said sourly. 'When pigs lay eggs.' I lay down and pulled her against me. 'Night-night, lady.'

'Goodnight, Marcus.'

Five minutes later I sat up again. Okay, I couldn't answer any of the questions, but at least I knew where to start. Piso's defence lawyers. And the guy who'd been given the phantom note to deliver in the first place, the freedman Carus. Carillus. Whatever. We weren't done yet. Not by a long chalk.

I thought about digging Perilla in the back and telling her, but she looked asleep. She was probably shamming, but even so I wouldn't've risked it. I like to wake up slow myself, and a grouchy Perilla at the breakfast table is more trouble than I can handle.

I curled up beside her and closed my eyes. Tomorrow was another day.

6

Perilla missed breakfast anyway. I left her sleeping it off in a beautiful huddle and went down for my morning crust dipped in olive oil.

Cotta hadn't mentioned who Piso's lawyers had been, but I knew anyway. There were three of them: his brother Lucius, a makeweight called Livineius Regulus, and Aemilius Lepidus, one of Rome's brightest and best who'd been an outside favourite for emperor when Augustus popped his clogs half a dozen years back. Lucius Piso was a touchy bastard who liked to make a big thing of his independence because he thought it pleased the Wart, while thinking five times before seriously crossing him. A crypto-arselicker, in other words, who'd only taken the case because it'd look bad socially if he didn't and gave him brownie points if he did. Him I wouldn't've touched with a ten-foot pole. Lepidus was a reasonable enough guy, but he was one of my father's cronies and I didn't want word to get round I was stirring the shit. Regulus was an unknown quantity but the weakest link, and so my best bet.

'Hey, Bathyllus!' The little guy was polishing the statues in the hallway. 'You happen to know where Livineius Regulus lives?'

Silly question. Bathyllus knows everything about everybody, if they're important enough.

'He has a house on the Pincian, sir. Near Pompey's Gardens.'

A good address for a makeweight: Bathyllus's tones were suitably reverent. Regulus was plainly a guy on his way up the social ladder.

'Will he be there now, do you know?'

'He's attached to the Treasury at present, sir. If you want to see him at this late hour' – he sniffed. Bastard!—' he will no doubt be in his office on the Capitol.'

'Yeah. Right. Thanks, sunshine.'

'A pleasure, sir.' He went back to rubbing brass bottoms while I gulped down the first of the day's cups of Setinian (well watered: he sees to that) and fastened on my cloak.

The litter slaves were hanging around outside but I waved them away. It was a good day for walking.

The first guy I saw on the steps of the temple of Juno Moneta was Caelius Crispus. He'd been giving me a wide berth since our run-in over the Ovid affair, which was fine with me because the oily little prat made my stomach crawl. However, he knew more about the ins and outs of the Treasury building than a cockroach knows a cookshop, so I gave him the big hello.

'Hey, Crispus! How're things?'

'Corvinus.' He looked wary as hell, but then that was his natural expression. 'What brings you up here?'

I told him. Not the details, of course. Just that I wanted to see Regulus. 'He around at the moment?'

'Probably.' The wary look deepened. 'Why do you want him?'

'Someone passed me a dud penny and I've come to complain.'

'Yeah?' His eyes shifted. 'Regulus is in Taxes. Quality Control's a different department.'

'He came recommended.' Crispus was pushing past me, but I stepped on his corn and wedged him against a pillar. 'So where's Taxes?'

'Why don't you ask at the desk? Now I've got business elsewhere, Corvinus, if you don't mind.'

'Sure.' I moved aside. Marginally. 'Go for it.'

He squirmed away in a mist of expensive hair oil. The guy was in a hurry to be gone; and knowing Crispus that could mean only one thing. I was interested. I was even more interested when instead of going down the steps – he'd been going that way when we met – he came back up them.

'You forget something?' I said.

'My writing-tablets.' He paused. 'Taxes are on the first floor. Regulus's office is the last on your right.'

'Thanks. See you around, Crispus.' But he was already gone, haring towards the Treasury annexe itself like someone had stuck a torch up his rectum. I followed more slowly.

Maybe it was my suspicious mind, but I asked at the desk to confirm Crispus's directions. The public slave looked me over as if I'd handed him a dead cat.

'Livineius Regulus?' he said. 'He's in Taxes, sir. Ground floor, east corridor. Fifth door along.'

'Not upstairs?'

'Nah.' The slave picked his nose absently. 'Upstairs is Senatorial. Regulus is Imperial.'

'Thanks, friend.' I set off the way he'd indicated, my brain buzzing. Crispus had tried to throw me a bouncer. So what was the slimy little prick up to?

I found out soon enough. I had my hand on the doorknob to Regulus's room when the door opened and Crispus came out. He shot me a look like a frightened rabbit's and took off fast for the tall timber. There was no point in chasing him, although I'd've liked to stamp on his balls, if he'd got any, and listen to him scream. I went in instead.

Regulus was on his own, but he wasn't at his desk. He'd obviously been planning to leave, too, because he had a bundle of tablets under his arm and a faraway look in his eye. I closed the door behind me and put my back against it.

'Yes?' he said.

He was an impressive guy, big and good-looking but running to fat; a sprint, not a marathon. And although the day wasn't all that warm he was sweating.

'You're Livineius Regulus?' I said.

'I am.' One of the tablets fell to the floor. He picked it up. 'What can I do for you?'

'You busy at the moment?'

He brightened. 'As a matter of fact I am.'

'Shame.' I folded my arms, and the bright look faded.

'If you'd like to wait,' he said, 'I'm sure I can make time later. Say in an hour. Perhaps two.'

'This won't take long. I just wanted to ask you a few questions.'

'What about?'

'You represented Calpurnius Piso? At the trial?'

'Yes. Yes, I did.' I could smell the sweat from here. 'Or partly so.'

'I was hoping you could tell me something about it.'

'About the trial?' There was a look in the guy's eye I couldn't quite place. He went back to his chair and set the tablets down on the desk in front of him. 'Yes, of course. Do have a seat, please. What did you want to know?'

There was something wrong here. It'd suddenly become too easy. The guy hadn't even asked my name or why I was interested. He probably knew the first already from Crispus, of course, but not to go through the motions was a serious mistake on his part. It showed he had something to hide. I filed that little fact for future reference, and stayed where I was between him and the door.

'My uncle Valerius Cotta, the consul,' I said – no harm in dropping a heavy hint that I had clout – 'mentioned something about a letter Piso wrote the night he killed himself.'

'Ah, yes.' Regulus was looking a lot less sweaty now. He almost smiled. Somewhere, somehow, I'd missed something. 'You mean the one addressed to the emperor. The suicide note. He – Tiberius, that is – read it out in court the next day.'

'Cotta didn't mention that.'

'Valerius Cotta was against my client from the first, Corvinus.' So the bastard did know who I was! I promised myself a quiet word with Crispus down some dark alleyway before we were much older. 'It's unlikely that he would mention it, I'm afraid. The letter revealed a more – ah – sympathetic side to the man's character than the consul would perhaps like to admit existed.'

'So what did this note say?'

'It was a protestation of innocence.' Regulus gave a deprecating smile; my fist itched to smash his even, pearly teeth in. 'Not that personally I believe that its contents were true in every detail, but by that stage it made no odds because Piso was already dead.'

'I thought you were defending the guy, friend.'

Regulus shrugged. 'Someone had to. I did the best I could. My personal feelings didn't come in to the matter.'

'Yeah. Sure.'

'Wait a moment.' He opened a drawer in the desk and took

out a sheet of paper. 'I made a record of the text. Not an exact
version, of course, since the letter was sealed and addressed to
the emperor. But as I say Tiberius read it out and I noted down
the gist.'

Hey! 'Oh, how frightfully efficient of you.'

He smiled again, and handed the paper over eagerly. I scanned
it. Gist or not, eagerness or not, it read real:

My enemies' plots and the hatred aroused by a false accusation
have destroyed me. Since there is no help in my own honesty
and innocence, I call on the gods to witness, Caesar, that I have
always been faithful to you and your mother, and I beg you
both to protect my children. The younger has been in Rome
all this time, and has not shared in my actions, whatever they
may have been. The elder, Marcus, begged me not to go back
to Syria, and I wish now that I had taken his advice, not he
mine. I pray therefore even more earnestly that he, being
innocent, should not pay the penalty for a crime that is my
own. By my forty-five years of faithful service, by our shared
consulship, I, whom once your father the Divine Augustus
once trusted and whose friend you yourself once were, beg
you, Caesar – as the last favour I will ever ask – to spare my
unfortunate son.

Tear-jerking stuff, right? Well written though, even if it did
sound stiff as hell.

'Can I keep this?' I asked.

'If you like. It isn't the only copy.'

I tucked it into a fold in my mantle. Something didn't add up.
Uncle Cotta had said the letter might not exist at all. Now this
smarmy bastard was handing me a notarised copy and telling
me the Wart had read it out to the Senate. Which included
the consul Valerius Cotta. An omission was one thing. Total
misrepresentation of the facts was another. Cotta might've been
against Piso, but he was no liar and he'd had no reason to lie. So
what was going on?

'This was passed on to you by Carus?' I asked.

'Who?' Regulus looked puzzled.

'Piso's freedman.'

'Oh, you mean Carillus? Yes. Yes, that's right.'

'You know where I can find him?'

'No. No, I'm afraid I can't help you there.' The smile had gone glassy. I'd touched a nerve, obviously, but what nerve? And how and why? 'I don't think Carillus is in Rome any longer.'

'Yeah? So where is he?'

'I really can't say.' Regulus was on his feet now and moving towards the door. 'Well, Valerius Corvinus, it has been a real pleasure talking with you but I have a considerable amount of work to get through today and I must be getting on with it. Please feel free to . . . ah . . . I mean, if you have any more questions don't hesitate to . . .'

Etcetera. Mumble mumble. I didn't listen to the rest because I recognised the bum's rush when I heard it, but I'd got all I wanted from him for the moment. Not all he could give, I knew, but Regulus wasn't going anywhere and I didn't want to raise any more dust than I had to. He'd been co-operative enough, suspiciously so, in fact. Nevertheless . . .

'So you know Caelius Crispus?' I said.

Regulus's hand, with its polished and neatly manicured fingernails, had been resting on my arm. Now he pulled it away like he'd been stung.

'We know each other, yes,' he said.

'Colleagues?'

The barest hesitation. Crispus may've known his way about the Treasury, but he wasn't an employee. Dirt and scandal, those were Crispus's business. His connections with the Treasury officials, or one especially pretty near the top, were more personal. Much more personal.

'No. Not colleagues. Just friends.'

'Yeah.' I grinned at him. 'Yeah. That makes sense. Give him my regards next time he drops by, will you? Thanks a lot, Regulus. I'll see you around.'

And on that cheap note I left.

7

After leaving Regulus I cut right across town to the Racetrack district and Scylax's gym. Not that I wanted a workout: I was getting enough exercise that morning without that dwarfish sadistic bastard beating the hell out of me as well. What I needed was information.

Scylax has lived in Rome most of his life. What he did before, where he came from, what his real name is – Scylax is only a nickname – Jupiter knows, though I doubt if even he'd've had the guts to ask straight out. He started as a gladiator trainer before going freelance, and taking him on as a client five or six years back and buying him his own place had been the best investment I'd ever made. Not just financially. The guy was a genius in teaching the kind of fighting that'd have you blackballed on any self-respecting training ground in Rome but made sure you walked out of an alley fight with all your appurtenances still attached. He also had a net of contacts among the city's underlife that would make the Imperial Secret Service hand in their cloaks and daggers and take up embroidery. That sort of return you don't get with trading.

When I reached the gym Scylax's slave and right-hand freak Daphnis was shifting the sand around the exercise yard with a rake: his normal occupation, except on slow days when you had to be watching closely to see the bugger move at all.

'Hey, Daphnis! The boss in?' I gave him the big smile. It's just as well to keep in with the staff, and the big Spaniard was no bonehead, whatever front he put on.

'Yeah.' The rake paused, not that you'd've noticed, and

Daphnis shifted his head towards the bath buildings. 'He's got a guy on the table, though. Help yourself, Corvinus.'

I nodded and picked my way between the wannabe bladesmen. The gym was getting popular. Even at this time, when most self-respecting Romans were out at work, there were three or four pairs slogging away with wooden foils. And I could hear the screams from the massage room up ahead already.

Scylax had the lucky punter face down and was rearranging the muscles of his back according to some arcane principle of his own. The guy's neck was the colour of raw liver and from the noise he was making he wasn't exactly enjoying the experience.

Scylax looked up, saw me and grunted. 'Hey. Be with you in a minute, Corvinus.'

'No hurry.' I sat down on the bench next to the door and watched while the little bald-head prised two plates of muscle apart and inserted a knuckle. The punter's feet drummed the table and he chewed on the towel Scylax had thoughtfully provided. The knuckle slowly worked its way in and down and I found my balls contracting in sympathy. Scylax might be the best masseur in Rome, but he was also an evil-minded bastard who liked his job far more than was decent. Finally, when he'd rearranged the guy's anatomy to his own satisfaction and rubbed the oil in, he let him up.

'That's all, sir,' he said. Polite as hell.

The customer swung his shaky legs over the side of the table, grabbed his towel and tottered off towards the changing rooms without a word. Supercilious bugger. Or maybe he was just afraid Scylax would change his mind and haul him back.

Scylax wiped his oily hands on a rag and looked at me. 'You next, Corvinus?'

'Uh-uh. No way.' I held up my hands. Having a massage from Scylax is like being mugged by a gorilla with a degree in anatomy. You may feel great afterwards but it's a pleasure to be rationed. 'This is business.'

'You want to go over the accounts? Corvinus, you can see how busy I am!'

'Not that kind of business. I need you to find someone for me.'

'Yeah?' He gave me a look and flung the rag on to the table. 'Okay. So tell me. But I can only spare you ten minutes, right?'

So much for the respect due from client to patron, but I was used to Scylax by now. If he'd called me 'sir' and licked my boots like your normal client I'd've had the doctors in. 'You ever heard of a guy called Carillus?'

'What kind of guy? Gladiator? Race driver? Knifeman?' Scylax sat down on the empty table. 'Pimp?'

'Freedman. I don't know what line he's in. Patron was Gnaeus Calpurnius Piso, before he slit his throat.'

A long whistle. 'You mixed up with that stuff again, boy?'

'Yeah.' I didn't go into details. Scylax would understand. 'You know him?'

'No. But if he was a freedman of Piso's I can put you on to somebody who does. Right now, in fact.' He got up and moved to the open door. 'Daphnis!' he yelled. 'Hey, *Daphnis!*'

There was a long pause while the ball of Spanish fire parked his rake, shambled over from the other side of the exercise ground and propped up the door frame with his shoulder.

'Yeah?' he said.

'Corvinus is asking about one of the Piso freedmen.'

'No kidding?' Daphnis looked unimpressed, but then he always did.

Scylax turned back to me. 'Daphnis's cousin's a litterman with the Pisos. Or was.'

Daphnis nodded glumly. 'The bastard's been cadging free drinks on the strength of it ever since the trial.'

'Is that right?' Someone up there liked me after all. 'This cousin of yours have a name?'

'Capax. Bought himself out after Piso's death. He runs half a chair now out of Augustus Square.'

'Great! He'll be there today?'

'Maybe.' The big Spaniard spat carefully on to the sand outside. 'You know the litter business, Corvinus. They don't work office hours. Stand around long enough in the square and you might get lucky.'

'Gee, thanks.' I got up and he moved aside. 'I owe you one.'

'Just tell Capax I sent you.' Daphnis was already heading back to his rake. 'Then if you can manage to leave him pissed the stingy bastard might feel obliged to return the favour for once.'

It had to be Augustus Square, of course; right back the way across town, not far from where I'd just come from. I could've taken a litter, but litters aren't thick on the ground in the Eleventh District except on race days. Besides, it was getting late and my belly was rumbling. I decided to go back home first and see what Perilla had been doing.

She was out, visiting her mother at the Fabius place further up the hill. I thought of going round to join her. Then I thought again. Call me a coward if you like, but as I think I've said somewhere else insanity's the one thing I can't hack, even if it's the gentle empty-headed kind Perilla's mother suffered from. When we'd got married I'd offered to give Fabia Camilla her own suite in the house, but I was relieved when Perilla turned me down. The old woman was happy enough staying with her cousin, and Marcia saw she was well looked after. There was no point in moving her. Luckily.

So I grabbed a slice of meat, a hunk of bread and a travelling flask of Setinian and took my own litter downtown. It'd be faster that way, and the litter slaves could do with losing a few pounds of unsightly flab. Eccentricity's fine, but unless you exercise them now and again chairmen can turn into real lardballs. I let them go just short of the Market Square, though, and walked the rest: picking up likely looking young chairmen from a litter of your own is a favourite game of a certain set of my acquaintance, and I didn't want to get myself that reputation.

As usual, there were a few chairs hanging about the south side of the square. I went up to the first one. The lead was a big Nubian, which more or less disqualified him for Daphnis's cousin unless the sisters'd had seriously different tastes in men.

'Hey, friend,' I said. 'You know Capax?'

The Nubian gave me a long careful stare that took in my slightly soiled but expensive mantle with its narrow purple stripe and my straight patrician nose. Obviously the guy had heard all about the young chairman dodge. From the look he gave me I'd've bet he could've written the script.

'Maybe,' he said at last. 'Tall thin man. Spaniard. Heavy breather. One eye gone.'

Shit. Hardly Chairman of the Year material. When his parents had named him Capax they must've had their fingers crossed.

'Yeah. That's the guy,' I said, and hoped it was. 'Daphnis's cousin.'

The Nubian relaxed; either at the mention of Daphnis or more likely because having mentally placed Capax he couldn't imagine him as any narrow-striper's sexual fantasy. 'He went out an hour ago with a customer for the Viminal, sir. He should be back any minute unless he gets another fare or stops off on the Sacred Way for a quick one.'

Yeah. That fitted in with what Daphnis had told me too; at least if by a quick one the Nubian meant booze, which wasn't necessarily so because the Sacred Way brothels are open all hours. To kill time I wandered over to the open booths behind the litter rank and bought a bilious-looking pastry peacock with squinty currant eyes for Perilla and a new hernia support for Bathyllus. I was turning over a collection of amulets and wondering what the chances were of being caught in an earthquake or catching leprosy, and whether or not I needed the insurance, when the Nubian shouted over. I looked up. A litter was coming in on a wing and a prayer, and its second man was obviously Capax.

Not a pretty sight. Forget Chairman of the Year. Capax wouldn't even've made the last five.

I pulled my eyes away. 'Hey, pal,' I said, turning to the stall owner. 'You got anything for flat feet?'

He rummaged around and held up two evil-eyed little figurines.

'One Greek, one Egyptian. Both good, sir. Which you want?'

'Give me the pair. Put them on the one chain.' I reckoned the poor guy needed all the help he could get. Besides, a silver piece covered it easy. Gods who look after flat feet come pretty low down in the divine pecking order.

I tossed another silver piece to the Nubian, who caught it and grinned. Then I went over to the tall thin guy on the new chair, who was busily engaged in trying to keep his lungs working.

'Your name Capax, friend?' I asked.

'Yeah,' he wheezed. 'So what?'

Obviously the open, cheerful type. I could see the family resemblance already. 'These're for you.' I gave him the amulets. 'Also your cousin Daphnis suggested I buy you a drink. There somewhere near here we can go?'

On the word 'drink' his one eye had lit up like Polyphemus the Cyclops's.

'Sure,' he said. 'The White Poplar. In Gaul's Alley.'

'Let's do it, then.' I turned to his partner: a short beefy German who must've been mentally subnormal to have hitched up with Old Capable here. 'Sorry, friend. You mind finding a jug of your own somewhere else?'

'*Was? Was hast du gesagt?*'

Jupiter! You'd think someone would teach these guys Latin before letting them come over. I slipped him another Wart's Head. The German may've been slow, but not that slow. He made the coin vanish. Then he vanished too, along with the Nubian and his mate, in the direction of an evil-smelling cookshop that sidled on to the square. I wished them luck. I'd bet whatever went into the rissoles would keep them running all afternoon.

We made our way to Gaul's Alley, a hundred yards off the square, and bagged a choice table under the eponymous poplar. From the state of the ground under the tree the neighbourhood dogs must've thought it was a prime site too, but I doubted if Capax could've made it inside and I didn't want the guy folding up on me before I'd milked him dry, so I just watched where I put my feet and tried not to breathe too often. Then I ordered up a jug of their best and grinned with professional appreciation while Capax sank his cup at one go. I tasted mine more gingerly. Not bad stuff, not bad at all; in fact, it might even be Calenan, and you don't see that stuff often these days since the vineyards deteriorated. Dog shit or not, this place was a find, and I tagged it for future reference. Old Capable might be a walking disaster but he obviously had the soul of a wine drinker.

'So.' He wiped his mouth with the back of his hand. 'Daphnis sent you, did he? You want to tell me why?'

No. That was one thing I didn't want to do, unless I had to. I ducked the question. 'He said you were Calpurnius Piso's chairman. Before he had the run-in with the razor.'

'It wasn't no razor, friend. But yeah, I carried him, off and on.'

'You were in Syria?'

'Nah.' He poured himself another belt of wine and drank it straight down. Jupiter! And Perilla thought I was bad! I signalled the waiter for a second jug. 'I was one of the house slaves.'

That made sense. Piso would've taken the cream with him, sure: major-domo, chef, his wife's maid, his own valet. Maybe even a coachman. Not the rest. It would've been cheaper to buy them over there and sell when he left; and of course the Residence would have its own staff.

'But he kept you on in Rome?' I asked.

'That's right.' Capax sank another cupful. For a thin guy he could really put it down; maybe he was well named after all. I just hoped he could hold it too. 'Some of us were farmed out to his brother, but mostly we just hung around.'

'He was a good master?'

'He was okay. Nothing special. Plancina was a bitch, though. I was sorry she got off.'

That gave me my opening. 'You think they did it, then? Murdered Germanicus?'

'How should I know?'

A fair answer; but then sometimes litter slaves overhear things, so the question wasn't exactly stupid. I tried my main tack. 'Okay. So tell me about Piso's freedman Carillus.'

Capax upended the jug into his cup after pouring me a token splash. 'Carillus? Why should you be interested in Carillus?'

'I'm buying, friend. Remember? And there's another of these on its way. Just answer the question.'

He shrugged. 'Fair enough. He worked in the kitchens. Skivvy, not chef. Bought himself out a few years back. He's got a butcher's business now in the Subura.'

So much for Regulus's statement that the guy had left Rome. But then I hadn't believed that for a minute anyway. 'You know the address?'

'Sure I do. Just behind the Shrine of Hermes, off Suburan Street.' I knew the place. Not a bad location, for the Subura. High class, in fact, comparatively speaking. 'He's doing quite well. Owns a slaughterhouse too now, up near Tannery Row.'

'What was his connection with Piso? Apart from the client-patron link?'

Capax shrugged again. The waiter came over and set the new jug on the table. This time I got in first and filled my cup before the bugger finished that one as well. At least the wine didn't seem to be affecting him, but at this rate Daphnis's request that I leave his cousin plastered looked like costing a small fortune.

'No idea. They may've had a scam or two going, though, because Carillus always was a bit shady. After he left the chef bought the family's meat from him and got his cut on the deal. The meat wasn't all that great, either.'

Something had been bugging me. 'You said Piso didn't use a razor to commit suicide.'

'Uh-uh. His barber kept the things under his own mattress. Said if the master wanted to kill himself he was keeping the fuck out of it.'

'So what did he use? A dagger?'

'Cavalry sword. We found it by him the next morning. Not me personally, of course, but the word got around.'

I sat back. The hairs on the back of my neck were lifting, always a sure sign that something is screwy somewhere. But thinking could wait.

'Okay,' I said. 'So let's talk about something else now. Were you with the family through the trial?'

'Yeah. Right from the moment they landed.' Capax helped himself liberally from the jug. 'We got the word they were coming downriver and to meet them at the mausoleum. Bloody stupid way to do things, especially the mood the mob were in, but that was Plancina for you.'

The tingling increased. I tried to put it to the back of my mind.

'Where is the Piso place, exactly?'

'City centre.' He jerked his head towards the mass of the Capitol. 'One of these big old-fashioned places overlooking the Market Square.'

'Uhuh.' I took a swallow of wine. 'So. Piso and Plancina get off the boat by Augustus's mausoleum and you take them all the way to Market Square. What time was this?'

'You mean what time of day?' I nodded. 'Must've been mid-morning because the streets were packed. Besides, Plancina had all their clients and hangers-on turn up. As well as the household, of course.'

'Okay. Then what? After they got home?'

'Not a lot. But they threw a party that evening. Thousand-lamp job. You could've picked the house out from right across the river if there'd been nothing else in between.'

Shit! This guy was pure gold! I could've taken him home with me, but it would've cost a fortune to keep him in wine.

'One last thing,' I said. 'You know anything about a letter? A suicide note?'

'Sure.' Capax nodded. 'The master left one with the emperor's name on it. They say Tiberius read it out in the Senate.'

'Any idea how it got to him? The emperor, I mean?'

'Search me, friend. How do these things usually get delivered? Somebody picked it up and passed it on, I suppose. You don't mess with the imperial mail.'

Forget the tingling at the back of the neck. What hit me now was a cold hook right deep in my bowels. '"Picked it up"? Picked it up from where?'

'Who knows?' Capax poured himself another full cup of the wine and drained it. 'The desk? The floor? Where do suicides usually leave notes?'

'Hold on, pal.' I had to have this right. 'You mean the note to the emperor was still in the room when Piso's body was found the next morning?'

He looked at me like I'd suddenly grown an extra head. 'Sure it was,' he said. 'Where else would it be?'

Where else would it be? Oh, Jupiter!

8

I left Capax a jug and a half ahead and a gold piece richer and went back to the Palatine (no, I didn't take a litter. If these guys in Augustus Square had been patronising the local cookshop I doubted if they'd make it as far as the Temple of Vesta). Perilla was already home, sitting by the pool and looking stunning in a light blue mantle. I kissed her.

'Did you have a successful day, Corvinus?' she said.

'Yeah. You could say that.' I gave her the cross-eyed peacock. 'Present.'

'Oh, how lovely. Just what I've always wanted.'

I grinned. 'You should see what I brought Bathyllus.'

She laid the peacock on the edge of the pool. 'So tell me. What did you find out?'

'In a minute. I've been three times across Rome today, lady, and I'm whacked. That rates a celebration drink.' On cue, Bathyllus came in with a jug of the Falernian on a tray. I gave him his hernia support, modestly wrapped.

'Thank you, sir,' he said. 'What is it?'

'Open it in private, sunshine, and enjoy. What time's dinner?'

'Meton says it'll be some while yet, sir. He's had an upset with the sauce.'

'No problem. We'll have a couple of liquid starters while we're waiting.'

Bathyllus poured and left.

'So,' Perilla said. 'You have your drink, Corvinus. Now tell me.'

'The Wart's in this up to the hairs on his boils.' I let the Falernian trickle gloriously past my tonsils. 'Maybe even Livia, whatever she says to the contrary. Jupiter knows what game she's playing.'

'Explain, please.' Perilla sipped at her own cup.

I started at the beginning, with the visit to the Treasury.

'You think this Regulus knows more than he told you?' she asked when I'd finished.

'Sure he does. But he thought I knew it already. Maybe it was relevant, maybe not, but I'll swear the guy was doing a runner when I nailed him. Funnily enough I don't think it had anything to do with the trial, though. He blossomed like a rose when I told him I wanted to talk about that.'

'Perhaps he has a guilty conscience. You say he works in the tax department.'

'Yeah.' I frowned. There had been something there, something I'd missed . . . 'Anyway, the main business was over the letter.'

'Uncle Cotta's missing letter?'

'Fuck knows, lady. That's one big problem with this case. Too many letters.'

'You've lost me, Corvinus. And please don't swear if you can help it.'

'Sorry.' I took a mouthful of Falernian and used it to marshal my thoughts. 'Okay. Let's take the letters. We've got three. Or three sets. Whatever. One, the private correspondence between Piso and the Wart that neither of them would let the Senate see. Call that A. Then there's Letter B that Cotta says Piso wrote the night he died and gave to his freedman Carillus to deliver. Check?'

Perilla smiled. 'Check.'

'Only I find out from a guy called Capax who was one of Piso's slaves that there's a third letter. Call it C. A suicide note addressed to the emperor and which the Wart read out to the Senate the next day, and Cotta never told us about.'

'But the answer's simple, Marcus! He did. B and C are the same. Piso wrote his suicide note to the emperor and gave it to Carillus to pass on through his lawyers.'

'No. I assumed they were the same when I left the Treasury, because that's what that bastard Regulus told me and I'd no reason to disbelieve him. But Regulus was lying.'

'How do you know?'

'Because Capax, who's got no axe to grind one way or the other, said C was found in Piso's room the next morning. If B were identical with C then Piso couldn't've given it to Carillus the night before, and we know he gave him a letter of some kind. So C's accounted for but B's still missing. We're back at what Cotta told us. The night he died Piso wrote a letter to someone, sealed it and gave it to his freedman to deliver. At which point it disappeared. Who it was to, what was in it and whether it was delivered we still don't know.'

'I see. Can't you ask the freedman directly?'

'Yeah. Sure I can. That's tomorrow's job. At least I know who he is now, and where to find him.' I sank another quarter-pint of the Falernian. 'And that's another thing, Perilla. This guy Carillus is some queer cookie. For a start he sounds as crooked as a Corinthian dice artist. Also I'd assumed he was Piso's secretary or some such, but it turns out he was in charge of plucking the chickens.'

'So?'

'An ex-kitchen slave's hardly a social giant, lady. They tend to smell of giblets and pick their teeth with the dinner knives. Patrons may take a percentage of their profits when they set up in business for themselves but they don't encourage an intimate acquaintance. So why should Piso choose a chicken plucker to give an important letter to? Or do you think that after a hard day in the dock he made a habit of sneaking down Suburan Street for a pound of sausages and a cosy chat?'

'But there must be some connection between them, Corvinus. After all, the man did carry the letter. Or did he?'

'Sure he did.' I paused. 'At least I think he did. At least . . .' Oh, shit. I didn't know what to think any more.

'He wasn't ' – Perilla hesitated – 'a *favourite* of any kind, was he?'

'You mean was he Piso's toyboy? Yeah, that's a possibility. Not a strong one, though. I haven't met the guy and I didn't know Piso, but Capax wasn't one to pull his punches and I'm sure he would've said.' My cup was empty. I got up and refilled it from the jug on the table. 'Perilla, I'm sorry, I can't think. I'm too tired. Let's leave it for now, okay?'

'Why did you say you thought the emperor was involved?'

'That was Capax too.' I sat down again.

'He told you?'

'Not in so many words. The guy was only a litter slave. But the way he told it the Wart had to be involved.'

'Why?'

I sighed. 'Okay, let's play charades. We're Piso and Plancina, right? We've just murdered the emperor's son and heir and committed ten kinds of treason. Germanicus's widow and half the Syrian staff are itching to get us up a dark alleyway somewhere for a quiet talk and the whole of Rome wants to see what we look like turned inside out and pegged up for the crows. Like it or not we have to come back to stand trial. So how do we do it?'

'We slip back quietly, of course. Probably at dead of night and in a closed carriage.'

'Right. Only in the event we don't. We sail down the Tiber in a barge scattering roses like Antony and Cleopatra, put in about as far upstream as we can get, let all our friends and enemies know we're coming and stage a public bump and grind through the middle of the city at a time when everyone's around to wave. Then we throw the biggest party of the season and blow raspberries at the crowd from the balcony. Does that tell you something about us, lady?'

Perilla smiled. 'It tells me we've lost our senses. Or perhaps that we couldn't care less for public opinion.'

'Okay.' I stretched my length on the couch. 'Let's take the second suggestion. Why shouldn't we care? Remember we're not just talking about a few yobbos throwing cabbages and calling us dirty names. Some of that public opinion's got a wide purple stripe down its mantle and it's pretty pissed off at us already.'

She was silent for a long time. Then she said slowly: 'We don't care because we know we're innocent and we can prove it. Because we know we've got right on our side. And because we know we're protected.'

I grinned. 'Smack on the button, lady. And who's big enough to protect us against everything the mob, the Senate and Agrippina's fan club can throw at us?'

'The Imperials. Tiberius and Livia.'

'Tiberius and Livia.' I drank my wine. 'Congratulations. You win the nuts.'

'But Livia swore she had nothing to do with Germanicus's death. And Tiberius may have saved Plancina but he went out of his way not to protect Piso. In fact, he abandoned him to the Senate.'

'Right. Only we're talking pre-trial here. Piso and Plancina didn't know that was how it would be played at the time. You see what I meant last night about a standing deal?'

Perilla shook her head. 'No. I'm sorry, Corvinus,' she said, 'but I simply cannot believe Tiberius had his son murdered. And if you are convinced that Livia was telling the truth too, then . . .'

'Wait. That's not all. Okay, as I see it we've got two possible scenarios. First that Piso and Plancina were guilty on all counts but they thought they had a deal with the Imperials that would get them off, because the Wart and his mother – or the Wart alone – had ordered them to commit the murder.'

'But why should Tiberius . . . ?'

I held up a hand. 'Second scenario. Piso and Plancina were innocent as new-born babes, and they knew that the Imperials knew and could prove it. Or at least make sure they didn't get chopped for something they didn't do. Only they were too trusting. In fact they were the fall guys. Tiberius set them up and then pulled the rug from under them. Rome wanted a scapegoat and the emperor gave her one, maybe to cover up his own guilt, certainly to cover up someone's.'

'Do you have any proof of this, Marcus? Any proof at all?'

I took the letter out of the belt in my tunic – the copy of Piso's suicide note I'd got from Regulus – and passed it over.

'Read this,' I said. 'Sure, it might be garbage from beginning to end but it rings true. I don't believe Piso did it. I think he was set up.'

Perilla read the letter. When she put it down she was frowning.

'You're right,' she said. 'About the letter, at least. It does sound sincere.'

'There's another thing. According to Capax Piso slit his throat with a cavalry sword.'

'That's rather unusual.'

'Difficult, too.'

'Perhaps that was all he had to hand.'

'Oh, sure!' I rubbed my eyes. The tiredness was coming back, and even although I was used to walking my legs felt stiff. 'Perilla, he was in his own house. His barber might be sleeping on the razors but he'd surely have a knife put away somewhere. And even if he didn't the best way to kill yourself with a sword is to put the point against your chest and fall on it.'

'You mean Piso was murdered? But, Corvinus, we'd already decided that!'

'Sure he was murdered. The question is, why that way? Why not with a razor or a knife, to make it look plausible? Or if the murderer did use a sword, why not a chest wound?'

'I assume you do have an answer.'

'Yeah. I think so. Say you were Tiberius or his agent, and you wanted to get rid of a political embarrassment by faking a suicide. How would you do it?'

'As you said. With a knife or a razor, or a sword between the ribs.'

'Right. Now listen carefully, because this is tricky. Let's say you were someone else, and you wanted to do things the other way round. Take a genuine suicide and turn it into a fake murder. Or maybe commit a murder, tart it up as suicide, but make sure the death looked suspicious.'

I could see her working that one out. Then she looked at me with startled eyes. 'You think that's what happened?'

'I'd risk good money, lady. So who did it, and why?'

'The why is obvious. To throw suspicion on a third party.'

'The third party being the Wart and/or Livia. Yeah. So what about the who?'

'Agrippina. Or one of Germanicus's friends.'

'Stirring the shit in revenge for the Wart quashing the murder charge?' I nodded. 'Right. It's possible.'

She was frowning again. 'There is another possibility, Marcus. That it was a genuine suicide, but that Piso himself wanted to disguise it as murder to get back at the emperor.'

I sighed. 'Or maybe the whole thing's a mare's nest, I'm being too clever and the sword was the only thing Piso had in his cupboard after all. We're going round and round in circles, lady. Call it a night. So how was your afternoon?'

We talked about Perilla's mother, or at least she did while I sank another cup of the Falernian and wool-gathered until dinner. Bathyllus must've opened his present because when the little guy came in to announce that the sauce crisis was over and we could eat he was beaming. Tomorrow was another day. I just hoped when I got there Carillus's butcher shop would be open and the guy wasn't already at the bottom of the Tiber in a pair of concrete sandals. If I'd been the Wart, or whoever the hell was responsible for all this, that would've been one of my priorities.

9

I found the place without any trouble, and the shutters were off. Capax had been right, it was one of the biggest shops in the street with a proper painted sign and two or three customers waiting to be served. I parked myself behind an old woman with a basket of onions and watercress and waited my turn.

The guy behind the counter was German: a mean-looking six-footer with red hair and a wart on his nose that wouldn't've disgraced the emperor and put me off chickpeas for a month. He swung a neat cleaver, too, and I promised myself I'd think twice before going up any dark alleyways in his company. At least this time around no one had decided yet that Corvinus would look better with his belly ventilated. That was something to be thankful for. I just hoped it would last.

The woman in front of me left with her half-pound of chitterlings. I moved up to the counter.

'Yeah?' Customer relations obviously weren't the guy's strong point.

'Your name Carillus?' I asked.

He jerked his head at the sign. 'How's your reading, friend?'

'There somewhere we can talk?'

'That thing says "Butcher". Butchers sell meat. So what can I get you?'

Jupiter! 'How are your collops this morning?'

'Pound?'

'Make it two.' I held up a gold piece. 'And ten minutes of your valuable time.'

He gave me a long measuring look; me, not the coin. Then

he set down his cleaver and wiped his hands on a scrap of bloody rag.

'Scaurus!' A thin lad with bad skin who was filleting a leg of lamb on the back bench looked round. 'Take over until I get back. Right?'

The thin lad nodded. Obviously, from the facial resemblance, the son and heir. Carillus came out through the gap in the counter.

'Ten minutes, pal,' he said. 'You drink beer?'

Oh, hell. 'When I have to. Yeah. Sure.'

He grunted and led the way across the street to a wooden shack that leaned against the side wall of a horsemeat seller's. The inside was bare and empty except for a counter, a couple of trestle tables and an old woman sitting in the corner. Carillus growled out a word or two in German and the woman poured us two foaming beakers from the barrel beside her.

'Right.' He tossed a handful of small change on to the counter and sat down at one of the tables. 'So what do you want that's worth a gold piece to you, friend?'

I took the bench facing him. 'You're a freedman of Calpurnius Piso's.'

'Was. The guy's dead. Or hadn't you heard?'

'I need to know about a certain letter he wrote the night he died.'

'Is that right, now?'

Jupiter! When he'd made that crack about butchers selling meat he hadn't been kidding. This guy had his mouth sewn up tighter than a gnat's arse. 'According to my information he gave it to you.'

'Your informant being?'

There was no reason not to tell him. 'A guy called Livineius Regulus. One of Piso's lawyers.'

'Uhuh.' He eyed me speculatively. 'Yeah, okay. Piso gave me a letter that night. So what?'

Well, that was one question answered. At least Letter B existed. 'You mind telling me who it was addressed to and what happened to it?' I said.

He took a long pull at his beer and set the beaker down three-quarters empty.

'What the fuck business is it of yours?' he said softly.

'Call it curiosity.'

That long measuring look again. Then, suddenly, he laughed.

'Okay, pal. I'll make a deal with you. What's your name, by the way?'

'Corvinus. Valerius Corvinus.'

'Okay, Corvinus. Here's the deal. Forget your money, I don't need it. You say you drink beer. Prove it. Finish that pot at one go, without taking a breath, and I'll tell you what you want to know for free. Leave enough inside to wet the table, or spill so much as a drop down your chin, and you can go and lose yourself. Bet?'

Shit. I was no beer drinker, and these things held two pints at least.

'Bet,' I said.

'Go for it, then.'

I picked up the beaker and took a deep breath. The stuff smelled like stale yeasty horse piss, and it had a head on it that sat and sneered. The taste was worse. Halfway down I knew I wasn't going to make it. Then my eyes met his over the rim of the beaker and suddenly twenty generations of cross-grained, bloody-minded Valerii were in my head and yelling, 'Screw you, pal!' So I finished it.

Carefully, my eyes still on his, I lowered the beaker and set it back on the table, topside down. Not a drip.

He clapped me on the shoulder. I belched.

'Not bad for a Roman,' he said. 'Maybe you can drink beer after all. You want another?'

No way. I wasn't doing that again, not even in exchange for a signed statement witnessed by the Wart himself. 'We had a bet, sunshine,' I said. 'Remember?'

'Yeah.' He reached inside his tunic, brought out a letter and handed it over. 'This what you want?'

The seal had been broken, so I opened it. I didn't know what Piso's handwriting looked like, but it had his signature at the bottom and there was no reason why it shouldn't be genuine. The letter was the deed to a slaughterhouse near Tannery Row, made out to Gnaeus Calpurnius Carillus.

*   *   *

So we were stymied, I thought as I walked back through the Subura towards town. Letter B had turned out to be a red herring: a transfer of property from patron to client paid for fair and square out of the profits of the big German's butcher-meat business. Sure, it had been a coincidence that the deal was finalised the day Piso had died, but coincidences happen. Carillus was just lucky he'd got his deed before Piso was beyond signing it. There was only one thing that still bugged me, and that was why Regulus had lied when he'd said the freedman had brought the suicide note. Maybe I should have another word with the smoothie bastard, somewhere people wouldn't come running if the furniture got a little disarranged.

I found myself within two streets of the Shrine of Libera. I hadn't seen Agron in six months, not since the wedding when he'd hit me a smacker in the ear with a celebration walnut, so maybe a quick courtesy call wouldn't go amiss. Besides, after that German beer I needed a drink.

Agron was the big Illyrian who'd saved my life over on the Janiculum after pushing my face into a Suburan dinner service. He'd severed his connection with the bastard Asprenas, of course, but he still had his metalsmith's business near the Libera shrine. I suppose you could call him a kind of client of mine. Just. Real patrons have real clients. I'm stuck with stubborn, independent-minded buggers like Scylax and Agron.

He was in, luckily, but he put up the shutters and we went round to a local wineshop and split a jug of half-decent Massic with a dish of good cheese and olives on the side: Agron's got a weakness for cheese. We talked about this and that for a while – he's no bonehead, for all his barleybread accent, and he can handle a conversation – and then he said: 'So what are you doing these days, Corvinus?'

Maybe it was the fact that I was on a downer after seeing Carillus. Maybe because I had a certain respect for the guy. Whatever the reason, I told him. Not everything, not about Livia, although he knew all about my past relations with the empress. Just that I was interested in the Piso case, and in how Germanicus died.

'You ever serve under him?' I asked. Agron was ex-army. He'd been one of the few survivors of the Eighteenth Legion when it was massacred in the Teutoburg.

'No. He was after my time.'

'Know anyone who did?'

He grinned. 'Sure. Dozens. You can't talk to a Rhine squaddie for more than two minutes before he starts boasting how he served under Germanicus. Whether he did or not.'

'The guy was that good, eh?'

Agron spat out an olive pip into his palm. 'To the Rhine legions Germanicus is god, Corvinus. As far as they're concerned there's only ever been one General – capital G – between Gaul and the Elbe. And that's Germanicus.'

'Not the Wart?'

'Not the Wart. Sure, Tiberius was good, better in some ways, but he still isn't the General. Not to most squaddies, anyhow.'

'Better in what ways?' I speared a piece of cheese.

Agron's eyes narrowed. 'You got a reason for asking?'

'No. Not especially.' I didn't, but now the Carillus angle seemed to have fizzled out I was groping around for a new one. And if the Wart was involved then I needed to know more about the relationship between father and adopted son. 'Just curious.'

'Yeah.' The suspicious look changed back to a grin. 'That I'd believe. Your curiosity'll be the death of you one of these days. Okay. So maybe better's the wrong word. Germanicus and Tiberius were different characters, heart and head, with Germanicus being the heart. And heart'll win over head with squaddies every time.'

That made sense of a sort, although I didn't completely agree with his views. The Wart's campaigns in Germany had been slow and steady, while Germanicus's were flashier and covered more ground but in the end they got us nowhere. Still, like he'd said, it wasn't totally fair to compare the two as generals. Agron wasn't stupid, he just thought direct like the soldier he was . . .

Something tugged at my brain. I reached for it, but it wasn't there any longer. Never mind, it would come in its own time.

Agron was saying something. I switched my attention back to him.

'Of course the guy had a lot of points with the squaddies from the way he handled the mutiny after Augustus died. Agrippina too. That's some woman, Corvinus. Iron hard, army to the bone and with more sheer guts than a dozen first centurions. You ever meet her?'

'Agrippina? No. No, never.'

'Pity.' Not the word I would've used. 'If Germanicus is the General then Agrippina's his second. That kid of theirs is going to be a red-hot soldier, too. Young Gaius. Caligula.'

'That right?' I drank my wine. I could feel the faint prickling at the back of my neck that was telling me that something was important here if I could only put my finger on it.

'Yeah. It was a shame the poor guy died,' Agron shared the last of the Massic between our two cups. 'He'd've made an emperor. Drusus is okay, but he's no Germanicus. He's like his father, all head.' He pushed over the plate. 'Hey, Corvinus, you want some of this cheese before I finish it?'

'No. No thanks, you have it. I'm going . . . *Shit!*'

'You okay, boy?'

'No.' The thought hadn't anything to do with the Germanicus business. It was much more serious. 'I just remembered. We're going out to a birthday dinner tonight. Perilla and me. At my mother's.' Oh, Jupiter! Perilla would kill me! 'I shouldn't be here, friend.'

'Relax! It's hardly two hours past noon yet. You've got lots of time. Anyway, it's my shout.'

I shook my head. 'Helvius Priscus is old-fashioned. He eats early. And I promised Perilla I'd look for an Etruscan relic for him in the Saepta.' Priscus is my mother's husband. He has this thing about tombs. 'Sorry, Agron. Some other time, okay?'

'If this is what marriage does to you then you can keep it.' Agron grinned. 'Yeah, okay. I'll see you around, maybe.'

I tossed the waiter a silver piece and took off at a run. I hadn't been kidding. Less than four hours to get all the way to the Saepta, find a second-hand Etruscan toothmug for Priscus, then hoof it back to the Palatine in time for a bath and a change of mantle. And I'd better do it, too, or Perilla would kill me slowly with sarcasm. Nevertheless, I felt a lot happier for having seen the big Illyrian guy.

You see, I knew now why the Wart had wanted to murder his son.

10

By the time I got to the Saepta I was in a muck sweat, with my mantle in a state that would have Bathyllus climbing the wall when he saw me. Not the best condition for a visit to one of Rome's most exclusive shopping districts, but where the alternative to keeping up my reputation as a narrow-striper is facing Perilla with a job undone then elegance loses hands down. Phlebas's was at the far end, just short of the Virgan Aqueduct, halfway up a cul-de-sac whose entrance was an anonymous narrow gap between two fashionable goldsmiths. Not a prime site, in other words, but that meant nothing except that Phlebas was a smart cookie who watched his overheads and knew his market. His customers were rich oddballs like Priscus who'd rather collect than eat, and a clientele like that is a licence to coin money. The guy was already making enough to run a house on the Pincian and a fast mistress whose collecting tastes certainly didn't include Babylonian clay tablets; which wasn't bad going for an ex-slave who'd started out selling junk from a stall in the Subura. But then, that's modern Rome for you. Give him another ten years and he'd probably be making the Wart an offer for his little place on the Palatine.

The shop was small and cramped, with just enough floor space to collapse on when you checked out the price tags. When I went in the man himself was dealing with another customer, so I poked around the larger stock arranged down the nearside wall. It was eccentric stuff: a podgy basalt lion like a kid's smudged drawing, a life-sized wooden statue of an Egyptian in a loincloth, and a hatchet-faced Athene complete with constipated owl. Not my style at all. Good garden ornaments, maybe, but too heavy to lug all the way to the Caelian, and pricey as hell. The knick-knacks on the shelves were more promising, and a lot cheaper; meaning the prices didn't overrun the labels. I picked up a small bronze incense burner shaped like a goose, checked the tag (no more than twice what I expected) and carried it over to the counter. Fast work. Maybe I'd be back home in time for a pre-dinner cup of wine after all.

'I'll be with you in a moment, sir,' Phlebas said.

'Yeah, okay.' I jiggled the bronze goose in my hand and tried to look as if I'd got all the time in the world.

I'd probably need it. The other guy had his back to me, and spread out on the counter between him and Phlebas were a dozen ivory door plaques. The two of them were debating the fors and againsts of each one in painful detail. Moment, nothing; there went the wine. Still, you have to be polite, and no one likes a queue-jumper. I went back to staring out the cross-eyed lion.

Ten minutes later they were still going. Politeness is one thing, but I was getting desperate; any longer and I'd have to turn up at Priscus's bathless, stinking of sweat and looking like an alley-cat's leavings, which was more than my life was worth: Bathyllus would die of shame, Perilla probably wouldn't even speak to me for a month, and my mother would be pointedly sending me mantles as Winter Festival presents for the next ten years. So with the goose in one hand and a gold piece in the other I stepped up to the counter and cleared my throat.

Phlebas gave me a warning look but I ignored him and tapped the customer's shoulder.

'Uh, excuse me, friend,' I said in my politest voice. 'You mind if I just pay for this and go?'

Phlebas's face set like concrete as his favoured customer turned round slow enough to give me time to realise I'd just made the biggest mistake since Remus jumped his brother's wall.

The guy buying door plaques was Aelius Sejanus.

'As a matter of fact,' he said, 'I do.'

Uh uh. I swallowed and took half a step back. The caution was natural: you didn't crowd the Wart's favourite, whoever you were, and all Rome knew it, Sejanus especially, and not only for political reasons. The guy was built like a Polycleitus original, out of pure Parian marble. One squeeze in the wrong place and you could kiss your ribs goodbye. There was no comeback, either.

He set the base of his spine against the counter and folded his arms. The counter creaked, and I could hear seams give in his tunic.

'Maybe you didn't notice, *friend*,' he said slowly, 'but I'm negotiating a purchase here.'

'I realise that, sir,' I said, 'but—'

He stopped me. 'You're Messallinus's son, aren't you?'

'Yeah. Yeah, that's right.' Shit. So much for anonymity.

'Then I'd've thought your father would've taught you better manners. He's licked enough arse in his time.'

Phlebas drew in his breath: I may've been in the wrong, but politeness goes both ways and there're some things that just aren't said, even if they're true. Especially if they're true.

'We may have our differences, sir,' I said quietly, 'but Marcus Valerius Messallinus is a highly respected ex-consul. And arse-licking has never been confined to consulars.'

He blinked; he hadn't expected me to answer him back, let alone with an insult of my own. Nor, for that matter, had I. But no one, *no one*, insults family and gets away with it. I took another step backwards, this time to give myself fighting room. Behind me a stone statue that was probably worth half the Aventine jiggled on its pedestal. Phlebas opened his mouth to protest, but thought better of it.

Sejanus was looking at me like I'd just squirmed out of the Tiber on six legs and bitten him.

'I doubt if the emperor would put me on a par with your father, boy,' he said at last. 'Respected ex-consul or not. There're some services more useful to the state than straddling a curule chair for a year.'

'More profitable too.' Jupiter! This couldn't be me talking. The guy only had to whisper a word or two in the Wart's ear to have me dining on beets in Lusitania.

Sejanus's face darkened. For a moment I thought I'd gone too far. Then, suddenly, it cleared again. He laughed and shrugged his massive shoulders.

'All right,' he said. 'Perhaps I'm in no real hurry after all. The emperor's present can wait.' He turned back to Phlebas. The shopkeeper was stone-faced as one of his own statues: new money may talk in Rome, but it knows when to keep its mouth shut. 'Go ahead, Phlebas. Make the sale.'

Without a word, Phlebas checked the tag and slipped the gold piece into his strongbox. He didn't ask me if I wanted the goose gift-wrapped. No change, either.

'Nice piece.' Without asking my permission, Sejanus took the incense burner and turned it over in his hands. 'For yourself? Or for that new wife of yours?'

I kept the surprise out of my face, or at least I hoped I did: for Sejanus to know your family details wasn't exactly a healthy sign.

'Neither,' I said. 'A birthday present for my stepfather.'

'Ah, yes. Old Helvius Priscus.' He passed the goose back. 'I'm sure he'll be delighted. Wish him happy returns from me.'

I tucked the goose into one of the few remaining folds in my mantle and turned to leave.

'Thanks,' I said.

'Don't mention it.' I'd been talking to Phlebas, but if the big guy wanted to think it was meant for him I wasn't going to argue. I'd played the hero enough for one day. All I wanted was to go. 'Oh, and Corvinus?'

The use of my name jerked me round.

'Yeah?'

'It's a shame you don't take after your father in other ways. We could use you. The state, I mean. Tiberius has always appreciated young men with balls.'

Maybe there hadn't been two sides to the remark, but he was grinning. Not a pleasant grin, either. I didn't trust myself to answer. Instead I gave him a wave and made for the door.

'Think about it,' Sejanus called after me. 'You know where to find us.'

I left, quickly. I could still feel his eyes on me halfway to Agrippa's Baths.

We made the dinner, just; by the time I'd got back home, kissed Perilla and changed into a fresh tunic and mantle, the litter slaves had to go hell for leather to arrive prompt. I swear when we pulled up the guys' feet were throwing up steam.

I had an unpleasant surprise when we walked in to the dining room. The man lying on the principal guest couch was my father.

'Uh . . . Hi, Dad,' I said.

'Good evening, Marcus.' Valerius Messallinus gave me a bland smile. 'Perilla.'

There were no other guests. I was thankful for that at least. I get on well enough nowadays with Dad, bar the occasional spat, but I still can't take his new wife. No way.

'Cosconia has a headache, son.' Dad must've read my expression, but then he always was sharp. 'She sends her apologies. And her love.'

Yeah. Yeah, sure. One of these diplomatic headaches. Still, I was grateful to her because it made things a lot easier.

'Sit down, Marcus. Beside me, please.' Mother was looking fantastic as usual in a mantle of the finest Coan silk. And not a day over thirty-five, which was a good fifteen years short of her real age. Priscus, on the other hand, looked gnarled as hell and old as Tithonus on a bad day. His head poked out of the top of his rumpled narrow-striper mantle like a walnut that'd been left too long in the pickle jar. Don't mistake me, though, they were happy enough: the old guy, as my mother had told me once, had hidden depths. He'd have to, to cope with Mother.

'Mmmaa! Perilla! You're next to me, my dear.' Priscus patted the couch. The guy bleats, and I won't mention it again because it's annoying as hell. But he's okay, if you like dried-up mummies who spend all their free time raking around cemeteries.

Perilla hadn't batted her beautiful eyelids once, which gave me the distinct impression that I'd been conned.

'I'll speak to you later, lady,' I whispered out of the corner of my mouth. She smiled demurely as she took her place. We washed our hands and the slaves served the hors d'oeuvres.

'So what are you doing with yourself these days, Marcus?' my father asked. Straight out, no messing. I knew what was coming. It was the reason I avoided him as much as I could.

'This and that.' I kept my voice neutral. I was pretty sure Cotta hadn't split on me, if he'd known anything at all about my involvement with the Germanicus business, but it was best to play things carefully. 'The usual.'

'I see.' He helped himself to some puréed cheese with fish pickle. 'Apropos of which, I haven't seen your name on the selection lists for any of the junior state offices yet. Don't put it off too long, will you, son?'

Perilla gave me a quick warning glance, but I was keeping my cool without her help, and I just nodded. Which was all he really expected. Dad never gave up. If I turned out the only Valerius Messalla who hadn't made at least a city judge's chair before I hung up my mantle for keeps he'd never forgive me. Still, that was the way he was made, I suppose, and I'd stopped minding the needling long since. Which didn't mean I didn't still get it at every opportunity.

'If you ask your father nicely, Marcus,' my mother put in smoothly, 'he might recommend you for one of the minor posts on that corn commission of his. If that oily pusher Sejanus hasn't filled them with his relatives already, of course.'

Ouch. I grinned, while Dad coloured and clammed up. My erstwhile pal from the antiques shop was pushing his finger into every pie around lately. Junius Blaesus, one of Dad's colleagues on the commission, was his uncle, and whatever Sejanus's expressed opinion of Dad was he had let him marry one of his distant cousins. That was a lucky coincidence for Dad, of course – in as much as anything Dad ever did was coincidence – but the shot had gone home and he'd think twice before having another go at me that evening. Saved. I smiled at Mother and she gave me the ghost of a wink.

'Oh. Before I forget.' I handed the incense burner across to Priscus. 'Happy birthday.' I wasn't going to mention my own little run-in with Sejanus, let alone pass on his good wishes. Not even to Perilla. No way. I didn't need the hassle, and I had no intention of taking him up on his parting offer. I may have balls, but I prefer to keep them intact, and sooner or later we'd've had our differences.

Priscus took the little bronze goose and examined it like it was made of cobwebs.

'Veian,' he said. 'About the time of Servius Tullus, I should think. Beautiful, Marcus. Where did you find it?'

'Phlebas's in the Saepta. I'm glad you like it.' I was. Priscus was a nice old stick, even if he was crazy.

'The differences between Veian bronzework and the Caeran type are slight but striking,' he said. 'Notice how . . .'

Jupiter. I groaned quietly while he took us through the Etruscans before moving on to Greeks and Phoenicians. The Celts got mixed in there too, somewhere along the line, but I'd given up by then. Maybe I should've brought him a new cloak pin after all and saved us all a lecture. As it was I learned more about ancient metalwork in the next half-hour than I wanted to; or I would've done if I'd been listening. If it was any consolation everyone else's eyes were glazed as well, except for Mother's. She was hanging on to the old guy's every word.

Somewhere about six hundred years back the slaves cleared away the starters. I sipped my wine and wondered how, when he finally did dry up, I could get Dad to talk about Germanicus's campaigns in Germany from the political side. Without showing that I was interested, naturally. Let on that I'd an ulterior motive and the guy would seize up tighter than a constipated mussel. Which was a pity, because Valerius Messallinus knew the musty back passages of politics as well as a bear knows how to scratch.

In the end it was Priscus himself who solved the problem. We were well into the main course by then – partridge in a raisin sauce, beets with leeks in wine, and pork with anise and chives – when my mother finally laid her hand over his.

'Titus, darling,' she said, 'I think our guests are just a little tired of hearing about the conjugation of irregular verbs in Oscan.' Jupiter! I'd missed that particular jump. But then as I say I'd given up listening long since.

There was an almost audible sigh of relief round the table. Priscus blinked at Mother like a surprised owl. Along with everything else the poor old bugger is blind as a bat to anything more than a tomb inscription's length from his nose.

'Really, dear?' he said.

'Really,' Mother said firmly. 'Do you think we could possibly change the subject?'

'Oh.' Another blink. 'Oh, my. Very well, then. If you're sure.' His brow furrowed and I could see him groping: as far as Priscus was concerned nothing that had happened in the last four hundred years had any relevance to human life whatsoever. 'Ah . . . I hear that nice young Prince Germanicus is dead.'

I stiffened. My father was slitting a beet. He looked up. Sure, it was old news, but as far as he was concerned it was streets ahead of Oscan verbs. Besides, this was his bag. I could see the relief in his face.

'A good job too,' he said.

'Oh, my dear man!' That was Mother. 'What a terrible thing to say!'

'I'm speaking politically, Vipsania.' Dad was using his pompous lawyer's voice; that put-down of my mother's over Sejanus must still be rankling. 'Germanicus was a liability. He may have had his good points and in a subordinate position he was competent to a certain degree, but had he succeeded to the supreme power he would have been disastrous for Rome.'

Uhuh.

'Really? How so, dear? I always thought Germanicus was a lovely boy.'

My father laid his knife aside. 'Oh, not through any baseness of character. Quite the reverse. The fellow was honourable, honest, charming and deservedly popular. But he was shallow. He reminds me very much of Marcus here.'

'Gee, thanks, Dad.'

He didn't smile. 'I don't mean that as an insult, son, only an observation. Germanicus didn't think things through, and as a result he overreached himself on several occasions. Take his German war, for instance. Showy, certainly, but far short of brilliant. And ultimately costly in men, money, prestige and territory.'

Priscus was grinning across the table like a delighted prune. The old guy probably reckoned he'd hit the bull's-eye in the snappy conversational stakes, and from my point of view he had. I couldn't've managed things better myself; it was pure gold. I kept my head down and ate my pork, but my ears were wide open.

'Then why on earth should the emperor have chosen him as his successor?' Mother again. One thing the couple had shared, when they were married, was intelligence. The difference was that Mother's range of interests didn't start and end with politics.

'But he didn't.' My father sighed as if he were explaining two times two for the fifth time to an idiot. 'Augustus had him adopt him when he made Tiberius his own heir.' Yeah. That fitted, once you'd worked the grammar out. The old emperor had had a soft spot for Germanicus, and his wife Agrippina was the imperial granddaughter. In a way he'd be keeping the succession in the Julian family. 'Then of course Germanicus now being the elder of the two sons took precedence over Tiberius's natural son Drusus.'

'And being as popular as he was Tiberius couldn't edge him aside without a very good reason. Especially since Drusus shares his father's antisocial tendencies. I see.' Mother set aside her partridge wing and rinsed her fingers in the finger bowl. 'How unfortunate for the poor dear. Still, I liked Germanicus. He had flair.'

Dad grunted and reached for another beet. 'Flair isn't everything,' he said. 'We're far better off with Drusus.'

'If you say so.' She patted her lips with a napkin. 'Although I do wish the man wasn't quite so terribly dull. Drusus is not a name to conjure with, I'm afraid.'

Priscus laid his spoon down suddenly, spattering Perilla's sleeve with raisin sauce.

'Oh, but I disagree, my dear!' he said. 'I disagree most strongly!'

Everyone looked at him. Hearing Priscus express a political opinion is about as rare as seeing the Wart bang a tambourine up and down Pullian Street sitting on an elephant.

'You do, Titus?' Mother said at last.

'Of course.' Priscus smiled at her. 'Oddly enough conjuring is exactly what the name does suggest. In my view, at least. The accepted derivation as you no doubt know is from the Gallic chieftain Drausus whom the original Livius Drusus is said to have killed in battle, but personally I find that explanation rather facile, if it is not indeed a simple tautology. I consider much more likely a link with the Greek *drus*, an oak tree, and by extension with the cognate Celtic *derwydd*. Which as you will be aware from its Latinised form *Druid* has definite mystical connotations. But perhaps I should explain the linguistics in more detail before considering the historical aspects . . .'

Oh, hell! I knew it was too good to last. We were off again down the highways and byways of esoterica. I suppose it was the old guy's party, but I could still cheerfully have strangled him, and I'm sure I wasn't alone, although Perilla was trying not to giggle. I switched off and sneaked an extra cup of wine.

Still, things weren't too bad. Dad had given me what I wanted, for a start. More, if anything.

That bit about Drusus was interesting, too, when you thought about it.

12

It wasn't late when we got back: Priscus goes to bed early, which from the glow my mother always has doesn't seem to worry her any. Quite the reverse, in fact. I was glad to see Bathyllus had a jug waiting. The little guy knows that the wine doesn't exactly flow like water over at Mother's place, although what there is is top of the range, and when I get home after one of her dinner parties my tongue's trailing the marble. I sank a quick cupful, poured myself another and settled down for a cosy evening of domestic criminology.

Perilla had nipped upstairs to change out of her raisin-sauced mantle ('I don't mind being bored, Corvinus, but why must your mother's husband *always* throw his dinner at me?'). She came back down in a fetching white tunic with gold edgings. I told Bathyllus to get lost minus the jug and patted the empty half of my couch.

'You want to sit over here?' I said.

She kissed me on the forehead and lay down. When you want to talk crime you may as well be comfortable.

'So,' I said. 'The Wart.'

Perilla sighed. 'Really, Corvinus, do we have to? I mean, after an evening of bronzeware, Oscan verbs and etymology I'd like to relax my brain a little, if you don't mind.'

She wasn't getting off that easy. Anyway it was her own fault.

'You owe me one, remember, lady?' I said. 'Oscan verbs I can take, but if I'm going to be shovelling the peas with Dad I like to know in advance. That's your job and you flunked it. So we talk about the Wart.'

She kissed my cheek and snuggled in a bit further. 'I'm sorry, Marcus. It wasn't my idea, and your mother didn't mention it until this morning. And then you were out, and I forgot I hadn't told you.'

'Hey, I'm not complaining!' I grinned. 'Not too hard, anyway, and not about the way things went. Dad was okay after Mother slapped him down over Sejanus and the corn commission. And what he had to say about Germanicus made my evening. Even with the Oscan verbs.'

She looked at me. 'You mean about him being a political liability.'

'Yeah. I was already getting there by myself after talking to Agron, but it's nice to have confirmation from a good source. And it gives us the missing angle on why the guy was murdered.'

'You still think Tiberius was responsible?'

'If he wasn't, lady, then I'm a blue-posteriored baboon with freckles.'

'Really. How interesting, Corvinus. Fruit for breakfast then, I assume?'

'Oh, ha. Okay, let's take it from the start. Stop me if I go off beam.' I shifted on the couch so that one arm was round her shoulders and the other could reach the jug and wine cup on the table. 'Thanks to Augustus the Wart's saddled with an extra son who outranks his own. Unlike Drusus – and unlike the Wart himself – the new guy's popular; he's the blue-eyed boy who can do no wrong, the universal darling. Trouble is, once you get down to dickering he's all flash and no corn meal, not the stuff good generals are made of. Let alone good emperors.'

Perilla nodded absently. She was winding a strand of her hair round her finger. 'So Tiberius has serious doubts about his fitness to succeed,' she said. 'Especially after the German campaign.'

'Right. Only the Wart's hands are tied. He may be emperor but in the popularity stakes Germanicus is streets ahead. The army think he's the best general since Julius, to the Senate he's a modest, regular guy without a boil to his name and the ordinary people want him to kiss their babies. In contrast the Wart's a morose antisocial bugger who hates the world and blue-eyed boys in particular. And who's got Rome's best interests at heart, too much at heart to stick her with Germanicus once he's gone.'

'So.' Perilla took my wine cup from me, sipped at it and gave it back. 'Germanicus makes a mess of Germany. Tiberius, seriously worried about the soundness of his stepson's judgment and his fitness to control events, recalls him and sends him straight out again with plenary powers on a sensitive diplomatic mission to the east.'

I blinked.

'Uh . . . run that one past me again, lady,' I said. 'I think I missed something.'

'Certainly. Having recalled Germanicus from Germany in disgrace and awarded him a triumph, Tiberius decides to use him as his representative in, among other delicate tasks, arranging the Armenian succession and resultant *modus vivendi* with Parthia. For which he gives him full powers as imperial plenipotentiary.'

'Ah.'

'*Ah* is right, Corvinus. Now don't you think that's just a little illogical?'

'Uh, yeah.' Shit. 'Yeah, it could be construed as a problem, I suppose.'

'Don't understate. If the man's judgment was flawed in dealing with a situation at least within his theoretical range of competence as an experienced soldier then for Tiberius to send him on a purely diplomatic mission involving Armenia and the Parthians was sheer madness. So if he was as dissatisfied with Germanicus as you claim then why did he do it?'

The lady had a point, even if she did use long words to make it. Armenia's a perennial pain in Rome's ass – and Parthia's, for that matter – because lying where it does it's vital to the security of both empires. Hence the tap-dancing involved in choosing a new Armenian king: a Parthian sympathiser with his backside on the throne makes Rome nervous and vice versa. The problem is that dickering with the Parthians is like mud wrestling with a greased eel. Try to get the better of those bastards and you're more than likely to come out missing your own back molars and wondering at what precise moment you were suckered. Sheer madness was right. The Wart had done the political equivalent of pulling Germanicus out of a kids' game of kiss-in-the-ring only to throw him into a high-stakes Corinthian dice match played with loaded bones. Stranger still, given my theory, the guy had done okay. Since Germanicus's settlement we had a better relationship with Parthia than we'd had for fifty years. Longer.

'Maybe he was just going through the motions, Perilla,' I said. 'Maybe Artabanus of Parthia and the Wart had made their deal already.'

'In that case why not send Drusus? He could have done with the extra kudos, and from all accounts he has the necessary deviousness to push things through if the Parthians did try a double-cross. Also Drusus is the emperor's son as much as Germanicus, even if he is junior. So there would be no question of outraged protocol.'

'Drusus wasn't free, lady. He had his own fish to fry in Pannonia.' I was clutching at straws. She was right; Drusus would've been a natural choice, given the circumstances. And the poor guy could certainly use a round of applause back at Rome.

Perilla was twisting her hair again. 'There's one thing that does support your theory, Marcus,' she said slowly.

'Yeah?' I tried to keep the surprise out of my voice. No point having her smug as well as smart. 'What's that?'

'Agrippina is a Julian. If the succession is an issue then it's relevant that one of their children would be next in line.'

'Explain.'

'Germanicus had three sons. Drusus only had a daughter. If Germanicus were to be the next emperor then his eldest son would be *a fortiori* the new crown prince.'

Uhuh. That made sense. Germanicus's eldest son Nero was fifteen already, with the second boy a year younger and Gaius – Agron's Caligula – rising ten.

'Right,' I said. 'Which would leave Drusus to do a Tiberian tap-dance in the wings.' Three sons. The succession. Tiberius's tap-dance. My neck was itching . . .

Ah, leave it.

'Marcus?'

'Hmm?'

'Your eyes have gone glazed.'

'Yeah? Oh, it's nothing. Just an idea, but it won't come.' I reached over for the wine cup: my brain needed lubrication. 'So what do you think? About the theory?'

'That Tiberius had Germanicus removed for incompetence? I'm sorry to say that it has its attractions. Apart from the Armenian problem, of course, which is crucial.'

The wine went down the wrong way. When I'd finished coughing my guts out, I said: 'Really? You like it? No kidding?'

She smiled. 'I wouldn't go quite that far, Corvinus. I still can't believe that Tiberius would commit murder, especially the murder of his own son, adopted or not. However I'm willing to accept that he might do it in one circumstance and one only. Where the future of Rome was at stake.'

The future of Rome. Perilla had hit it smack on the button. The Wart, as I've said before, might be six different kinds of bastard but he was straight. If the reasons behind the murder were purely dynastic, or purely personal, then I'd've believed Livia was responsible, but never the Wart. He was a soldier, he didn't think that way. To Tiberius what mattered was the empire and his duty to it, and screw popular opinion.

I had that itch again. There was something . . .

Three sons. Tiberius's tap-dance. The succession . . .

Sons . . .

'Oh, Jupiter!' I said softly.

'Corvinus? What's wrong?'

I waved her down. I had to get this straight. Another cup of wine would help . . .

'Maybe it wasn't the Wart,' I said. 'Oh, sure, it could be, despite the problems. In fact, Germanicus's success with Parthia makes it even more likely he didn't do it. But if not there's someone with an even bigger reason for getting rid of the guy than the emperor.'

'And who might that be?'

'Drusus himself.'

Perilla was quiet for a long time. Then she said: 'Yes. Yes, you're right. I hadn't considered Drusus.'

'He's got a motive, Perilla. He's got one hell of a motive. The Wart, whether he likes it or not, has edged him to the sidelines, exactly like Augustus did to him twenty years back. Germanicus had three sons old enough to be groomed for the purple, while

Drusus was stuck with a daughter. Only about a year ago the situation changed, didn't it?' Our eyes met. 'Because Drusus's wife Livilla got pregnant.'

Perilla nodded. 'And had twin boys. Yes. Drusus wasn't to know that at the time, of course. She gave birth after Germanicus's death.'

'The chances were fifty-fifty, lady. Good odds. And Imperials are good breeders.' Jupiter, it made sense! 'Suddenly the ante's gone up. Drusus has responsibilities, or he soon will have. He's a family man in the only way that matters in the succession stakes. Only as things are he hasn't a hope in hell of getting his bum off the bench. Worse, after Armenia Germanicus is riding even higher than ever.'

'So Drusus takes matters into his own hands and has his stepbrother murdered.' Perilla looked thoughtful. 'Would he do that?'

I shook my head. 'I don't know. I don't know enough about the guy. Not many people do, because he's spent most of his life out of Rome. Sure, he and Germanicus were supposed to be close but like my father said he's a pretty cerebral character. Maybe he's always secretly hated Germanicus's guts. Jupiter knows he's had reason. Or maybe the temptation was just too much, especially with Livilla pushing. From all accounts that lady's a tough cookie.'

'She's Germanicus's own sister, Marcus!'

'So what? You think that would stop her?'

'I don't know.'

'Nor do I, but I wouldn't take bets. The Imperials aren't exactly a togetherness family.' I lifted the jug, but it was empty. An omen. I'd had enough for one night. 'Anyway, it's too good to miss. That's our next project. We check out Drusus.'

Perilla looked at me. 'Bed first?'

I grinned and kissed her. 'Bed.'

We were on our way up when Bathyllus oiled through from the kitchen. Obviously he'd been lying in wait.

'Yeah, Bathyllus?' I said in the most discouraging voice I could manage. 'What is it?'

'I'm sorry to disturb you, sir,' he said. 'I would have told you earlier, but I'm afraid it slipped my mind.'

'These things happen, little guy. Just make it quick, will you?'

'Yes, sir. It concerns Livineius Regulus. You recall you asked me recently where the gentleman lived?'

'Yeah. Yeah, I recall that.' Jupiter! Didn't Bathyllus have any sense of occasion? 'What about him?'

'I heard earlier this evening that he's dead, sir. Murdered. I thought you might be interested.'

Jupiter Best and Greatest! 'You have the details?'

'His body was found at the foot of the Gemonian Stairs, sir, with a hook in his throat. He had been stabbed in the back.'

Perilla gasped. I felt pretty shocked myself.

'They have any idea who did it?'

'No, sir. Robbers, presumably.' A sniff. 'The Aventine is quite an uncultivated district. Goodnight, sir.'

'Night, Bathyllus.'

We carried on upstairs in a more sober frame of mind than we'd left the hallway. I'd wanted another word with Regulus and now it seemed I wouldn't get the chance. Someone, somewhere, evidently considered that he'd flapped his mouth once too often already and shut it for him. Permanently.

There was one other thing; maybe it was coincidence but I doubted it. Whoever had knifed Regulus had a pretty sick sense of humour. The Gemonian Stairs run down from Aventine to Tiber. After their execution unpopular criminals, particularly traitors, are dragged down them with hooks and tossed in the river for the rats to gnaw. I'd been sent a message. No more pussyfooting around. Now we were playing for real.

13

Next morning I checked with Watch headquarters. They put me on to the guy who'd found Regulus's body. He was off duty, and I took the address: a tenement not far from the Appian aqueduct. When I found it there was a kid sitting on the step outside, shelling peas into a bowl.

'Hey, sonny,' I said. 'You happen to know where I can find Flavonius Lippillus?'

The kid set the bowl down. 'You already have, friend. And less of the sonny.'

I did a double-take. He didn't look old enough to shave, let alone help keep order in one of the toughest districts of the city. '*You're* Lippillus?' I said. 'Of the Aventine Watch?'

'That's right.' I could see him take in my narrow-striper mantle; you don't see many of those south of the racetrack. He sounded older than he looked. No slob, either. There were good vowels there.

'Uh, sorry, pal,' I said, trying a grin. 'No offence.'

'None taken. It happens all the time.' He hadn't smiled, though. 'So what can I do for you?'

'Name's Marcus Corvinus. I understand you came across a corpse yesterday night at the bottom of the Gemonian Stairs.'

'Livineius Regulus. Works at the Treasury.' His mouth twisted. 'Worked. He was a friend of yours?'

'No.' There were a few old wickerwork chairs against the wall, and I pulled one up and sat on it. Most tenement dwellers prefer living in the open air when they can, and there's more furniture outside these places than in. Stick your nose inside a city tenement flat and you'll realise why.

'Just an acquaintance. You were pretty quick off the mark identifying him.'

He shrugged. 'My brother's one of the junior clerks. You get to know a few faces. And a few names.'

The guy might look like he'd just dedicated his toy chariots to the household gods, but he was razor sharp. I blessed my luck. 'Can you tell me anything about how it was done?'

'You have a reason for asking?'

I had an unpleasant feeling that if I tried to lie he'd be on to me like a dog on a rabbit. And that that wouldn't be too good an idea. 'Not one I can give you straight out, no,' I said. 'Except that it's not friendship. And not just curiosity.'

The eyes gauged me.

'Okay,' he said at last. 'Regulus was stabbed once, in the back, at the top of the Stairs, some time between ten o'clock and midnight. He was then dragged down towards the Tiber by means of a hook under the chin. The hook stayed with the body. His purse was missing but that was done as a blind, or maybe it was taken later by some other bastard. He came alone, he knew the man who did it, and he trusted him. Probably he'd gone there specially for a meeting. And the murder was premeditated. That do you for starters?'

I whistled softly. 'You tell fortunes for an encore, friend?'

The serious look vanished, and he laughed. 'It's simple enough. We found blood above the top step and traces all the way down. It was raining before ten, the ground under the body was wet and we got there ourselves just after midnight. Hence the timing.'

'Okay. What about the rest?'

'From what I've heard of him Regulus wouldn't be seen dead on the Aventine. No pun intended.' I grinned: I was beginning to like this guy. 'So he must've had a reason for being there. Especially somewhere out of the way like the Stairs. Hence the clandestine meeting. Right?'

'Right.'

'Also, he was a narrow-striper. Broad- and narrow-stripers don't go out alone at night because they can afford not to; they've got torchmen, probably a few hefty slaves with clubs. Aventine toughs go for easy pickings. Solitary drunks, that sort of thing. They steer clear of guys like that. Yet there was no sign of a fight, and no subsequent report. So Regulus came alone.'

I frowned. 'Wait a minute, friend. You can't have it both ways. Narrow-striper or not, if he was alone what was to prevent whoever put a knife into him being one of your local yobbos?'

'How many yobbos do you know who carry hooks around on the off chance? And how many would waste valuable drinking time dragging a corpse down a flight of steps?'

Yeah. Sharp as a new-ground razor. 'So you think the murderer brought the hook along specially? Meaning to use it?'

'Sure. Premeditated, like I said.'

'Why?'

He shrugged. 'Search me. Ask me again when I've got more to go on.'

'Okay. And the bit about Regulus trusting the guy who killed him?'

'Would you turn your back on someone you didn't trust at that time of night, Corvinus? Alone? In a neighbourhood like the Stairs?'

'No. I wouldn't.' Shit. He had it all stitched up. I'd bet he was right, too, in every detail. Fresh-faced kid, nothing. This guy had a future. 'So where does the case go from here?'

'We reported it to the city prefect's office, naturally. Regulus was an important man. There'll be an investigation.'

Sure there would. At least the start of one. But it wouldn't go very far before it was quashed, and when it was I'd pay good money to know who put the dampers on. 'Listen, Lippillus,' I said. 'The investigation may not happen. Don't ask me why, just take my word for it.'

He gave me a slow, careful look. 'And just what the hell is that supposed to mean?'

I shook my head. 'I can't tell you. If I'm wrong then there's no harm done. But if I'm right I want to know. And I want a name.'

He wasn't smiling now. 'Corvinus, I've been pretty patient, although none of what I've told you was a secret. You could've found it out anyway through your uncle.' Shit. On top of everything else the guy carried a copy of the social register around in his head. He was even smarter than I'd given him credit for.

'But the least you can do in return is tell me why a consul's nephew should be interested in the death of a Treasury official. Personally interested, I mean. You say he wasn't a friend.'

'No way!'

The frown vanished, and he grinned like a twelve-year-old.

'Yeah, okay,' he said. 'I believe you. But like I said Regulus was an important man. Even shits like him don't just get forgotten. So why should there be an official cover-up? That's what we're talking about, isn't it?'

'Yes, that's what we're talking about. But I'm sorry.' I was. Really sorry. 'I can't tell you, Lippillus. Not yet, anyway.'

'You mean it's political?'

'Yeah. Very. At least I think so.'

'Dirty political?'

'The dirtiest.'

'Uhuh.' He picked up the basin of peas again and began to shell them slowly and methodically. I could almost hear his brain tick. 'Okay. Maybe I'll trust you. Or half trust you. Provisionally, anyway.' Jupiter! Talk about hedging your bets! Still, if I'd been the guy I would've been cautious myself. 'So what do you want?'

'Nothing much. Keep your ear to the ground. If – when – the case is closed, let me know who's responsible for closing it. That and only that. And another thing.'

'Yeah?'

'Whatever you do, don't try to keep the investigation going single-handed.'

His eyes came up, and I saw he believed me after all. He nodded, slowly. Maybe he swallowed. If so, I didn't blame him.

'Okay. You've got it.'

'Thanks.' I stood up and put the chair back. 'You know where to find me?'

'I'll find you.'

'Good. It was nice meeting you. A real pleasure.'

He grinned suddenly: fresh-faced kid again. 'Likewise. Good luck with the sleuthing.'

As I turned to go another thought struck me. Not a pleasant one either. 'You said the hook was still in the body. What kind of hook was it?'

'Just the usual. The kind butchers use to hang up carcasses. Why?'

Uhuh. 'No reason. See you, Lippillus.'

'Yeah. Yeah, well, let's hope so.'

I left with the hairs on the back of my neck crawling and a strong sense of guilt. The kind of hook butchers use to hang up carcasses. Jupiter and all the gods! I'd fingered Regulus myself.

Maybe I should have another talk with my butcher friend.

The shop was open, but the guy behind the counter was Carillus's boy Scaurus. I waited my turn.

'Your father around, son?' I said.

'He's away at the moment.' The kid's eyes didn't shift. He even smiled. 'Up north.'

'Yeah? Anywhere in particular?'

'No. Not that I know of.'

'When do you expect him back?'

A shrug. 'Ten days. Maybe twelve.'

'This happen often?'

'Now and again. He goes round the farms buying stock. Checking quality. Arranging delivery. You know the sort of thing.'

'Yeah, I know.' That made sense, especially since the guy owned his own slaughterhouse. He'd have more than his own business to supply. Still, it was too pat. Much too pat. 'So when did he leave?'

'Early this morning.' Scaurus looked past me. A queue was starting to form. I recognised the chitterlings lady; this time she'd been buying spring greens. 'Now what can I get you, mister?'

'Uh . . . you got any sows' wombs?'

'Sure. How many you want?'

'Two. No, make it three.' While he was fetching them I looked up at the meat rack. Hooks there and to spare: he'd never have missed one. Nice sharp knives, too.

Immortal Jupiter! And I'd believed the guy!

I took my sows' wombs wrapped in straw and paid for them. I thought of giving them away to the first passing dog but then I changed my mind. They looked fresh, and roast sows' wombs with a nut and sausage stuffing is something you don't see every day. Besides, if Meton ever found out I'd chucked them he'd probably poison the soufflé in revenge. The guy was like that. A real professional.

Okay. So if the murderer was Carillus then the bastard was either very careless or very confident. And I didn't think Carillus was the careless type. That hook had been part of the message. He was saying, in effect, 'So I did it. So nail me if you can. But watch your back if you try because I've got friends!' That didn't sound too good. Also there was the matter of the letter. If the murderer was Carillus then all the bets were off. Maybe the deed of transfer he'd shown me had been genuine. The date had certainly checked, but that didn't mean the deed had to be the letter Piso had written on his last night. Carillus could've got both from Piso at the same time. In which case we were back to square one, with a phantom note that'd been written and possibly delivered.

Or not, as the case might be.

14

Perilla was out when I got back. I had a quick lunch and then set off for the Caelian to see Gaius Secundus, the nearest thing I'd got to a Drusus expert. Until six months ago he'd been a junior staff officer in Pannonia; at which time the silly bugger had fallen down a cliff, smashed the bones in his right leg to smithereens, and been invalided back to Rome. We'd split a few jars together in the past and I reckoned I could rely on him to give me some straight answers.

The slave showed me through to the garden. Secundus was sitting on a chair with his leg stretched out in front of him and a stick within easy reach. Not that he'd been able to use it yet, but that would come. Maybe. If he was lucky.

'Hey, Corvinus!' he said. 'How's the lad?'

'Not bad.' I sat down on the garden bench facing him and tried not to stare at the shapeless, seamed disaster stretched out between us. 'How's Secundus?'

'Never better. Phidias!' He shouted to the retreating slave. 'Bring us a jug of the Reserve and two cups, okay?' The slave turned and grinned. 'Perilla tired of you yet?'

I laughed. 'Sod off!'

'Yeah, well, just let me know when it happens.'

Having only one leg doesn't cramp Secundus's style. In fact if anything it's an advantage because he's got playing for female sympathy down to a fine art. I was lucky to find him on his own. Disappointed, too, in a way: some of his volunteer nurses are real honeys, with a bedside manner you wouldn't believe.

The wine came and we drank it and swapped insults for a while. Finally, halfway down the jug, he set down his cup.

'So, Corvinus. Pleasantries over. Let's get down to business. Tell me what brings you to the Caelian. Besides my riveting conversation, naturally.'

'I wanted to pick your brains.' I sipped my wine. 'About your old boss Drusus.'

'Yeah? Any special reason?'

'Yes.'

He waited. Then, when I didn't elaborate: 'You mixed up in something, Marcus?'

I wasn't smiling now. Secundus was a friend, and I'd no intention of conning information out of him under false pretences. Also I hadn't been near him for two months, and I felt guilty as hell turning up now just because I needed a favour.

'Yes,' I said again.

'Uhuh. Feel like telling me what it's about?'

'No. I can't do that.'

'Sure?'

'Sure.'

He was quiet for a long time. Then he shrugged. 'Okay. So move that stool over here and we'll talk.' I looked round and found the stool he meant. As he lifted his bad leg on to it I could see the sweat spring out on his forehead, but he wouldn't've wanted my help, or my sympathy, so I didn't offer either. Finally, when he'd got himself settled, he picked the wine cup up, drained it and held it out for me to fill.

'Right,' he said when I'd done it. 'So what do you want to know?'

'Everything.' I poured wine into my own cup. 'Let's start at the beginning. What sort of man is he?'

'How do you mean?'

'Friendly? Bastard?'

'He's a good soldier. One of the best.'

'That's no answer, pal.'

He grinned. 'Yeah. I know. But I'm not sure I can give you much more. Drusus isn't exactly the kind to invite confidences.'

'No jolly ragging in the mess with the lads after dinner, then?'

'The Pike?' Secundus laughed. 'No way!'

'That what you called him?'

'Some people make it the Dead Pan. I think Pike describes him better.'

'Why?'

He hesitated. 'You ever see Drusus, Corvinus?'

'Not that I can remember. Not from close up, anyway.'

'You know that little twist the Wart gives to his mouth sometimes? Like he's smiling at some particularly nasty joke no one but him would understand or find funny if they did?'

'Yeah. Yeah, I know the one you mean.' It usually came just before some arselicker or thick-head found himself flattened by an imperial one-liner. 'Like whoever he's talking to wouldn't measure up intellectually to a backward chicken.'

Secundus nodded. 'That's the one. Drusus has it too. It lifts his upper lip over the canine. When it happens the rest of his face doesn't move, not even the eyes. Just the lip. Like a pike eyeing up a breakfast guppy. Scares the shit out of you, even if you're only watching.'

'You're saying Drusus is like his father,' I said. 'A cold-blooded bugger with too much going on between the ears.'

'Uhuh.' He nodded again. 'That would describe him pretty well. He's fair, mind, and that's like the Wart too. I never heard Drusus chew anyone out over nothing, squaddie, officer or civilian. And he'd make sure he had all the facts weighed before he gave his verdict.'

'And then Jupiter help you if the scales came down on the wrong side.'

'Yeah.' Secundus didn't smile. 'He can be a cruel bastard, when he's in the mood.'

I reached over and helped myself to more wine from the jug, topping up Secundus's cup at the same time, although he hadn't touched the last batch.

'How did he get on with his stepbrother, do you know?' I said.

'Germanicus?' Secundus shot me a sharp look: the guy wasn't stupid, and I'd overdone the attempt at casualness. 'He what all this is about?'

I hesitated a fraction too long. 'Maybe.'

'Maybe, hell!' Secundus laughed. 'Okay, Marcus, I'll play as dumb as you like. I've got nothing better to do this afternoon anyway. When Germanicus called in on his way east—'

'Germanicus went to Pannonia?' I was shocked into interrupting, but Secundus didn't seem to notice. Or pretended he didn't.

'Sure,' he said. 'Not for long. Ten days, max. You didn't know that?'

'No,' I said slowly. 'I didn't know that.'

'It was just a courtesy call. The usual thing. Exchange of presents, formal review of the legions. Handing over of dispatches from Rome. Anyway, the two got on fine, in public at least. And don't try to read anything into that qualification, either, because although I only saw the public side I've no reason to think the private one was any different. They hugged each other like . . . well, like long-lost brothers. I'm not sure there wasn't a manly tear in Germanicus's baby blue eyes.'

Uhuh. I'd caught the tone loud and clear. 'So you didn't like him,' I said.

Secundus shifted in his chair. The breath hissed between his teeth and his eyes screwed shut. He looked grey as death and I thought for a moment he'd passed out, but before I could shout for Phidias the eyes were open again.

'Hey, pal,' I said. 'You okay?'

'Yeah.' He took a deep breath. 'Sure. Sorry, Marcus. I forget sometimes to pamper this lump of meat and it gives me a gentle reminder.' Jupiter! If that was a gentle reminder I'd hate to see what a twinge was like. 'To answer your question, no, I didn't like Germanicus. Not a lot, anyway.'

'You mind telling me why?'

He grinned, or tried to. 'He was an actor, and I don't happen to like actors all that much. No, I don't mean he was playing a part, he was sincere enough as far as I could see. In fact the bastard oozed sincerity. But he had the actor's temperament. Whatever he did he couldn't help pitching to the gallery. Not his fault, it was the way he was made. And it certainly made him popular.'

Yeah. That fitted. It explained the histrionics in Germany and his visit to the site of the Varian massacre where, by all accounts, Rome's blue-eyed boy had literally wept over the bones of her slaughtered legions before collecting what he could find of them for burial. Pious as well as sensitive. I saw what Secundus meant; Germanicus oozed so much sincerity it set your teeth on edge. But then I've never had much time for pious heroes. I hated Virgil's Aeneas at school, for a start; and like with Aeneas I would've found Germanicus a more sympathetic person if just once in his life he'd hauled off and metaphorically slugged the cat. Ah, well, maybe Dad was having more of an effect on me than I thought and I was getting cynical. If this weary world could still throw up the occasional hero then who was I to grouse?

'You know he called in at Troy?' Secundus was saying.

'What?' Following on to my thoughts about Aeneas the question startled me.

'Yeah. After he left us. Wrote a poem to be inscribed over Hector's tomb. Recited it at the dedication ceremony, too. Strange guy, for a Roman.'

'It's odd he and Drusus got on as well as they did, then.'

'Yeah. They were chalk and cheese.' Secundus paused. 'You heard the story of the two of them in the mutiny?'

Agron had mentioned the mutiny, too, although he hadn't gone into detail. It had been six years back, the year old Augustus died and the Wart took over. There had been two separate outbreaks at roughly the same time, in Pannonia and on the Rhine. Tiberius had sent Drusus to deal with the first, and Germanicus, who was the overall commander in Germany, had dealt with the second.

'No,' I said. 'No, I haven't.'

Secundus sipped his wine. He was looking a better colour now, but the sweat was a permanent oily sheen on his forehead. I was still trying to avoid looking at his leg. Just thinking about that formless mass of pulped flesh less than a yard from me made my balls shrink.

'The story tells you a lot about both of them,' Secundus was saying. 'The different ways their minds worked. Drusus went through the mutineers with his two battalions of the Guard like a dose of salts. No flash, just hard cunning and brute force. He had the ringleaders' heads spiked on the Tribunal before the month was out. Meanwhile Germanicus fucked around appealing to the Rhine squaddies' better feelings. He could've called on the two loyal legions further upriver for help, but he wouldn't do it and eventually it was too late. The result was an even bigger bloodbath than would've happened if he'd gone in hard to start with.' Secundus's lips pursed. 'No, I didn't like Germanicus, Marcus. That was him in a nutshell. An idealist who couldn't resist the grand gesture, however impractical it was and whatever it cost.'

'I thought the Rhine legions idolised him,' I said.

Secundus scratched his good leg absently. 'Sure they did. But he was sticking up for Tiberius, and that may've been honourable but it wasn't popular. If they hadn't felt so shamed by the fact that he was sending Agrippina and the kids away for safety they might even've got round to murdering him.' He grinned. 'That brat Caligula may need his backside tanning but he and his mother had more to do with putting down the mutiny than Germanicus did.'

'How did the two wives get on, by the way? Agrippina and Livilla?'

'We're talking about Pannonia now, right?' Secundus said. I nodded. 'Like fire and ice, Agrippina being the ice. I wouldn't care to bed either of those two, and they're both stunners so that's not the reason. Making love to Agrippina would be like screwing a marble statue. And Livilla's got too much of her grandmother in her for anyone's liking.'

'Her grandmother? You mean the empress?'

'Yeah. She and Drusus are well matched, maybe too well matched. The lady may be a hot little cookie in some ways but she's got a cold calculating streak a yard wide, and there's more in her head than fluff. Also she knows Tiberius has been playing favourites, and she doesn't like it above half.'

Uhuh. This was something I hadn't thought of. I pricked up my ears.

'Is that right? Tell me.'

Secundus took a swallow of wine from his cup and set it down again. 'You've just got to look at the consuls for the past few years,' he said. 'Most of them've been Germanicus and Agrippina's friends. And Drusus may've got his own consul's chair five years back, but he didn't share it with the Wart. Germanicus did, twice.'

I sat back. Yeah. Yeah, that was true, and it was important: joint consulships with the emperor are the accepted way of showing imperial favour. Taking that together with Germanicus's prestigious eastern command and her dislike of Agrippina, it was no wonder if Livilla had been pissing her pants with jealousy. Then there was the matter of the children. As suspects Drusus and Livilla were beginning to look pretty promising material.

Someone coughed behind me: Secundus's slave Phidias. I turned round.

'Excuse me, sir,' he said, 'but the Lady Furia Gemella has just arrived.'

I looked behind his shoulder and grinned. Furia Gemella was a curvy little brunette with tinkling earrings and breasts that'd knock the eyes out of an octogenarian priest. She was carrying what looked like a bowl of soup.

'I'm sorry, Gaius,' she said. 'I didn't know you were busy.' Nice voice, too.

I took my eyes off her just long enough to give Secundus a quick wink.

'No, that's okay,' I said. 'I was just leaving.'

'You sure, Marcus?' Secundus didn't exactly sound pressing. 'Gemella won't mind, I'm certain. Will you, Gemella?'

'Of course not.'

Yeah, I thought, and I'm a blue-rinsed Briton. The lady was sending me looks already that would've scuttled a trireme. I know when I'm not wanted. I got up.

'Thanks for the talk, pal,' I said. 'It's helped a lot.'

'I'm glad of that.' Secundus grinned. 'You married men need a bit of stimulation.'

I gave him the finger under the cover of my mantle. He beamed back at me and I turned to the brunette.

'Watch he doesn't dribble down his tunic when you feed him that soup, lady,' I said.

Her rosebud mouth made an 'oh' of disapproval. Secundus chuckled and jerked his head.

'Piss off, you bastard,' he said.

I waved at him, grinned and left.

*   *   *

Perilla was getting changed after a bath when I got home. Too good a chance to miss.

'Marcus, for heaven's sake!' She squirmed away, or tried to. 'It's the middle of the afternoon!'

'You noticed.' I took a mouthful of ear.

'Someone will come in. One of the slaves.'

'Not unless they want to be sold for cat's-meat.' I'd edged her over as far as the bed. Finally. I really would kill that architect. 'Ha! Gotcha!'

But I hadn't, because at the last moment she pulled back.

'What did you have for lunch, Corvinus?' she said.

Non sequiturs get me every time. I paused.

'What the hell does that have to do with anything, lady?'

'Just curious.' She kissed me. A long kiss, while I removed one of the few bits of clothing she'd been wearing when I grabbed her. 'After all, there must be some good reason for this. Not that I'm complaining, you understand. Academic interest only.'

'Okay. Left-over pork liver with bacon. Cold chickpeas with fennel. And half of a chicken and parsley dumpling. Satisfied?'

'Wine?'

'Uh . . . yeah. Just a few cupfuls.'

'Maybe it's the weather, then.'

'Mmmm.'

At which point she gave up on academic interest and co-operated; and by the time we came up for air dietary considerations were forgotten.

We lay side by side for a while, staring at the plaster key pattern on the ceiling.

'Marcus?' Perilla said finally.

'Yeah?'

'Your brain's buzzing. I can hear it through your skull. What're you thinking about?'

'How lucky I am to wear my sandals in pairs.'

She sat up and stared down at me. '*What?*'

'Sorry.' Well, she had asked me. 'My mind's going. Must be the booze.' I pulled her back down and we watched the cornice again. It didn't move at all. 'Hey, Perilla.'

'Mmm?'

'You ever wear these earrings with little chime bars in? The Egyptian things?'

'Of course not. I'd sound like part of a street band.'

I grinned and turned my head to kiss her cheek. 'Yeah. You're right. Terrible things, chime earrings. In the wrong hands. Ears.'

She stared at me. 'Marcus, are you all right?'

'Never better.' I winced. 'Yeah. Yeah, I'm fine, lady. Why?'

'It's just that you seem a little strange this afternoon.'

What can you do when the woman in your bed says something like that? I kissed her, put the events of the morning out of my mind and set about proving to her and myself that I felt absolutely fine.

Really.

15

We made it down for dinner. Just. Which was lucky because
Meton had cooked my stuffed sows' wombs specially, and hell
hath no fury like a chef insulted. After we'd finished I sent
Bathyllus for another jug of wine and brought Perilla up to
date on the case.

'The plot thickens, lady,' I said. 'According to Gaius Secundus,
Livilla's on the make.'

Perilla was nibbling at some dried fruit. 'How is Secundus?'
she said.

'He's doing okay. Coming along slowly.' I didn't mention the
cute little stunner with the musical earrings; she might've made
the connection. 'He tells me Germanicus called in at Pannonia
on his way east.'

'Pannonia's rather too far off the ordinary route to Syria for
calling in in passing, Corvinus.'

'Sure. That's what I thought. Mind you, the guy was paying
an official visit with dispatches from the Wart. And I'd give a lot
to know what was in that particular diplomatic bag.'

She sighed. 'You still think that Tiberius was responsible for
Germanicus's death, don't you?' She made it sound like it was
evidence of insanity.

'Yeah.' I took a swallow of Setinian. 'Maybe the Wart and
Drusus had cooked something up between them. Germanicus
was in Pannonia for ten days. That's enough time for Drusus
to make a deal with one of his servants. Or Drusus and Livilla
could've acted off their own bat.'

Perilla set down the dried apricot she was holding. 'Marcus,'
she said, 'you really will have to make your mind up. First it's

the emperor getting rid of an embarrassment, then it's Tiberius
and Drusus together. Now you seem to be accusing Livilla of
having a hand in things. They can't all be responsible.'

'Yeah? And why not?'

'Because it's ridiculous, that's why not.'

'It could work, lady. Don't knock it.'

Bathyllus padded back in with the new jug. I held it up, but
Perilla shook her head.

'No, thank you,' she said. 'So you're seriously suggesting that
in the short time available to them Drusus and Livilla suborned
one of Germanicus's personal servants and instructed him to
poison his master?'

'Yeah. Sure I am. You got a problem with that?'

Instead of answering, Perilla raised herself on one elbow and
snapped: 'Bathyllus!'

The little guy had been on his way out. He jerked round like
she'd planted a hook in the tail of his tunic and pulled.

'Yes, madam,' he said. Cringed.

'I want you to poison Corvinus for me, please,' Perilla said
calmly. 'How and when you do it is up to you, but I want
a professional job with no fluffing around and no awkward
questions asked later. Is that clear?'

'Ah . . .' She sounded convincing as hell. I'd never actually
seen the little guy lost for words before. He looked at me and
swallowed.

'Oh, go away, Bathyllus,' I said wearily. He did, with a nervous
backward glance at both of us. 'Okay, Perilla, point taken. But I
had envisaged something just a bit more subtle.'

She picked up the apricot again. 'Perhaps so. But in a case of
poisoning the family slaves are the first to be suspected. None
of them was, in this instance. That, I think, is significant.'

'That's because they'd already fixed on Martina.'

'Marcus, if a slave were to poison his master society would
collapse. It just isn't done.'

'Then we're up shit creek without a paddle, lady.'

'Really? Oh how interesting.'

'I'm serious.' I poured myself another cup of Setinian. 'We
can't work on nothing, and nothing's all we've got at present.
Sure, the Wart could've been responsible, in theory. So could

Drusus and Livilla, ditto, together or separately, with or without the emperor's backing. Or Piso and Plancina. They've all got motives of some kind or another for wanting the guy dead. Our trouble is there are too many suspects and not enough hard facts.'

'Means and opportunity?'

'They've all got them, too. At first or at second hand. Or maybe the murderer was some crazy bastard who just decided that killing a Caesar was a good idea and happened to have an afternoon free.' Jupiter! The more I thought about it the more depressing it was. I glared into my wine cup. 'Theories're fine, Perilla, but we need leads. Regulus is dead, Carillus is somewhere out in the sticks pricing goats and I can't even get decently beaten up so I can trace the bastards who did it.'

'You've forgotten someone.'

'Yeah? And who might that be, clever clogs?'

'Didn't you mention a man called Crispus?'

My head snapped up. 'What?'

'Caelius Crispus.'

I set the cup down. She was right. Shit. Caelius Crispus. The rumour merchant. The guy who had warned Livineius Regulus that I was coming to get him. Little oily Crispus, the doyen of the Treasury! I leaned over and planted a smacker due south of Perilla's perfect nostrils.

'I love you,' I said. 'You know that?'

'Yes, Marcus. I do, actually.'

'Hey, Bathyllus!' I yelled.

He came running; that new hernia support had done wonders. 'Yes, sir.'

'Scratch the poisoning, little guy. Fetch my mantle instead. And whistle up the litter and half a dozen torches.'

Perilla was staring at me. 'You're going to see him *now*?' she said. 'At this time of night?'

I kissed her again. 'Sure I am. This is when Crispus comes alive. If you can call it living.'

She got up. 'Then I'm coming with you.'

That stopped me in my tracks. 'No way, lady!'

'Corvinus, this was my idea and I'm coming. Finish. Or we can go tomorrow. One or the other.'

Bugger. Stymied. Finding Crispus in daylight would be tricky: he didn't have an official daytime job and I'd no idea where he lived. Nights were a different matter. But taking Perilla along was something else again. I was tempted to pull head-of-the-household rank and hope that for once she'd knuckle under. Then I took a good look at her face and decided to save my breath.

'Okay,' I said. 'You can come, so long as you dress warm and keep a tight rein on your mouth. Only don't say I didn't warn you.'

Crispus spent his evenings in a certain house on the Pincian: expensive and far enough out to guarantee the Watch didn't go knocking on the door unless they had good reason to. Not that that'd ever happened, or ever would: a raid would've netted some of the biggest names in Rome, the Watch Commander's included. I hadn't given up trying to persuade Perilla even when we were on our way there. Now, while we parked the litter outside the anonymous front door, I made one final appeal.

'You want to wait here for me, Perilla?' I said as casually as I could manage. 'This shouldn't take long.'

'Don't be silly, Marcus,' she sniffed. 'I haven't come all this way just to wait in a litter.'

Yeah, right. Oh, well, what the hell. It was her choice; and against the pig-headed stubbornness of women even the gods shrug their shoulders and call it a day.

'Okay.' I shrugged myself. 'But prepare to have your education broadened.'

'Certainly.' She smiled. 'I'm looking forward to it. I've never seen the inside of a brothel before. It is a brothel, isn't it?'

'Uh . . . yeah.' Jupiter! 'Yeah, sure. In a way. But not the kind you think it is.'

'You mean there are different kinds?'

Oh, Priapus on a see-saw! This was no time to explain the murkier facts of life. 'Sure there are. When we get inside just behave as normal, okay?' I paused. 'Revise that. Just don't say anything at all.'

'Very well, Corvinus.'

We got out and I rapped on the door. A spyhole slipped back.

'Caelius Crispus in there, friend?' I said.

Maybe it was the name, or my seductive tones. Or it might've been the gold piece I was holding that did it. Anyway, the door swung open. I pushed Perilla ahead of me – she was muffled so you couldn't see that she didn't comply with the club's first rule of membership – and squeezed in behind.

I knew I'd asked too much of her. She took one wide-eyed look round the glittering hallway with its fancy Corinthian decor and proceeded to remove any doubt over her credentials. Loudly.

'Corvinus, what are those two men doing over there?' she said. 'And why is that boy naked?'

Shit. I clapped a hand over her mouth before she could do any more damage, smiled my apologies and turned to the slave who'd let us in.

'Quick!' I snapped. 'Where's Crispus?'

The guy pointed silently and disapprovingly to a curtained alcove between two bronze satyrs. Bathyllus couldn't've done it better, even without the frizzy gilded hair and the tutu.

'Thanks, friend,' I said. Then, putting my mouth to Perilla's ear, I hissed: 'Okay, lady. Listen up. One more comment like that last one and you're divorced. Understand?' She nodded and I felt her mouth widen in a grin. I took my hand away carefully. 'Now stay right here and don't move a muscle until I tell you otherwise.'

I scratched at the curtain: whatever his bag was, Crispus had a right to privacy.

'Come in.'

Crispus's voice. I pushed the curtain aside. Luckily he was alone, reclining on a couch behind a low table set with a selection of expensive nibbles, including a pineapple. His jaw dropped a yard when he saw me. Two yards when he saw Perilla. That woman never listens.

'Corvinus!' he said. 'What the hell are you doing here?'

'Broadening my wife's education.'

'For Jupiter's sake!' He whipped a napkin over his naked appurtenances. 'You can't bring a woman in here!'

'Is that right?' I dropped the curtain behind us. 'Sorry. It must've slipped my mind.'

'This is an exclusive club!' He was fussing like a dowager whose butler has just appeared in the middle of a dinner party wearing nothing but a G-string. And I'd thought the guy was unshockable. Well, you learn something new every day.

'Okay, okay!' I sat down on the couch facing him. 'Calm down, Crispus. No problem. We'll be gone soon, promise.'

Perilla smiled sweetly at him. She was beginning to enjoy herself. I could tell.

'Delighted to meet you, Caelius Crispus,' she said. 'What a lovely club you have here. Who does the costumes?'

He went beetroot red and started spluttering. I turned round. 'Will you behave, lady? Please?'

'I'm sorry.' She sat down demurely on a stool to one side and folded her hands in her lap. 'There. Better?'

I glared at her. 'Look, cut it out, Perilla! Check out the wall paintings or something.' I checked them out myself. Jupiter! 'On second thoughts don't. Have a slice of pineapple.' I turned back to Crispus. 'Sorry, friend. Domestic dispute. Where were we?'

'Corvinus, just go.' The guy was fiddling with his napkin. Now he was an interesting shade of puce. 'Both of you.'

'Sure.' I sat back. 'Gladly. Right after you explain why you lit a fire under your pal Regulus. And don't try to flannel or call for help because I can be very nasty when I like. If not now then later.'

'Look, I swear to you . . .'

'Don't swear. The lady doesn't like it.' I helped myself to a handful of raisins. 'Never mind the frills. Just the straight explanation, please.'

'Corvinus.' Crispus was sweating now. Really sweating. I should've thought of bringing Perilla along myself; she beat thumbscrews any day. 'Marcus. If it were just my secret, or even Regulus's, I'd tell you. Believe me.'

'I don't.'

'Sure you do! We're pals, Marcus. Only this thing's dangerous. You know what happened to Regulus.' Nervously, his fingers rubbed the space under his jawbone where a hook might just've fitted nicely. 'There're other people involved in this. Big people. You start sniffing around them and we're both dead.'

I was getting tired of this, and it was way past my bedtime.

'Come on, Crispus! Cut the crap and give! Or next time we meet you'd better have on a fast pair of sandals.'

The guy wasn't acting. I could smell his fear across the table, even above the smell of the perfume. However he was the only lead I'd got. I couldn't let up on him. No way.

'Okay,' he said at last. 'Okay. A compromise. I tell you one thing and you leave me alone. Otherwise I yell for help and you can go and fuck yourself. Deal?'

I didn't like it but I knew this was the best I'd get. 'Deal.'

'Fine.' He swallowed. 'Regulus was Piso's middleman.'

I waited. 'And?'

'That's it, friend. All you get. Take it or leave it.'

I stared at him. 'Jupiter, Crispus! What the hell is this? Middleman for who? Doing what?'

'Find that out for yourself. That's all I'm saying.'

I thought about the napkin, then remembered Perilla. Maybe not. Instead, I reached over, grabbed the guy by his hair and pulled. 'Crispus, you bastard! Unless you . . .'

Which was as far as I got before the curtain was jerked open and a guy the size of the Capitol and made out of the same material stuck his head inside.

'You having problems with your guest, sir?' he growled. He was pointedly ignoring me. And Perilla. They breed their gorillas polite in the luxury market.

Crispus tore himself free and lay back gasping. I wiped my hair-oiled hand on my mantle.

'No, that's okay, Scorpio,' he said at last. 'Just a friendly argument. Valerius Corvinus was just leaving.' The bouncer held the curtain aside for me to walk through. Beyond it an exotic assortment of club members goggled. 'I'll see you around, Marcus. Maybe. No hard feelings, okay?'

'Yeah, sure.' If it hadn't been for Perilla I might've argued the toss, although more out of principle than sense with Tiny itching for an excuse to see how hard and how far I'd bounce. As it was, we left peaceably.

Maybe the bastard would be drummed out for bad form after all. I certainly hoped so.

Perilla kept pretty quiet on the way home. She opened her

mouth once or twice and took a breath as if she were going to ask a question, but the question never came. I watched her covertly and grinned to myself.

Yeah, well, I had to admit I'd enjoyed myself, and so had she. We should go out clubbing more often.

16

Next morning I went for a haircut down to one of the barber shops off the Market Square. Sure, I had a barber of my own at home, but people don't go to one of those streetside places just to get scalped. You can pick up some juicy bits of gossip, and they're great for sitting thinking about life, the universe and murder. Which was more or less what I had in mind. I sat down in the chair, told the guy with the shears to use his own judgment, and settled back with my eyes closed.

So. Regulus had been Piso's 'middleman'. That meant a deal, or maybe a scam; and given Regulus's predilections one that was illegal or at least shady. The obvious deal was the one with the Wart, but I dismissed that out of hand. Not because I didn't believe it existed; it had to for anything to make sense. But Crispus would've cut his own tongue out before he gave me anything that might lead me to Tiberius. The same went for Drusus. Parting with information that might bring an angry Imperial down on his greasy neck wasn't something the guy would risk. Not under any circumstances. Besides, if we needed an imperial middleman then our best bet was Carillus. He was Piso's ex-slave, and Piso had used him as his messenger to carry the mysterious phantom letter to whoever the hell's name was on the front, which could well have been the Wart.

No, Piso and his lawyer Regulus must've had another scam going, one that didn't involve the emperor and that I didn't know about yet. A private scam that had nothing to do with Germanicus. Or nothing directly to do with him . . .

'You want more off the sides, sir?'

'Hmm?' I opened my eyes.

'I'm sorry, sir.' The barber was waiting with a mirror. 'Is that okay for you or do you want me to cut some more?'

I looked into the polished bronze. Jupiter! Did I always look this worried? Maybe I needed a holiday. 'Uh, yeah,' I said. 'Yeah, that's fine, pal.'

I sat back again while he clipped away at the top. Piso's lawyer. Yeah. That was something else that didn't fit. Why had Piso asked Regulus to represent him in the first place? And why had Regulus agreed? The unwritten rule in court cases is that lawyer and client share some sort of common bond, social or political. The other two guys fitted the rule: Lucius Piso was his brother and Lepidus had followed him as governor of Tarraco. Regulus was the odd man out. Politically and socially he was a nobody, he wasn't Piso's type, and as far as I knew there'd been no existing link at all between them.

The operative phrase there was *as far as I knew*. That was where the 'middleman' came in, naturally. If I could ferret out the missing connection then maybe I'd understand what Crispus was telling me.

Yeah. If. The only problem was that Piso and Regulus were both dead, Carillus was Jupiter knew where and liable to stay lost until hell froze over, and that particular avenue was closed. Crispus had been a good idea, sure, but the bastard hadn't helped all that much. We still needed a major lead, and I hadn't the slightest idea how to go about getting it . . .

'You think the Reds have a chance tomorrow, sir?'

Oh, bugger. I opened my eyes again. Most barbers can gauge a customer's mood straight off and gab or shut up accordingly; the tips are better that way. This guy was evidently new, or he had all the sensitivity of a brick. Still, you have to be polite. And some subjects are sacred.

'About as much chance as a Vestal in a dice game, pal,' I said. 'The way these morons've been driving lately Green'll wipe the sand with them.'

'Right. Right.' He nodded. 'It's a crying shame. If Felix cut in on the turns different he could grab another five yards easy.'

'You think so?' I kept my voice neutral. Felix was the Reds' principal driver, a total incompetent who couldn't cut a decent turn if he practised between now and the next Winter Festival.

But I wasn't going to say that, oh no: my barber was obviously a Red supporter, and you don't disagree with the guy with the scissors.

'Sure,' he said. 'Listen . . .'

Luckily I had my experiences with Priscus to fall back on, so at least I managed to look vaguely interested. It was good stuff, though, smack on the button, even I could see that and I'm no expert. If I'd been the Reds' trainer I'd've had enough to fill a notebook.

'You seem to know a lot about racing, friend,' I said when he'd finished gabbing and cutting together.

'Used to be in the business myself, sir.' He flicked the stray hairs off my mantle and held the mirror up. 'Not a driver, just one of the stable hands, but you get a feel for the cars. Besides, I'm a Syrian. From Antioch. You ever meet an Antiochene who doesn't like racing?'

'No. No, come to think of it I haven't.' Certainly not a barber. Half the barbers in Rome were Syrians, and you always saw more stubbly jowls around on race-meet days.

'Have you been to Syria yourself, sir?' The barber was shaking clippings off his cloth.

'No. Never east of Athens.'

'You should go some time. Nice place. Lovely country. Except for the tax-collectors, of course.'

He didn't smile, and I wondered if he used that exit line for all his customers. My hand was in my purse to pay. I stopped.

'Shit!'

The barber paused. 'Some problem, sir?'

'No. No, no problem.' I gave him my best smile and half a gold piece. 'Thanks, friend.'

He stared at the coin like it was the key to the mint. 'Hey, I'm sorry,' he said. 'I can't change that.'

'You don't have to.' Bells were ringing. It was going to be a good day after all. 'Keep it, and thanks again. Thanks very much.'

'Uh, yeah. Likewise.' He was still looking after me, jaw hanging, when his next customer took the empty chair. Probably waiting for the minder to leap out from behind a pillar and cart me off somewhere quiet.

I'd meant to kick around the Market Square in the hopes of running into Crispus and bending his arm a bit more. Now I didn't have to. Sure, I could've gone up to the Capitol and asked the guy on the desk at the Treasury itself for the information, but he'd've wanted to know why the question. Probably passed me on to someone higher up, too, and that I didn't want. The fewer waves I made the better. Anyway, there was someone else I could ask. I headed back for the Palatine.

Who says oracles always speak in riddles? I'd just heard one, and short of grabbing me by the scruff of the neck and giving me the answer in words of one syllable it couldn't've been clearer. Thanks to the guy with the magic shears I knew now what the connection between Piso and Regulus had been.

When I got back home Bathyllus was outside the front door, chewing our young door slave to shreds for getting muddy sandalprints all over his nice clean mosaic. I collared him while the kid slipped away.

'Hey, Bathyllus, pal!' I said. 'I've a job for you.'

'Really, sir?' I got the little guy's best boiled turbot look; Bathyllus has a fixed routine and he doesn't appreciate any sudden alterations.

Hard cheese. Even Bathyllus had to be prepared for a few loose cobbles in the paved road of life. 'Yeah. I want you to run down to the Aventine for me. Now.'

'The Aventine, sir?' He reeled, a bit too dramatically to be convincing. 'Me, sir? Now, sir? *Run*, sir?'

I'd forgotten his hernia. Supported although it now was. 'Yeah, okay, walk. Only walk fast, right, sunshine?'

'Thank you, sir. Most generous.'

Jupiter! I didn't have the time for temperament. 'Hey, cut it out, little guy! This is important and I want you to go yourself because I know you'll get it right first time.' Oil oil, smarm smarm.

'Your estimation of my capabilities is most gratifying, sir. However I had planned to—'

The hell with this. 'Look, just go, okay?' I snapped. Jupiter's balls on a string, did everyone have these problems with the bought help or was it just me? I gave him directions to Lippillus's place and told him what I wanted. 'And if he's not at home then try the Watch headquarters. You know where they are?'

'Of course. Not a very prepossessing building, as I remember.' He sniffed.

'You starting a cold, Bathyllus?'

'No, sir.' Stiffly.

'Fine. The mistress in?'

'As far as I know, sir, yes.'

'Good. Bugger off, then.'

He buggered off fast as a speeding tortoise. I went inside, being careful to wipe my feet on the mosaic in the process.

Perilla was in the garden, deep in a book. I crept up on her and bit her neck. She didn't look round.

'Go away, Corvinus,' she said. 'You smell of barber's talc.'

Good start. 'That's because I've just had a very interesting haircut, lady.' I peered over her shoulder and examined the book. Heavy stuff, and in Greek: Nicander's *Theriaca*, a study of poisons and their antidotes. 'You doing some research, or were you serious the other night about poisoning my breakfast porridge?'

'The former, actually, but the latter is becoming rapidly more attractive.'

Ouch. What with Bathyllus and Perilla both in moods the home team weren't doing too well this morning. Maybe I should go out and come back in again as somebody else. 'You want to watch that reading, lady. Too much of it drives you mad.'

Perilla closed the roll with a sigh. 'Are you especially trying to be annoying, Corvinus, or does it come naturally?'

'Both.' I came round the front and kissed her. 'I know what scam Piso and Regulus were involved in. Or at least I think I know. Bathyllus has just galloped off to get the proof.'

That got her interest. 'Tell me,' she said.

I sat down next to her on the stone bench. 'I'd assumed it had something to do with the trial. It doesn't, or not directly. Regulus worked in the tax office. Imperial division.'

'So?'

'So I'll bet my boots he looked after Syria.'

She was quiet for a long time. Then she said: 'I see. You think

Piso and Regulus were fiddling the taxes between them while Piso was governor?'

'That's the theory.'

'It's possible, I suppose.'

'Sure it's possible. It's every governor's dream to have a friend at the tax office who can juggle the figures and level out the bumps in the balance sheet. And it explains why Regulus practically hugged me when I told him all I was interested in was the trial. The guy was heading for the hills with a ton of documents under his arm, and one gets you ten they weren't the Residence's laundry bills.'

'Mmm.' Her brow creased. 'So what, if anything, does this have to do with Germanicus?'

'Simple. One reason Germanicus was sent out east – besides to clinch the Parthian deal – was that the locals were screaming over the amount of tax they had to pay. It's an unwritten law that within reason a governor's entitled to his perks, but I reckon Piso was getting greedy. Taking two bites at the cherry and counting on his personal friendship with the Wart to keep him out of trouble, like it did in Spain. So then suddenly he finds a strait-laced Imperial banging on his door and asking to see the receipts, and he panics.'

'Are you saying now it *was* Piso who killed Germanicus after all? Piso personally, to cover up embezzlement?'

I shifted uncomfortably. 'Well, no. I wouldn't go quite that far. But it'd help to explain why the two were at daggers drawn right from the start. If Germanicus were building up a case against the guy – a valid case – then Piso would be keen to get rid of him. Maybe even keen enough to agree to act as someone's agent for murder. Someone with the clout to protect him when the feathers started to fly.'

'Whose agent? Presumably not Tiberius's, for obvious reasons. Drusus and Livilla's?'

'I don't know, lady. I really don't know. Maybe.' I sighed. 'I'll tell you one thing, though. We won't get many more answers in Rome. We're going round in circles as it is, and we need to break fresh ground.'

'Then what would you suggest? Or could we possibly just give this whole thing up? It has nothing to do with us, anyway.'

I ignored that. She didn't mean it, really.

'You ever been to Syria?' I said.

Her eyes widened. 'You're not serious!'

'Sure I'm serious. Lovely country, so I'm told. Good barbers. Cheery locals. They like racing.'

Perilla was frowning. 'No, I haven't been to Syria, Marcus,' she said slowly. 'But I know someone who has. He's there now, in fact. Very much so.'

Shit. I'd forgotten about her ex. Rufus had been on Germanicus's staff, and now he commanded one of the Syrian legions. Not only was the guy there, he was one of the top brass.

'Uh, yeah,' I said. 'Well, that's certainly a drawback, I suppose.'

'Marcus.' There was the barest touch of ice in her voice. 'I'm sorry, but this is *not* a good idea. Please forget it altogether.'

I back-pedalled rapidly. 'Yeah, maybe it is a bit of a bummer at that. Never mind, just a suggestion.'

'I don't even want to be in the same *country* as Rufus, never mind the same city.'

'Uh, Syria's pretty big, Perilla.' Bugger. I hadn't considered checking things out at the other end until my pal the barber had put the idea into my head. Not consciously anyway. But the more I thought about it the more I liked it. 'The guy's probably up country somewhere sticking pigs.'

'The Third Gallic's based in Antioch, Corvinus, as you well know. I assume that would be where you would be conducting your investigations.' She bent down and picked up her book. 'Now if you don't mind I want to get on with this. The librarian at the Pollio gave me it on special loan and he needs it back by tomorrow.'

She'd frozen up on me. I knew the signs. Not that I blamed her: I'd never actually met Rufus, but from what she'd told me about him at our first-ever dinner together and the few times she'd mentioned him since he sounded a real thoroughgoing gold-plated bastard. Also, as I knew, he hadn't wanted to agree to the divorce. If I hadn't had Livia pitching for me, and through her the Wart, it never would've happened. That must've made the guy pretty sour. I didn't particularly mind having to meet him face to face, but I wasn't going to bust a gut arranging dinner.

We needed a new angle on the case, though. We really did. And taking things from the Syrian end would've given us it.

Well, maybe Lippillus would come up with something. I kissed the top of Perilla's head and went inside to catalogue my pottery collection.

17

Bathyllus got back late in the afternoon: forget 'run'; the bastard must've had problems overhauling snails. Also he was smirking when he came into the study, which is always a bad sign.

'Hey, little guy,' I said. 'You find Lippillus?'

'Yes, sir. Eventually. He was out shopping for his mother.'

'Get her cheap, did he?' Not a flicker. Jupiter knows why I bother. 'Okay, so spit it out.'

'Livineius Regulus worked in the department dealing with Noricum, sir.'

I looked at him. 'Where?'

'Noricum. It's one of the minor northern provinces. Beyond the Carnican Alps. Between Rhaetia and Pannonia.'

'I know where Noricum is, you smart bugger! Regulus didn't have any connection with Syria? None at all?'

'No, sir. Before that he was in the Sicilian department.'

'Fuck. Double fuck.'

'Quite, sir.' Bathyllus paused, his hand on the doorknob. 'Now if you don't require me any further I'll get back to my normal duties. Such as there remains time for.'

'Yeah. Yeah.' I waved him away wearily. 'Go and count the spoons. And bring me a jug of Setinian. Easy on the water.'

'Yes, sir.' I expected him to scuttle out, but he didn't. 'Oh. I almost forgot, sir. One more thing. Favonius Lippillus asks if the name Vonones means anything to you.'

I sat up straight. 'Who?'

'Vonones. It was your enquiry about Syria that prompted the question, sir. Although Regulus had no connections with the province *per se* he was a very close personal friend of a young

Parthian gentleman by that name when the latter was resident in Rome.'

'Almost forgot', nothing! Bathyllus could give an elephant memory training. The bastard had kept it back intentionally. I could've taken the little guy by the throat and beaten him to death with his own floor mop.

'Okay, Bathyllus,' I said. 'Just tell me, right? What exactly did Lippillus say?'

'Only that while the eastern gentleman was in the city Regulus was very much attached to him, sir.' Bathyllus's mouth was pursed in disapproval. 'The two were quite inseparable, in fact.'

I translated that into straight Latin. 'In other words they were lovers?'

'Such would seem to be Lippillus's impression, yes.'

'Uhuh.' Bathyllus was still hovering. 'That all this time, little guy?'

'Yes, sir.'

'You sure?'

'Except that Lippillus asked specially that his name be kept out of any subsequent enquiries.'

'Yeah. Smart cookie. Nothing about the murder investigation?'

'No, sir.'

'Okay, off you go and play with your dish-rag. Don't forget the wine.'

When he'd gone I lay back on the reading couch to think. We'd really opened up a parcel of worms here. I hadn't known about Vonones's predilections, but I knew who he was: an ex-king of Parthia, no less, who'd spent his early years as a hostage at the court of Augustus. Which explained the 'ex' part of the title: he'd turned out too much of a Roman for the Parthians, who'd washed their hands of him four years after he'd succeeded to the throne. Driven from Parthia he'd trotted off to neighbouring Armenia and taken up the vacant kingship there.

Which was where the Syrian connection came in. Under diplomatic pressure from Parthia, Piso's predecessor Silanus had forced Vonones to abdicate and brought him back to Antioch, where he was kept under what amounted to luxurious house arrest. Then came Piso's governorship and Germanicus's mission to dicker with the new Parthian king Artabanus. One of Artabanus's terms of settlement had been the request that Vonones be moved away from Syria, which he duly was. Only at some point – I didn't know the details – he'd tried to escape and been ever so slightly killed.

There were holes, but that was the general drift, and the implication of the last bit was pretty clear: Vonones had been playing the Parthian conspiracy game from behind the Roman border and Artabanus had finally had enough and pulled his plug. The question was, was any of this relevant? Sure, Regulus had known the guy when he was young and not so innocent, and Vonones might've had fond memories of balmy evenings on the Pincian, but that'd been a dozen years at least before Piso's time in Syria. A lot had happened since, and if Piso did have a scam going with Vonones then twelve years were too much water under the bridge to account for Regulus's claim to middleman status. Or were they?

I didn't know, and it was becoming increasingly apparent I wouldn't find out sitting on my butt in Rome. Ah, well. It was a shame about Rufus . . .

Someone scratched on the door: Bathyllus with the wine.

'Come in, little guy!' I shouted; but it wasn't Bathyllus holding the tray, it was Perilla.

She set it down on the side table and kissed me.

'Marcus, I'm sorry I bit your head off earlier,' she said. 'I didn't mean it. Honestly.'

'Hey, that's okay. Although frozen balls would describe the effect you achieved better, lady.'

She hid a smile. 'Really. The apology still holds. But I've been thinking it over and I've reached a decision. You really, truly think going to Antioch is necessary?'

'It'd certainly help, sure. Antioch was the scene of the crime, after all, there're people there who can tell us exactly what happened. As far as being necessary's concerned, well, yeah, I'm beginning to think we have to take things from the other end. At least that'd make them easier.'

'Very well. In that case we'll go.'

I simply stared at her. She sat down on the edge of the couch and poured a cup of wine. 'The sea lanes are open again now, aren't they? There will be a ship available?'

'Yeah. Yeah, there'll be a ship.' My head was spinning. I picked up the wine cup and drank. 'You sure about this, Perilla?'

'Yes. Quite sure.'

'Swear on your grandmother's hoary old head and spit on the ground for luck?'

'Yes.'

'What about Rufus?'

'We're divorced, Marcus. Quite legally. There's no reason why I should even talk to him if I don't want to. And Syria – Antioch, even – is a big place. As you so rightly said.'

'Hey! Okay!' I hugged her. 'Great! Thanks, lady.'

'Drink your wine.'

I did, while she leaned against me. Finally I said: 'How's the book coming along, by the way? Thingummy's Poisons?'

'I've just finished it. Fascinating reading.'

'I can imagine. You know how it was done yet? The Germanicus business?'

'No, of course not. It could've been any of a dozen different methods using a dozen different substances. If the poor man was poisoned at all. I did discover one thing that might interest you, though, Marcus.'

'Yeah?'

'It seems that if the . . . sexual parts are touched with aconite death ensues within a day.'

I winced. Jupiter! 'No kidding.'

'No kidding.' She kissed me again; a longer one, this time. 'Don't worry. I wouldn't even know what it looked like.'

'The aconite?'

'The aconite.'

Uhuh. I can tell when I'm being propositioned. Study couches, however, are designed for chaste solo reading. Five minutes later we gave up in favour of upstairs.

Bathyllus was waiting in the hall to ask about dinner; tactfully, because the little guy had seen the direction we were heading.

'Tell Meton something light,' I said. 'Oh, and Bathyllus: send someone down to Puteoli to ask about boats for Antioch, okay?' Big ships don't sail from Ostia: the harbour's too full of Tiber mud to float anything bigger than a kid's toy yacht, and for serious sailing you have to go south. 'To leave as soon as possible, right?'

'Would that be Antioch in Syria, sir?'

'Is there another one, sunshine?'

'Not that I know of. Would fish suit? Broiled tunny with a vegetable mousse and some Clazomenean wine?'

I looked him over carefully. Sometimes I suspect the little guy of having a sense of humour after all, but it's buried pretty deep and it's pretty weird. The fish gag slipped past me – if it was a gag – but not the wine. Wine I know, and Clazomenean's got sea water added to it: the locals say it gives it a certain unique tang.

Bathyllus was staring back with bland innocence. What the hell, I was probably only imagining things. 'Yeah,' I said. 'Tunny's good. Not the wine, we'll have Setinian as usual.'

'If you insist, sir.'

'I insist, little guy. I insist. And don't forget Puteoli.'

'Certainly not, sir.' He left in the direction of the kitchen.

One of these days I'll see the bastard fazed. One of these days.

18

We were lucky; a passenger-carrying merchantman called the *Artemis* was sailing for Antioch in ten days' time. No problem with berths, either: it was early in the season, and most punters wait until June when they can do the journey in two quick hops via Alexandria. I'd've taken Bathyllus along but Rome would've ground to a halt without him and he gets sick crossing the Sublician, so we settled for Meton the cook, Perilla's maid Phryne and three general skivvies.

We got ourselves down to Puteoli with a day to spare and I checked the boat out. She looked okay: just short of two hundred tons, well built, with a new set of rigging and a crew that didn't look like they'd jump ship at the first sign of a squall. The captain was a solid-looking guy called Theon, with a big gut and legs you could've driven a wagon between without worrying about your paintwork. Also he was an Alexandrian Greek, which was a definite plus. Most Italians can't tell a frap from a luff, but Alexandrians come ready wrapped in sealskin and if you take their sandals off nine times out of ten their feet are webbed. I didn't quite go that far with Theon, but I reckoned he knew his job. You tend to make sure of these things for yourself before you start, or you regret it later. If you've got a later. Especially if you happen to be someone like me and swim like a brick.

We sailed the next day, across the harbour bar and smack into what felt like the biggest storm in living memory. I was on the poop deck with the captain at the time.

'A good following wind, lord.' Theon picked his nose with a marlinespike and rocked back and forward on his portico legs. 'We're lucky.'

'Lucky?' I clung to a strut or a spar or whatever the hell the technical term is while Neptune and all his bloody nymphs and tritons tossed us in a blanket and Puteoli did a bump and grind behind us. Shit. Maybe the word meant something different in Greek. 'That what you call this, friend?'

He gave an evil laugh: all ship's captains are born sadists. 'Don't worry, lord. You won't feel a thing in a day or two.'

'Yeah.' The boat lurched sideways like something had kicked her in the belly. Theon never moved. I nearly went over the side. 'Yeah. That's what's worrying me.'

'Of course Cape Scyllaeum'll be quite another matter. Things might get a touch rough there.'

'Oh, whoopee.' Bastard! I looked out over the heaving green mess between us and land. There were no dolphins; the smart buggers knew better than to venture out in this weather. Probably they were all holed up in a cove somewhere with a good supply of sardines, laughing their beaks off.

Perilla's head appeared over the edge of the poop deck's ladder. The captain held out a steadying hand which she didn't need.

'Everything shipshape below, ma'am?' he said.

'Yes, thank you, captain.' She gave him one of her best smiles and I could see the nautical bastard's mainbrace splice. How the hell the lady could look this good and this cool when I was within an inch of losing my breakfast beat me, but she did. 'Quite homely, in fact.' We'd been lucky as far as accommodation went, anyway. Us being the only passengers, and purple-stripers to boot, Theon had given us half the deckhouse, which beat the pants off camping out in the scuppers any day of the month.

'If there's anything else you need, ma'am, just ask,' he said. Preen, preen. I grinned. Give Perilla two days and she'd have Agrippa here wound round her little finger.

She'd been looking round her with more interest than I could've mustered. Suddenly she pointed to the top of the mast, where someone had hung what looked like an old leather cloak.

'What's that?' she asked. 'Some sort of flag?'

'That, ma'am?' Theon turned his weather-eye aloft. 'No, no flag. It's a sea-cow's hide. It protects us from lightning.'

Oh, Jupiter! Being hit by lightning was something I hadn't

thought of. Drowning I can handle. Getting fried from above comes extra.

'Really? But how interesting!' She wasn't kidding, either. Scientific titbits like that fascinate Perilla. 'How does it work?'

'Lightning doesn't strike sea-cows, ma'am. Nor their skins.'

'Oh, of course. Neither it does. How silly of me.' Perilla glanced at me, then stared. 'Marcus, are you all right? You're looking grey. Green, rather. Both.'

'Ah . . .' I'd made the mistake of looking up at Theon's patent bolt-deflector myself and I was wishing now that I hadn't. As an idea it had been a real bummer. When you're on a moving boat and not enjoying it the trick is to keep your eyes on a fixed point. Like Italy. The trouble was, even Italy had started jumping around. I swallowed and tried to put everything back where it belonged. 'Yeah, well, actually no, Perilla. Maybe I should go and lie down for a while.'

'Hardly wise, lord.' That was Agrippa putting his grapnel in. 'If you're feeling queasy then . . .'

Too late! Oh, Jupiter! Jupiter Best and Greatest!

Heave!

'Marcus!'

Forget the deckhouse, I never even made it to the ladder. My only consolation was that I caught the bow-legged bugger fair and square.

Things couldn't get much worse over the next few days, I thought. They did. Theon had been right; Scyllaeum was rough. By the time we rounded it and were into the straits I couldn't've cared less if Jupiter had blasted that bloody sea-cow's hide with every lightning bolt in his quiver, so long as he made it quick. Perilla wasn't much help either. The last thing you want when you're dying of seasickness is to have a perky and very sexy lady coming in every five minutes saying how invigorating she finds the sea breezes and what a charming attentive man the captain is. It took me five days to decide that maybe I'd live after all. When I opened my eyes Perilla was sitting in front of her mirror having the maid fix her hair.

'Hey, lady?' I said. No answer. I tried again. This time I got some sound to come out.

She whipped round, scattering pins.

'*Marcus!*'

'Yeah, that's me. Maybe.'

'How are you feeling?' Cool fingers touched my forehead.

'How the hell would I feel? Like I've been turned inside out.'

She sniffed and took her hand away. 'You did that yourself, dear. All over the floor. Several times.'

'Yeah, well . . .'

'Phryne.' She turned to the maid. 'Go and tell Meton to make some soup.'

'Hey, let's not get carried away, Perilla.' I tried to sit up. Mistake. The cabin heaved. 'A cup of wine'd be nice, though.'

'Soup, Phryne.' The maid left. 'Unless you'd prefer a pint of sea water, Corvinus. That's what the captain suggested.'

'Sadistic bastard.'

'Not at all. It's a well-known cure for seasickness. Besides, he's a lovely man once you get to know him.'

'*Lecherous* sadistic bastard.'

She gave me a bright smile and a kiss. 'Feeling better, so I see. Don't overdo things, though.'

'If this is better, lady, then I'm a porpoise.'

'Nonsense. A mug of sea-urchin soup with the spines boiled in will work wonders.'

My stomach crawled. I tried to sit up again. This time I made it, although the walls still spun. 'That another of your nautical pal's remedies?'

'My old aunt's, actually. She sailed the Mediterranean end to end four times before she was ten.'

'Yeah, that figures.' The walls were slowing down now. 'It had to come from somewhere. Where are we anyway?'

She sat down on the edge of the bed. 'Off the Greek coast, not far from Methone. Theon says conditions have been excellent and we're making good time.'

'Theon can take a flying . . .'

'*Marcus!*'

'. . . jump. And don't shout, lady. Please. It goes right through me.'

She grinned. 'This was your idea in the first place, remember.'

'Yeah. Yeah, okay.' I kissed her and swung my legs out of the bed in the direction of the floor. 'Maybe I'll just go and see how things are for myself.'

'Corvinus, I don't think that is such a terribly good idea at the moment.'

I waved her back. 'You do it your way, I'll do it mine. Forget the soup, okay? All I need's a breath of fresh air. Oh, and maybe a cup of neat Setinian and a bit of bread to soak it up with.'

The floor felt strange beneath my feet but it didn't move around as much as I'd thought it would. With Perilla's help I made it to the door and out.

It was a beautiful morning, and I had my dolphins. They were playing all round the ship; throwing themselves into the air, tossing rock-crystal droplets of water at the sun, plunging back into the waves and shooting through the water like greased arrows. I leaned against the rail for a long time and watched them.

'Aren't they marvellous?' Perilla said from beside me.

'Yeah.' I put my arm round her. 'Yeah, they're okay. For fish.'

We were hugging the coast, just far enough out to avoid the rocks and get the benefit of the land breeze. I could even smell a hint of pine and goat-shit on the air. When Meton appeared with the soup I gave him his new orders.

The wine when it came hit my empty stomach like a warm football, but I kept it down and bit into the bread. Lovely stuff, fresh-baked, hot and crusty from the oven. Before I knew it I'd finished the loaf. A pity. I'd meant to throw the last bit to the dolphins.

'You've got your sea legs finally, lord, I see.' Theon was coming down the poop deck ladder.

'Uh, yeah.' I brushed my tunic free of crumbs. My head was still spinning, but that could've been the wine. 'Sorry I brought my breakfast up over you, friend.'

'Nothing to be ashamed of. We can't all be born sailors like your lady here.'

Uhuh. I'd only been up five minutes and he was needling me already. 'Now, look, pal . . . !' I began.

'*Marcus!*' Perilla snapped. I grinned and held my palms up.

'Okay. Okay. No hassle. It's too nice a day, anyway.' I leaned against the rail and he joined me. 'So we're making good time.'

'Good enough. We should be into the Messenian Gulf soon. Maybe even sight Taenarium in two days' time. If the wind holds.'

'That so?' Geography's never been my strong point, let alone maritime geography, but the guy sounded pleased. 'How much longer, you reckon?'

'Depends on the wind and the weather. We've been lucky so far. If they both hold we'll cut as straight as we can for Rhodes. Then an easy run along the Asian coast. Eighteen days, maybe twenty depending on landfalls. We're sailing light.'

'What are you carrying?'

'Crockery mostly. Samian. Some private consignments. But that's just for ballast. Most of our trade's the other way. Spices and perfumes. Jericho balsam. A few jars of Laodicean wine.'

I pricked up my ears. 'Is that right? Laodicean wine, eh?'

He grinned. 'You know it, lord? As good in its way as the best Italian. Very popular in Alexandria.'

'Yeah?' Maybe the guy's heart was in the right place after all. 'You . . . ah . . . happen to have any lying around loose at the moment?'

'Marcus . . .' Perilla began.

But Theon was still grinning. With a gut like his I should've expected the guy to turn out to be an oenophile. Or maybe he just liked wine. 'One or two jars,' he said. 'Not for trade. Just private consumption. You'd care to try some?'

'You've just twisted my arm, friend.'

'Before dinner tonight, then? The Lady Perilla as well, of course.'

'Sure,' I said. 'Why not?'

Maybe sea travel wasn't so bad as I'd thought it was. I felt better already.

19 ∫

In the end Perilla didn't come on the wine-tasting binge; a ruse to get me back in time for dinner and sober enough to eat it. I was glad I'd made the effort, though. Once you got Theon alone and off his mysteries of the deeps crap he turned out to be good company. Useful, too, because he knew Antioch like the back of his hand, and without Perilla there to cramp his style I got a fair run-down of the parts of the city tourists don't get told about. The Laodicean, incidentally, wasn't bad stuff, but it wasn't half as good as Theon had promised. I wouldn't've backed it against an ordinary Setinian, let alone my best Falernian. Far too spicy on the palate, which was probably why the Alexandrians went for it. These over-civilised bastards add perfume to their wines anyway. No wonder Cleopatra lost Actium. Half her sailors were probably down with rose petal poisoning.

I left, as I'd promised Perilla, as soon as we'd sunk the first jug and before the sun was properly below the yardarm. Not that I'd've stayed much longer anyway. My head still felt pretty woozy and the wine hadn't helped my balance any. It was a beautiful evening. We'd lost the dolphins but the Greek coast was still slipping past like a long strip of purple ribbon: presumably while the captain and I had been swapping details of Roman and Antiochene night life one of his crew had been making sure we didn't hit Crete or Egypt or whatever the hell was in front of us. I took a moment to lean over the rail and generally think how great it was to be alive . . .

Another second and I wouldn't've been. What made me turn I don't know, maybe the rush of air as the guy brought back his knife-arm. As it was I just had time to spin round, move to the right and bring my left knee up for his groin as he knocked me against the side of the boat.

I missed. Maybe it was because I'd been on my back for five days, maybe I was just out of practice; but I missed. And when you're facing a guy with a knife you don't get a second chance.

The knife came at me again in a vicious upward stab angled under my bottom rib. I caught his wrist before it struck and pushed down and out, feeling the blade slice through the left side of my tunic and bite into the ship's timbers.

I didn't have a knife myself; walking in Rome I usually carry one strapped to the inside of my forearm, but I wasn't in the Subura now. In any case, my left hand was busy. This was no time for heroics. I yelled blue murder while I went for his balls again. This time my knee connected. He gasped and his grip slackened.

Right, you bastard! I thought, and brought my forehead down hard on to the bridge of his nose. He fell back, blood streaming, then came on again. He still had the knife, only this time he held it wide, waiting to see which way I'd move. I brought my foot up to kick his liver through his kidneys . . .

And the ship shifted. Whether it was a rogue wave or a change in the wind I didn't know, but suddenly I'd lost my balance completely and I was sprawled face-up half over the side. The guy was handier on his feet than I was. He moved forward, grinning. I rolled away, but I was years too late . . .

There was a thump, and a horrible crunching sound. The guy stopped, sagged, and slipped to the deck. Behind him stood Theon, holding what looked like a major part of ship's equipment.

I turned and leaned over the rail, gasping for breath.

'You okay, Corvinus?' The captain's hand pulled me back.

'Yeah. Yeah. Thanks.' I was glad we'd got beyond the *lord* crap. But then it doesn't sound so bad in Greek.

'What the hell happened?' He looked more shocked than I was.

'Shit knows. One of your crew went for me. You know who he is?'

He reached down, grabbed the man by the scruff of his tunic

and lifted him like he was a doll. The head lolled sickeningly: whatever Theon had hit him with it'd stove in the brain pan like an eggshell and he was definitely an ex-assassin.

'His name's Albianus,' Theon said. 'He's our galley skivvy.'

Suddenly something white rushed across the deck and threw itself at me. I grabbed in reflex and found it was Perilla.

'Marcus, are you all right?' she said.

'Sure. Why shouldn't I be?'

'I heard you yell.'

'You and the rest of the ship, lady. Probably half the Greek coastline from here to Corinth.'

'Don't exaggerate, Corvinus. We're nowhere near Corinth.'

'Yeah, well.' I detached her gently, without letting go altogether. 'Wherever.'

She looked down at the dead man – Theon had dropped him again – and shivered.

'What happened?' she said quietly.

'A brush with the shipboard staff.'

'Marcus . . .'

'Perhaps you should go back inside, ma'am,' Theon said.

'If you think . . . !'

'Go on, Perilla.' I kissed her cheek. 'We'll be right there. Promise.'

She went. Once she was safely out of sight Theon picked the dead guy up and tossed him to the fish.

'He joined the ship at Puteoli,' Theon said. He was sitting on the deckhouse's only stool. Perilla and I sat chastely on the bed, side by side. 'Our normal skivvy'd gone out on a bender and never come back.'

'Was that usual?' I said.

'Not unusual. Though so far we've known where to find him.'

'But not this time?'

'Not this time.' Theon made to spit, and then remembered where he was. 'So when this Albianus turned up asking for a job an hour before we sailed I took him on. You get a lot of that sort hanging about Puteoli harbour. Any harbour. Not real seamen, but if they can peel an onion, clean out a pan and stay sober nobody asks too many questions.'

'So you didn't know him?'

'No.' He scowled. 'Did you?'

'Uh-uh.'

'Then why did he attack you?'

'Jupiter knows,' I said. Yeah, sure. He probably did, but I could make a damn good guess myself. 'Maybe the heat got to him.'

'What heat?'

'Okay, make it the endless empty wastes of the briny, pal.' I reached for the cup of wine – my own Setinian – on the side table. 'Whatever. How should I know?'

'You'll report it when we get to Seleucia, naturally.'

'No.'

That rocked him, I could see. Sure, he was relieved: no ship's captain wants it to get around that his crew might try to puncture the passengers. The fact that I was a purple-striper and a current Roman consul's nephew made things worse. One word from me to the authorities in Syria and he'd spend the rest of his days hauling cabbages in the Black Sea. But he was puzzled, and a guy like Theon hated to be puzzled.

'You care to tell me why not?' he said.

I shrugged. 'Because it wasn't your fault. Because you saved my life. And because the bastard's dead anyway. What did you slug him with, by the way?'

'A belaying pin.'

'Yeah?' Jupiter! Maybe I'd've understood that in Latin, but I doubted it. 'Okay, so we'll agree to blame it on the heat, right? No questions either side.'

'Well, Corvinus, so long as you're satisfied.' Theon got to his feet. 'Nothing like this has ever happened before on a ship of mine. You've my apologies. And my thanks.'

He was a straight guy. Straight but puzzled. We shook hands and I saw him out and on his way to keelhaul the bilges or whatever the hell captains did at night. Then I poured myself another cup of wine and settled back against the bolster.

'That man was supposed to stop you getting to Syria, wasn't he?' Perilla said.

'Yeah.' I took a mouthful of Setinian. After the Laodicean it went down like liquid velvet. 'Yeah. Sure he was.'

'So who sent him?'

'Jupiter knows, Perilla. I'll tell you one thing, though.'

'Yes?'

'It means we're on the right lines.'

She was quiet for a long time, her head on my shoulder. Then she said: 'Now I'll tell you something, Corvinus.'

'Yeah?'

'Antioch isn't Rome. You don't know it, you've no friends there. Right lines or not, if whoever sent Albianus tries again then next time they may succeed. And they might well have people already there and waiting. I want you to be very careful, please, because I don't want you dead. It isn't worth it. Do you understand?'

I kissed her forehead.

'I understand, lady.'

Sure I did. I didn't want me dead, either. But after that evening's little incident it might be pretty tricky avoiding it.

20

Twenty days later, we stepped ashore at Antioch's port of Seleucia in the middle of a major earthquake. At least that's what it felt like. The weird thing was that although the ground was jigging about like the lid on a soup pot the buildings seemed to be holding together okay, and none of the locals who turned up on the quayside trying to sell us things were paying any attention. But then that's Greeks for you. It'd take more than an earthquake to stop these guys turning an honest drachma.

Normal people planning a foreign trip arrange things the other end months before they put the doorkey under the mat and stop the oil deliveries. We'd had ten days max, which meant we were starting cold. Theon had suggested that we use his cousin's guest house south of the city on the Daphne road as a temporary base, which seemed a good idea. So we left most of the baggage and one of the skivvies behind for collection later and took a ferryboat the fifteen miles upriver to Antioch itself. We got there late in the afternoon and disembarked at a landing stage just beyond the Bridge Gate.

'Isn't it lovely, Marcus?' Perilla was looking round her as I supervised the unloading and dickered with the carriers for the last stretch to Theon's cousin's place. We were smack in the middle of the Old Town, where most of the buildings dated back to the original founding of the city. Honey-coloured marble, shady porticoes. Lots of greenery and water, too, and at Rome you only get those two things together with the scum on the Tiber.

'Yeah. Great,' I said, wrestling with a rogue optative.

'So wonderfully Greek. I really feel we're on holiday.'

Personally I was feeling pretty sour. Dickering in street Greek with a pack of evil-minded sharks who wilfully misunderstand your stress patterns isn't my bag, added to which I had serious problems with the exchange rate and I hadn't had a cup of wine since breakfast. There's a lot to be said for foreign travel, no doubt, but for an amateur it can be a real bummer. I wished I'd brought Bathyllus after all. With his organisational genius the little guy would probably have made all the arrangements telepathically while we were somewhere west of Crete.

Perilla stopped soaking up the local colour and came over.

'Having problems, Corvinus?' she said.

'You could say that, lady.' Jupiter! I was being eaten alive here! Meton was no use either; he'd wandered off to check out a fish stall. Take that bastard away from his kitchen and he'd got no more idea than a dowager in a cathouse. 'Yeah. Problems describe what I'm having pretty well.'

Perilla frowned. 'But it's simple, Marcus! What was the name of Theon's cousin's guest house?'

'Uh . . . the Three Bay Trees. Two. Two Bay Trees. Cedars.'

'The Two Cedars. Fine.' Turning to the gang of carters who were squabbling over us, she pointed at random. 'You, you and you. You know the Two Cedars? On the Daphne road?'

The guys looked at each other and swallowed. I didn't blame them. When Perilla's in this mood you just grin and nod and go with it. Unless you can run for cover, of course, which these bastards couldn't because there wasn't any. Her stress patterns were pretty good, too.

'Yes, ma'am,' they said.

'We'll need two carriages and a wagon. Any problem?'

'No, ma'am.'

'A tetradrachm each. And you can keep the change. *If* you drive carefully and don't break anything.'

'Yes, ma'am. Thank you, ma'am.'

'Don't mention it. The rest of you can go.'

Five seconds later with the exception of our three carters the landing stage was empty, apart from a sandal or two that'd got left behind in the rush. Even the birds had shut up. Perilla turned back to me.

'There,' she said. 'Everything all right now?'

'Uh, yeah. Yeah. That about does it.'
Shit.

We left the city by the Daphne Gate. Even I'd heard of Daphne, and Theon had waxed lyrical about it on the boat. It's one of Syria's most famous tourist spots, a little town in the hills five miles south of Antioch with a precinct of Apollo and more greenery and springs than you can shake a stick at. The walk there's popular in summer, too, and your average tourist – or Antiochene, for that matter – won't go far without stopping off somewhere on the way, which means that the road's lined with places offering everything from a cup of chilled fruit juice to full bed and board with ten-course banquets and a dozen dancing girls as optional extras.

No one with any regard for his skin or his stomach stays in an Italian guest house. If the owner doesn't get you the fleas will, and doing the tour of the kitchens is about as safe as a walk through a plague pit. The Syrian Greek variety's different. It puts ours on a par with a shack on the Danube. Even on this scale the Two Cedars, when we finally got to it, was top-of-the-market stuff: a long, two-storey building with a flat roof and a first-floor balcony running its length, set in a grove of trees a stone's throw from the river. Round the side I could see a garden with a stream and tables shaded by trellised vines. Cool in summer, just as good in spring, especially with a jug of cold crisp white wine and a plateful of the local olives served by . . .

Served by . . .

Jupiter!

'Marcus?' Perilla said.

'Hmm?'

'Would you mind getting down and letting me out, please? When you've finished ogling the waitress, of course.'

'Uh . . . yeah. Yeah, okay, Perilla.' Jupiter! She was a big girl, though. Lovely ankles, too. I liked the Cedars already.

We unloaded. I paid off the carters and watched them hare back down the road towards town like their postilions had been struck by lightning. Meanwhile Perilla was talking to a little fat guy with ringlets. Presumably Theon's cousin.

'I've taken half the first floor, Marcus,' she said when she'd finished. 'It's self-contained, with a private kitchen downstairs and use of the baths at the rear. Will that do?'

The little guy looked punch-drunk and his eyes were glazed. It'd do. Sure it would. We'd probably got his best suite for half the normal price.

'Yeah. Yeah, that sounds fine, Perilla,' I said. Meton had already wandered off with a single-minded look in his eye and his best set of knives under his arm to find the kitchen. I motioned to the other two slaves. 'Hey, just take everything inside and stow it, guys, okay?'

'Philotimus, lord, at your service.' The fat owner was bowing. 'You had a pleasant trip?'

'Yeah, it was okay. Lovely place you have here.' An arselicker, obviously; but then you have to make allowances. Manners are different out east.

'The lord is gracious to say so.' He waved a ringed hand towards the garden. 'Perhaps some cool wine and fruit? The city can be tiring. My own slaves can help yours with the luggage while you and the lady relax.'

Maybe he was okay after all. The guy had his priorities right, anyway.

'Sounds good,' I said. 'Okay, Perilla?'

We left the lads shifting our bags and boxes upstairs for us and went into the garden.

'So.' I took a swallow of the wine – it was Chian, chilled in the stream that flowed past our table – and tore my guilty eyes away from the girl with the ankles who'd served it. Probably Philotimus's daughter, although if there was a family resemblance the mother must've been a real honey. 'What's our plan, lady?'

Perilla sipped her own drink: chilled pomegranate juice. 'I'd suggest that once we're settled we should start enquiring about properties to rent,' she said. 'And pay a courtesy visit to the governor, naturally.'

Jupiter! 'You think so?' That I wasn't looking forward to. Not that I knew anything bad about Aelius Lamia, he was probably a nice enough guy, but the thought of the diplomatic tap-dancing involved in a visit to the Residence made me want to go somewhere quiet, pull a bag over my head and wait till spring.

'Of course, Marcus. It's only polite. As well as politic. And you are the consul's nephew, after all.'

'Yeah. Yeah, sure.' I frowned. 'Actually, though, I was thinking more along the lines of Plan with a capital P. Contacting the guys who were directly involved with Piso. His pals Celer and Marsus, for a start. The prosecutor Vitellius. Maybe someone who knew the poison lady Martina. That sort of thing, you know? The really useful stuff.'

Perilla sighed. 'Marcus, we have just got here after being at sea for a month. Not an unpleasant trip, but certainly tiring. I don't suppose you'd consider just relaxing and enjoying yourself for a while? Having a holiday? Doing a little sightseeing?'

'I am enjoying myself, lady.' I was: the wine was good, the girl with the ankles was an easy eyeful and there was the prospect of scaring up a decent new lead in the Germanicus case. What more could I ask out of life? 'This is a holiday. And as far as sightseeing's concerned you can take it and drop it down a very deep hole and put the lid on. Okay?'

'Marcus, you are *not* serious!' Perilla's eyes had widened. 'Antioch is one of the most beautiful cities in the Greek east! Of course you have to see some of it while you're here!'

Uh-oh. We obviously had a major concept clash somewhere. This was no time for pussyfooting around. 'Believe me, lady, prolonged exposure to three-hundred-year-old bronzes brings me out in boils. Watch and marvel.'

That got through. She sat back.

'Mmm. Very well, Corvinus. Then I suggest we divide forces. You deal with the . . . the business aspect while I look around for suitable accommodation. I think from our experiences so far that I may be better at that than you are.'

'No argument there, sweetheart.' With Perilla's track record we'd probably end up rent-free in the imperial wing of the Residence while Lamia dossed down on a couch. 'So long as you're happy.'

'Oh, I am.' Yeah, that was obvious. She was looking more relaxed than I'd seen her for a long time. 'Coming to Antioch was a lovely idea after all, Marcus. I'm glad you thought of it.'

So was I. Which reminded me . . .

'Uh . . . you seen our rooms yet, Perilla?'

'No. But Philotimus says we have a view over the river.'

'You want to check it out?'

'You mean now? I haven't finished my fruit juice. And you haven't finished your wine.'

'The fruit juice can wait. And the wine.'

It was strange making love again in a bed that didn't move. The view across the river wasn't bad either, when we got around to looking at it.

21

We compromised over the sightseeing; meaning we did it after all. Philotimus's cousin Zoilus (Hey! Surprise! You ever meet a Greek who *didn't* have a handy cousin?) was a tourist guide and would give us special rates; which meant the bastard soaked us for half again over the going price. I spent the next three days glaring at statues – including one of the Wart looking constipated on top of a column – and having my ears driven into my head with who'd built what temple when, how big it was, how much marble had gone into it and how much the bugger who'd thought of it had stung the taxpayers to put it together. Perilla lapped everything up. She even asked questions. Me, I just got sore feet, a headache, and a tongue that was permanently dry as a razor strop. The only place I perked up, in fact, was the New Market; 'new', of course, being a relative term. When Antiochus Epiphanes had laid it out old Cato was boring the pants off the Roman Senate, and Carthage was still a viable proposition.

With a party of Greek punters Zoilus would've started by pointing out the Shrine of the Muses or the Senate building. Five years ago for us Romans he'd've kicked off with the Temple of Capitoline Jove, which was the biggest lump of marble in the city and looked as out of place as an elephant in a jeweller's. Now only one line was possible, whatever the nationality.

'This,' he said, 'is where we burned the Lord Germanicus.'

'Yeah?' I straightened. 'No kidding!'

'Marcus!' Perilla glared at me. 'Behave, please!'

Zoilus beamed: nothing pleases a tour guide more than having an awestruck punter in the group. 'Yes, lord, indeed,' he said.

'The city fathers had constructed a magnificent cenotaph on the site of the pyre. You'd care to see it?'

'Sure!' I took the guy's arm. 'Lead on, friend!'

Maybe I'd overdone the eagerness, because Zoilus looked fazed for a second. Then he recovered and gave me a flash of teeth.

'But certainly, lord,' he said. We pushed our way into the crowd.

Smack in the middle of the square was a mass of new marble representing a funeral pyre. 'Here, lord,' Zoilus said, mounting its steps, 'Prince Germanicus lay in state for three days and nights, his noble blood soaking the rich tapestries which swathed the catafalque . . .'

'You mean the guy was stabbed?' I said.

'. . . while a whole city – a whole province – mourned. The blood, lord, is metaphorical.'

'Uh . . . right.' I cleared my throat. 'Metaphorical blood. Got you.' Perilla smiled. 'You were there?'

'I was. Everyone was.'

'Hey!' I beamed. 'That's great!'

'I was even fortunate enough, lord, to acquire two of the seed pearls which fringed the young prince's robe. Should you be interested in purchasing a souvenir . . .'

'Maybe later, pal. How did he look? The body, I mean? Any signs of poison? Facial distortion? What about the colour? Any blueness round the mouth? What about his fingernails?'

'Marcus! I told you to behave!'

'Just asking, Perilla.'

Zoilus had come back down to ground level. I could see the guy was struggling between his professional instincts and his conscience. Officially Germanicus had died of a fever. If Zoilus claimed that the guy's face had been bright blue with the tongue sticking out it might be good tour-guide stuff but it'd be lousy tact. There could be repercussions, and not metaphorical ones, either.

'No, lord,' he said at last. 'There were no external signs. But when we burned the prince his heart was unconsumed, which is a sure indication of poison. There is the famous parallel of King Philip's toe, which after his cremation—'

'Pyrrhus's toe,' Perilla said.

Oh, hell! 'Perilla!' I hissed. 'Not now, lady, please!'

The guy was looking blank. 'Your pardon, ma'am?'

'The toe belonged to Pyrrhus, King of Epirus. He cured a man's diseased spleen with it by touch, as I remember. And Pyrrhus wasn't poisoned, he died in a street fight, so the parallel doesn't apply. I'm sorry, Zoilus. You were saying?'

Jupiter! Now wasn't the time for historical nit-picking! I dug her in the ribs. 'Look, Aristotle, just cut it out, okay?' I whispered in Latin. 'Stop rattling the guy. This is interesting.'

She grinned and ducked her head. I turned back to Zoilus, who was still looking gobsmacked. 'Forget the toe, friend,' I said. 'You know anything about how Germanicus died exactly?'

He shook himself. 'Yes, lord. Who doesn't?' Me for a start, sunshine, I thought; but the poor bugger had been slapped down by Perilla once already in the past five minutes and it wouldn't've been fair. 'The prince fell ill after his return from Egypt. He began to recover, and thank-offerings were made in the temples, although our governor Piso' – he spat politely – 'discouraged them, for reasons which the lord will understand.'

Yeah, sure. Like hell I did. 'And Germanicus had the idea that Piso and Plancina were poisoning him, right?'

'Not only poison but witchcraft was involved, lord. Things were found' – he spat again, for different reasons this time – 'behind the walls and beneath the floors of the prince's house. Wicked things.'

'Is that so? Inside the house itself, right?' Hey, this was good stuff. Maybe sightseeing wasn't so bad after all. I knew about the witchcraft, of course, but not the details. 'Give us a for instance.'

'Decomposing parts of corpses. A deformed foetus,' Zoilus said sombrely. Jupiter! The guy was enjoying himself more than I was! 'Other objects too disgusting to name, of remarkable filthiness and evil.'

'Marcus, we've just had lunch,' Perilla whispered in Latin. 'Do you *really* have to go into this now?'

'Sure we do, lady. It's fascinating.' I turned back to Zoilus. 'And this woman Martina was responsible?'

'Yes, lord. Or so the story goes.'

Perilla opened her mouth to say something else but I shut her up with a look. 'So tell me about Martina.'

'An evil woman. A friend of the governor's lady Plancina.'

'You know that for a fact?'

'No, lord. Not from personal knowledge. But certainly the woman was a witch. My cousin's wife knew her sister. They were children together in Litarba, and she, too, is an evil woman involved with magic and drugs. Such things run in families.'

Hey! Score another point for the cousins! I noticed Perilla stiffen. 'Let's get this right, pal,' I said carefully. 'Your cousin's wife knows Martina's sister?'

'Yes, lord.'

'And the woman's in Antioch?'

'The sister? Yes, lord, of course.'

'Uhuh.' I took out a gold piece and held it up. 'Can you find out where she lives?'

He blinked, his eyes on the coin. A gold piece was half what we were paying for the whole three-day tour. Good money. 'Possibly,' he said. 'If the lord is interested.'

'The lord is fascinated.' I handed him the coin. It disappeared. 'We have a deal?'

Zoilus cleared his throat nervously. 'We have a deal,' he said.

'Okay. So what happened next?'

He slipped back into the patter like a rabbit going to safe ground. 'The noble prince died, blaming the governor and his lady for his death. Syria grieved, but not its governor. We burned him and built the empty tomb. He was a great man and a great benefactor to Antioch, lord, as I have told you.'

Yeah. He had, at that. Several times, ad nauseam, over the past three days. In his few months here Germanicus had made quite a splash. Fresh marble paving in the main streets, a dozen new statues that the place needed like a hole in the head and dedications in the temples you couldn't count without using an abacus. No wonder the guy rated a five-star encomium.

'And now, lord.' Zoilus turned away. 'To happier things. Perhaps you'd care to see the Temple of Jupiter? An exact copy of your own great temple in Rome . . .'

Okay. The guy had done his bit as far as I was concerned, and he deserved the nuts. The address of Martina's sister was definitely worth a temple or two on top of the gold piece I'd given him. And at least with all our trailing around in the past few days I had a fair idea where everything was. None of the dives Theon had mentioned, though. Maybe another time I should leave Perilla behind and get Zoilus to give me the alternative tour. If we were both up to it.

Not today, though. I sighed and followed Perilla up the steps of the temple.

22

It was too late when we got back home to make an appointment with the governor: Antioch's a lot more laid back than Rome, and nobody who can avoid it works later than mid-afternoon, just as nobody starts before the sun's halfway through its first quarter or goes to bed until an hour or two before dawn. So it wasn't until the next day that I left Perilla househunting and went over to the palace to pay Aelius Lamia his courtesy visit.

The palace complex in Antioch fills most of the big island in the river to the north-west of the city; Greek-designed but Roman-built, by our Marcius Rex about a hundred years back as a calculated goodwill gesture to the locals. It's impressive as hell. The Greeks may be stuck-up bastards where aesthetics are concerned, but when it comes to architecture they've got cause. Even where the guy picking up the tab is Roman.

The Syrian governor being one of the empire's top men I didn't expect any red-carpet treatment, even on the strength of the introductory letter I'd screwed out of Cotta before we left. Sure enough, I was kept waiting in the anteroom for a good half-hour. Not that I minded. Clerks and military adjutants were constantly in and out with reports and messages, and I picked up some useful information just by keeping my mouth shut and my ears flapping. Like the fact that Vibius Marsus, who'd been Piso's deputy before he fled the country, had the same job under Lamia. That surprised me, but then apart from his name I didn't know much about him. I gave the young tribune who'd mentioned him time to clear and drifted over to the secretary's desk.

'Uh . . . excuse me?' I said.

The secretary looked up from his desk and raised a carefully plucked eyebrow. 'Yes, sir?'

'Vibius Marsus. Would he be any relation to Vibius Postumus at all? Guy who served as legate under my father in Dalmatia a dozen years back?' I'd heard Dad mention Postumus more than once. Whether they'd been concurrent I couldn't recall, but if he and Marsus were related then it would give me a definite in with the deputy.

'Possibly, sir.' The guy carried on transferring figures from one set of writing-tablets to another. High-powered stuff. 'I'm afraid I can't say.'

I tried again. 'Marsus is based in Antioch, anyhow?'

'Yes, sir. Of course.' A slight sniff that said only a moron would've asked the question.

'You happen to know where he lives?'

The pen stopped and the guy's lips pursed. Maybe he'd hit a vulgar fraction.

'No, sir,' he said coldly. 'I'm afraid I can't give you that information. But if you'd like to make an official appointment I'm sure his secretary would be happy to arrange one.'

'No. No, that's okay.' The discussion I had in mind couldn't be held across a desk. I backed off. Jupiter! These Syrian bureaucrats were as bad as the Roman ones. Worse; they froze you out in Greek. 'Just a thought. No hassle, pal, none at all.'

Just then the door of the governor's office opened and a grey-haired man in a broad-striper's mantle came out.

'Valerius Corvinus?' he said.

'Yeah. That's me.'

He smiled and reached out to shake hands. 'I'm Aelius Lamia. Terribly sorry to have kept you waiting. Endless paperwork. The bane of any decent man's existence. Come in, please.'

I followed him in to the office and he closed the door behind us.

'Now, Corvinus,' he said. 'Some wine.'

'Yeah. Yes, please.'

'It's only Laodicean, I'm afraid' – my heart sank – 'but it's not a bad vintage.' He poured from a tall glass jug into a pair of stemmed glasses and handed me one. I examined it with interest. I'd seen Phoenician glassware before, sure, but nothing this good. The glass was thin as eggshell, absolutely regular and almost transparent, and the wine shone through it like blood.

'Nice wine set,' I said.

'A present from one of the client-kings. It was made in Tyre, I believe. Beautiful, isn't it?'

'Yeah. Very unusual.' I sipped. The spicy taste of the Laodicean was toned down and mellowed, and it wasn't bad stuff, not bad at all. Still not Falernian, but getting there. Certainly beyond the swigging stage. Maybe Theon had been right. 'The wine's not bad, either.'

'I like it. Mind you, I'm no connoisseur.' He set his own glass down after the barest taste. 'So. How is your uncle the consul?'

I had the impression from the way he said it that he didn't like Uncle Cotta much, but then that was par for the course. Cotta was an acquired taste, like the wine. You either liked him or you loathed him. Most people took the second option, and Lamia seemed no exception. A pity, but I could live with that. Also, I was on my best behaviour and nervous as hell: Lamia could make or break me in Syria, and I had to make a good impression.

'He's fine, sir,' I said. 'He sends his regards.'

'Kind of him. Sit down, please.' Lamia gestured towards a chair: there were three in the room besides the one behind the desk. Once I'd sat he took one of the others. 'Your uncle tells me in his letter that you're recently married. My congratulations.'

'Thank you, sir. Perilla's looking for a house for us to rent at the moment, or she'd be here with me.'

He frowned. 'You mean a house in Rome?'

'No. Here in Antioch. We've been staying in a guest house on the Daphne road.'

'Ah.' The frown deepened. 'So the lady Rufia Perilla came out with you?'

'Sure. Yes, she did.' I noticed he'd used Perilla's family name where I hadn't; but then he'd probably got it from Cotta's letter. 'Uncle didn't mention that?'

'No. Or at least he didn't make it clear.' Yeah, that I'd believe: Cotta's epistolary style reeled like a drunken rhino and his letters had more gaps in them than a boxer's grin. 'You do realise, of course, that her presence here causes certain complications?'

'I know Perilla's ex-husband commands the Third Gallic, sir, yes,' I said carefully. 'And that the Third is based in Antioch.'

'Mmm.' His fingers drummed on the desk top. 'Well, there's no reason why they should meet, naturally, but it's worth remembering that Rufus is still . . . disgruntled. Seriously disgruntled. You understand me?'

Sure I did, and I was grateful for the warning. Translated out of diplomatic-speak *seriously disgruntled* meant given half the chance the guy would have my guts for bootlaces. 'Yes, sir,' I said. 'I understand perfectly.'

'Good.' Lamia nodded and inspected his glass. 'I'm not interfering, Corvinus, but Suillius Rufus is one of my officers and I do have a certain interest in the matter. I'll bear your wife's presence here closely in mind.' The eyes came up. 'Very closely in mind.'

Uhuh. 'Thank you, sir.'

Lamia sipped his wine. 'Thanks aren't necessary, young man. It's for my own sake as much as yours. As far as a house goes we'll see what we can do there as well. Sometimes properties do become temporarily vacant, and the owners are delighted to have them taken care of in their absence. Tell my secretary where he can get in touch with you when you leave and we'll ask around. Now.' He set the glass down. 'What exactly are you doing in Antioch, if you don't mind my asking?'

The tone was polite and I'd expected the question, but my mouth still went dry. I couldn't tell him the truth, but then again he was a smart cookie and I couldn't risk a direct lie. 'We were only married last winter, sir,' I said, looking (I hoped) innocent and ingenuous as hell. 'I thought we might do the eastern tour. A sort of holiday.'

'You chose a strange time for it.' His eyes on mine were like chips of marble. 'The sailing season's only just started, Corvinus. And from what you say about looking for houses you made no prior arrangements.'

'Uh . . . yeah. I mean no. No, we didn't.' Shit. I'd been afraid that this would happen. The interview was turning into an interrogation, and I wondered how much Lamia knew already.

Or just suspected, which would be bad enough. I tried to look innocent. 'Uh, maybe it was a pretty half-baked idea at that, sir.'

'Half-baked is right, young man. Especially with Rufus in the offing.' He paused; another frown. 'Well, it's no real business of mine. At least I hope not. You're welcome here in any case.'

I said nothing. If I'd been through some sort of a test I'd passed it, seemingly. Just. But if I'd expected the usual diplomatic chit-chat to follow I was disappointed because suddenly, without any warning, Lamia got to his feet.

'Now I really do apologise,' he said, 'but I have a very tight schedule today.'

'Uh, sure, sir.' I was left clutching my glass. I swigged down the wine and stood up. 'Certainly.'

'We'll meet again less formally soon, of course.' He smiled. 'And I'm looking forward to making the acquaintance of your charming wife. Bion will arrange things.' Bion must be the mathematical wizard with the sniff. 'A pleasure to meet you, young man.'

'Me too, sir.' I set the glass down on the desk. 'Oh, by the way. Your deputy's Vibius Marsus, I understand. My father knew a Vibius Postumus in Dalmatia.'

'That's right. Postumus is Marsus's uncle. Or was, poor fellow. He's dead now, of course.'

'Yeah. Yes, I knew that.' I'd've asked for an introduction, but I didn't want to push things, not with this guy. The information was enough. Besides, Lamia obviously wanted me out, fast. Maybe I should've wondered why, but I was too relieved to care and too happy to oblige. 'Thank you for giving me so much of your time, sir. And for the wine.' Gabble, gabble. Smarm, smarm.

'Not at all. The pleasure was mine. I'm sorry our first meeting has been so short.'

'Uh, that's okay. I know how it is.'

We shook hands, and he took my arm and led me to the door. The secretary looked up.

'Bion,' Lamia said, 'Valerius Corvinus needs a house urgently. Get the details, will you? Quickly, there's a good fellow.'

'Yes, sir. Certainly, sir.'

'Very nice to have met you, Corvinus. My apologies again.'

Lamia disappeared back inside his office and closed the door. I breathed a mental sigh of relief. The secretary turned to me and smiled. Obviously I'd gone up a notch, even with the brusqueness; but like I said, the Syrian governor's a busy man, so maybe even that hadn't been unusual. 'Now, sir,' he said. 'If you could just tell me where you can be contacted.'

'You know the Two Cedars guest house? Philotimus's place?'

'Of course.' He reached for a pad and made a note. 'On the Daphne road.'

'Right.' Someone was coming up the stairs: a big guy in army uniform. I nodded to him. He gave me a sharp look, then sat down on one of the benches with his helmet under his arm. Not one of life's natural socialisers, evidently. 'That's where we're staying. Philotimus will pass on any messages.'

'Good. That seems quite in order, Valerius Corvinus.' He made another note in his pad. 'I'll send a messenger as soon as something comes up. Enjoy your stay in Antioch, sir.'

'Yeah, thanks, pal.' I turned away, trying to remember where the nearest wineshop was. The governor's Laodicean had been welcome, but after that minor grilling I needed the rest of the jug.

The gorilla in uniform was on his feet again. The secretary smiled at him.

'You're a little early, legate,' he said, 'but I think the governor is free now if you'd like to go straight in.'

The big guy ignored him. He was staring at me like I'd just pissed on his lunch. Legate. Oh, Jupiter! Coincidences like this I could do without. No wonder Lamia had wanted shot of me so fast. I knew what was coming. I just knew. And there wasn't a thing I could do to stop it.

23

Rufus didn't go for me after all. It was a close-run thing, though, and I suspect the only thing stopping him was the fact that there were only two inches of wood between us and the governor. The Roman imperial system doesn't encourage brawling on its home ground.

'Your name's Corvinus?' he said slowly. 'Marcus Valerius Messalla Corvinus?'

'Yeah. Yeah, that's me, sunshine. All four of them.' I sat back against the desk, but I was still holding myself ready and my heart was thudding in my chest. 'You want an autograph?'

'Legate . . .' The secretary was on his feet now, and looking worried as hell: secretarial skills don't include dealing with homicidally inclined gorillas who also happen to command a quarter of Rome's army between Egypt and the Black Sea.

Rufus ignored him. 'Is Perilla here with you?'

'I don't think that's any of your business, friend,' I said quietly.

'Legate, please . . . !'

'You're lucky, Corvinus. Very lucky.' The eyes were still boring into me like hot wires into cheese. 'We can't talk properly now. But I'm glad we've met, and it won't be the last time. Understand?'

'Sure.'

'Good. I look forward to it.' He turned his back on me, moved towards the governor's door and raised his hand to knock.

'Hey, Rufus!' I said.

He paused. I thought he'd answer or at least turn round but he did neither, just waited.

'You understand something too, pal. Perilla divorced you because you're a bastard. A twenty-four-carat, thoroughgoing bastard. As far as she's concerned – as far as both of us are concerned – you don't exist. You go anywhere near her and I'll kill you. Okay?'

The fist came down. Inside the office Lamia shouted: 'Come in!' Rufus opened the door and went through. He didn't look back.

When I got home the lady had found us a house to rent.

'It's lovely, Marcus.' Her face was one big smile. 'Very central, in Epiphania. And such marvellous grounds.'

'Yeah?' I sat down in the chair opposite – we were out in the garden under the trellised vine – and waved to the girl with the ankles. She grinned at me and hurried off for the Chian. 'Epiphania, eh? Nice neighbourhood.'

It was: Epiphania was in what the locals called the New Town on the hill slopes to the east of the city. Big villas, big gardens, big bank balances. We'd taken it in on the sedan-chair ride which was part of Zoilus's package tour.

'Beautiful.' Perilla was still beaming. 'And the rent is so cheap you wouldn't *believe*.'

Sure I would, especially with her doing the dickering. 'Don't tell me. Philotimus has another cousin in the real-estate business.'

'No, the owner's one of Uncle Cotta's friends. He has to go to Corinth unexpectedly and he was simply going to leave it empty until he got back. We won't have to worry about staff, either. They're included.'

'Hey, great!' I leaned over and kissed her. 'So when do we move in?'

'The day after tomorrow.'

'Fine.' My wine arrived. Lovely ankles. Beautiful. I poured a cup and drank it down. 'I could get a taste for this stuff, you know that?'

'Really?' Perilla watched the girl's retreating back and sipped at her own cup of fruit juice. 'So how was your day?'

'Not bad. The governor's a nice guy. We had quite a chat.' I didn't even think of telling Perilla I'd met her ex: it would only worry her. It worried the hell out of me. 'Which reminds me. Lamia offered to help with accommodation. I'll send one of the lads to say he needn't bother.'

'We'd better let Gratianus know as well.'

'Hell! I'd forgotten him!' Gratianus was the skivvy we'd left behind with the baggage at Seleucia. Mind you, he was probably having the time of his life: I'd been generous with expenses and some of the docklands girls looked like they'd rattle their bangles just for the promise of a free drink. Nice bangles, too. 'Hey, incidentally, I found out Marsus is deputy governor.'

'Marsus?'

'Vibius Marsus. You remember? Piso's sidekick?'

'Oh, yes. The poet.'

'What?'

'He writes poetry, Corvinus. Only in an amateur sense, of course.' I detected the barest sniff. Perilla's a poet herself, and she's pretty hot by all accounts; but then with a stepfather like Ovidius Naso you couldn't expect anything else. 'He comes from a very literary family. He wrote an ode for Mother once. Mind you, he was very young at the time.'

I set down my wine cup slowly. 'Perilla, are you saying you know this guy personally?'

'No, not really. Certainly not well enough to trade on the acquaintance. He was a friend of Mother's. But that was years ago.'

I kept my voice calm. 'Why the hell didn't you mention this before?'

'Because he's sure to have forgotten all about me. I was only a child at the time.'

Jupiter give me patience or strike me dead! Didn't the woman have any idea how these things worked? I waved for the girl with the ankles. She came over.

'Your father about?'

'He's inside, lord. You want to see him?'

'Yeah. Oh, and Theano . . .'

'Yes, lord?'

'Have another jug cooling, yeah?'

She smiled. 'Yes, lord.'

I turned back to Perilla. 'You may not know it, lady, but I've been cudgelling what few brains I've got all morning thinking about how I can corner Marsus in private, and you had the answer all the time.'

'But surely if he's the deputy governor all you have to do is make an appointment.'

'*In private*, Perilla! Lamia's suspicious enough already. I may've persuaded him that I'm just a spoilt young smartass with more money than sense . . .'

'You mean you aren't?'

'. . . but the guy's no fool. So I need to go carefully.'

'Which is where I come in, I suppose.'

'Sure it is.'

'But Marcus . . .'

'You wished to see me, lord?'

Philotimus had oiled his way up, and stood smiling. Not the whole twenty-four-carat job: Perilla had told him we'd be gone in a couple of days, and apart from us this early in the season the guest house was empty.

'Yeah. Philotimus, you happen to know where Vibius Marsus lives? The deputy governor?'

'No, lord. But I can find out.'

'You do that,' I said. 'Let me know as soon as you can, okay?'

'Yes, lord.' He paused. 'Incidentally, I had a message from my cousin this morning. Zoilus. You wished a certain address?'

Hey! Things were moving! 'Sure! He's got it already?'

'The woman lives in the Old Town, lord. She has a small perfume shop near the Taurian Gate.'

'Yeah, I know where you are.' The Taurian Gate was at the end of one of the bridges leading to the island. 'What's her name?'

'Baucis, lord.'

'Fair enough. Thanks, pal.' I took a swallow of Chian. 'Don't forget Marsus's address, okay? Now whistle me up a carriage and tell Theano to keep the wine on ice.'

'You're going to see her now, Marcus?' Perilla was frowning. 'But you've just got back.'

'I thought I might, yeah.'

'Very well.' She stood up. 'Then I'm coming too this time.'

*   *   *

We found the shop no bother. Small was right: it was no more than a shack against the inside of the city wall fifty yards from the gate itself; but whatever Baucis traded in it wasn't perfumes. Sure, the word was written up on the sign but all I could see were stacks of dried herbs and roots. The smell wasn't within a mile of rose water either, and the place looked a tip. Me, I'm used to tips, but not ones as weird as this. Cockroaches I can take, shops that deal in whacky roots and dried bats' giblets give me goosebumps. I wasn't looking forward to the next bit.

'Uh . . . you want to wait here a minute while I check this out?' I said to Perilla.

I thought she might object, but she'd got a clean mantle on, and if Perilla is one thing it's fastidious.

'All right, Marcus,' she said and turned to examine a bunch of herbs hanging from the outside eaves. Maybe they were for soup, but I wouldn't have placed any bets. I took a deep breath and ducked under the lintel.

There were two people inside: a wizened crone who looked old enough to be Aeacus's grandmother and another woman. The crone was waving a handful of dried dung and muttering what sounded like a terminal curse. I was going to speak to her but she turned and squeezed out past me into the sunlight. Which left the other woman.

She was tall, a half-head taller than me, easy, and I'm no shrimp. Also from what I could see of her in the darkness she was a stunner.

'Uh, excuse me,' I said. 'Your name Baucis? Martina's sister?'

She moved forward without any warning. Strong fingers closed round my upper arm and I found myself yanked outside to where Perilla was staring wide-eyed. Outside, she looked even more impressive. Stunner or not, this lady had enough muscle for a couple of Amazons.

She let go and stood glaring at me.

'What the fuck do you want, Roman?' she said.

Beside me I felt Perilla stiffen, but she didn't speak. Very wise.

'Just a little information, lady,' I said as mildly as I could. 'If you have the time.'

'First you tell me what's happened to my sister. Is she alive?'

Uh-oh. This was one angle I hadn't thought of. Martina had been sent to Rome in the winter and the sea-lanes hadn't been open for commercial traffic more than a couple of months. We were the first chance for news Baucis had had.

'No, I'm afraid not,' Perilla said very gently. 'I'm terribly sorry, but she's dead.'

The woman's face didn't change. She nodded. Then, suddenly, her eyes still open, she sagged against the side of the shack. I made a grab at her but she weighed a ton. It took both of us to hold her upright and prop her sitting with her back to the wall.

'Get some water, Marcus,' Perilla said.

'From in there? You want to poison her, lady?'

'Don't be silly!' Perilla snapped. She disappeared into the shop and reappeared a minute later with a full cup. Most of the water – at least I hoped that was what it was – went down Baucis's chin, but finally she gave a cough and swallowed. The eyes lost their empty stare.

'Hey, Baucis?' I said. 'You okay?'

'Go away please, Marcus.' Perilla was still speaking very quietly. 'Come back in ten minutes.'

I didn't argue. Perilla's bedside manner has mine beat every time, and I know my limitations. Nursing witches isn't my bag. I went.

When I got back they were sitting side by side on the bench beside the shop. Baucis was staring straight ahead. Her face was set in the same stiff expression she'd had when Perilla gave her the news.

'How did Martina die?' she said to me.

I sat down on the other side of her. 'I don't know. Not for sure. They say she took poison before the trial. At Brindisi.'

'No.' The word came out flat.

'It's possible, though?' Perilla probed gently. 'In theory?'

Baucis nodded. 'It's possible. Martina knew about poisons. If that's what you're asking, lady.' Perilla said nothing. 'I don't deal in them myself. Not even for rats.' Oh, yeah, sure. And I was Hecate's grandmother. 'You know who killed her?'

'No,' I said. 'That's one of the things we're trying to find out.'

'When you do, give me the bastard's name and I'll kill him myself. Slowly. You hear me?'

'I hear you.' Jupiter! The hairs on the back of my neck crawled. 'But you have to tell us something first. Did she murder him? Germanicus?'

The barest shrug. Baucis's eyes hadn't wavered. They were still staring into nothing. 'Who knows, Roman? Who cares?'

'We do,' I said. Perilla glared at me but I ignored her; this was too important for pussyfooting. 'And if we don't know that, lady, we'll never find out who killed your sister. So just tell us, okay? Did Martina poison Germanicus or not?'

Baucis was quiet for a long time. Then she said: 'Maybe.'

'For Piso and Plancina?'

'Maybe.'

'The story is that your sister was a friend of Plancina's.'

'So I've heard.'

I felt myself sweating. 'And was she?'

'Far as I know she never met the bitch. But then maybe she just never told me.'

This was like wading through glue. 'Did . . . ?' I began.

'Marcus, let me handle this,' Perilla said suddenly. 'I'll meet you by Seleucus's statue when I'm finished. The one by the gate.'

I looked at her, then at Baucis who was still staring into empty space. This I didn't like. I didn't like it at all. Still, she was probably right.

'You sure, lady?'

'I'm sure.'

'You'll be fine here on your own?'

'Of course I will! Corvinus, just *go*!'

So I went.

24

There was a wineshop at the edge of the Old Marketplace, so I parked myself there, ordered up a jug of Chian and a plate of Damascus figs and waited. Finally Perilla came round the corner. There were two or three people hanging round the statue but she never so much as glanced at them. She came straight towards me.

'I thought we'd an arrangement, lady,' I said as she sat down.

'We did. But then I remembered seeing this place.'

Yeah, well. If you can't be smart be predictable. I sighed, signalled to a waiter and ordered her a chilled pomegranate juice. She must've got through gallons of the stuff since we'd arrived. I hoped she wasn't getting addicted.

'So,' I said. 'What did you find out?'

'Yes, it was Martina.'

'Uhuh.' I sipped my wine. 'So who put her up to it? Baucis give you any names?'

'Yes and no.' Perilla helped herself to one of the figs.

'Yes and no?' I set the cup down. 'Come on, Perilla! Don't fool around!'

'I'm not. Baucis said that at the beginning of the affair – or what must've been the beginning – Martina talked about a certain Mancus. Mancus, she said, would make her fortune.'

'Hey, now! That's great! All we have to do is find this Mancus guy.'

'Corvinus, you obviously didn't pay much attention to your religious studies as a child. Mancus is the Etruscan god of the dead. And by association, like our Pluto, of wealth.'

'Yeah? Is that so?' I digested the implications. 'Oh. Oh, right. You mean it's a pseudonym. Shit.'

'Exactly.' Perilla's drink arrived. 'However at least we know now that Martina had no contact with Plancina. No direct contact anyway, because of course Mancus could still have been her agent. And if we can't identify Mancus then at least we know how the murder was arranged.'

'Baucis told you that?' I leaned forward.

'Not in so many words, but it's clear enough reading between the lines.' She sipped at the pomegranate juice. I winced. 'You've noticed that Baucis is a striking woman.'

'She'd turn a few eyes down Pullian Street, yeah.' An under-statement: set her on Pullian and the lady would cause a major traffic jam just by breathing.

'So was her sister. A little older, a little smaller, but also strik-ing. On Mancus's instructions she gained access to Germanicus's household as a laundress. She then seduced one of the slaves; Baucis never knew the man's name, and the affair was kept secret, but he was evidently high up the domestic pecking order. After that matters were comparatively easy to arrange.'

'Meaning the poison and the bits and bobs?'

'Her lover had the free run of the house. Also being a senior slave he could arrange for rooms to be empty or dishes left unattended when necessary.'

'Did Baucis mention what happened to him?'

'He was crushed by a runaway cart the day after Germanicus died.'

'Surprise, surprise.' I took a swallow of wine.

Perilla hesitated. 'I gave Baucis my word, Marcus, that if we ever found out who this Mancus was we'd tell her.'

'Seems fair, lady. And I can't think of a better way of putting the fear of hell into the guy than have him know she's on his tail.' I shook the jug. The Chian was almost gone, and I poured the last of it on the ground as an offering to Martina's ghost. I doubted she'd get many offerings, not from Romans, anyway, and I wouldn't like to think of her going thirsty. 'So. Was that all Baucis told you?'

'That's all she knew. And I'm convinced she wasn't holding anything back. Martina was very close-mouthed, especially latterly.

The acting governor picked her up straight away; and that, of course, was the last Baucis saw of her.'

'Uhuh.' I indicated her empty glass. 'You want another of these pomegranate concoctions?'

'Not at the moment, thank you, Marcus.'

'Good. You fight it, lady.' I called the waiter over and paid. 'Okay, so we'll whistle up the carriage and get back. And we can ask the driver to take us the long way round by Epiphania and gawp at this house of yours.'

Which was why we got home pretty late, and after our usual dinner hour. Meton was going spare because his seafood pancakes were like leather and his egg sauce had hatched out. Philotimus was going spare, too, because we'd had a visit from Rufus.

'He refused to believe me when I said you were out, lord,' he said. 'I'm sorry, but he searched your rooms. I couldn't stop him.'

The guy was almost weeping, and it wasn't just on our account, either. The last thing a hotelier wants is to fall out with the local authorities, especially the military: a word from Rufus to the junior ranks of the Third Gallic's officer corps and Philotimus would find his place wrecked by a regimental romp. No compensation, either. Entertaining these braying half-wits is supposed to be an honour.

'That's okay, Philotimus,' I said. 'Not your fault.' I was furious. Quietly furious, which doesn't happen too often.

'Corvinus, why didn't you tell me you'd seen Rufus?' Perilla was angry too; more with me than with her ex-husband.

'Because I didn't want to worry you.'

'That's silly!'

'I'll decide what's silly where Rufus is concerned, Perilla.' It must've come out flatter than I meant because she shut up straight off. 'Philotimus. Any of my lads hanging around, do you know? Apart from Meton?'

'Yes, lord. Sextillus is in the garden.'

'Get him, would you?'

'Marcus,' Perilla said. 'Be careful. Please.'

'Oh, I'll be careful all right. But if that bastard thinks he can get away with . . .'

'You wanted me, sir.' Sextillus. He must've been hanging around outside all the time, listening. At least it saved explanations.

'Yeah. Get your backside over to the island,' I told him. 'I know the public offices'll be closed just now but you camp out on the fucking doorstep until they open again. Okay?'

He grinned and nodded.

'You want to speak to a guy called Bion, the governor's secretary. Two messages, one for the governor, personal, one for Bion himself. Got me?'

'Yes, sir.' I was glad it'd been Sextillus. He wasn't much more than a kid, but he was smart as a whippet.

'First. Tell Lamia what's happened. Say if it happens again or anything like it he'll be short one legate. Exactly those words, no fancy wrapping. Right?'

The kid grinned again. It wasn't often he got to deliver a message like that, especially to a provincial governor. Maybe I was out of line myself but I didn't much care at the moment.

'Right.'

'Second. To Bion personally. Tell that little fucker if I find he was responsible for giving Rufus our address I'll wring his scrawny neck and peg his carcass out for the crows. Okay?'

'Okay, sir.' The grin widened. 'Any reply?'

'You think there will be?'

'No, sir.'

I took a silver drachma out of my pouch and threw it to him. 'Here. Don't spend it all in the one shop.'

Sextillus caught it, gave one final grin and disappeared at a run.

'Now, Marcus, *that* was silly,' Perilla said.

'I meant it, lady. Every word. And Lamia will be as mad as I am. He may even peg Bion out to dry himself.'

Philotimus was hovering and smiling nervously. 'Incidentally, lord,' he said. 'Perhaps it's the wrong moment, but I have that other address you wanted. The deputy governor's.'

'Yeah? Great! Where?'

'He has a house in Epiphania. Not far from the Temple of Dionysus.'

'Temple on a podium with a portico? Couple of statues of the

Twin Gods flanking it?' One thing about Zoilus's tour, I knew my Antioch temples.

'Yes, lord. On the southern side, directly below the citadel.'

'Got you.' It was too late to send tonight, and anyway we only had one skivvy left, but I could do it tomorrow. 'Thanks, pal.'

There wasn't much else to be done, so we called it a day there and had our belated dinner. It wasn't one of Meton's best. I was just sorry Rufus hadn't stayed to join us. He could've had the pancakes, for a start.

25 ∫

There wasn't much we could do the next day either. I sent our last skivvy Troas round to Marsus's place with a note: he wouldn't be in, but he'd get it later. In it I just said who we were and mentioned Perilla's mother. The rest was up to Marsus, but if he'd an ounce of hospitality in him the least we could expect was a free meal. I thought maybe this being our last day at the Cedars we might spend it lounging around the garden soaking up the atmosphere and being pampered by Theano. We didn't. Perilla hauled me off for another day's sightseeing, this time in the other direction, up into the hills to Daphne. Temples and statues again. A lovely place but believe me you don't want to *know*!

When we got back Sextillus was already there, with a letter from Lamia apologising and promising it wouldn't happen again. No mention of Rufus, but reading between the lines it was clear that the governor had talked to him, and if he wasn't singing soprano in the Third Gallic's next glee club concert he could count himself lucky. With the letter was an invitation to a party in two days' time. That I could've done without. Dinner parties and party-parties I enjoy, but I'd bet my bootstraps this would be the kind of formal occasion where you stand around drinking second-rate booze and making inane conversation with people you'd normally run a mile to avoid and who'd run twice that to avoid you. Still, it might be useful, and we could be sure it was the only place in Antioch we wouldn't bump into Rufus.

The day after, we moved in to the new house. It was over in the north-east corner of Epiphania near the Parmenius, the open stream that locals call the Donkey Drowner. Like I said, a nice area, laid out with plush urban villas each set round a pillared courtyard and with a scrap of garden attached that back at Rome wouldn't've fallen far short of a public park; in fact you could've just about fitted one of our Janiculan villas in amongst the rose beds. Forget comfort, as soon as we stepped inside the place I had the definite feeling we'd moved upmarket.

The chief slave met us at the door. He was a local Greek by the name of Critias.

'Welcome, lord and lady,' he said. 'I hope you'll be very happy here.'

'We'll try hard.' While he pocketed the huge tip I gave him to make sure we were, I looked round at the pricey decor. Barring the subject matter, it reminded me of Crispus's club. Inlaid marble by the square yard. Frescoes. Oh, and statues, of course. A good dozen of the buggers, enough bronze wrestlers and river gods to stock a minor square back home. And this was only the hall. 'Hey, Critias. You ever worked for Romans before?'

'No, lord.' He sniffed. 'However, I'm ready to make allowances. Now if you'd care for a tour of the house the main rooms are this way.'

He led off. This bastard would need watching, I could see that already. And the sniff was pure Bathyllus. Next time I saw the little guy I'd have to ask him if they were cousins.

We were up on the first floor inspecting the linen closets when what sounded like a full-scale battle broke out below. Perilla and I looked at each other.

'You got a private arena tucked away downstairs we haven't seen yet, friend?' I asked Critias. 'Or are the Parthians giving us a house-warming?'

He never even blinked: Bathyllus again. Maybe it was something dietary.

'Neither, lord. I imagine that will be the two chefs, ours and yours, discussing future menus.'

Oh, shit. I remembered now, and it was too late. A full complement of staff, Perilla had said. We should've thought of that before we let Meton wander off on his own. I took the stairs at a run, hoping I could get to the kitchen before any serious blood was spilled.

It was a close thing. Arena was right, these guys weren't kidding. I'd seen tamer scraps at the midday Games. Our guy was backed up against the table swinging a chopper while his colleague held his wrist with one hand and throttled the life out of him with the other.

'Hey, Meton,' I said as calmly as I could manage. 'Put the cleaver down, okay? Down! That's the boy. And you, whatever your name is, just slacken off, will you?'

'Lysias!' Critias snapped.

The other chef gave Meton's throat one last squeeze before reluctantly taking his hand away.

'That's better,' I said. 'Now listen. I know two chefs in one kitchen isn't such a hot idea but you'll just have to come to some arrangement. You think that's remotely possible?' They glared at each other. Yeah, well, maybe it wasn't, but that was hard luck on them. Stray ears in the soufflé I could do without. 'Because if you don't, sunshines, we'll call in an outside caterer now and you can spend your time boiling barley mash for the horses in the stables. Eating it, too. You get me?'

I left them to it without waiting for an answer. Perilla was waiting in the hall, examining the statues.

'Staff problems already, Corvinus?' she said.

'It's no joke, lady. We nearly had one blue chef and two halves in there. Critias.' He'd followed me out. 'You keep an eye on these two, right? The first one to use a filleting knife on anything other than a chicken is cold meat.'

'Yes, lord.' The guy was grinning like a drain. Jupiter! Was I the only sane person around here? 'Incidentally, one of the lord Vibius Marsus's slaves brought a message earlier. He would be delighted if you would drop in for dinner tonight if it isn't too short notice. Sundown would be convenient.'

'Hey, great!'

'May I send a message to that effect, lord? It may also ameliorate the kitchen situation a little. Temporarily.'

'Yeah. Yeah, you do that.'

'And then perhaps you'll wish an early lunch. I will inform the chef. Chefs.' He paused. 'Lamb chops and a cold tongue, perhaps.'

Oh, ha ha. Bathyllus's cousin, for sure. Perilla giggled, and I glared at her.

'Look, sunshine, just do your job and leave out the gags, okay?'

'Yes, lord.'

This place was going to be fun. Oh, sure. I could tell that now.

Vibius Marsus was a lot younger than I thought he'd be; a fit man in his late thirties with a nose like the business end of a battleship. When the slave showed us into the dining room he bounced up from his couch like someone had wired him with springs.

'Valerius Corvinus! Come in, my dear fellow!' he cried. 'Delighted to see you! No, you take the chief guest couch, we're on our own this evening, strictly family. This is my wife Sulpicia.'

They could've been brother and sister. If anything, Sulpicia's nose had the edge. When they kissed it must've been like a refight of Actium.

'Pleased to meet you, Valerius Corvinus.' I got a smile like a well-bred parrot's. 'Welcome to Antioch.'

'And this must be Perilla!' Marsus was beaming. 'Good grief, you have changed, haven't you? You're quite ... ah ...' He paused.

'Yeah, she is, isn't she?' I said. 'Very.'

'Sit down and behave yourself, Publius,' Sulpicia murmured. I grinned, and so did Perilla. 'Simeon, serve the wine, please.'

The slave took the jug from its cooler. Marsus was still gripping Perilla's shoulders like an absent-minded octopus. 'How long has it been, my dear? Fourteen years? Fifteen?'

'Longer,' she said. 'It was just before Stepfather was exiled. I was seven. I didn't think you'd remember.'

'Nonsense! Of course I do!' He gave her one last hug before stretching out next to his wife. 'Sulpicia, don't fuss! Sit down, Perilla. How's your mother?'

'Not well,' Perilla said gently, taking the other half of my couch.

'Ah. I'm sorry.' Marsus didn't pursue the matter: maybe he

knew about Fabia Camilla, or maybe he was just responding to the tone. 'Corvinus, your glass. Make sure we've all got some wine, Simeon, and then bring in the starters. Come on, boy, stir yourself!'

They were glasses, not as good as Lamia's but still lovely work. I held mine up for the guy to fill just so I could see the wine shining in the lamplight. I'd have to find a dozen of these to bring back before we left. Certainly there was nothing in Rome to touch them. All they needed to set them off was a good Falernian.

'And how are you enjoying Antioch?' Sulpicia's look took in both of us.

'It's wonderful,' Perilla said.

'You've been up to Daphne?'

'Yes. We went yesterday.'

'A lovely town.' Marsus nodded. 'Mind you, I can't stand sightseeing myself. Once you've seen one statue you've seen them all. Sulpicia dragged me round when we first arrived but now I can't be bothered. You look as if you agree, Corvinus.'

'Yeah.' I was beginning to like the guy. His wine was good, too, although I couldn't place it. Cypriot, maybe; I wasn't too well up on white Cypriot. 'You know how many statues there are in Daphne, sir?'

'Three hundred and twenty-six,' Marsus said promptly. 'You counted them too?'

'Yeah.'

We laughed. The slaves brought in the appetisers: a big plate of steamed shellfish, little rissoles, cold beans with fennel and the usual olives and raw vegetables with fish pickle dip.

'And how is your new house?' Sulpicia selected a rissole. 'It belongs to old Athenodorus, doesn't it?'

'That's right,' Perilla said. 'He's gone off to Corinth for two months.'

'Ah, yes. His sister. A lovely man, Athenodorus, although his head slave Critias can be a pain, as I remember.'

'I think Marcus can handle him. It's the chef we're having trouble with.'

'Lysias?' Her eyes widened. 'Oh, surely not! He's one of the best cooks in the city!'

We told the story of the fight in the kitchen. Sulpicia laughed.

'Well of course that's different,' she said. 'Professional jealousy. It happens all the time here.' She turned to Marsus. 'You remember when Parthenius's coachman took a knife to that other fellow, dear? Poor Vonones's groom?' I stiffened. 'They disagreed over the best treatment for a split hoof, as I remember.'

'Vonones.' Perilla's eyes were on her plate. 'Wasn't he some sort of Parthian pretender?' Good girl! Very nicely done.

'Oh, no.' Marsus was frowning slightly. 'No, not quite, Perilla. He spent some time here before we shipped him off to Cilicia, that's all. But speaking of grooms . . .'

'Yeah, I've heard about Vonones.' I couldn't let Marsus off the hook now; we might not get another chance. 'One of Augustus's tame Parthian princes, wasn't he? Got himself killed in the end trying to break house arrest and escape to Scythia.'

'Yes, Corvinus, that's right.' Marsus's frown had deepened and the bounce was gone. 'You're very well informed. Remarkably so, in fact.'

'How did it happen exactly?'

'I don't remember, to tell you the truth. Not my province. In both senses of the word.'

'Don't be silly, dear.' Sulpicia had picked out another rissole and was neatly quartering it. 'It was Cousin Fronto who rearrested him. And then he was stabbed by that fool of a man in Fronto's troop. The gaoler with the same name as that slave we had with the drink problem. Remmius.'

Marsus leaned over and took a spoonful of clams. His face was expressionless.

'Quite correct,' he said. 'I'd forgotten.'

'Nonsense, Publius.' Sulpicia chewed her piece of rissole delicately. 'Cousin Fronto's a cavalry commander, Corvinus, with the Sixth in Laodicea. He was seconded to Vonones's guard.'

'Who by? The governor?' I gave her my best smile. 'That'd be Piso then, wouldn't it?'

'Yes, it would.' Marsus tried a smile that didn't quite work. 'Perilla, do have some of these clams before I eat them all. They really are delicious.'

'They are, aren't they?' Perilla took one or two on to her plate. 'Where do you get them?'

'The best place is just up from the Old Market. I'm sure our chef can give you details.'

'Really? Now what about eels? Meton was asking only the other day whether . . .'

Lovely. While she kept Marsus talking I turned to Sulpicia. 'Did you know Vonones well? Socially, I mean?'

'Oh, yes. He was a charming man. A little' – she paused – 'well, he wasn't very fond of women, if you understand me. Most unusual for a Parthian. But perfectly charming. And of course terribly generous. I remember once Plancina showing me a necklace that he . . . Oh, Publius! You are clumsy! Now look what you've done! Simeon, get a cloth, please.'

'I'm sorry, dear, I didn't see it.' Marsus dabbed at the spreading pool of wine from his overturned glass. 'Perhaps we should have the main course now in any case. Simeon, get your lads to clear away, will you? Now, Corvinus.' He gave me a very sharp look. 'Let's have the really important news. How are the Reds doing in Rome this season?'

About as well as I was, seemingly. Like the accident the change of subject was intentional, and there wasn't a whole lot I could do about it. We talked about this and that, and the evening turned out pretty pleasant, but when I tried to bring the conversation round to Piso again I found myself politely stonewalled. It was quite deliberate; Marsus knew what he was doing, and he knew I knew he knew. So I wasn't exactly surprised when after the dessert had been cleared away and Sulpicia had taken Perilla off for a private chat he sent Simeon out of the room and turned towards me.

'Now you listen here, young man,' he said. I swallowed: the guy didn't sound nearly so bluff and hearty as he had through the dinner. Not even particularly friendly. 'I don't know what your game is in Antioch, but I'd advise you to give it up. Now. Before it lands both of you in trouble.'

'Is this an official warning, deputy governor?' I said.

I got a slow stare like I was one of the clams he'd been spooning down that had sat up and spat in his eye. 'No. Not yet,' he said at last. 'Although it might be, later. At the very least. And not from me, either.'

'You feel like telling me why?'

'Why you're being warned off?' Well, that was straight enough. 'No, Corvinus, I don't. All I'll say is Piso and Germanicus are touchy subjects of conversation in this city and the case is closed on both of them. Closed, locked and barred. If you're wise you'll leave it like that. All right?'

'This go for Vonones too, sir?'

'Especially for . . .' He stopped himself. 'Yes. For Vonones too.'

'Uhuh.' I sipped my wine. 'One question. Just one. Why should Piso have had Vonones killed?'

I'd expected to shock him, and I did; but not in the way I thought I would. In fact, Syria's deputy governor almost laughed out loud. Which told me just what I wanted to know.

At which point Sulpicia and Perilla came back, and Marsus pretended we'd been discussing something else.

When it was time to go, he clapped me on the shoulder, kissed Perilla and saw us out.

'Goodnight, Corvinus,' he said. 'I've enjoyed this evening. Look after yourself, and look after this girl here.'

'Sure.' I waited while Perilla climbed into our carriage. Marsus's hand held me back.

'Don't forget what we talked about, either,' he said.

That I didn't answer. I liked Marsus; I liked him a lot. But I knew the bastard was hiding something. Eventually I'd find out what it was.

26

We talked about it in the carriage on the way back.

'So,' I said. 'Piso definitely had a scam going with Vonones.'

'It certainly seems that way.' Perilla paused, and then said neutrally: 'You think Marsus was involved?'

I shook my head. 'I don't know the guy well enough yet, but my gut feeling says no, although being Piso's deputy he'd probably have an inside line on what was going on. And I liked him. He seemed genuine even when he was covering up for his boss.'

'Yes. I liked him too. Very much. And that's just what Marsus would do.' She shifted uneasily. 'He was a great fan of my stepfather's, Marcus. And he stayed loyal when Stepfather was exiled. He used to write a lot to my mother, even after he was sent abroad on his first posting. If they'd been more of an age I might have thought there was a romantic attachment. A genuine man, as you say.'

'Yeah, but still the deputy governor. Very much so. He may not've been involved with the scam but he's doing his best to cover it up. He had a word with me while you were powdering your nose. We've been warned off, lady.'

She looked at me, her eyes wide. 'Really?'

'Chapter and verse. It means we have to be careful, but it also means we're digging in the right part of the garden. And that's something worth knowing.'

She was quiet for a long time, her head against my shoulder. Finally she said: 'I don't suppose you'd consider not digging anywhere at all?'

'No.'

'I didn't think so.' She sighed. 'Well, at least if we're packed off back to Rome tomorrow we've had a nice holiday.'

'Yeah.' I kissed her cheek. 'So. What was this scam?'

'Vonones was giving Piso bribes. Obviously. Probably money, definitely gifts.'

'Plancina's necklace. Yeah. I spotted that too.' I frowned. 'But how much was it just a rich exile keeping in with the governor and how much was it constructive bribery? Vonones had been thrown out of Parthia on his ear and King Artabanus had winkled him out of Armenia with our full backing. Piso may've been the Syrian governor but his general political clout was limited, and if Vonones expected his help to get his backside on to one of the two thrones again the guy was being pretty optimistic.'

'Perhaps Vonones had other reasons for hope besides Piso.'

'Yeah. Yeah, that's what I was thinking.' I looked out of the carriage window. The streets were full of people and almost as bright as day: unlike Rome, most of Antioch doesn't sleep at night. There's even public street lighting in the centre, and most private houses burn torches outside their front doors. 'Maybe we should find out more about that angle.'

Perilla was quiet for a bit. Then she said: 'Vonones had a house here, didn't he?'

'Presumably.'

'So if we could find where it was then perhaps there might be a servant or two we could talk to.'

'Unless he took them with him to Cilicia.'

'It's still a possibility.'

'Sure it is.' I put my arm round her shoulders. 'Critias would know. And it'd cause fewer waves if we started at the bottom of the scale. Slaves tend to pick up loose gossip, and they see who comes and goes. Yeah, good idea.'

'There's another thing, Marcus.' Perilla was hesitant. 'Sulpicia was telling me the Roman wives meet at the Residence every afternoon. It appears that I will be very welcome if I want to attend.'

'Hey!' I let go and beamed at her. 'That's great!' Never underestimate a diplomatic honey-wine-and-cake clatsch. These harpies run the empire, and what they don't know about what goes on in the sticky corridors of power you could write on a sandal strap and forget about. 'You said you'd go?'

'Not in so many words,' Perilla said primly. 'No.'

'Why the hell not, lady?'

'Marcus, I like Sulpicia, but these women's groups are dreadful. Yes, of course I'll go, if you want me to, because it could be useful. But I'm not looking forward to it.'

'Yeah. I can imagine.' I grinned. 'You'll survive.'

'Physically, yes. Mentally and intellectually I'm not so sure.'

I kissed her. 'Be careful, though, right? It cuts both ways. One gets you ten that right now Marsus is warning Sulpicia to keep her mouth stitched. You start asking the other wives pointed questions and it'll get back. We may find ourselves on a boat out of here before you've baked your first cake.'

'I'm not altogether gormless, Marcus. Not yet, anyway.'

'I know that, lady.' I settled back against the cushions. 'There's another thing that puzzles me.'

'What's that?'

'When we had our little heart-to-heart Marsus said as far as Piso and Germanicus were concerned the case was closed. Closed, locked and barred. That suggest anything to you?'

'An interesting choice of words.'

'Yeah. Very interesting. As if there's an official cover-up going on.'

'But we know there is! Piso . . .'

'Not just Piso. Piso, Germanicus and Vonones. All three of them, bracketed together. Like that's how they belonged.'

'Mmm.' She looked thoughtful. 'Yes. Yes, that is interesting.'

'There's something else as well. I asked Marsus straight out why Piso should have Vonones killed. Sure, I was shooting the wind, but with Marsus's cousin being sent specially and just happening also to be the arresting officer it was a fair assumption. Especially since one of Fronto's troop took it on himself to stab the guy.'

'You think the man was acting under orders?'

'You have a better explanation?' She was silent. 'Squaddies don't do that sort of thing, Perilla. Not off their own bats. Anyhow, Marsus's reaction was interesting. He laughed. Like he was expecting something different and I'd got hold of the wrong end of the stick. So maybe I had.'

'Meaning?'

'Meaning someone else was responsible.' I paused. 'Germanicus himself, maybe.'

Perilla sat up. 'Marcus, that's nonsense. Why should Germanicus want Vonones dead?'

'Search me, lady. It's only an idea.'

'Vonones was a spent coin. The new Armenian king was Germanicus's own appointee, and he'd been moved to Cilicia at the Parthians' request. He had no power or importance any more whatsoever.'

'Yeah, I know. That's what's worrying me. There is no reason, or none that I can see. Piso I could understand. If he'd been taking bribes he might well want Vonones's mouth shut permanently. But spent coin or not Vonones was a genuine Parthian royal, and it was in Germanicus's interests to keep him alive. But if Piso didn't have him chopped then Germanicus is the obvious bet.' The carriage slowed: we were turning into our own street. 'Ah, leave it for tonight. Big day tomorrow. Governor's party. And you've got your first women's social to look forward to.'

'Marcus, that isn't even remotely funny.'

'Come on, lady! Diplomats' wives can't be all that bad.'

I never thought I'd hear Perilla swear.

Critias was waiting up for us.

'You had a pleasant evening, lord?' he said as he took our cloaks.

'Yeah, it was okay. How've things been here? All quiet in the kitchen?'

'Yes, lord. When I called in the chefs were exchanging tunnyfish recipes.'

'That's great.' I stripped off my mantle and handed it over. 'Any other news?'

'Your slave arrived from Seleucia with the baggage.'

'Fine.' I headed for the stairs. 'Hey, by the way, Critias, you ever hear of a guy called Vonones?'

'Of course. The Parthian gentleman.'

'You happen to know where he lived?'

'Not far from here. Near the small shrine of Pan, down from the Iron Gates.'

'Uhuh. Any of his servants still around?'

'Not in the house itself, lord, no. But I understand his coachman was bought by a neighbour. A gentleman by the name of Apollonius.'

'He the guy who was involved in the knife fight? The coachman, I mean?'

'Indeed. Rather an irascible fellow. A Cretan.' Critias sniffed. 'His name is Giton, if I remember correctly.'

The Antioch slave grapevine was obviously as good as the Roman one. I'd been counting on that, and it was good to know.

'Thanks, Critias. You're a gem.'

'Thank you, lord.'

So. I followed Perilla upstairs. We were doing okay for leads so far, and if I could get this Giton character into a quiet corner alone for ten minutes there might be more. Certainly Vonones was important. And if the guy was a spent coin like Perilla had said then that was curious. Then there was the question of Germanicus . . .

'Marcus?'

'Yeah, Perilla?'

She was inside the bedroom.

'Quickly, Marcus! Please!'

There was something wrong about her voice. I took the last four steps at a run and burst through the door, my heart thudding. Perilla was standing staring at the bed, her hand pressed to her mouth . . .

A huge spider leered up at us from the bedspread. And if there's one thing Perilla can't stand it's spiders.

Panic over. Ah, well, it was better than having to face Rufus. I frog-marched the eight-legged bastard to the door and made sure he left peaceably.

27

While Perilla was at her cake clatsch I took a walk up towards the Iron Gates to see if I could find Apollonius's place. No problems: the fruit-juice seller I asked was parked less than a dozen yards away, and he pointed it out to me.

The coaches – Apollonius must've been loaded, because he had five, different sizes – were in the stables round the side of the house. Giton, if he was around, would be there too. Sure, I could've knocked on the front door but I didn't want to do that: a strange Roman turning up on the doorstep and asking to speak to the family coachman might've raised a few eyebrows. Set a few tongues wagging, too. So it had to be the stables.

Loaded is right. The horseflesh that eyed me over the cutaway doors would've made the Greens back home curl up and die with shame. And you ain't never been sneered at until you've been sneered at by something with two clear yards separating its hooves from its ears. Still, horses are okay if you take the time to get to know them. By the time I'd scratched a few noses we were old friends.

'Hey! What the fuck you think you're doing?'

I turned round to see a big guy with a head of hair like a black wire mop coming towards me. Giton, for sure. Critias had said he had a way with people.

'Sorry, pal,' I said. 'Just admiring your stock. Real beauties. What are they, Arabian?'

'Yeah.' He'd cooled down when he'd heard the Roman accent and seen the stripe on my tunic; I wasn't wearing a mantle, even in this mild heat I'd've suffocated. 'Straight off the desert south of Palmyra. Finest in Antioch. You looking for the master, lord? He's out.'

'No. It was you I wanted to see. If your name's Giton.'

The suspicious look was back. 'That's me. So what?'

'No hassle.' I took a pair of tetradrachms out of my purse. 'Nothing to do with you or Apollonius, and nothing illegal. I just want a word. Ten minutes of your time, okay?'

His eyes were on the coins. Eight drachs was as much as he'd earn from tips in a month.

'Okay,' he said at last. 'Let's go to the tackle room.'

He led the way across the yard to a shed against the side wall. Inside a couple of lads were sprawled out on the straw shooting dice. He jerked his head and they scuttled out. 'Right.' He pulled up a bench for me and sat opposite. 'So what's on your mind?'

'You used to belong to a Parthian exile named Vonones.'

'Yeah. So?'

So was right. I had to tread carefully here, and there was no point in asking directly about anything political because the guy would just've clammed up. 'He was pals with the Roman governor? Calpurnius Piso?'

'They had dinner about twice a month, yeah. Lord Piso and his wife came round just as often.'

'Just that? Dinner party stuff?'

'Far as I know.' He was scowling by this time, but the eight drachs were still working their magic. 'I drove him to the Residence sometimes in office hours. Maybe he went to see Piso, maybe someone else.'

'He have any other bosom cronies that you know of? Romans, that is?'

'Bosom cronies I couldn't say. Not that I'd've put it past him. But yeah, he was friendly with a couple of Romans, on and off.' The scowl deepened. 'What's this about, pal?'

'Just curiosity.'

'Sure. Eight drachmas worth of curiosity. That's a lot of metal, considering the guy's dead.'

'Let's just say I'm doing a favour for a client of mine in Rome.' Oh, the empress would love that!

'Uhuh.' He held out his hand. 'In that case maybe you

wouldn't mind opening that big purse of yours a bit wider. It might refresh my memory.'

I put the two tetradrachms into his palm. 'The same again when you've earned them, sunshine. But remember I want names not flannel. And after that you don't talk to no one.'

'Who would I talk to?' The coins disappeared inside his leather belt. 'You know Marsus? The deputy governor?'

'Yeah.' My stomach did a turn. Shit. I hadn't wanted Marsus to be involved. 'Yeah, I know him.'

'He was one. But the man you really want is Celer.'

'Domitius Celer?'

'That's him.'

'He's still in Antioch?'

'Sure. Commands the Third's cavalry. For what it's worth. These screw-kneed hacks they ride wouldn't even make good glue.'

'Why should I want Celer in particular?'

He shrugged. 'You asked what Romans the boss was thick with. He was thick with Celer. And not just what you called dinner party stuff, either.'

Uhuh. 'Tell me.'

'Same again, you said?'

'If the information's worth it. Sure.'

'It's worth it.' A pause, but I wasn't giving. Not until he did. 'We used to drive sometimes out along the Beroea road, towards the Third's camp. There's a grove of trees down a track just beyond Agrippa's Baths. I'd stop there and he'd go on foot to meet the guy further up the hill.'

'So how do you know it was Celer?'

'He left his horse in the clearing. Black gelding, patch above the eye like a crown. Nervous tail.'

'This happen often?'

'Not often. And not regular. Now and again. Maybe once, twice a month.'

'You know what they talked about?'

'You think I'm a fool? I stuck to the coach. Ears shut and eyes on the horses.'

'It wasn't . . . ah . . . a romantic assignment?'

'With Celer? No way! Celer's not that type.' He held out his hand again. 'That's the story, pal. All you get.' I passed over the other coins and he slipped them under his belt. 'A pleasure doing business with you. I always had a soft spot for Romans.'

'Yeah, sure.'

'Truth.' He stood up. 'You want a tip for the races tomorrow? Back Green in the third heat. Not the second or the fourth, the third. Okay?'

'Okay.' I stood up too. The Orontes would freeze over before I bet on anything this guy recommended, and not because he didn't know horseflesh. A bastard like Giton would tell you to put your shirt on a team just for the fun of knowing you'd lose it.

Perilla got back late afternoon, and we exchanged notes.

'You do realise, Corvinus,' she said when I'd told her about Giton, 'that you are talking to the current Antioch expert on how women in Rome are wearing their hair at present?'

I grinned. 'No kidding?'

'No kidding. I was also interrogated on what was the chicest way when we left of draping a mantle, what authors were popular – of the lighter Alexandrian sort, naturally – and who was having an affair with whom.' She took a morose swallow of her pomegranate juice: I was becoming seriously worried about the effects that stuff was having on her. 'These topics not necessarily in the order I've given.'

'So you had a nice time?'

'Marvellous.'

'Think of it as work, lady. You find out anything interesting? Besides how to make upside-down egg pudding?'

'No. Not anything specific. Sulpicia was being very close-mouthed and I didn't dare ask anything overtly.'

'So who was there?'

'You want a list? There were at least a dozen.'

'Just the key names.'

'All right.' She paused. 'Sulpicia. The governor's wife Caecilia Gemella . . .'

'How about Mrs Celer?'

'Yes. Popilla, I think her name was. Then there was Acutia, of course. A rather plump lady with artistic pretensions. Several others I can't recall.'

'And you got nothing? Nothing at all?'

Perilla stared into her juice glass. 'I wouldn't exactly say nothing, Marcus. It's difficult to explain. There was a certain . . . atmosphere.'

'Yeah?'

'I mean, there are undercurrents to any group. Parties. Factions. Petty jealousies. Nothing an outsider can identify, just . . . undercurrents. But these ones were particularly strong.'

'Come on, lady! You can do better than that!'

'I'm trying. Let me think. Sulpicia, for example, didn't get on with Popilla. And Acutia wasn't popular with anyone. Not that she was left out but she simply wasn't . . . included. Oh, she was a bit of a pain, but that wasn't the reason. Some of the rest were worse.'

'Who's this Acutia?'

'Publius Vitellius's wife.'

Yeah, that made sense. Vitellius had been one of Germanicus's main supporters; he'd helped to prepare the case against Piso in Rome. Marsus and Celer, on the other hand, had both been Piso's men. Given the feud that'd be plenty to account for a certain coolness still among the wives.

'You think it's a hangover from Germanicus's time?' I said.

'Maybe. Probably. But it seemed more general. Caecilia was distant with Acutia as well, and Caecilia wasn't in Antioch when Germanicus was alive. Nor were some of the others.'

I was out of my depth here, and I knew it. Simple facts like guys being knifed in the back or holding secret meetings beyond the city limits I could understand, even if I didn't know the whys and the wherefores, but all these women's names just made my head spin. Not that what Perilla was saying wasn't important: sure it was. But there was nothing I could latch on to. Not yet, anyway.

'Okay. Let's leave it,' I said. 'You feel up to going again tomorrow?'

'Not really. But I will, of course.'

'Good.' I kissed her. 'So. Any of your lovelies coming to the governor's party tonight?'

'Most of them. It is his birthday, after all.'

'It's *what*?'

'The governor's birthday, Marcus. Sulpicia told me.'

'Then why the hell didn't it say so on the invite?' Oh, Jupiter! That was all we needed. To turn up at Lamia's birthday party without a present would be the diplomatic equivalent of blowing a raspberry in the guy's face. He wouldn't say anything, of course, but we could forget any little future indulgences.

'Don't worry. I bought something in town on the way back home. An alabaster perfume jar. He's interested in antiques, seemingly.'

Like my pal Sejanus, although I'd bet his interest wasn't aesthetic. I breathed a sigh of relief. 'Quite a cultured lad, all told. First Tyrian glass, now antiques. You think he's a poet as well, like your friend Marsus?'

'Perhaps. I don't know, Corvinus. Do you have a reason for asking?'

I didn't, not as such; but I had a suspicion that we were going to have to stir up some shit soon. And when that happened we'd need all the goodwill we could get.

Incidentally, I checked the race news with Critias the next day. The Green team in the third heat lost. They lost by a nose, but they lost.

28 ∫

I hate these formal parties. The booze is always slow and second rate, you never know what to do with your plate and the guy you end up talking to (it's always a guy, or a fifty-plus harpy with a face like a camel's worst angle) is either a total bore or he thinks you are. He's usually right, too: I'm never at my snappy conversational best when I have to talk vertical. And when I'd been through the problems of travelling out of season and the beauties of Antioch for the tenth time in a row with the tenth political smoothie I was ready to jack it in in favour of solitaire draughts.

Which was when I felt a hand smack me between the shoulder blades so hard I almost spilled my wine. I turned, and recognised Statilius Taurus.

'Hey, Corvinus!' He was grinning like a drain. 'What the hell are you doing here?'

I could've asked him the same question. The last time I'd seen Taurus was in Rome two years back, when he'd been packed and ready to go to Crete as junior finance officer. Now here he was in Antioch, and in a tribune's uniform instead of an administrator's mantle.

'Taurus!' I grinned back. 'What happened to Crete? They kick you out of the diplomatic?'

'I was never in, Marcus boy. I did a swap with a friend who was chasing the collector's daughter. Anyway, it was a fair deal. He juggled accounts ten times better than I could.'

Yeah, that made sense: Taurus never did have a head for statistics barring vital ones, but he was a born soldier. I doubted if the friend had needed to twist his arm much. And I was glad to see a familiar face.

'You with the Third?' I asked.

'The Tenth. Over at Cyrrhus. I'm delivering a report for the boss.' He emptied his wine cup and held it out to a passing waiter. 'You?'

'Call it a holiday,' I said.

'Hey, that's right! Someone mentioned a narrow-striper from Rome. That you?'

'Must be.'

'A honeymoon, then. I heard you'd married that Perilla girl. Congratulations.' He hesitated. 'You know Rufus is here?'

'We've met.'

'No kidding.' I could see he wanted to ask what'd happened but he was too polite. 'So where's the lady?'

I looked around. Perilla was deep in conversation with Marsus, and I didn't want to risk another brush with that guy. 'Over there. I'll introduce you later.' I paused. 'Hey, Taurus. How long've you been here, exactly?'

'In Syria? Well over a year now. I came out two Novembers ago.'

'Is that right?' So he'd overlapped pretty considerably with Germanicus. Maybe I'd struck lucky and the draughts could wait after all. 'Did . . . ?'

I never finished the question. A movement at the edge of the room caught my eye. The governor was on his way over, with a thin-faced military man in tow. Obviously this wasn't the time or the place to go into things. Not if I wanted answers.

'Look, Taurus,' I said quickly. 'You in Antioch for long?'

'Two or three days.'

'Okay. So let's split a jug. Tomorrow?'

'Make it the day after.' His left eyelid drooped. 'Tomorrow night I'm busy. Or I hope to be.'

'Fair enough. You know Athenodorus's house? In Epiphania?'

'I can find it.' Lamia was almost up to us by now. 'Marcus, you okay? What the hell's going on?'

'Later, pal.' I turned to face Lamia.

'Ah, Corvinus!' The governor was smiling. 'I'm sorry to interrupt. Can I introduce Domitius Celer, the Third's commander of cavalry?' Hey! Great! 'I think your wives met earlier today.'

'That's right.' I shook Celer's hand. 'Pleased to meet you, sir.'

'Fine.' Lamia smiled again. 'Now if you'll excuse me I think my wife is trying to attract my attention. Some domestic crisis, no doubt. Lovely present, by the way, Corvinus. Thank you.'

He left, and I turned my attention to Celer.

'Rufus sends his regards,' he said.

As the Third's commander of cavalry, Celer would be Rufus's second. I stiffened. 'Yeah? That was nice of him.'

Taurus was looking between us. Celer hadn't so much as acknowledged his presence, but he did it now. Turning to him, he said: 'Don't let us keep you, tribune.'

Taurus blinked and reddened. I got ready to grab his arm in case, governor's party or not, he decided what the hell and punched the bastard out. He didn't, although it was a close-run thing. Instead he gave him a long careful stare, nodded, and with a 'See you later, Marcus' walked off to join another group.

Celer watched him go, then turned back to me.

'You're enjoying Antioch?' he said.

'It's okay.' I found that my own right hand had made a fist, and I had to will myself to relax: I hadn't liked the crack about Rufus, I hadn't liked the way he'd dismissed Taurus, and I was rapidly coming to the conclusion that I could live without Celer full stop. 'You want the travelogue, pal?'

'No. I know how you've been spending your time, Corvinus. In fact that's why I thought a little talk with you was in order.'

'Is that so, now?'

'That's so.' He moved closer in, and I caught the smell of metal polish and beeswax from his armour. 'A friendly warning. Leave it alone. Carry on and you'll only get hurt.'

He'd dropped his voice almost to a whisper. I stepped back and spoke normally. 'Uhuh. And does Lamia know about this "friendly warning" of yours?'

Several heads turned; Celer's eyelids flickered, but he didn't move, and this time he made no effort not to be overheard. 'Oh, the governor agrees with me,' he said calmly. 'In fact I'm afraid you're in a minority of one here. Not a very popular minority, either.'

'I can take that.' I held out my empty cup to a hovering wine slave. I'd misjudged Lamia: the wine wasn't bad although a bit sweet for my taste. Probably local, because I couldn't place it at all, but good local. 'Hey, talking about sightseeing as we weren't, pal, I hear you know a nice spot in the hills on the road to Beroea. Good place for a picnic, you think?'

I'd rocked him; I could see that. His face shut. 'You be careful, Corvinus,' he said slowly. 'You be very careful. As I said, you could get hurt. And Antioch isn't your city.'

'Yeah. So I've been told.'

'Remember it, then.' He turned his back without another word and walked off to join two other officers by the ornamental pool.

I was so angry I was shaking, but short of going after the guy and holding his head under the water until his toes turned blue there wasn't a lot I could do. At least we knew where we stood, and the fact he'd been so blatant showed he'd probably told me the truth; that most of the people who mattered would back him, including the governor. Like he'd said, I was on my own. I looked over to where Taurus was chatting to a little honey in red silk, but I decided not to join them: we'd made our appointment and the less I saw of Taurus before then the safer it'd be. Maybe he thought the same, because although I was sure he'd seen Celer go he was ignoring me. Besides, I'd be cramping his style. I went off to look for Perilla instead.

She'd moved on from Marsus and was talking to a pale plump woman in a subfusc mantle and a big guy with baggy jowls like a pig's cheeks.

'Oh, Marcus, there you are,' she said. 'Come and meet Acutia and her husband Publius Vitellius.'

We nodded at each other. Vitellius gave me the look I was beginning to recognise: a sharp, summing glance that was just on the polite side of unfriendly.

'Your wife's just been telling us about her stepfather.' Acutia may've looked like a pigeon but her voice and manner were pure mouse. I had to bend close to hear all the words. 'So fascinating, to have a famous poet for a relative. And how rewarding it must have been artistically.'

'Did you ever meet Ovidius Naso, Corvinus?' Vitellius asked. The guy had all the presence his wife lacked. You felt that if they ever caught you these jaws would crunch you up.

'No. My uncle knew him well, though.'

'Ah, the present consul. How is that gentleman?'

Ouch. I could recognise sarcasm when I heard it. I was beginning to wonder if Cotta had any friends at all. 'He was fine when I left.'

'I understand he had . . . well, certain circumstances to thank for his elevation. Not unconnected with yourself.'

'Yeah? Is that so?' I was surprised, and cautious: it wasn't often I met anyone who knew about the Ovid business. But then Vitellius had been pretty close to Germanicus and the guy had other high-powered connections. 'You know more than I do, then. Cotta deserved his consul's chair. As much as anyone usually does.'

Vitellius pulled at his earlobe – I noticed the tip of his right index finger was missing – and frowned: on that face it was like a crease in a lump of dough. 'Perhaps you're right,' he said. 'Certainly Cotta Maximus is in good company. If that word isn't inappropriate where favouritism is concerned.'

Bastard! 'You mean company like Sejanus?' He paused; then said, distastefully:

'No. *Not* like Sejanus.'

'Vitellius is the governor's assistant, Marcus,' Perilla said quickly. 'On the finance side.'

'Really?' I tried my best for a polite smile. 'I wondered why you weren't in uniform, sir. You were a legate on the Rhine, weren't you?'

I caught a look in his eye I couldn't quite place, but maybe I was imagining things: the eyes were so sunk into the podge that you hardly noticed them. 'That's right. I was. But I've found my talents lie more in administration.'

'And in forensics.'

He frowned again. 'No, Corvinus. Not at all. Certainly my last venture into that field was . . . unsuccessful.'

'You mean nailing Piso and Plancina on a poisoning rap?'

'Indeed.' I'd gone too far, even with that innocent little probe. The guy had stiffened up like he'd been cemented from the inside. 'So how are you finding our city? A change from Rome, no doubt?'

Hell. We were back to temples and statues. Acutia blossomed, and talked column proportions with Perilla. Then Lamia drifted over with a horse-faced female on his arm.

'You're enjoying yourself, Corvinus?' he said.

'Uh, yeah. Yes, very much, sir.' I avoided Perilla's eye.

'That's good. My wife Caecilia Gemella.' The horse face nodded benignly at me. I remembered Giton's stable and wondered if maybe I should scratch her nose, or even blow up her nostrils. 'And so this is the lovely Rufia Perilla. We haven't had a chance to talk, my dear. I hear you don't need my services after all over accommodation.'

'No, governor.' Perilla smiled at him. 'But thank you in any case.'

I'd been watching the interplay between Lamia and Vitellius. It was interesting: the two were friendly enough – they'd nodded to each other when the governor had come over – but there was a wariness I couldn't account for. And the wives, as Perilla had said earlier, obviously didn't get on at all: Acutia was stuck to her husband's arm like a limpet, and her eyes never left his face. Caecilia had ignored her completely.

'Apropos,' Lamia was saying to Perilla. 'Domitius Celer was telling me you were enquiring about possible picnic sites.'

Perilla gave me a sharp glance. 'Well, yes,' she said. 'Marcus did mention picnics the other day. He's quite a fresh-air fiend.'

The governor laughed. 'A more common trait of character here than in Rome, although even so as a good Roman not one I'd endorse.' He turned to me. 'Celer said someone recommended the Beroea direction to you, Corvinus. Personally I would've thought the other way would be better, south towards Daphne. You'd agree, Vitellius?'

The pudgy eyes were fixed on me. 'Oh, yes,' Vitellius said. 'Most definitely. Certainly from the health aspect.'

Uhuh. 'Yeah, thanks, gentlemen,' I said. 'Thanks a lot. Nice to know you're all together in this. I'll bear it in mind.'

'You do that, Corvinus,' Lamia said blandly. 'Daphne's perfect for fresh-air fiends like you. Stick to that side of the city and you won't go far wrong.' He turned back to Perilla. 'And now, my dear, you must tell me where you found that beautiful Egyptian perfume jar.'

* * *

So. Lamia, Celer and Vitellius. Whatever the exact relationship was between these guys – and it wasn't a straightforward one, I could see that – they were all on the same side against Corvinus. That didn't augur well, not well at all. Like Celer had said, I was in a minority of one. Whatever was being covered up it was major, and the cover-up was official; at least official as far as the local authorities were concerned. The thing was, with beef like that on the opposition benches would we get anywhere at all?

The party was still in full swing when we said our thank-yous and went home. Sure, I was glad at least to have run across Celer and Vitellius, but the whole affair had basically been a downer. I'd expected someone, somewhere to be on my side, or at least neutral. What I'd got was a general conspiracy of silence; and I was beginning to feel like a sprat in a pond of hungry lampreys.

Still, I had to talk to Taurus yet.

29 ∫

He came round the following afternoon. I was taking a nap out in the garden when Critias showed him through.

'Hey, Taurus!' I said when he'd prodded me awake. 'We said tomorrow.'

'Count yourself lucky I came at all.' The guy looked jaundiced as hell. 'I'm standing Junia up for this.'

'That the girl in red you were talking to last night?' I indicated a chair and sent Critias off for the wine.

'Yeah.' He sat down. 'So you owe me one, pal. A big one. Okay?'

Perilla came through from the direction of the kitchens. 'Corvinus,' she said, 'Meton and Lysias are quarrelling again over the best way to truss a chicken. Honestly, this has to stop.'

Taurus's eyes had lit up when he saw her. I knew the signs. 'Whistle and I'll kill you,' I said. 'Perilla, this is Statilius Taurus. He broke my wrist when we were kids. He also gets his days mixed.'

'Really?' Perilla smiled at him and sat down on the bench beside the box hedge. 'Pleased to meet you, Taurus. I was sorry to have missed you at the governor's party.'

'I'm sorry about that too,' he said. Personally, I wasn't. The guy was leering, and that was bad news.

Critias came back out with the wine and Perilla's fruit juice. I was gradually getting him trained; another month and there'd be no time lag at all. 'So,' I said as he poured for us. 'What caused the change of plan?'

Taurus drank. 'The bastard's sending me back to Cyrrhus.'

'Who? Celer?'

'Celer's got no jurisdiction over me, Corvinus. The order's personal, from the governor.'

'Lamia?'

'Yeah. Lamia. I should've been gone already. Would've been if he'd got official hold of me straight off, but I was round at Junia's so the messenger missed me. I'm keeping a step ahead.'

'Did he give a reason?'

'Urgent dispatches.' He finished the cup and reached for the jug that Critias had left in its cooler. 'Though if they're urgent enough to lose me three days' leave I'll eat my helmet.'

Right, and I'd pass my plate and help him do it. Syria may have more legions than anywhere else east of Pannonia, but they're cold war troops and you can't say they're overworked; over here even the Eagles're laid back, and words like 'urgent' aren't in the manual. Our little confab at the party had evidently been noticed.

'Does the governor often act so arbitrarily?' That was Perilla.

'No, Lamia's okay.' Taurus pulled a few grapes from the bunch Critias had brought with the wine. 'Sejanus's cousin or not, he's straight.'

Yeah. Given the name, I'd known that there had to be some sort of connection. But then as I said the Wart's favourite had his fingers into all sorts of pies these days.

'What happened to Saturninus, by the way?' I drank my own wine. 'The temporary governor?'

Taurus shrugged. 'Went back to Rome. Or maybe he was transferred someplace somewhere else.'

'In disgrace?'

'No, he did all right. He kept Piso out, anyway.' Taurus was beginning to look suspicious. 'Hey, Corvinus, this isn't like you. What's all this about? You suddenly gone political or something?'

I'd known Taurus for years; like I'd told Perilla, the guy had broken my wrist when we were kids in an argument over an apple. What I hadn't told her was that we'd shared the same girl, off and on as it were, for two years. So we knew each other pretty well, and much too well for lies. Besides, I needed a friend. Like Vitellius had said, Antioch wasn't my city. It may not've been Taurus's either, technically, but he was the best I'd get. Added to which I trusted him.

'Okay, pal,' I said. 'Pin your ugly ears back and I'll tell you a story.'

'Piso was still guilty,' he said when I'd finished. 'Sure he was. Guilty as hell.'

'Jupiter!' I leaned back in my chair and put my hands over my eyes. 'Taurus, you just have not been listening, have you? Sure, he *could've* been guilty, but if he was then it still leaves too much unexplained. Maybe he and Plancina did murder Germanicus. But it could just as easily have been half a dozen other people, for half a dozen other reasons, any one of which is just as good.'

'Perhaps it wasn't even murder at all,' Perilla put in quietly. 'Germanicus may have died of a fever. You see, Taurus, we simply do not know. All we know is that the authorities here are trying to cover something up, and that something is connected with Piso's treason and Germanicus's time in Syria. We thought perhaps that you might be able to help.'

Taurus was quiet for a long time. Then he said: 'Hey, Marcus.'

'Yeah?'

'You remember the time that girl in Fidenae tied her bra to the pig's tail?'

'Uh.' I glanced at Perilla. She was busy with the grapes, or pretending to be. 'Yeah. Yeah, I remember that.'

'You remember trying to explain to me why she did it?'

'Sure. It took me an hour and you still didn't understand.'

'Okay. So what do you want to know?'

I laughed. That was one of the things I liked about Taurus. Intellectually gifted he wasn't, but the guy knew his limitations and didn't worry too much where they left him short. Still, I was glad we'd gone through the motions. 'Fair enough,' I said. 'So let's start at the easy end with Piso's treason. What happened? Exactly?'

Taurus helped himself to more wine. 'It was straightforward enough. After the row with Germanicus, Piso and Plancina boarded their yacht and took off for Greece.'

'Why did they do that?' Perilla put in. 'After all, for a governor to leave his province unauthorised is a culpable act in itself.'

'Let's not get bogged down, Perilla, okay? Taurus has enough problems.' I held out my own cup for Taurus to pour. 'Carry on, pal.'

'Piso got the news of the death on Cos. Marcus Piso wanted to go on to Rome and face the Wart but Celer suggested they go back to Syria.'

'Marcus Piso being the son?'

'Right. Anyway, Piso took Celer's advice and sent the guy down to Laodicea to bring over the Sixth Legion. Only Celer never reached them because their legate sent a cavalry troop to tell him he wasn't taking orders from anyone now but Saturninus.'

'I'm sorry, Taurus.' Perilla again. 'Germanicus appointed Saturninus *before* his death?'

'No. The top brass elected him as a temporary replacement.'

'But what about Vibius Marsus? He was Piso's deputy.'

I nodded; a fair point, because Marsus hadn't left Antioch when his boss did and so unlike Piso hadn't put himself outside the law. All things being equal, and barring a direct ruling to the contrary by someone with overriding authority, he'd be the natural caretaker. And there hadn't been anyone with overriding authority, because Germanicus was already dead.

'Marsus was in the running, sure,' Taurus said. 'But he backed down.'

'Uhuh.' I took a swallow of wine. 'Leaving Germanicus's man in control. Politic. Or maybe he was just being realistic.'

'Yeah.' Taurus chewed on a grape and spat the pips into his palm. 'In the meantime Piso lands in Cilicia. He calls on the Asian client-kings for troops, grabs a crowd of raw squaddies on their way to Antioch and occupies a fortified town called Celenderis.'

I sat back. Jupiter! Talk about escalation! What we had here was a full-blown civil war! No wonder the Senate had called for Piso's guts on a pole. 'So what was he trying to prove?' I said.

'I should say that was obvious.' Perilla sipped her fruit juice. 'Technically Piso was still the Syrian governor. That part of Cilicia was part of his province. He could argue, I suppose, that Saturninus's election was invalid, his armed resistance illegal and, since Germanicus was dead, that he himself was now Tiberius's sole accredited representative.'

'Even though he'd left the province illegally and possibly in disgrace?'

'But he hadn't been officially dismissed, Marcus.' Perilla turned to Taurus. 'Or had he?'

'No. Not that I know of.' Taurus was scowling into his wine. 'Anyway, it didn't matter in the end because the Cilicians caved in. Piso wanted to stay at Celenderis until Tiberius had given a ruling, but Saturninus packed him straight off to Rome.'

'And when he and Plancina arrived they did their Antony and Cleopatra act on a gilded barge down the Tiber.' I reached for the jug. 'It doesn't add up. Syria's an imperial province, under the emperor's direct jurisdiction. After a mess like that the Wart would've been fully within his rights to nail Piso to the Speakers' Platform without stopping to scratch his boils, let alone consult the Senate or bother about a murder charge. And Piso must've known it. So why was the guy so confident he'd get off?'

'Bravado?' Perilla said.

'Fuck bravado. Even without the poisoning rap he was on a hiding to nothing.'

'But, Corvinus,' Perilla said gently, 'of course he was. Whether his death was suicide or not, Piso died because he committed treason.'

'Yeah, but . . .' I subsided into silence. None of this made sense. None of it.

'Very well,' Perilla said. 'So what about the earlier events, Taurus? The quarrel, especially?'

'Okay.' Taurus sat back in his chair. 'You know Germanicus did the grand tour on his way out?'

'Yes.' Perilla nodded. 'Stopping off with Drusus in Pannonia and then visiting the Greek-speaking provinces.'

'Right. While he was swanning around Asia Piso went straight to Antioch. He replaced a lot of Creticus's staff with his own men, Celer and Marsus included. And he got the squaddies on his side by easing up on discipline and extending their town privileges.'

'What about Creticus? Didn't he have a say in this?'

I sighed. 'He was the outgoing governor, Perilla. As the new man Piso was within his rights to make his own appointments. Of course Creticus didn't have a say. He wouldn't expect to.'

'Perhaps not. But I just wondered what his reaction was.'

'Syria was his last posting. He was on his way to retiral and a prime seat in the Senate while his daughter was marrying Germanicus's eldest, so he'd have an in with the Imperials. Why the hell should he stick his neck out about Piso?'

'I expect you're right.' Perilla lowered her eyes. Hell. I never trusted that lady when she went demure on me. It usually meant she thought I was completely wrong, and was working out the most devastating way of telling me. 'So. Piso took control of Syria. And then Germanicus arrived and the quarrel began.'

'Yeah.' Taurus scooped up a last handful of loose grapes. 'When Germanicus went to dicker with the Parthians over Armenia he gave Piso a direct order to join him with two Eagles. Piso ignored it.' I winced; some things you just don't do, and ignoring a direct order from the heir-apparent comes pretty high on the list. 'Then of course Germanicus went off on his Egyptian tour. When he got back Piso had cancelled or ignored all his arrangements and the shit really hit the fan.'

'At which point Piso left Syria. Or was thrown out. And Germanicus popped his clogs. Or had them popped for him. End of story.' I lifted the jug, but it was empty. 'You want more wine, Taurus?'

'Sure.'

'Perilla? Another prune juice?'

'Pomegranate.'

'Whatever.'

'No, thank you. I've had my quota for the day.'

Very wise; like I said, I wasn't sure about her and that stuff. Critias had disappeared, so I went inside with the empty jug to look for him.

I found the guy in the hallway. He was talking to an army tribune. They looked up as I came through.

'Valerius Corvinus?' the tribune said in a voice that was trying to be ten years older than its real age.

'Yeah, that's me.' For a minute I was worried, but the kid was on his own and he didn't look old enough to shave, let alone mean enough to cause trouble. Maybe I wasn't being deported quite yet. Or beaten up, if he came from Rufus. Unless there were a dozen squaddies with brickbats waiting outside.

The tribune cleared his throat. 'I'm sorry to disturb you, sir, but I wonder if you have Statilius Taurus with you.'

'I might have. So what, son?'

He went beetroot red under his helmet. 'Could I talk to him for a moment, sir, do you think?'

I hesitated, weighing the pros and cons of throwing the guy out on his squeaky-clean superpolite ear. The cons won hands down.

'Yeah, sure,' I said. 'He's in the garden. You want to follow me?'

'Should I bring out some more wine, lord?' Critias asked.

'Uh-uh.' I shook my head: Taurus's official orders had obviously caught up with him, and Junia was in for a major disappointment. 'Forget it, sunshine. I think our guest's just leaving.'

I couldn't help feeling just a little smug as the tribune delivered his message. Sure, I was sorry to see Taurus go, especially since I'd been the one responsible for lousing up his trip to the big city, not to mention his plans for sweet Junia. But at least the home team had got off its backside for once and scored before the opposition moved the goalposts. That deserved a celebration, if anything did. So I collared Critias and got him to bring the wine anyway.

30

Perilla was on cake-clatsch duty again next day when Critias brought me a message from Giton the coachman. That surprised me; I wouldn't've thought Giton could write much past his own name, if that.

Then again, maybe he couldn't.

'Hey, Critias.' The strip of paper had been torn from a receipted grain bill. I held it out. 'Who delivered this?'

Critias came back over. 'One of Apollonius's boys, lord.'

'You sure?'

'So he told me.'

'Uhuh. What did this kid look like?'

A sniff. 'Squint-eyed, as I remember, lord. With warts.'

Yeah, that checked out. I remembered that one of the lads who'd been throwing dice in the tackle room had had a vicious squint. Still, it was just as well to be careful. Especially since I hadn't told Giton who I was, let alone where I lived.

'He say what it was about?'

'No, lord. Only that the message came from the coachman.'

I read the thing again. It was neatly written and well spelled: *To Marcus Valerius Corvinus, at the house of Athenodorus. Meet me at the Shrine of the Dryads at two hours before sundown. Bring some real money.* 'So where's the Shrine of the Dryads?' I said.

'In Iopolis, lord, on the western side of the Capitol. Above Caesar's Baths.'

'Yeah. Got you.' It hadn't figured on our tour, although we'd been all over Iopolis. 'Not one of Antioch's major monuments, I take it?'

'No, lord. The shrine is a ruin, and quite isolated.'

'Uhuh. Thanks, sunshine.' It would be isolated. Isolated was par for the course. Taken all in all this whole thing smelled. Giton had told me all he knew when I'd seen the guy last. Why should he want to meet again? On the other hand 'bring some real money' sounded authentic Giton. And promising. Too promising to pass up just on a suspicion. Still . . .

I'd go, sure; but I'd go careful.

I found the shrine eventually. Isolated ruin was right: it was nothing but a tumble of old masonry half hidden by rocks and bushes at the end of a path that would've given a goat vertigo. When Critias had said 'above Caesar's Baths' he hadn't been kidding; I could practically have spat down the furnace chimney. If Giton wanted privacy inside the city limits he couldn't've chosen a better place.

He was there all right, sitting with another guy on the broken steps of the shrine.

'So you got the note, Corvinus,' he said.

'Yeah.' I scratched my left wrist under the long sleeve of the tunic, checking that my knife was taped in place. So far so good, but I still wasn't taking any chances. 'How did you know where to send?'

'I've got my methods. Young smartasses fresh from Rome aren't thick on the ground. You bring the money? Real money, like I said?'

'Maybe.' I indicated the other man. 'Who's this?'

'My name's Orosius, lord.' He was a weaselly little runt with the look of a clerk, or maybe a school teacher. 'A pleasure to meet you.'

'Orosius is a friend of mine,' Giton said. 'He works in the records office. Listen to him, Corvinus. He's smart.'

Yeah. And working in the records office he could spell, too. That was one mystery cleared up. I sat down with my back against a lump of column.

'So what's this about?'

It was Orosius who answered. 'You were enquiring about the Parthian Vonones, lord. I knew him.' The guy gave me a smile like third-rate olive oil. 'Perhaps I can give you the information you need.'

'If the price is right,' Giton grunted.

They waited. I waited longer. I'd got Giton's measure at our last encounter.

'Three names, lord,' Orosius said at last. I noticed for all his smile he was nervous as a cat, and sweating. 'Archelaus, Epiphanes and Philopator.'

'That supposed to mean something to me, pal?'

'Archelaus of Cappadocia. Epiphanes of Commagene. Philopator of Amanus.'

I'd got them now. 'The client-kings?'

'Ex-client-kings, lord. That's the point. Very much the point.'

Giton laid a hand on his arm. 'Okay, Corvinus, that's all you get for free. You want more, you pay for it. Fifteen silver pieces. Sixty drachmas. Each.'

I whistled. Whatever Giton thought he'd got here he wasn't selling it cheap. Which meant the information might just be worth it.

'Thirty tetradrachs is a hell of a lot of gravy, pal,' I said. 'I haven't got that much with me.'

'Then screw you, Roman.' Giton stood up. 'I said bring real money and I meant it. You know where to find me.'

'Wait.' Orosius pulled him back. 'You agree in principle, lord? To the price?'

'If what you've got's that valuable, yeah. Fifteen on account, fifteen later.'

'Very well.' He turned to the coachman. 'Giton, sit down, please. We'll trust to the lord's good faith.' The guy wasn't used to this, I could see, and that was another point in his favour. He belonged behind a desk or in a library, not out here in the real world. I began to relax. 'First, lord, you know where these places are? Commagene and the others? It's important.'

'Sure.' Geography may not be my bag but I'm not a total bone-head. 'Commagene and Cappadocia are to the north, between us and Armenia. Amanus straddles the main land route through the Syrian Gates to Asia.'

'Good. And the kings?'

The guy should've been teaching school. 'Archelaus of Cappadocia was hauled off to Rome three years back on a treason charge. The other two are just names to me.'

'Very well. Do you know the details of Archelaus's trial?'

'No. Except that it was held in the Senate House, behind closed doors, and that the guy killed himself before the verdict was given.' Like Piso. I felt the first prickle of interest. 'The Wart annexed Cappadocia and turned it into a province.'

'Correct.'

I was getting tired of this. 'Look, friend, you want to do the talking for a change? I'm paying for answers, not questions.'

'Patience, lord. So Archelaus died. The other two kings died too, in their own countries but at roughly the same time. Of, it was said, natural causes. Their kingdoms were also annexed.'

Uhuh. 'Obviously what you're implying is that the deaths weren't natural.'

'I'm stating it, lord. Both kings died by poison.'

'So you say.'

'So I say.'

The answer had come straight back. Whether he was right or wrong the guy believed it himself. 'And Archelaus?'

'The Lord Tiberius had a personal dislike for the old man. Perhaps he wanted that death to be more . . . personal.'

I sat back. This was high-powered stuff. If what Orosius was telling me was true then a hundred and twenty drachs was a fair price. More than fair. 'You've got proof of all this?'

'No, lord.'

Well, at least the guy was frank. 'So where does your pal Vonones come in?'

'He caused the kings' deaths.'

I hadn't been expecting that. 'You're saying *Vonones* poisoned them?'

'No.' Orosius smiled. 'Forgive me, lord. I'm being melodramatic. Vonones killed them with money. And unintentionally. The kings died because Vonones had bought them and the emperor found out.'

'Why?'

'He was paving the way for a return to Armenia. Probably more, probably Parthia itself. And an alliance with the northern client-kings would guard his southern flank.'

Oh, yeah. Sure. I was disappointed; seriously disappointed. If all the guy had to offer was unsubstantiated rumours and pie-in-the-sky strategic theory two centuries out of date then I was wasting my time here after all. I could've saved myself the climb.

'There's only one fly in the ointment, friend,' I said. 'Or two flies, rather. Us and the Parthians. Artabanus wouldn't take kindly to Vonones setting his bum back on the Armenian throne, let alone the Parthian one. And a couple of our legions could roll up all four of your client-kingdoms inside of a month without breaking sweat.'

If I'd expected that to faze him I was wrong. He just smiled his oily smile.

'This is the east, lord,' he said, 'and you're thinking like a Roman. Give us Greeks credit for a little subtlety.'

'Okay. So convince me.'

'First of all Parthia. Artabanus is royal only on his mother's side, whereas Vonones's father was a king. That, to Parthians, is important. Vonones was driven out with difficulty after a civil war, and he still had considerable support inside Parthia itself when he died. Second, Armenia. The Armenians themselves invited Vonones to rule. Furthermore, to the Parthians Armenia is Parthian. A Roman king would be a standing insult, and any Parthian king who accepted him would be seen as betraying his own people.'

'But that's the point, surely. Vonones was a Roman puppet with a Roman outlook. That was the reason the Parthians threw him out in the first place.'

'Wait, lord, please.' He cleared his throat. 'Third, Rome. To us easterners, Greeks and others, Rome means – forgive me, but I must speak frankly – brute force and taxes. Increasingly so in recent years. You are not . . . *sympathetic*. Left to ourselves, we would rather do without you.'

'Gee thanks, pal.' I didn't blame him, mind. He had a valid point. When you get down to it we are a set of rapacious sods. Right, but rapacious.

'You may govern Syria proper directly,' Orosius went on, 'but you control the territories to the north and south through local rulers. They aren't . . . *committed* . . . to Rome except at the crudest level. And the common people don't like you at all. You understand?'

'Yeah.' The guy was right again, despite the high-flown rheto-
ric. Between Syria and Egypt Roman civilisation has always lain
pretty thin. In Judaea even thinner: the Jews have always been
a pack of touchy stiff-necked bastards. And there's a lot of
hatred around just below the surface, even in the Romanised
coastal cities.

'So, lord.' Orosius smiled again. 'That is the situation. Now a
scenario. Vonones returns to Armenia. At the same time, on his
instructions, the three northern client-kings break with Rome
and Amanus fortifies the pass at the Syrian Gates against help
from the west. The result?'

The smug little bastard's lecture style was beginning to get to
me. 'I told you. The Syrian legions would march north and wipe
the floor with them. And the Parthians would throw Vonones
out on his ear.'

'True. Unless the kings were supported by a universal – and
popular – revolt of the southern territories also. Coinciding with
the murder of Artabanus by Vonones's Parthian supporters and
a resulting threat from Parthia. As the orchestrator of the revolt
Vonones would certainly no longer be regarded as in any sense
a Roman puppet. And despite what you said the client kingdoms'
armies are not negligible. Especially when one considers they
would be fighting within their own territories.'

Jupiter! My scalp tingled. Sure, with four legions on the spot
we might weather something like that, but it would be touch
and go; far worse than what had happened a dozen years
back in Pannonia, and that had been bad enough. Armies and
garrisons were cut to the bone throughout the empire already,
and Rome's security was the result of a fine juggling act that
left no room for major changes. Man for man the client-kings'
troops might not be a match for the legions, but they were
well armed and well trained. Far better than the Germans or
the Pannonians had been. It was possible, sure it was. And if
the revolts were synchronised like Orosius was suggesting, and
Parthia piled in on the rebel side, then the whole Roman east
could go down the tube inside a month. As a scenario it was a
potential nightmare.

'You're saying that's what happened?' I said.

Orosius shook his head. 'No, lord. Of course not. I'm saying

that's what *almost* happened. With the deaths – executions – of
the three northern kings the revolt was quietly abandoned. The
emperor Tiberius is a clever man, lord. Much too clever for a
Roman.' Again the oily smile. 'That of course was Vonones's
downfall.'

I sat quiet and thought it through. Sure, there were problems,
but the way Orosius had described the plan I could see it
working. Especially if Vonones had made his move in winter,
when with the Syrian Gates blocked it would've been difficult
getting reinforcements in by sea or land. The rebels would've
had a good three months to consolidate. Time enough, easy.

'So how do you know all this, friend?' I said at last.

'Vonones talked in his sleep. That gave me the main points.
The rest – well, it comes from various sources, including my own
poor powers of reasoning.'

'One point. Why didn't the Wart have Vonones killed as well?
He was behind the whole scam, after all.'

'You're forgetting, lord. Vonones had a strong claim to the
throne of Parthia. So long as he was genuinely powerless within
the Roman marches he was a useful bargaining chip with
Artabanus; certainly too useful to kill out of hand. And with
the three kingdoms now under direct Roman control the plot
was dead beyond remedy.'

Giton was grinning. He'd sat through Orosius's spiel like
the guy was his own personal performing monkey. 'You see,
Corvinus?' he said. 'I told you he was smart.'

'Yeah, he's smart, okay.' He was, despite the weasel face and
grubby fingernails. Too smart for his own good.

'So.' Giton's grin broadened, and he held out his hand. 'Let's
have the money.'

'Wait a minute.' My brain was still spinning. 'All this may be
right but it's old history. Piso didn't get to Syria until after the
kings were dead, and he's the guy I'm interested in. And if the
plot was stone dead like you say then what did he and Vonones
have on the boiler together?'

Orosius spread his hands. 'Nothing, lord.'

I frowned. 'Run that one past me again.'

'Nothing for the Lord Piso's part, in any event. Oh, Vonones
believed that Piso was furthering his interests, and he himself was

certainly still in touch with his Parthian allies. But I'm afraid that by this time he was . . . shall we say in a rather over-optimistic and unrealistic frame of mind, and too ready to catch at any straw that was offered. When a friend in Rome contacted him to say that the new governor would be . . . more amenable than the last it built up his hopes considerably. And out of all proportion.'

Yeah, that would fit. And the 'friend', of course, had been Crispus's middleman Regulus. It fitted. Still . . . 'The guy couldn't've been that much of a fool,' I objected. 'Piso would have to give something in return for his bribes besides promises. Something more concrete.'

'Oh, but he did, of course!' Orosius sat up. 'You see, thanks to his imperial connections Piso was able to tell Vonones that the present situation was unlikely to last very long because the emperor had . . .'

The trees behind the shrine rustled. There was a sharp hiss and a dull thud. The guy jerked, his mouth still open and his eyes wide. Then, slowly, he fell forward to reveal the arrow-shaft buried in his back.

I threw myself to one side. Giton was slower: the second arrow caught him on the left shoulder and he screamed like a stuck pig. A third skittered over the rocky ground and broke against a boulder. By that time I was up and running, my knife out, keeping low and weaving. I'd got maybe ten yards when a fourth arrow stung my cheek and I caught sight of the guy through the scrub. He lowered his bow and took to the mountain.

'Go left!' I shouted to Giton; he was on his feet now and he had his own knife out. '*Left*, you bastard! Cut him off!'

Giton nodded. He was holding his arm but the wound couldn't've been serious because there was no sign of the arrow. I broke through the screen of bushes and found myself at the foot of a narrow ravine. The man was about fifty yards ahead, his bow looped over one shoulder, clambering up the scree. He was fit, I'd give him that: my own chest was beginning to burn with the effort and I wasn't gaining any.

The ravine ended in a lip of rock, and that was where he was headed. Halfway towards it I knew I was in trouble because he'd reach it while I was still struggling up the watercourse.

There was no cover and no place to go except up and down, and whichever one I chose he'd pick me off as easy as a duck in a bucket. I swore hard and concentrated on closing the gap. I was still a good forty yards short when he swung himself over the lip, scooped the bow off his shoulder and fitted an arrow to the string. I waited, ready to dive whichever way it wasn't going; but the arrow never came.

The guy had been squinting down at me, waiting for a good line of shot. Suddenly he looked up and back. A second figure loomed behind him and he shouted and pitched backwards arse over tip. I went hell for leather up the scree, my head low and my lungs bursting, and threw myself across the lip on to the plateau.

I landed right on top of him. He was dead. Very dead; Giton's knife had all but taken his head off. His bow lay to one side. No sign of the arrow, so he must've loosed it after all and I hadn't noticed.

Giton was sitting on a boulder, staring at the corpse.

'Thanks, friend,' I said, when my ribs had stopped hurting and I could breathe again.

He didn't look up. 'Fuck that, Roman. You think I did it for you?'

I put my knife back into its wrist sheath and said nothing.

'He was smart, wasn't he, though?' Giton still wasn't looking at me. 'A right smart little bugger.'

'Yeah, he was smart.' I knelt down beside the dead man. He was a soldier, that much was obvious from his leathers and army boots. 'Hey, Giton. You know if the Third have an archer troop attached?'

He was quiet for so long I didn't think he'd answer. Then he said: 'Sure. The Seventh Cretans. Mostly from the west, around Mount Leuca.'

Uhuh. I'd forgotten he was a Cretan himself. 'You know this guy, by any chance?'

Giton got up, walked over and spat very deliberately into the upturned face. 'His name was Lyncaeus. Julius Lyncaeus. I killed his uncle years back in Dictynnaeum.'

'Is that so?' I paused and touched the corpse with my foot. 'You want to help me bury him?'

But Giton was already on his way back down to the shrine. He didn't even look round.

'I owe you thirty silver pieces, friend,' I shouted after him; but I was talking to his back.

31

The Third's camp was five miles out the Beroea road. I could've gone back home to get my own carriage but that would've taken too long. Instead I picked up a public one from outside Caesar's Baths and left the driver twiddling his thumbs while I crossed the camp's main causeway and introduced myself to the gate guard.

'Yes, sir?' The guy in charge was a big decurion who looked like he'd been boiled in his leathers and then dried over an oakwood fire.

'Your legate on base at the moment, soldier?' I said.

The hard eyes raked me like I was a fifth-rate rookie who'd just fumbled his throwing spear at the present. Maybe I should've gone home first and smartened up after all, but I'd been too angry to put this off, and I'd hoped my patrician vowels and the purple stripe on what was left of my tunic would make up for appearances.

'Who wants him?' The guy was polite enough, but I noticed he'd dropped the 'sir'. I dabbed at the arrow scratch on my cheek. It'd stopped bleeding now but I'd bet good money my face didn't look too respectable either.

'The name's Valerius Corvinus. Marcus Valerius Messalla Corvinus. Rufus knows who I am. Tell him he's just lost himself an archer.'

The decurion stiffened, and I thought for a moment he'd have his squaddies throw me out. Then he nodded slowly.

'Wait here,' he said. 'Geminus!' One of the squaddies stepped forward. 'Message to the duty adjutant. Visitor for the legate at the main gate. Give him the b—' He stopped himself. 'Give him the gentleman's name and ask for instructions.'

'Thanks, sunshine.' I sat down uninvited on the bench inside the gatehouse to wait.

Ten minutes and not a word of social chit-chat later the guy reappeared, panting.

'The adjutant says I'm to bring him up, decurion,' he said.

'Do it, then.' The decurion turned his broad back on me.

When I strode into Rufus's office he was standing beside the desk, his face dark with anger.

'All right, Corvinus,' he said. 'What's this about an archer?'

'His name was Julius Lyncaeus. One of your Cretans. He shot one of the people I was with over by the Shrine of the Dryads, wounded a second and near as hell put an arrow through me. I thought maybe we should discuss it, Rufus.'

'Where is the Cretan now?'

'Last I saw he was lying on a plateau under the Capitol with his head hanging off. Pick him up any time you like, friend.'

I was hoping he'd go for me but he didn't. 'You killed him?'

'Not me. The other guy, the one he wounded in the shoulder. Personally I'd've preferred the bastard alive so I could sweat him.'

Rufus turned abruptly and crossed behind me to the door.

'Sabinus!' he shouted. 'In here! Now!'

The adjutant who'd met me in the outer office came running. He was a young guy, no older than me, and he looked scared. Rufus glared at me. 'I want you to listen very carefully to what this . . . gentleman says, Sabinus,' he said. 'And to remember it.'

The adjutant swallowed. 'Yes, sir.'

I was cooling down now, although my anger hadn't lost any of its edge. Quite the reverse. 'Lyncaeus was one of your men. You sent him, you or Celer.'

'Understand this, Corvinus.' Rufus came so close I could smell his breath. 'I've been ordered to stay away from you and I've done it. I don't know what Domitius Celer has to do with anything, but if I really wanted you dead I'd kill you myself. You've come in here uninvited and confessed to being involved in the death of one of my auxiliaries. When the governor gets to know about that, which he will as soon as I can send a despatch rider, you'll be out of Syria so fast your feet won't touch the ground, consul's nephew or not. Is that clear enough for you?'

'Sure it is.' There was a camp stool next to me. I pulled it up and sat on it. 'Now you understand me, Rufus. This wasn't a personal thing. Nothing to do with Perilla.' He'd been staring at me, and he didn't blink. 'The first arrow wasn't meant for me, unless the guy was the worst shot in the army. I don't know yet what bit of political garbage you and your mates are covering up, but I'm getting there. What I do know is it stinks, and throwing me out of Syria isn't going to alter the fact that now you've gone the length of murder and attempted murder. So you just shove that bit of information in your despatch rider's bag while you're at it, sunshine. Unless Lamia knows already, of course.'

Rufus was breathing hard and his fists were clenched. 'Sabinus, escort Valerius Corvinus back to the gate, please. Tell the guard he's not to be readmitted. Under any circumstances.'

'Yes, sir.' The young officer snapped a salute; I noticed he didn't look at me. Or, more to the point, at Rufus. I stood up to go.

'Wait. One more thing, Corvinus.' Rufus was stiffly formal. 'The name of your dead friend, please. And the name of the man who actually killed my Cretan.'

I held his eye. 'I think you know both their names already. Or if you don't you can always ask your pal Celer.'

'Get him out of my sight, Sabinus.' Rufus turned back to his desk.

I didn't feel too proud of myself on the way home. No, I'd no regrets about facing Rufus, but I'd let my temper rule my head and that'd been a mistake. He hadn't been bluffing when he'd said he'd contact the governor, I was sure of that, and if we weren't on the first ship out we could count ourselves lucky. Still, there hadn't been much else I could do. We had the whole of the Syrian top brass against us. To keep things under wraps would be playing into their hands. The only way we were going to come through this was to scream blue murder as publicly as possible and hope they'd be too embarrassed to try anything else.

I'd told Rufus that as far as the cover-up was concerned I was getting there. Like hell I was. What Orosius had told me about Vonones was interesting but it didn't help much. The only really useful part had been the bit at the end just before the guy had been shot. Piso had told Vonones that the situation was only temporary. And that the Wart was involved. The implication being that Piso, as a friend of the emperor or maybe as governor, knew something that most people didn't.

I settled back against the cushions. Okay. What situation? Presumably the only one Vonones had an interest in, namely Parthia and Armenia. Parthia was unlikely: Roman writ stops at the Orontes, and anyone who isn't a Parthian themselves born and bred would go mad inside a month trying just to make sense of Parthian dynastic squabbles, let alone manipulate them. Armenia then. Only the Armenian question had been solved once and for all by Tiberius's rep Germanicus. But then if Piso had told Vonones not to worry about Germanicus's arrangements because they wouldn't last then the implication was . . .

No. No, that wouldn't wash either. Tiberius hadn't cancelled his son's arrangements. They'd lasted even after Germanicus's death, because whether he was acting on orders or not Germanicus had done a good job. The Parthians were happy, too. Or at least they couldn't afford to pretend otherwise. So that wasn't it. Not Parthia, and not Armenia.

Okay, I thought. So let's go back a bit. Maybe Piso had meant Germanicus himself; that Germanicus was only temporary. That angle was more interesting. Sure, Piso could've been spinning a tale to keep the pennies coming in, but I didn't think so: Orosius had been certain that he had something solid to offer, and I trusted the smart little clerk's judgment. We were back to the theory that Piso had a private scam cooking with Tiberius. A special relationship. But if so then what was it?

Okay. What if the Wart had sent Piso out because the Armenian situation was too important to louse up? In other words, as the blue-eyed boy's official-unofficial minder?

It made sense. Germanicus had ballsed up the German campaign; he was on probation, crown prince or not. Piso was an experienced diplomatic hand and the emperor's personal friend. Let's say Tiberius had called him in, given him Syria, and told him to ride point. Make sure Germanicus handled the diplomatic juggling the way the Wart wanted it handled; simply and with none of the lad's usual flash. Which meant Tiberius also had to give Piso secret discretionary powers that overrode Germanicus's official ones. That would explain why Piso had been so blasé about crossing a ranking Caesar; it would explain the friction, especially if Germanicus knew the arrangement; it would explain why the two of them had been so cagey about letting the Senate see their correspondence; and it would explain Piso's cockiness when he got back to Rome. He'd followed the Wart's orders and he expected support. When he didn't get it it must've felt like a surprise boot up the backside . . .

Only that theory didn't work either. I kept hitting the objection that as far as Armenia and the Parthians were concerned the boy had done good. Tiberius was a sour bugger but he was fair. If he'd been testing Germanicus as a diplomat, or maybe just for his willingness to follow orders and take advice, then the guy had passed with flying colours. If anyone deserved to be ridden home on a rail it was Piso; which was exactly what had happened. Piso had had his knife into Germanicus from the start. He'd been rude, obstructive, petty-minded, and he'd finally caused more trouble than a rhino in a flower shop by committing an overtly treasonable act. If Tiberius had let the Senate claw the guy's balls off he'd thoroughly deserved it.

Yeah, sure. But I still couldn't get round what Orosius had said. Piso had practically told Vonones that Germanicus's days were numbered. Which would imply, in the event, that the Wart had had him killed. And *that* just made no sense at all. Germanicus was a long way from deserving poison in his porridge and a trip home in an urn, even if that was the way Tiberius did things, which it wasn't. Livia, sure, but not the Wart. It didn't explain this Syrian cover-up, either. So I was still missing something . . .

Ah, hell! Leave it! I looked out the carriage window. We were halfway along Epiphanes Street, just beyond the central plaza with the Shrine of the Nymphs and the Caesarium. Maybe I should spend more time just taking in the sights. If Rufus had his way this might be the last trip through Antioch I'd get. Perilla would be disappointed, too; she'd enjoyed it here. And Antioch wasn't a bad place. Not Rome, but then you can't have everything.

We turned up towards Epiphania and the hills, the sunset behind us covering the mountain ahead with purple like an emperor's cloak.

When I got back, I found a message from Lamia waiting for me. He wanted to see me in his office the next morning. First thing.

32

I knew things were bad as soon as his slimy secretary Bion showed me in.

'Ah, Corvinus.' Lamia was urbane as ever, but I could see he wasn't happy. Not happy at all. 'Good of you to be so prompt. Have a seat.'

I sat down and waited. This was official: the guy was behind his desk this time, and he had a letter in front of him. No prizes for guessing who that was from.

'Suillius Rufus tells me you visited him at the camp and became quite abusive.' His frown didn't lift. 'Something about a dead auxiliary. Perhaps you could give me your version of the story.'

'Did Rufus tell you the man shot one of the people I was with?' I said. 'Wounded another and tried to kill me?'

Lamia's eyelids didn't flicker. 'Yes, he did. Or at least that so you'd told him.'

'You don't believe me?'

'I might have been more inclined to do so if you hadn't been so reticent about giving Rufus your friends' names. And that cut on your cheek could easily have been caused by a clumsy barber.'

I stood up. 'Very well, sir. It seems whatever I say isn't going to carry much weight. Maybe . . .'

'Sit down, Corvinus.' It was said quietly, but it was an order. I sat. He indicated two slips of paper that were fastened to the letter. 'My Greek colleagues in the records office tell me that one of their clerks by the name of Orosius is missing from his desk this morning. And I have a report from the city guard that a certain Giton, coachman to one Apollonius, brought a corpse to an undertaker's establishment in the Aphrodisian district yesterday afternoon. The cause of death was an arrow wound in the back, although the arrow itself had been removed. The coachman is being held for questioning.'

Uhuh. 'Very efficient, sir. Especially since the records office can't've been open more than an hour yet. And do the city guard report every suspicious death direct to the governor?'

'No.' Lamia was watching me carefully. 'Of course not. I simply wanted you to know where you stood. And where I stand. Am I succeeding?'

'Yeah. You're doing okay.' I paused, trying not to let the anger show. 'Sir.'

'Good. I'm glad. Now.' He laid the papers to one side. 'As far as the murder of the Cretan is concerned I'm willing to believe that although you were involved you were not directly responsible. Also that there were extenuating circumstances' – I opened my mouth to say something but he held up a hand – 'which we won't go into.'

My temper snapped. 'Like hell we won't! You sent the guy to—!'

'That's enough!' Lamia's hand came down hard on the desk. 'I did not send anyone to do anything, Corvinus. The coachman Giton, as I understand, has admitted to knowing the dead man personally and to there being bad blood between the families. That is sufficient motive for the attack as far as I am concerned, and that particular aspect of the situation is closed, whether you like it or not.' He paused. 'I would, though, very much like to know what the three of you were doing in such an out-of-the-way spot in the first place.'

'Would you believe a serious dice game? Sir.'

'Don't be flippant. I'm asking you officially as the emperor's representative in Syria, and I want a proper answer, please.'

'Okay.' If I was going to go down – and it looked more than likely – I'd go down fighting. 'I'm on a commission from the empress to find out who killed Germanicus and why. Orosius was helping. Giton was just a friend of his.'

Lamia's eyes had widened when I'd mentioned Livia. 'But the empress . . .' he began.

I waited. 'The empress what?'

He laid the letter to one side. 'Nothing. At least nothing that concerns you. And please understand that none of this does concern you, Corvinus, empress or not. The situation is under control, neither I nor any of my colleagues have anything to feel guilty over, and you, young man, I'm afraid, are simply being a complete damn nuisance.' It was the first time ever that I'd seen the guy lose his cool, but it only lasted a second. Then he was his usual polite, polished self. 'Thank you at least for your frankness. However, I have the welfare of my province and staff to consider, as well as my duty to the emperor. The *Castor* leaves for Rome in five days' time. I'd like you to be on it, please. Bion will make the arrangements.'

Well, I'd known what was coming, I suppose. I stood up.

'And thank you, sir,' I said, 'for your time and your . . . sense of justice.'

'Sense of justice?' Lamia's mouth twisted. 'Yes. Well perhaps that's a little more developed than you think it is. Goodbye, young man. I don't believe we'll meet again, in the near future anyway. Certainly not in this room. Safe voyage, and my regards to your uncle.'

He didn't offer to shake hands, and neither did I. Bion didn't even look up as I walked past.

When I got back home we had a visitor. Perilla's pal Acutia. They were sitting over cakes and fruit juice in the portico.

'Hi, lady.' I kissed Perilla on the cheek. She gave me a worried look, but I shook my head. 'Tell you later.'

'You remember Acutia, Marcus? Publius Vitellius's wife?'

'Yeah, sure.' I collapsed into a chair and Critias put a full cup of Chian into my fist. Hell. The guy had got it right just when we had to leave. There was a deep philosophical truth hidden there somewhere, but I was too knackered to work out what it was. 'How are you, Acilia?'

'Acutia, Marcus,' Perilla said.

'Oh, don't worry.' Acutia gave a nervous smile. 'I'm quite used to people getting my name wrong.'

'Hey, no. It's my fault.' She was so mouselike I didn't believe it, and I felt as guilty as if I'd slapped her. Nice eyes, though. 'I just don't listen.'

'Acutia called round to ask if I'd like to go shopping with her.' Perilla's voice was carefully neutral.

Despite my downer, I grinned. 'Sounds great.'

'But we're busy this morning, Marcus. Remember you wanted to take me to the Philadelphan Gallery. To see Zeuxis's *Flower Girl*.'

'Uh, yeah. Yeah, that's right. Zeuxis's *Flower Girl*. I'd forgotten.' Jupiter! Intellectually, Perilla might be capable of giving Aristotle a run for his marbles but as far as thinking up plausible excuses went a parrot could've done better. And if she really expected me to go and look at a four-hundred-year-old painting just to avoid picking over material with Acutia she'd have to drag me there with a hook.

'Perilla said you'd made other plans.' Acutia looked like a kid who'd just had her Winter Festival pastry swiped. 'Such a pity. Still, the Zeuxis is beautiful. You'll enjoy it.'

'Maybe some other time,' I said.

It could've been something in my voice, but Perilla looked at me sharply. 'What's wrong, Corvinus?' she said.

There wasn't any reason not to tell her, really, even with Acutia there. It'd be all over Antioch by now anyway. 'Lamia's just kicked us out,' I said. 'We're leaving in five days, on the *Castor*.' Perilla's eyes widened, but she didn't say anything. Nor did Acutia. I wondered if she knew already, and why, or if it was just tact or part of her murine act. 'He was pretty good about it, but five days is all we've got.'

'The *Castor* is really very nice.' Acutia finally broke the silence. 'It's a government warship fitted out for passengers. So much faster and more comfortable than these terrible merchantmen. Luckily Publius being on the senior staff we don't have to use them ourselves, but still . . .' Her voice faded away as if she didn't have the energy to finish the sentence, or keep up the act. 'And Antioch gets so busy in the summer. Not to mention Daphne. It's not nearly such a nice place, you'd hate it.'

Perilla was still looking at me. I wished we'd been alone, but short of picking our visitor up by the scruff of the neck and dragging her to her carriage there wasn't a lot I could do. Acutia took a cake and bit delicately. I just knew she'd chew thirty-three times before swallowing. She did.

'Are you going straight back, have you decided?' she asked me. 'Or will you be stopping off on the way?'

Small talk's not my bag. 'If the *Castor's* a government boat, lady,' I said, 'we won't have that option.'

'Oh, but you will! Of course you will! You don't have to stay with the *Castor*. I mean, you could change ships at Rhodes. Such a nice place! And if you're not in any hurry you could see some of the Greek cities.' She turned to Perilla. 'Ephesus is so lovely. And I have friends there who would be delighted to put you up. Then my sister is married to a marble exporter in Corinth. Corinth has some simply marvellous statues, and as for the temples, of course . . .'

'I don't think so, Acutia,' Perilla said gently. 'I imagine Marcus will be glad to get home. Won't you, Marcus?'

'Yeah.' Too right I would. Especially if the alternative was more temples and statues. I swallowed the wine in my cup at a gulp and lifted the jug that Critias had left in its cooler.

'Of course,' Acutia was saying, 'if you did leave the *Castor* in Rhodes you could cross over to Alexandria and sail up the Nile. I've always wanted to do that, but Publius being a senator it's impossible. At least without the emperor's permission. Such a silly rule, I always think, not to allow senators into Egypt. But naturally since you haven't held senatorial office yet, Corvinus, there's no reason why you can't . . .'

'Shit!'

'*Marcus!*'

I grabbed a napkin and mopped up the wine that had spilled all down my mantle, while Perilla glared at me and Acutia watched with her big, wide, beautiful brown eyes. I could've kissed her. I almost did.

'Uh, sorry,' I said. 'The jug slipped.'

'That was no excuse for the language,' Perilla said primly. 'Acutia, I apologise. Marcus can be terribly crude.'

'Not at all.' Acutia took another cake. 'Publius is just as bad at times. But honestly, dear, do think about going to Alex and doing the Nile. They say that the sunset on the pyramids is absolutely fantastic. And as for the temples . . .'

But I'd stopped listening. I had other things to think about. And as I thought everything slid smoothly into place.

You see, I'd just realised why Germanicus had had to die.

33

'The guy was a traitor,' I said when I finally got Perilla alone.

'*What?*'

'Germanicus was engaged in active treason against the emperor.'

'Marcus, Germanicus was Tiberius's named successor! Why should he commit treason?'

I poured myself a fresh cup of Chian. 'Why I'm not absolutely certain about yet. But he was planning to knock the Wart off his perch sure as eggs is eggs.'

'All right.' Perilla sat back and folded her arms. 'Prove it.'

I leaned over and kissed her. 'Okay. Only I'll start at the end, because that's what set me off. Your little fluffy pal Acutia's point about Egypt. No one above the rank of knight's been allowed in Egypt without the emperor's permission since Augustus, right? Especially members of the imperial family.'

'Correct.'

'Why not?'

'Because Egypt supplies most of Rome's grain. Technically whoever holds Egypt, and Alexandria especially, could starve the city in a month.'

'Yeah. And by that time the city mob, who are no respecters of persons where the corn dole's threatened, would have the emperor strung up from the nearest architrave. So who's the blue-eyed boy who goes swanning off to Egypt for a winter break after he's settled the hash of the Parthians?'

'Corvinus, he might've had permission!'

'Like hell he did.'

'But he went as a tourist! A cruise up the Nile isn't treason!'

'Sure. But there was a corn shortage in Alex that winter and Germanicus opened the granaries to the mob. Simple tourists don't have that sort of clout, or if they do they're politic enough not to use it in case it gets misconstrued. Added to which, if you believe the stories, the guy swapped his toga for the duration for a Greek mantle. No self-respecting Roman's done that since Africanus two hundred years back, and he was half Greek anyway.'

'Now stop it! You're twisting things!' Perilla was staring at me. 'If the emperor had been aware of the famine he'd have authorised opening the granaries himself. And Scipio Africanus wasn't even part Greek.'

I grinned. 'Okay, so forget the mantle. But it sure as hell made an impression on the locals. And you take my point about the corn.'

'No. I don't. Just because Germanicus acted humanely to relieve a food shortage . . .'

'Perilla, be realistic! We're talking basic economics here. Egyptian corn's Rome's life blood, and we don't give it away for the asking. Not to nobody. Right or wrong we've got our own priorities.'

She ignored me. 'If he had shown the least sign of improper conduct – real improper conduct – in Egypt I might be inclined to believe this theory of yours, but he didn't. He simply used his own initiative and if he erred he erred from the best motives. Now tell me what happened at your interview with the governor. That's far more important at present.'

'Uh-uh.' I shook my head. 'No it isn't. Maybe it doesn't even matter any more.'

'Marcus, you might not mind being given five days to leave a province before you're frogmarched to the boat but I do. Perhaps if I see the governor myself, or maybe Vibius Marsus, I can . . .'

'It wouldn't do any good. Believe me. You've met Lamia. You think he's the kind of guy to give way to a pair of batting eyelashes?'

'No.' She sighed. 'Perhaps not. All right, then, let's go back to your theory. Suppose we forget the corn issue and you tell me why you think the simple fact of Germanicus's taking a holiday in a politically incorrect province should make him a traitor.'

'Okay.' I sat back and cradled my wine cup. 'Like I said that's just the end point in a series. Let's start with Germany six years back. You remember what happened then?'

'Of course. After Augustus died the northern legions mutinied. Or some of them did.'

'Right. There were two outbreaks, one in Pannonia, one in Germany itself. Drusus put down the first, Germanicus was responsible for dealing with the second.'

'You're not saying, I hope, that Germanicus engineered the mutinies?'

I shook my head. 'No, it isn't as simple as that. They were spontaneous, and I don't think at that point betraying the Wart had even occurred to the guy. In fact I doubt if left to himself he'd ever have really made the grade in the treachery stakes. Unless he was a lot more devious than I give him credit for.'

Perilla groaned. 'Corvinus, be sensible! One minute you're claiming that Germanicus was a traitor and then you say the man didn't have the capacity for treason. Don't you see any inconsistency there?'

'No, lady, I don't. Left to himself, I said.'

'But . . . !'

'Just bear with me, okay? Gaius Secundus told me about the Rhine mutiny back at Rome. Drusus waded in and had the whole thing sewn up inside a month while Germanicus screwed around on the sidelines tut-tutting like a sixty-year-old virgin and appealing to the squaddies' better natures. Finally the senior officers had to take matters into their own hands. Now what does that tell you?'

'Nothing whatsoever.'

'Jupiter!' I closed my eyes. 'Perilla, it's obvious. The mutineers were on to a loser from the start, but as far as the rank-and-file were concerned Germanicus came out smelling of roses. The real hard men were Drusus in Pannonia, the officers of the German army who did the dirty work, and the Wart himself. Especially the Wart. Roman squaddies may have the moral standards of Ostian brothel-keepers, but they like to believe that they're sensitive souls and they don't forget their enemies. Or their friends. Germanicus was on their side, he was an okay guy saddled by the emperor with a dirty job not of his choosing. Am I making sense or do I have to draw you a picture?'

'You're saying,' she said slowly, 'that Germanicus ended up with the legions' sympathy. Whereas Tiberius and Drusus didn't.'

'Right.' I nodded. 'And that's the key to the whole business. Sympathy and popularity. Whether Germanicus acted consciously or whether he was the simple-minded idealist he seemed I don't know. The main thing was he had something else going for him as well. Or rather someone.'

She had it now. 'His wife Agrippina.'

'Yeah. It was her and young Gaius who were largely responsible for changing the soldiers' minds and ending the mutiny. More, she's army to the bone, and squaddies appreciate that.' I took a swallow of wine. 'So. The mutiny was put down. What happened next?'

'Germanicus led the troops against the tribes on the other side of the Rhine.'

'Right. And whatever the political ins and outs were, as far as the lads on the ground were concerned he went further and did more than any other general since his father. Only the Wart pulled him back before he'd finished the campaign. Result?'

'Germanicus left Germany a hero to the troops. And again Tiberius was cast as the villain.' Perilla was looking thoughtful. 'Corvinus, I'm afraid you're beginning to make sense.'

'Good.' I took another swig of wine. 'Okay. So now we come to the eastern trip. The Wart sends our blue-eyed boy east. The first place he goes is Pannonia. Why would he do that?'

'Drusus is there. And Germanicus has despatches from the emperor.'

'Yeah. Both true. Anything else? Remember we're assuming the guy's a rotten apple. Or that he's planning to be. Think army.'

'Pannonia has the biggest concentration of legions between ...' Perilla caught her breath, then finished more slowly: 'Between the Rhine and Syria.'

'Correct. And the next legionary base down is Egypt. Where Germanicus later chooses to spend his winter holiday. Am I still making sense?'

'Yes.' She was frowning. 'Yes, you are. Very much so. Go on, please.'

'Secundus told me one of the things Germanicus did in Pannonia was to review the troops. Maybe there was nothing more to it than that but I think there was. The army's a tight family, especially along the Rhine and Danube frontier. A lot of the Pannonian squaddies would know Germanicus, by reputation at least. The officers, too. Especially the junior ones and the NCOs, and they're the ones that count. A personal visit would be something they'd appreciate.'

'You think he was canvassing for support?'

'Sure. Maybe not overtly, but the guy had charm and he would've used it. Like he did in Egypt. Sympathy and popularity, remember?'

She was definitely with me now. 'The Greek tour fits too. And the visit to Actium. Most of the client-kings come from the old Greek families who supported Antony in the civil war. It'd be a reminder to them that he was Mark Antony's grandson as well as an adopted Caesar, wouldn't it?'

'Yeah.' I paused with my hand on the wine jug. Antony's grandson. That was an angle I hadn't thought of. 'Hey, well done, lady.'

She was right, of course, and it fitted. Even after fifty years, to the Greek-speaking half of the empire Antony was still a hero because together with the Greek queen Cleopatra he'd led them against Octavian's Rome. The fight off Actium had been Greece's last stand, and even although Antony had been beaten the Asian Greeks had never forgotten him. I remembered what Orosius had said about them not finding Romans sympathetic. They'd liked Germanicus, though. They'd liked him a lot. He'd made sure of that. And not just Greeks, either. To the native Egyptians Cleopatra was still their greatest queen ever. And an interest in the local culture, expressed by a trip down the Nile to look at the monuments, would go down a bomb with them. Added to which they had even less cause than the Alexandrian Greeks to be grateful to Rome, because all we meant to them was oppression and taxes. Shit. It worked. It all fitted together like the bits of a mosaic . . .

'Marcus?' Perilla was looking at me.

'He had it all sewn up,' I said quietly. 'He and Agrippina were popular with the Senate and the mob in Rome, far more popular than the Wart and Livia. He had the northern legions in his pocket, maybe even the Pannonian ones. He'd only have to lift his little finger and the whole Greek east including the Alexandrians who sent the corn ships and the Egyptians who grew the corn would've been behind him. Only he had to have Syria too, because if he wanted to play Antony in a rematch against the Wart's Octavian Syria's four legions were too important for him to ignore. Meanwhile, Tiberius's hands were tied because the guy hadn't made a single overtly treasonable move. And he wouldn't, either. Not until he'd got all the sympathy and support he needed and he was good and ready to use it, by which time it'd be all over bar the shouting.'

I swallowed half the wine at a gulp. Perilla was sitting very still.

'So, Corvinus,' she said. 'What happened in Syria?'

34

'What happened in Syria,' I said, 'was that the Wart pulled the plug and sent him down the tube.'

Perilla shifted. 'You mean Tiberius knew?'

'Sure he knew. That's the whole point. He knew what Germanicus had in mind before he sent him east.'

'And how do you work that out?'

'Simple.' I poured myself more of the wine. 'It explains Piso. And it explains the cover-up here. Piso wasn't sent out because Tiberius didn't trust his son to do a good job; he was sent because the Wart didn't trust him full stop. And he was right.'

'But, Marcus, if the emperor thought that Germanicus intended to commit treason then why didn't he simply have him arrested?'

'Jupiter, Perilla! We've been through that! Germanicus was the empire's blue-eyed boy, and like you said he was his named successor. If Tiberius had called in the heavies he'd've had a full-scale rebellion on his hands before the ink was dry on the warrant. The same would hold if he just had him chopped. Especially since everyone knew – or thought they knew – that he was jealous as hell of his own crown prince. Besides, what proof did he have? Popularity isn't a crime, and Germanicus hadn't said one word or done one thing out of place. The Wart's fair, too fair to act out of hand. All he could do was give the guy enough rope and leave him to prove to his satisfaction that he deserved hanging. Which Germanicus did.'

'But you said yourself, poisoning isn't Tiberius's way.'

'Yeah.' I sat back scowling. 'That's the problem. The more I think about it the more I'm convinced Livia was involved right up to her eyebrows. Lamia as good as admitted it. When I said

I'd come from the empress it really threw the guy. I swear he was going to say the empress knew already. And personally, fancy oaths or not, I wouldn't put it past her.'

'But why should Livia poison Germanicus? Especially for the emperor? They haven't got on for years.'

'That's where Agrippina comes in. Sure, Germanicus was a traitor, but I'd bet a gold piece to a rotten cabbage his wife pushed him into it. Like I say, I doubt if left to himself he'd've had the heart for treason. Agrippina's different. That lady's got the heart and the stomach. And she has a pretty big axe to grind because thanks to the empress's little efforts over the years the Wart's on the throne and she's the last of the Julians.'

Perilla nodded. 'Yes. Yes, that makes sense,' she said. 'Agrippina certainly hates Tiberius and Livia, and it's mutual. If the Imperials were responsible and she knew it it would explain her conduct in bringing Germanicus's ashes back; she was bringing his murder home to his killers, in both senses of the phrase. Another thing. With Germanicus dead and Drusus Tiberius's heir the succession would be firmly back in the Claudian line. That would certainly weigh with Livia.'

'Too right it would, lady!'

'But why should she actually go out of her way to ask you to investigate the death if she was partly responsible?'

I shrugged. 'Jupiter knows. She could have her reasons, oath or not. What I do know is that trying to second-guess the empress is like playing tag with a leopard, there's no future in it. Leave it for later. We've got enough to keep us going here already.'

'What about Piso? You say Tiberius sent him to Syria to keep an eye on Germanicus?'

'Yeah.' I took a swallow of wine: the chill was off it now, and I topped it up with fresh from the jug. 'That must've been a real facer for the lad. Germanicus had made the last governor Creticus sweet with the promise of a marriage between the guy's daughter and his eldest son. Now Piso comes out from Rome, gets in ahead of the game and changes everything round. Not for reasons of favouritism like Taurus said. Piso was acting on the Wart's instructions: cancel all the old appointments just in case they'd been got at, replace them with his own men, people he trusted. And while he's at it, finesse Germanicus at his own game by getting the squaddies on his side so when the blue-eyed boy does arrive Piso's well and truly in the saddle and there's nowhere left to go. No wonder the two couples hated each other right from the start. Germanicus and Agrippina had been rumbled, and they knew it. Knowing they couldn't let on, because they weren't at the stage yet of open revolt, must've driven them spare. It explains why Piso wouldn't let Germanicus have the legions he wanted in Armenia, too. They represented half his force and he couldn't risk them being got at, or used to trigger the revolt itself.'

'Do you think Germanicus and Agrippina knew? That Piso had been sent to keep them under observation?'

'Maybe not for sure. But they must've suspected. And in any case Germanicus would have to keep up the pretence by sending the Wart regular complaints. He couldn't afford not to; to admit even tacitly that Piso was acting under orders would've been to confess his own guilt. Or at least bring the issue out into the open, and that was something he couldn't afford to do until he was ready.' I took a mouthful of wine. 'Which, incidentally, was where the Vonones scam came in.'

Perilla frowned. 'Vonones was involved with Germanicus?'

I shook my head. 'No. That part of it was completely separate. Vonones's problem was that from Germanicus's point of view he was a prime nuisance. His plan for a general revolt in the east had been too like Germanicus's own for comfort, and it may even have put the idea into the Wart's head. Germanicus's other down on the guy was that he was muddying the waters. Even after Tiberius wrecked his plans Vonones carried on plotting, and he was drawing too much attention. Sure, Germanicus probably knew, maybe through Celer, that Vonones was bribing Piso, but he was trapped. He couldn't blow the whistle on Piso without calling attention to his own plans.'

'And so he had Vonones killed.'

'He had Vonones killed. To keep the bribes coming Piso had told the guy that Germanicus was under suspicion, and so long as Piso seemed to have the upper hand Vonones was happy to wait. But when Germanicus was riding high after the Parthian deal Vonones lost confidence. He cut and ran, probably with

Germanicus's connivance. The poor bastard never even made the border.'

Perilla was quiet for a long time. Then she said: 'So you've got it all.'

I tipped the last of the wine into my cup. 'No. Not all. There're too many loose ends. If Germanicus was a traitor it explains a lot, but it doesn't explain everything. Sure, Piso's so-called treason makes sense. Even though Germanicus was dead his friends still held Syria because he'd reversed Piso's appointments, and Piso was only doing his job in trying to retake his province for the Wart. It explains why Piso and Plancina were so confident of Tiberius's support when they went back to Rome. It explains Lamia's cover-up. But it doesn't explain the *way* Germanicus died. It doesn't explain Regulus's murder or Carillus's missing letter. It doesn't explain why I was attacked on the ship or even why Orosius was shot. And it doesn't explain Martina's pal Mancus, either. Along with half a dozen other things that're simply wrong.'

'But Corvinus, surely if the emperor is responsible it could explain most of these things?'

'No.' I closed my eyes and leaned back. 'No, that's the point, lady. This whole business isn't like the Wart, none of it, not even at second hand. It's clumsy, it's ragged at the edges, it creaks like hell, it throws up too much dirt and it doesn't have his signature. Orosius said Tiberius was too clever for a Roman, and he was right. He'd've done things different and managed them better. Sure, he was the one to benefit from Germanicus's death and he must've approved it, but the way things panned out he might just as well have had the guy knifed or strangled and saved himself the hassle because everyone thinks he was responsible anyway. Livia's the same.'

'But . . .'

'Yeah, I know what I said, and maybe I'm still wrong. The poison angle, yes, that's her all over. But Livia would've managed things better as well. This way there's far too much mud flying around, and a lot of it sticks to her as well as to the Wart. Besides, if Livia's involved then we've still got to explain why she should get me to go through the motions. No, the case isn't solved yet. Not by a long chalk.'

'And now we only have five days.'

'Sure. But like I said I don't think it matters any more. Syria's played out.' I shook the jug. 'Like the wine. If we're looking for more answers than we've already got, lady, we'll find them back in Rome.'

Yeah. Maybe.

35

Acutia was right. The *Castor* was a lot more comfortable than the *Artemis*. Faster, too, even although the wind was against us all the way: being a trireme we didn't need the sails, and these boats can shift when the rowers hit form. Not that there was much difference otherwise. The captain was probably Theon's cousin, but I never asked; I lost my breakfast before we'd cleared Seleucia harbour and threw up all the way to Puteoli.

It was good to see Rome again, even in the dark (we got back after sunset). Smell it, too. Maybe it was my imagination but the first whiff of the Tiber seemed to hit my nostrils just as our hired carriage passed through the Appian Gate, and to a Roman coming home from abroad there ain't no better smell than ripe Tiber mud.

Bathyllus was waiting outside the front door when we pulled up. Jupiter knows how he knew we were coming, but he even had a flask of my best Falernian standing on the table in the hall, with a red ribbon round the neck and a tag saying 'Welcome home'. I was touched. While Meton shot off to check that nobody had filched his best omelette pan while he'd been away I gave the little guy the stoppered jar I'd picked up in the Old Market before we left.

'Thank you, sir.' He pulled the plug and took a cautious sniff. 'How interesting. What is it? Cockroach killer?'

'Hair restorer, you ungrateful bastard. The best in Antioch.' I was pouring my first cup of Falernian for two months. Slowly. Some pleasures you spin out. 'Made to an ancient Indian recipe based on silphium and tiger urine, handed down from father to son for six hundred years.'

'The urine or the recipe, sir?'

'Cut it out, sunshine.' Jupiter! Now even Bathyllus was making jokes. 'The shopkeeper swore it'd grow hair on the Golden Milestone, but if you don't want it . . .'

'Oh, Marcus!' Perilla was wearing her look of prim disapproval. 'You didn't actually buy that stuff, did you?'

'Sure I did.' I lifted the cup of Falernian and sipped, letting the liquid magic find its own way past my tonsils. Bliss! 'Don't knock it, lady. Come the next Games we'll have the hairiest major-domo in Rome.'

'Or possibly a total dearth of cockroaches, sir.'

'You say something, Bathyllus?'

'No, sir. Nothing of any importance.'

'Fine, fine.' I took in some more Falernian. Jupiter, that was good! Almost worth going the length of Syria for. I'd brought back a few jars of Chian, but it wasn't the same out of context. The glasses I hadn't had time to find. 'So how've things been? Any messages while we were away?'

'One from your client Scylax, sir. Almost a month ago now. He said the butcher was back in Rome. I hope that makes sense.'

'Yeah. Yeah, it does. That's great.' It was. Before we'd left I'd asked Scylax to keep his ear to the ground for news of Carillus, and with Piso's messenger boy (and possibly Regulus's murderer) home from the sticks we might be in business again. 'Anything from Lippillus?'

'Who, sir?'

'The guy from the Aventine Watch.'

'Oh, yes.' I noticed that Bathyllus had surreptitiously recorked the hair restorer. Smart move: it was strong stuff. Jupiter knows what these Indian guys had fed the tigers on, but I could feel the hairs in my nostrils beginning to curl. 'Much more recently, within the last ten days. The enquiry has been discontinued, sir. The young gentleman hasn't yet been able to ascertain who apart from the Watch commander himself was responsible.'

'Uhuh.' That was a name I badly needed, but I was glad Lippillus wasn't busting a gut to find it for me. Men like him were thin enough on the ground in the Watch already without me putting them in the way of a quiet knife in the ribs. 'He'll let me know if and when he does find out?'

'Yes, sir. He said on no account to contact him in the meantime.'

Lippillus was clever all right, and I was glad he'd taken my warning to heart. Maybe I could ferret out that particular goody from Uncle Cotta; but not tonight. It could've been the wine on an empty stomach – I never eat when I'm travelling – but I suddenly felt dead beat. I looked at Perilla. She'd taken off her hooded cloak and was handing it to Phryne to fold, and her hair shone in the light from the hall candelabrum.

Well, it was good to be home. And maybe I wasn't that dead beat after all.

I went round to Scylax's gym the next morning. It looked just the same as usual; some things don't change. Daphnis was pushing the same bit of sand with the same rake. I wondered what the guy did when he went home at night to relax. Probably watched rocks growing.

'Hey, Daphnis!' I called. 'Is the boss around?'

I got the long slow stare. I doubt if he'd even noticed I'd been gone.

'Yeah. He's in the office.'

'Right.' I set off across the empty yard – no punters today, it seemed – then stopped and turned. 'By the way, you got any hobbies?'

'Hobbies?' Daphnis's jaw slumped.

'When you're not working. What do you do?'

'I look at statues.'

'Uh . . . yeah. Right.' Well, I'd asked.

'You know how many statues there are in Rome, Corvinus?' He'd dropped his rake and he was following me like a dog. There was a light in the bastard's eyes that I hadn't seen before and I didn't want to see again. '*Real* statues?'

'Tell me some time.' I moved off again. Quickly. 'I'll catch up with you later, Daphnis, okay?'

'Temples are pretty interesting, too. I like temples.'

Shit. The rot was spreading. First Bathyllus's jokes, now Daphnis. Maybe you could catch it, like eczema. I wasn't taking any risks.

When I got to the office Scylax was fixing a broken sandal strap. He looked up. 'Hey, look what the cat's dragged in,' he said. 'Take a seat, Corvinus. You have a nice time in Antioch?'

Well, at least he'd remembered. I sat down on the bench. 'You know your yard skivvy was a connoisseur of art?'

'Daphnis? Sure.' He worked the bradawl through the leather. 'He knows a lot, too. Mention Polycleitus's Canon to him sometime and he'll talk the pants off you.'

'Is that right?' I didn't think I could take this. Not on my first day home. I changed the subject. 'Bathyllus says you left a message for me. About Carillus.'

'Your butcher pal?' Scylax laid the bradawl aside, threaded a needle with catgut and tied a knot in the end. 'Yeah. He's back. I had someone stake out the shop and follow him around like you asked.'

'And?'

He shrugged. 'And nothing. Nothing you'd want to know about, anyway. The guy's squeaky-clean, Corvinus. He sells meat, goes back and forward to his slaughterhouse up by the tanneries. Drinks beer. You sure you're interested in him?'

'Yeah. Very. No particular friends?'

'Locals, in the meat trade mostly. And the beer and barley bread contingent in the German beerhouse, of course.'

No mileage in that. 'What's his address?'

'He lives over the shop.' Scylax put the needle through the first of the holes and pulled the gut tight. 'First-floor flat.'

'He ever leave the Subura at all?'

'Not that I know of.'

Hell. I'd been hoping Carillus had kept in touch with his boss, whoever that was. He'd be a middleman, sure, especially if Tiberius was involved, but I couldn't imagine the Wart in a fake blond wig and moustaches, swilling beer and hacking chops. If I wanted to find out more about Piso's death, and that elusive disappearing letter, I'd have to do it the hard way, starting with Carillus himself. I stood up.

'Yeah, okay,' I said. 'Thanks, pal. I owe you one.'

'Forget it.' Scylax stuck the needle through the last hole in the strap, knotted the gut and cut it. 'Take it easy, okay?'

'Sure. Thanks again. See you later.'

Outside, Daphnis was still pushing sand. This time I gave him a wide berth.

There wasn't any point in going straight round to the butcher's shop. I wanted my second interview with Carillus to be private, and he wouldn't finish work until nearer sunset. A bit of extra back-up wouldn't go amiss either, from someone I trusted. So it meant the Subura in any case, Agron's metalsmith business near the Shrine of Libera.

I spent the time it took to cross the city thinking. The Wart was involved, sure; he had to be, because Germanicus was definitely a traitor and his death had been necessary for the safety of Rome. The cover-up in Syria had been official as well, and something like that needed top-level clout. So the emperor knew and approved, and the final responsibility had to be his. End of story, close the book, you might say. The trouble was I had a beginning and an end, but no middle. Like I'd told Perilla there were too many loose ends, the biggest one of which was the way the whole affair had been managed. Sure, Tiberius couldn't risk having his son arrested and openly charged; that would've sparked off a civil war that the Wart might not have won. Not when the guy had so many legions in his pocket and so much support; at the very least it would've torn the empire apart, and Tiberius wouldn't've risked that. He'd had a rough enough time as it was. An accident I might've believed – a boating accident, say, on the way back from Egypt, or a straightforward killing. But not poison. I'd never believe poison of the Wart, not directly.

So. We were back with Livia, or Plancina, or Drusus's wife Livilla. They all had motives of different kinds, they all had the clout to arrange things at second hand, and they could all count on getting away with it as far as the emperor was concerned.

I didn't believe Livia, not when it got right down to it. Sure, the empress would be the best bet: she hated Agrippina, she saw herself as the guardian of Rome and despite everything I couldn't see her allowing the Wart to be toppled and a Julian dynasty set up in his place. But unless she was playing a very deep game indeed swearing an unnecessary oath and getting me to dig the dirt after it'd already begun to settle made no sense at all. Plancina was more possible, and from what I'd heard of her she could've carried it through. She and Piso knew about Germanicus's treason and had secret orders to watch him. She was on the spot, and she had her friendship with the empress to protect her. Maybe she'd just used her own initiative, with or without her husband's knowledge, and relied on the end justifying the means. Even although Baucis had said she'd had no connection with her sister, Mancus, whoever he was, could easily have been her agent. And Plancina had a direct link with Carillus, who'd been Piso's freedman. Sure, the Wart had dropped Piso like a hot brick, but that wasn't Plancina's fault. She could've just miscalculated.

I was into the Subura now. You can keep the colonnades of Antioch, this was home. I cut down Cheesemakers' Alley specially to buy Agron one of the wicked-smelling blue cheeses from the Po valley he was so fond of, stopped off to watch a juggler at the corner of Spice Street (he wasn't very good, but he was getting plenty of laughs so maybe it was intentional) and found Perilla a pair of pomegranate earrings that she'd never wear but would be good for a laugh when I got back.

So. Livilla. We hadn't really considered Livilla on her own, but maybe we should. With her new pregnancy she had the motive, and Secundus had said there was a lot of the old empress in her. Enough, maybe, for her to want her husband on the throne rather than her brother after the Wart was fitted for his death mask and not balk too much over how she went about it. She could count on Tiberius's support, too, and I'd heard that she and the empress didn't get on despite – or maybe because of – the similarity in character. And I'd bet a gold piece to a brass button that she could twist Drusus round her little finger, which wouldn't make her too popular with his grandmother Livia either. Yeah, Livilla was a real possibility. The only problem with her was the means; but then maybe she had friends. Maybe even a friend like Plancina . . .

I stopped just in time to watch where I was putting my feet and stepped over a pile of donkey droppings. Pairing the two was an interesting scenario. The problem with fingering Plancina on her own was she'd be taking one hell of a risk without the promise of anything definite at the end. But if Plancina had been working for Livilla just as her husband was working for the emperor a lot of things would make sense. The Wart couldn't last for ever: he was in his sixties now, he drank too much and he lived hard. By poisoning Germanicus for Livilla Plancina would be getting the best of all possible worlds: she'd have the Wart's blessing, even if it was a sour one, for executing a traitor; she'd stand in well with the next empress; and she'd be doing herself and her husband a favour at the same time. It would explain Livia's attitude too, and her desire to see the case reopened: her friend Plancina would be safe under the amnesty but Livilla herself would be compromised. And I doubted if the empress would shed any tears if that happened.

Yeah. I liked Livilla. I liked her a lot. But then there was the question of finding the missing connections . . .

I turned into Metalsmith's Row, where Agron had his black-smith's shop. The shop was open, but the guy swinging the hammer was Agron's assistant.

'Hi, Sextus. Where's the boss?' I said.

Sextus hefted whatever he was making – it looked like part of an iron gate – and pushed it back into the forge to heat.

'Making a delivery,' he said. 'He'll be back later.'

'How much later?'

'Two hours. Maybe three. Customer's on the other side of the Tiber.'

'Can I leave a message, pal?'

'Sure. I'm not going anywhere.'

There wasn't any way round it. I left my name and asked him to get Agron to meet me at Carillus's shop at sundown. Which, considering what Fate had up her sleeve for me in the next few hours, was one of the smartest moves I ever made.

36

It wasn't worth going home. I went down to the Market Square to tell my banker I was back in town and pick up some of the latest gossip, then killed another hour or two in Gorgio's wineshop off the Sacred Way. The sun was already setting by the time I got to Carillus's. There was no sign of Agron.

Carillus was there, though, putting up the shutters: he must've been working late. He saw me at the same time as I saw him. If I'd expected the guy to look or act guilty I was disappointed.

'Hey, Corvinus!' he said. 'How's the Roman beer-drinker?'

'Okay.' I went over and waited while he fixed on the padlock.

'Good.' He slipped the key into the pouch at his belt. 'You have time for a quick jar?'

That I didn't need. 'I was hoping for a quiet word, friend. Somewhere private.'

'Yeah?' He shot me a look. 'Well, then, you're out of luck. I usually spend an hour at Hilde's after we close up. You want to tag along, that's fine with me.'

'Hilde's is the beer shop we were in last time?'

'That's right.' He was grinning.

'She sell wine as well as horse piss?'

The grin broadened. 'Don't call good beer that in Hilde's hearing if you value your skull, pal. Yeah, she's got a flask or two put by for delicate stomachs.'

'Right. Let's go, then,' I said. I didn't like it more than half, but I didn't have much choice. And if the talk wasn't to be particularly private at least there'd be a crowd, which was the next best thing.

The beer shop, if I remembered right, was further down on the other side of the street. Sure enough Carillus moved off in that direction. 'You been out of Rome?' he said.

'Yeah. In Antioch.'

'Uhuh.' I couldn't see his eyes, but his voice didn't alter. 'Business?'

'You could call it that.'

'Never been east myself. They say it's something else.'

'It's okay.' I was beginning to have my doubts about Carillus. The guy seemed straight. Maybe he hadn't murdered Regulus, the letter was a red herring after all, and his slaughterhouse deed was all there'd ever been. Cotta wasn't the most reliable informant of all time, and a butcher's hook could've come from anywhere.

We reached the beer shop. The place wasn't as crowded as I thought it would be: there were only four guys there, all Germans from the look of them, and as we went in two of these got up and left. Carillus sat down at the empty table and gave our order to the old woman. I was no linguist but it sounded okay, and sure enough Hilde went off grumbling while the two Germans sniggered into their pots and swapped guttural comments.

Maybe they knew something I didn't because the wine when it came was as bad as the beer, third-rate Massic just a step this side of vinegar. Still at least it was made from grapes not horse fodder, and with that in front of me I wouldn't be faced with a drinking bout like last time.

'So.' Carillus set down his half-empty beaker and wiped the suds off his face. 'What can I do for you now, Roman?'

'You know a guy called Regulus?'

I was watching his eyes. I caught the tell-tale flicker and I knew beyond all doubt that I hadn't made any mistake. Carillus was a good actor, sure, and he was expecting the question, but it still hit him where it hurt. Straight, hell, the guy had beans to spill. It was just a question of getting him to spill them.

'Piso's lawyer, right? Or one of them.'

'Yeah. He was found at the bottom of the Gemonian Stairs just before I left Rome.' I took a second sip of wine and decided that a third would be one too many. 'Just before you left Rome too.

Someone had knifed him and put a hook through his throat. A butcher's hook.'

'A butcher's hook. Is that right, now?' Very deliberately Carillus lifted his beaker, drained it and set it down. Unasked, the old woman came across and refilled it. 'And just because of that you think I killed him.'

'I know you did, sunshine,' I said quietly. 'What I don't know is who for and why. But then that's what you're going to tell me.'

This time he didn't blink. 'You're crazy, Corvinus.'

'Because I think you killed Regulus? Or because I think you'll tell me why? I'm right on both counts.'

'I never even met the guy.' He wasn't angry and he didn't raise his voice. The bastard even had the beginnings of a smile. 'I'm a butcher. I don't move in these circles. So why should I want to murder him?'

'That was my question.'

He made to stand up, not quickly but like he'd finished his beer and was going home. I grabbed his wrist. The two Germans at the other table looked over with bleary-eyed interest but he growled something and they snickered and went back to humming lieder. I'd expected him to break free – with his size and weight he could've done it easy – but he didn't. He only glanced down at my hand, grinned and lowered himself back on to the bench.

'Okay. I'll say it again, friend, because maybe you didn't hear me the first time,' he said. 'I may know who Regulus was but I never met him, I had nothing against him, and you are crazy. That answer your question?'

'Okay.' I let go of his wrist. 'Now I'll tell you something. You're in this up to your eyeballs, pal. You know that, I know that, so let's cut the crap. Now you may be working for the emperor, and if so then I'm making a bad mistake. But if you aren't, and I'm willing to bet you aren't' – did his eyelids flicker? I couldn't be sure – 'then you're up shit creek without a paddle. Because unless your patron has a hell of a lot of clout and he's willing to use it to keep you safe I'll make it my business to nail your hide to a cask of beer and roll it down the Gemonian Stairs myself. You understand?'

He was watching me carefully, like he was trying to make up

his mind. He still looked cocky but the grin had slipped a bit. Maybe I was getting through to him after all.

Was I hell. Or at least not the way I wanted to. With his eyes still on me he said something to Hilde that made the two crooners at the other table sit up sharp. The old girl shuffled over to the door, slipped the bolts top and bottom and then went back behind the counter.

We were all on our feet now, crooners included. One was hefting a solid-looking blackjack like he knew how to use it. The other absently broke his pottery beaker against the table and inspected the jagged edge. I pulled my knife and slowly backed up until I felt the wall of the beer shop grate against my spine.

Carillus hadn't moved, and his arms hung loose. 'Okay, Corvinus,' he said. 'You've convinced me. Maybe you're safer dead after all.' He added something in German.

The guy with the blackjack moved round to my right while Beaker crossed behind Carillus and came up on the other side. They were weaving a bit and belching but they weren't as drunk as I'd hoped they'd be. Or as neutral. Teutonic solidarity, let's all get the Roman. Shit. I cursed myself for nine kinds of smartass fool and wished I'd stayed home with Perilla pressing flowers.

Beaker moved first, then Blackjack a split second later. After twenty days on a ship and no exercise for the best part of two months I was way out of shape. My kick missed Beaker's groin, but got him in the thigh. The knife was years too late and my head exploded as the blackjack hit my ear like a sackful of rocks. Carillus leaped forward, and I could just see the glint of metal in his hand. I yelled and twisted, but not far or fast enough, and the pain lanced through my ribs . . .

I don't know what happened then. It seemed like the far wall burst apart and the roof fell on me at the same time. Then things got confused. Someone – I think it must've been Hilde – was screaming and there were a lot of bodies thrashing about. Then everything went quiet and dark and all I could hear for a while was the drip . . . drip . . . drip of liquid on the floor.

'You okay, Corvinus?' It was Agron. His face bending over me in the darkness looked twice its usual size and he sounded worried as hell.

'Probably not,' I said. 'You tell me.' It was like trying to speak through a woollen blanket. I felt hands against my ribs, and a dull ache.

'Hey! Get a light over here!' Agron again. He repeated it in German and I tried to grin, but it was too painful. Hell. Saved by a polyglot. A lamp appeared somewhere above me and I heard and felt cloth ripping. Then silence and more fingers, probing.

Finally Agron let out his breath. 'You're bleeding like a stuck pig and you've a lump like an egg over your ear,' he said, 'but you'll live. Maybe. Now what the fuck do you think you're doing alone in a German beer dive, you stupid bastard?'

'Being a smartass,' I whispered. It must've got through because I heard him chuckle. 'Where's Carillus?'

'That the big lunk who knifed you? He's gone. Minus a tooth or two, but he got away.' He heaved me to my feet and I almost doubled over with the pain. 'Can you walk?'

'Walking I can manage. Maybe. Running a marathon might be tricky.'

He chuckled again and handed me a piece of rag. 'Okay, Corvinus. Keep that pressed against your ribs, lean on me and take it easy, right?'

My tunic was sodden with blood, and through the rip that Agron had made I could see the damage: a long, deep cut right across the side of the ribs about halfway up my chest ending in a ragged hole. Bad enough, but like Agron had said I'd live. I wouldn't be wrestling pythons for a while, though, that was sure. I'd thought the dripping liquid might be me, but the flask of Massic was on its side on the table and the wine was running over the edge. Well, that was one good thing anyway. At least I hadn't had to drink the stuff, and now no one ever would. I grinned and tried to tell Agron, but the words wouldn't come. Instead I found myself blacking out.

I woke up in bed at home with a splitting headache and a feeling in my chest like an elephant was standing on it with spiked sandals.

'Marcus?' Perilla, of course. She was sitting by the bedside looking like she'd just come back from a wake.

'Yeah. I think so. Where's Agron?' My tongue felt thick, and somebody had filled my mouth with glue.

'He left an hour ago. He said he'd be back later. Marcus, what the *hell* did you think you were doing?'

'Being a smartass. I told him that already.' I tried to sit up and then decided I wouldn't after all. My head was pounding like the worst hangover I'd ever been through, I was bandaged up like an Egyptian mummy, and someone was playing funny buggers with the balance of the room. 'And don't swear, Perilla, it doesn't suit you.'

'If I want to swear I'll swear,' she snapped. 'And smartass describes you perfectly.' Shit. Tied up like this and feeling weak as a kitten I couldn't even run for cover. 'Don't you *ever* do anything like that again, Corvinus, do you hear me?'

'You want to put that in writing, lady?'

She got up quickly and walked over to the door. I thought she was leaving but she just stood there with her forehead pressed to the panelling.

'You could have been killed, Marcus,' she said quietly. 'You almost were. The doctor said another inch to the left and the knife would have punctured a lung. So stop joking about it, please.'

I didn't say anything for a long time. Finally she came over and kissed me. Her cheeks were wet.

'Besides,' she added. 'I'd make a terrible widow.'

I pulled her down on to the bed and put my arm round her waist. It hurt, but it was worth it. 'Agron say how he managed it?'

'Saving your life or getting you home?'

'Whatever. Both.'

'He was passing the beer shop on his way to Carillus's when he heard you yell. He kicked the door down.' I winced, remembering the bolts. Maybe the wood had been rotten, but I wouldn't like to lay any bets. That guy was big. 'Then he carried you round to his workshop and woke up a couple of littermen neighbours.'

'Uhuh. He do anything about Carillus?'

'Marcus, forget about Carillus! He doesn't matter!'

'Sure he does.' I closed my eyes. I suddenly felt sleepy again, and unreal. 'Perilla, will you do something for me? If I'm not awake when Agron gets back ask him to check Carillus's flat. He won't be there, but it's got to be done. Then send round to Scylax's and get him to put the word out.'

'Corvinus . . .'

'Just do it, okay? Please. Tell Scylax.' Maybe the doctor had given me something. My mouth and tongue weren't working properly again and I doubt if she heard me. I felt her hand on my cheek before everything slipped away again into nothing.

37

I was awake when Agron got back after all. Not too bright, but awake.

'You need a minder, Corvinus,' he said when he came in with Perilla. 'That was the stupidest thing I've ever come across.'

'Yeah, and I'm glad to see you too, pal.' I struggled to sit up. It still felt like going through the Straits of Messina in a rowing boat with someone sawing my head open, and it hurt like fury, but this time I made it. 'What about Carillus?'

Agron pulled up a stool. 'Like I said. He got away.'

'You checked his flat?'

'Sure. The place is empty. No wife, no kids. Nothing. He didn't even lock the door when he left.'

Well, I'd been expecting that. And if he'd taken the family with him it looked permanent. Or at least indefinite. 'Maybe Scylax can trace him.'

'Yeah, maybe. Smart thinking, Corvinus. Then you can go round to his new place and let him punch another hole in you.'

'Don't make me laugh, you bastard. It hurts.' I looked at Perilla. 'You sent the message?'

'Yes, I sent the message, but . . .'

'Good. Thanks, lady.' The room was deciding to spin. I closed my eyes and waited until it had finished before opening them again. 'Maybe I should tell you what all this is about, Agron. So next time you save my neck you'll know why you did it.'

'Perilla already told me. While the doctor was patching you up.' Agron wasn't smiling. 'Corvinus, can't you leave this political stuff alone? Or there just might not be a next time.'

'No. Listen, Perilla couldn't've told you all of it because she didn't know. We were right. Sure, the Wart was in on Germanicus's death, but there was someone else involved, someone with a personal axe to grind, and that's who Carillus is working for. He's our only lead. We've got to find him and make him talk.'

'Marcus, you are not going anywhere or doing anything.' Perilla was using the voice that she saved for special occasions like reducing guard dogs to a quivering jelly. 'That is final.'

I was still looking at Agron. 'How about it? Want to deputise? If Scylax can track him down?'

'If it's that important to you, sure.' Agron shifted uncomfortably. 'But he's left Rome for keeps. Maybe Italy, even. The guy wouldn't stick around after knifing a patrician in front of witnesses, whatever clout he thinks he's got. And if he isn't in the city Scylax hasn't a hope in hell of finding him.'

'Yeah. Yeah, I know.' I felt exhausted, mentally as well as physically. 'But like I said he's the only lead we've got. He came back before, he's got too much going for him here just to pull up sticks and leave. So maybe he's hanging on somewhere after all until he thinks it's safe.'

Agron looked at me. Finally he said: 'Okay. You've got it. It'll never happen, but if it does you've got it. Leave the guy for now anyway. You look like a month-old dish-rag. Get some more sleep and I'll come back later.'

'Yeah, maybe I will.' I closed my eyes again, then opened them. 'Hey, Agron. One more thing. You ever meet someone called Caelius Crispus?'

But it must've been later already, because they were gone.

It was three days before I felt fit enough to get up, and even then the main reason was I was sick to death of Meton's chicken broth. There was no one around, but I held on to the banister and got to the foot of the stairs without falling over before yelling for Bathyllus. He came racing along the kitchen corridor like there was a fire in the hypocaust.

'You want to watch your hernia, friend,' I said.

'The mistress gave strict instructions that you were to stay in bed, sir.' His bald head gleamed with sweat and prim disapproval.

Not a single hair marked the smooth expanse. So much for the magic tiger piss. Mind you, I hadn't checked out the Golden Milestone yet. 'The doctor also.'

'Perilla wants the doctor to stay in bed?'

Not a flicker. I could see that one go straight past him without even nicking the edge. Well, maybe it'd been a false alarm after all. 'No, sir,' he said. 'Not the doctor. Only you, sir. I'll get one of the kitchen slaves to help you upstairs again.'

'I'm fine here, thanks, sunshine.' Yeah, well, I was having second thoughts about that already myself, but I managed to make it to the couch before my legs gave way altogether and dumped me. 'What you can do for me, though, is fetch a cup and a great big jug of Setinian. And go easy on the water, okay?'

He fizzed a bit, but at least I was lying down and looking more like an invalid so he didn't have that grievance any longer. 'Yes, sir. Setinian, sir, well watered, sir. At once, sir.'

I sighed. He'd heard me perfectly clearly, of course, and I hadn't missed the heavy sarcasm either. I remembered an epitaph I'd seen once on one of the Appian Way tombs: 'Here lies so-and-so. Killed by his doctors.' I knew how the poor bugger felt.

'Hey, Bathyllus!' I called him back. 'Have there been any messages from Agron?'

'No, sir.'

'How about Scylax?'

'Not today, sir.'

Ah, well. If nothing was happening then I didn't feel so bad about taking it easy. I lay back on the couch and closed my eyes. Just for a moment . . .

I was woken by Perilla. The lady didn't look too happy, either.

'Corvinus, what on earth are you doing downstairs?' she said. 'You should be in bed.'

'Yeah, well . . .' I struggled to sit up.

'And you've been drinking.'

Bathyllus must've put the jug and cup down on the table while I was asleep. I hadn't touched a drop. What a waste. 'I swear to you, Perilla . . .'

She ignored me. *'Bathyllus!'*

He was there in two seconds flat, all rolling eyes and teeth. Half an ounce of encouragement and he'd've been on his back with his paws in the air. Sickening. Jupiter knows what would've happened to the little guy if at that moment someone hadn't knocked at the outside door. He shot off like he'd been greased, and Perilla turned her attentions on me.

'I'm fine, lady,' I said quickly. 'No problems. Honest.'

'Nonsense.' She sat down on the couch next to me. 'The doctor gave strict instructions that you should stay in bed. Bathyllus knows that perfectly well. Marcus, how can you possibly expect to get better if you don't follow instructions?'

I wasn't listening, because Bathyllus was sidling back in with Scylax in tow.

'Hey!' I said. 'Scylax!'

'Marcus.' Perilla glared at him. 'I really do not think that you should trouble yourself with . . .'

I waved her down. 'Any news, pal? You find Carillus? Bathyllus, get the guy a chair. Two chairs. Three. And another cup.'

'Carillus?' Scylax was looking puzzled. 'You still want me to find *Carillus*?'

I poured myself some of the Setinian and took a moderate swig. Even watered to within an inch of its life, I could feel it doing me more good than all the doctors and bowls of chicken broth in Rome.

'Sure I do,' I said. 'Why shouldn't I?'

A shrug. 'I just wouldn't've thought it was necessary any more. Not once you knew where he'd gone after he'd cut you.'

I looked blank. Perilla groaned. 'Scylax,' she said, 'I will personally kill you for this.'

'Wait a minute, lady.' I was staring at him. 'Run that one past me again, pal. Slowly.'

Scylax was looking nervous as a virgin in a cathouse, which was a thing I thought I'd never see this side of the grave. He glanced at Perilla. She was sitting straight as a ramrod.

'Oh, go on,' she said. 'You may as well tell him now.'

'I was having Carillus watched, Corvinus,' Scylax said. 'Like we arranged. By Daphnis's young nephew. He hadn't been told to stop watching, so he didn't. When the guy ran out of the beer shop after knifing you our boy was waiting over the road.'

'And?'

'I've told you all this. Or at least I told Agron. Two days ago.' Another glance at Perilla. 'Uh, yeah, well, maybe you haven't heard after all. Carillus went all the way to the Pincian.'

'Crispus,' I said slowly. 'Fucking Crispus.'

'What Crispus? Carillus didn't go to see no Crispus. He went straight to a guy called Fulcinius Trio.'

I frowned. Fulcinius Trio? Who the hell was Fulcinius Trio? Then I remembered. Trio had been one of the prosecuting panel at Piso's trial; in fact, the opportunist who'd brought the charge in the first instance and been cold-shouldered by Germanicus's friends, who thought he'd no right muscling in. So. Lucius Fulcinius Trio. It looked like we were in business again.

'Bathyllus, pal,' I said. 'Take this dishwater away and bring us some wine.'

Perilla sniffed.

38 ∫

I compromised with Perilla, the deal being that I'd behave for three days and after that Trio was mine, so long as I promised to go easy and take Agron along as a babysitter. A fair bargain. Even so, I nearly didn't make it, fitness-wise; after three more days on a diet of chicken soup and wine-flavoured water I wouldn't've backed myself arm-wrestling a five-year-old.

We took a litter: the Pincian's way up in the north of Rome and Trio's place was off Pincian Street itself, near the old gate in the Servian Wall. From my first view of the property it was obvious that social lightweight or not the guy wasn't doing too badly, which made me wonder straight off where the money had come from.

The slave who opened the door was young, pretty-faced, fair-haired and well groomed, and he wore a natty little tunic that showed a lot of thigh. Uhuh. So that was another angle I could follow up later. If Trio's taste in domestic servants ran that way then he might have more in common with Regulus than I'd thought.

'What name, sir?' The kid's look travelled from my face to the purple stripe on my mantle and then past me to Agron.

I pushed past him with Agron following. 'Just tell your master I've come about his meat deliveries. He'll know what I mean.'

Goldilocks wasn't happy, that was for sure. 'If you'd care to wait here, please,' he said, 'I'll ask if he's at home.'

'You do that, sunshine.' I looked around. Nice mosaics and a lot of good marble, all new and in the latest style. Wherever the money had come from it had only just arrived.

A minute later the slave was back. 'Follow me,' he said. No 'please' or 'sir' this time, and he didn't even look at Agron.

Trio was in his study. He was a pudding of a man in his mid-thirties with eyes as shifty-sharp as a third-rate horse dealer's and no smile. He didn't get up from his desk to shake hands.

'Close the door behind you, Flavillus,' he said. 'I'll call if I need you.'

The kid left. I sat down univited on the reading couch while Agron took up a stance by the door. Trio's eyes shifted between us and settled on me. His lips pursed.

'Now,' he said. 'Maybe you'd like to tell me what you want.'

'I think you know that already, pal,' I said.

'I'm not a mind-reader. My door slave mentioned something about meat deliveries. I assume that was a joke, although I can't quite see the point of it.'

'No joke.' I sat back against the wall. 'I understand you had a visit a couple of days ago from a mutual friend. A butcher by the name of Carillus.'

'Then you understand wrongly. I have no butcher friends. And Flavillus didn't catch your own name, by the way.'

'I didn't give him it. Corvinus. Valerius Corvinus. You know that too. And I'm not mistaken about Carillus, Trio, because he was followed here. You're telling me you don't know him?'

He gave me a long considering look before he answered. 'No. I know Carillus. A freedman of Calpurnius Piso's whom I prosecuted several months ago. If you say he's a butcher then I'll take your word for it, although I wasn't aware of the fact myself. In any case I haven't seen him since the trial.'

'You're lying, sunshine,' I said cheerfully. 'I told you, Carillus was followed here. Did he tell you he'd just tried to kill me?'

There was a long silence. Then Trio heaved himself to his feet, his face flushed.

'I'm not used to being called a liar in my own house, Corvinus,' he said. 'I'll let it pass this once, because you've obviously been ill and perhaps you haven't fully recovered yet. But I must insist you either tell me the reason for your visit or leave immediately.'

I glanced at Agron. The big Illyrian leaned his back against the door. I heard the panels creak.

'Sit down, Trio,' I said.

He didn't move, but a muscle on his cheek twitched. 'Tell your friend to stand aside, please.'

'When I'm good and ready. But first I'll tell you what I know and then we'll take it from there. If you're wise you'll listen.'

It was touch and go. Sure, he could've shouted for the slaves – there'd be beefier specimens around than Goldilocks – or he could've tried to get past Agron on his own, in which case Jupiter knows what would've happened. An innocent man would've done both, but Trio wasn't innocent. He sat.

'Very well,' he said. 'Tell me.'

I hoped the relief didn't show on my face. That bit had been tricky.

'Okay,' I said. 'Let's start with the letter.'

The eyes were inscrutable. 'What letter?'

'The one Piso wrote the night he died and gave to Carillus to deliver.'

'Carillus admits this? You've talked to him, I assume.'

'He claims what Piso gave him was the deed to a slaughter-house he'd just bought. And the only other letter extant – the suicide note – was found with Piso's body the next morning.'

'Then I don't see the problem.' Trio tried a smile. On that face it was as out of place as a whore at a Vestal's supper party. 'Carillus showed you the deed in question, presumably?'

'Sure he did.'

'And the emperor read out Piso's other note to the Senate. So both pieces of paper are accounted for.'

'Yeah. Unless Carillus was lying. The letter I mean was addressed to Piso's lawyers. Only it never reached them.'

'That has nothing to do with me. I was acting for the prosecution.'

'Sure you were.' I smiled. 'That's the point. If Piso did give Carillus a letter to deliver – and I think he did – then it came to you. The question is whether it got sidetracked, or whether Piso meant you to have it in the first place.'

He went very still. 'Now why would you think that?' he said.

'Because you were a double, Trio. You were on Piso's side from the start. Or at least he thought you were.'

'That's nonsense. I brought the original charge. And I think, Corvinus, that you had better leave after all.'

'Later. You ever hear of a thing called a steam engine?' I used the Greek word.

I'd caught him on the wrong foot. 'A what?'

'A steam engine. Maybe not. One of these clever-clever gizmos the Greeks dream up for fun every now and then that don't lead anywhere. My uncle took me once when I was a kid to meet a crazy Alexandrian philosopher who fooled around with hydraulics and water organs. He'd worked out that if you heated the water in a closed system until it boiled and led the steam through a pipe you built up a head of pressure that would turn a wheel at the far end.'

Trio's eyes narrowed. 'Young man, fascinating though this is I don't see the relevance.'

'Oh, it's relevant. The guy's problem was there was no way to control the pressure. If it built up too high it blew the boiler or ruptured the seals in the pipe. So he fitted a weighted plug and that got blown out instead before the whole thing went up. Trouble was, one day the plug blew and smashed his skull. Served him right for being a smartass, I suppose.' I smiled again. 'That was you, Trio. You were the plug in the boiler. It was your job to take the pressure off before it blew the case apart. You see the relevance now?'

Trio stared at me, but this time he didn't say anything.

'I didn't think of it until I found out you were tied in with Carillus,' I went on. 'But it's the only explanation that makes sense. Agrippina and her cronies had a carefully prepared case. If they'd been allowed to bring the charge themselves they would've done a proper job of it and not pulled any punches. Things could've got nasty, with all sorts of embarrassing shit floating to the surface.'

'Embarrassing to whom?'

'To the emperor, of course. Who else?'

I had his full attention now. 'And why should Tiberius be embarrassed?'

'Come on, Trio! You want me to spell it out for you? You know as well as I do.'

'Humour me.'

'Okay.' I was still smiling. 'Piso and the emperor had a private agreement. Tiberius didn't trust his stepson further than he could throw him, and he'd told Piso to keep an eye on him for signs of treason. Maybe even given him the authority to take drastic measures if he found he was right.'

'These drastic measures being?'

'To put the guy away, naturally. Which is what happened. Only it leaves the Wart in a difficult position, right? Agrippina and her Syrian pals who've been involved in the treason plot won't take Germanicus's death lying down, and they're out for what revenge they can get. Once Piso's back in Rome they're going to make as big a stink as they can. Which will be pretty big because they have the Wart over a barrel.'

'Go on.' Trio was watching me through narrowed eyes.

'Tiberius is stymied. He can't claim squeaky-clean Germanicus was a traitor because he's got no real proof and no one would believe him anyway. On the other hand, Piso will expect him to get him off the hook because he was only obeying orders. So the Wart does what he can with a bad job. He makes sure the guy who brings the charge is a secret sympathiser who'll do his best to pull the teeth from the prosecution's case, and he also makes sure Piso knows it. Then to guard his own back he steers the question away from the death itself to Piso's own actions after the event, but to keep Piso playing the game he gets his agent – you – to dangle the hope of a last-minute pardon in front of him. Only it's a double-cross, and Piso gets chopped with the Wart's blessing. You following all this, or do you want me to draw you a picture?'

'Piso committed suicide, Corvinus.'

'Like hell he did! That brings us back to the letter. Maybe I was wrong. Maybe it wasn't addressed to you after all.'

'That' – Trio grinned sarcastically—' is the first bit of sense you've come out with so far.'

I grinned back. 'Oh, Carillus still brought it to you all right. Whether you were supposed to have it or not. But let's say you weren't. Let's say Piso had had second thoughts. Maybe he distrusted you, or the Wart himself, I don't know and it doesn't matter. Anyway he decides to spill the beans by giving the whole story to his lawyers, on the reasonable grounds that if

Germanicus and his pals were crooks then in using armed force to retake his province he was only doing his duty as a responsible governor. He seals the letter and gives it to his faithful freedman Carillus, who takes it straight to your greasy little paws. You read it and the guy's goose is cooked.' I paused. 'How am I doing?'

Trio's face was impassive. For a long time he didn't say anything. Finally he leaned back in his chair and steepled his fingers.

'All right,' he said. 'Let's say for the sake of argument that you're correct. Except for the fact that Piso's suicide may have been . . . assisted.' Yeah, okay, I could take that. The suicide note at least had sounded genuine. 'Wouldn't it be far better to leave things as they are? After all, as you've described it, the situation has turned out not too badly. A traitor to Rome has met a well-deserved end, and the matter has been settled without undue fuss or bloodshed. The emperor has done as much as he could reasonably be expected to do to help a faithful subordinate who is also a personal friend, but has been unfortunately constrained by political realities to sacrifice him for the sake of the common good. Tiberius is an experienced general, Corvinus. He knows that to win a battle one must be prepared for casualties, even be ready to send men one knows personally to certain death if the situation demands it. Piso himself would be the first to admit this. And if my own role was as you've outlined it then I have done nothing to deserve censure. I acted from the most honourable of motives and with full, albeit clandestine, official backing.'

'Sure. So tell me why Regulus died.'

He hadn't been expecting that, especially after the fancy lawyer's speech. The eyes blinked. 'Regulus?'

'Piso's lawyer. The guy Carillus knifed at the Gemonian Stairs. That wasn't his own idea, *friend*. So why did you put him up to it?'

'I know nothing whatsoever about Regulus's death. And I certainly didn't arrange his murder.'

I knew bluster when I met it, even quiet bluster. The guy was rattled. Not before time, either; my ribs were starting to hurt. I shifted my position on the couch.

'Regulus's death doesn't fit the pattern, you see,' I said. 'Piso's, sure. Like you say, he was a necessary casualty, although getting Carillus to cut his throat with a sword was one touch too many. But you slipped up badly with Regulus.'

'This nonsense has gone far enough.' Trio stood up abruptly. 'I want you to leave. Now.'

'Not until I've finished, pal. We've just got to the interesting part.' I glanced at Agron. He'd stood like a statue all the way through this. Now without a word he came forward and pushed the guy back into his chair. Trio sat glaring, and breathing hard. 'Regulus died a traitor's death, with a hook through his gullet. Tiberius had no reason to have him killed, and certainly not like that. So who did Regulus betray? And how? You, or whoever you're really working for?'

Trio said nothing. If looks could've killed we'd've been dead meat.

'You want me to sweat him, Corvinus?' Agron growled.

The hell with my promise to Perilla. I was pretty angry myself now. I stood up, my hand pressed to the aching wound in my ribs. 'Yeah, why not? Go for it.'

Suddenly, without warning, Trio shouted.

'*Flavillus!*'

Agron's huge hand pressed over the guy's mouth; but he was too late. In the atrium beyond, feet thudded across the marble. The door was thrown open: only Flavillus, but there'd be a few other, bigger reinforcements along soon. Ah, well. Maybe I had been too optimistic, at that.

'Let him go, Agron,' I said.

Trio's face was livid. A red mark showed where Agron's fingernails had bitten into the pasty cheek. He stood glaring at us while his pretty home help shifted in embarrassment from foot to foot.

'I hope you've made a will, Corvinus,' he said softly, 'because you're dead. Dead and buried.'

Yeah. Still, I'd got what I came for, and you don't make fish sauce without flattening a few anchovies. I pulled myself up straight and tried not to wince as I made for the door.

'Maybe so, sunshine,' I said. 'But I've been threatened before and I'm still around. And I think maybe the emperor just might

• David Wishart

want to have his pennyworth to contribute before all this is over. In which case you'd better have your own will made out. I'll see you around.'

We left. Trio didn't say goodbye.

39

I wasn't sure about being dead and buried, but by the time I got back home I felt ropy as hell. Also, when I'd threatened Trio with Tiberius I'd been bluffing: I couldn't risk an interview with the Wart, or not yet anyway, not until I had the whole thing wrapped up in a nice parcel with a bow on top. Sure, at the end of the day the emperor had been responsible for his son's death, but somewhere along the line he'd been sold a pup and didn't know it, and unless I could come up with the proof it could be bye-bye Corvinus.

I dropped Agron at his shop and got back home to find Uncle Cotta parked in solitary splendour on the guest couch, his fist wrapped round a wine cup.

'Hey, Marcus!' He lifted the cup to me as I came in. 'Hear you got beaten up.'

'Yeah, well. It happens.' I lowered myself gently on to the couch facing him and poured wine into a second cup. Bathyllus had come through, but he was ostentatiously looking the other way. The little bugger was playing it safe this time, and I didn't blame him.

'You want to stay out of bar-room brawls if you can't hack them, boy,' Cotta said.

So much for sympathy; but at least it showed he hadn't heard about Carillus. I took a swallow of the wine. Shit, my best Falernian! Jupiter knew how Cotta had wangled it, and I didn't grudge him, but the last time I'd checked the cellar we were down to three jars, and Cotta had a throat like the Great Drain. I made a mental note to hand Bathyllus his head when I got him alone later.

'Where's Perilla?' I said.

'Round at the Fabian place seeing her mother.' Cotta absently sank a straight half-pint. I winced. 'That's a dutiful little wifelet you've got there.'

'Uhuh.' I was glad the dutiful little wifelet wasn't around to hear it or there'd've been more than one loose head up for grabs. 'So what can I do for you, Uncle? Or did you just come round to snicker?'

'Would I do that?'

'Sure you would. Not that I hold it against you.' He'd ducked my question; which should've made me suspicious but didn't.

'You want to tell me what happened exactly, Marcus?'

'I stood on a guy's corns, that's all. He was bigger and faster than me.' I sipped at the Falernian. It was practically neat, my first real wine for days, and I felt a warming, relaxing glow spread up from my stomach. 'How did you hear about it?'

'Oh, us consuls hear everything eventually.' He paused and looked into his wine cup. 'Including reports about pushy young smartasses who get themselves thrown out of imperial provinces.'

I stiffened. 'You don't say?'

Uncle Cotta set his cup down, and he wasn't smiling any longer. So this was an official visit. I should've expected it, of course, but somehow for me the words 'Cotta' and 'consul' never did go happily together.

'The *Castor* brought a formal complaint from Aelius Lamia to the emperor,' he said. 'I don't know the details because I wasn't told, but that's enough for me. Marcus, what the hell do you think you're playing at, boy?'

I tried a grin. 'Pissing around. What do I usually play at?'

'Well, cut it out as from now. I'm serious.' He was, I could see that. 'The Wart's fit to be tied; Jupiter knows why, personally I don't and I don't want to either because whatever his reasons are he isn't giving them out to anyone and that isn't healthy.'

'You've seen him?' I took another swallow of wine: a big one, this time. I needed it.

'It was the other way round. Tiberius saw me, first thing this morning. He wants to keep the warning private but it is a warning, don't make any mistake about that. A final one. Any more pissing around, as you put it, and you'll find yourself hauled up the Palatine so fast your arse won't touch the ground. And you may not come down again, either. That's official, Marcus. You understand me?'

'Yeah. Yeah, I understand.' My stomach now felt cold and empty, and the wine lay on it like a lead weight. 'Thanks, Uncle. Thanks a bunch.'

If he noticed the tone he ignored it. 'Don't thank me, I'm only the messenger boy. Just drop whatever you're up to. Or next time I might be passing on an order for you to slit your wrists, and I don't want to do that.' Jupiter! 'Okay? Enough said?'

'Enough said.' More than enough: I couldn't go against a direct order from the emperor, and I knew it. Tiberius had just put the lid on the case and screwed it down hard.

'Good.' Cotta reached for the jug and I saw that his hand was shaking. Bathyllus had made himself scarce. 'Now let's change the subject. Tell me about Antioch. You come across a dive called the Garden of Aphrodite? In Three Springs Street, just off the Old Marketplace?'

We talked wineshops and brothels, but my heart wasn't in it. This was what I'd been afraid of, and it was something I couldn't ignore or laugh off. My only hope was that our visit to Trio's place wouldn't be reported; and there was a chance it wouldn't, because if I was right about Trio working for someone else – and I knew I was – then the slimy bastard wouldn't want to make too many waves either, despite his parting threat. It was hard, though, when I'd been so close.

'Perilla enjoy herself out there?' Cotta was saying.

I pulled my mind back to the conversation. 'Yeah. Yeah, I think so. She could've stayed another month, at least if it hadn't been for the social side. Diplomatic wives can be pretty wearing.'

'Tell me something I don't know!' Cotta chuckled and absently pulled at his ear; now the official proceedings were over he was his usual easy-going self. 'Hairstyles and harmless gossip, right? And Rufia Perilla isn't exactly one of the soirée crowd.'

'She made one pal.' I reached for the jug. 'Girl called Acutia. Not my taste, and to call that birdbrain sharp is about the most unlikely . . . *shit!*' The wine splashed over the table. 'Sorry.'

Cotta lowered his hand. He was looking at me curiously. 'You okay?' he said.

'Just a twinge in the ribs.' I poured more carefully – only half a cup because the Falernian was already beginning to get to me – and reached for a napkin. 'Catches me sometimes when I stretch. Hey, now you've made consul you'll be on the diplomatic circuit yourself soon, right? You got any preferences for a province?'

'One of the senatorials, Asia or Africa, I don't mind which. So long as someone does for that African bastard Tacfarinas first.' Cotta held his own cup out and I filled it. 'With my background the Wart wouldn't look at me for an imperial, but screw that, I'll settle for the easy life any day.'

'Yeah.' I was trying to keep my voice level and half my brain on small talk while the other half worked like fury. Jupiter! *Sharp* . . . ! 'Yeah, I don't blame you. Syria'd be nice, though. I could take Syria.'

The front door banged.

'Marcus?' Perilla shouted.

'Through here, Perilla.'

She came in. 'Marcus, I'm glad you're back. I had the most interesting conversation with . . .' She paused. 'Oh, Uncle Cotta. I'm sorry, I didn't know you were coming round. I would've stayed in.'

'Didn't know myself until this morning.' Cotta was on his feet. 'Bathyllus looked after me. No problem.'

'So I notice.' Perilla's disapproving eyes were on the almost-empty wine jug. 'Corvinus, you're remembering what the doctor said about lots of water, I hope.'

'Yeah. Sure I am.' That was true enough. The fact that I'd ignored it was another thing entirely. 'Bathyllus will tell you.' Let the little bastard squirm. Jupiter knew where he'd got to, but he was keeping a low profile. 'You have a nice time? How's your mother?'

'It was one of her bad days, I'm afraid. They've been getting more frequent recently.' She turned to Cotta and said in her most unpressing voice: 'You're staying for dinner?'

'No, I'll push off now.' Cotta drained his cup and winked at me. 'A private engagement of my own. I just called in to see how the invalid was doing.'

'He'd do better if he took more care of himself.'

'Maybe he will from now on.' Cotta shot me a look. 'That right, Marcus?'

'Sure. I'll try, anyway.'

'You try, boy. You try very hard. Catch you later, okay?'

I walked Cotta to the door and saw him out. When I got back Perilla was lying on the couch. She was frowning.

'What was that all about?' she said.

'Nothing. You know Cotta.'

'I thought I did, but he sounded serious. And I don't think he and I were talking about quite the same thing.'

'He was canned, lady, that's all.' I kissed her. 'So would you be with the best part of a flask of Falernian inside you. I was surprised he made it to the door.'

'Cotta wasn't drunk, and you're hiding something, but we'll let that go. How was your talk with Trio?'

Talk. Yeah, well, I suppose that was one word for it. 'Okay. No hassle.' I crossed my fingers and hoped she didn't notice: one lie at a time was enough to risk with Perilla. 'Quite friendly, really.'

'Only I had a very interesting conversation with Aunt Marcia about him. Have you ever heard of a man called Libo? Scribonius Libo?'

The name rang a faint bell. I got down on to the couch and reached for the Falernian . . .

'*Marcus!*'

'Yeah?'

'I am not going to tell you this unless you promise not to touch another drop of wine for the rest of the evening.'

'Oh, come on, Perilla!'

'I mean it.'

I sighed and set the flask down again. Well, maybe she was right and I had had enough after all. 'Okay, lady. What's this about Libo? The name's familiar, but that's about it.'

'He was prosecuted by Trio five years ago. For treason.'

'Is that right?' My interest sharpened. I'd missed the case and I hadn't known that Trio was the prosecutor, but I remembered Libo himself now: a fast-living rich kid with expensive tastes and nothing between the ears to stop the wind blowing through.

'Aunt Marcia didn't know the full details and I didn't want to press her. But what she did recall was quite fascinating.'

'Yeah? Go on, lady.'

Perilla reached for my half-full wine cup and took a sip. 'The charge was manufactured, for a start. Obviously so. Then Libo was supposed to be dabbling in magic and witchcraft. Trio's crucial piece of evidence was a list of names, including the emperor's and other members of the imperial family, with coded notes against each one, all written in Libo's own hand. And Libo committed suicide before the Senate reached its verdict. Is any of this sounding familiar?'

'Uhuh.' I felt the hair stirring at the nape of my neck. 'Libo admitted writing the list?'

'No, he denied it. Tiberius had his personal slaves put to the torture, and they confirmed that the handwriting was his.'

I lay back frowning. Sure Libo would've denied it; like Perilla said, proof of authorship would've been crucial to the verdict. But the thing stank right enough, even without the tie-ins with Piso. Libo might've been stupid, but he'd've had to be a complete headbanger to consider murdering the Imperials wholesale, let alone put his plans down on paper. And the logical conclusion was that Trio's crucial piece of evidence was a forgery. Which, given the events of the Piso trial and Trio's involvement in both, suggested an angle that was interesting to say the least . . .

'How did the Wart handle all of this, Perilla?'

'Quite dispassionately, Aunt Marcia said.' Perilla took another sip of my wine. 'But he obviously wanted a conviction.'

'The Piso trial again, right?'

She nodded. 'That was what I thought. The circumstances of Libo's suicide were curious, too. He may have stabbed himself, but there is' – she paused – 'a certain doubt and confusion about the matter.'

'You mean the guy could've been helped on his way?'

'Yes. Very easily.'

There were too many parallels for coincidence, and that made the forgery angle even more worth chasing up. It was a pity I'd been warned off. More than a pity, because I was just itching to dig further into this.

'So what did Trio get out of it?'

'Libo's estate was divided up among his accusers. As the chief prosecutor he had the major share.'

Uhuh. That explained where the money had come from to pay for the fancy house on the Pincian. If I needed any more proof that Trio was crooked as a Suburan landlord I'd got it.

'There's one more thing, Marcus. The most important.' Perilla hesitated. 'Aunt Marcia didn't exactly give it as a fact, and you know how snobbish she can be at times, but I think it's worth passing on. The rumour was that Trio had a silent partner in the Libo prosecution. One very close to the emperor.'

My skin prickled. 'Yeah? And who was that, lady?'

She paused again. Her eyes held mine.

'Aelius Sejanus,' she said.

40 ∫

Everything suddenly went very quiet. I reached over for the jug and filled the wine cup Cotta had left on the table. This time Perilla didn't stop me. Her eyes were still on mine, and they looked scared. As well they might.

Aelius Sejanus. Commander of Praetorians and well on his way to becoming the Wart's principal sunbeam. Lamia's relative, the relative of Junius Blaesus whom Dad was so keen to keep in with these days and of half a dozen other prominent men in the Wart's government system. And, incidentally, a lethal bastard to cross: messing with Sejanus was about as safe as putting your head in an arena cat's mouth to check out its tonsils, as I'd almost found out for myself.

'You're sure he was involved with Trio?' I said. 'I mean, Marcia's sure?'

'She wasn't specific.' I could see that Perilla was trying to keep up her dispassionate front, and she wasn't doing too well. 'But you know her hints.'

Perilla's Aunt Marcia was Fabius Maximus's widow, and a long-standing friend of the Imperials. She had more pride and sense than to gossip, especially after the way her husband had died, but when she felt confident enough to drop a hint about something you could have the thing cast in bronze and hang it up with the law tables. I nodded. 'Yeah. That's good enough for me. She's sure, okay. Sejanus explains the poison as well.'

'How so?'

'Tiberius would balk at poison, but not Sejanus. One gets you ten that when the Wart found out Germanicus was crooked he threw the whole thing into Sejanus's lap and left him to it;

which was the best thing he could do, because it had to be handled carefully, and cloak and dagger stuff's right up that bastard's alley.'

'Sejanus arranged the murder on Tiberius's instructions.'

'Yeah.' I sipped the Falernian. 'If Germanicus had to be got rid of it had to be done secretly. So the Wart gives Sejanus *carte blanche* to put the guy away. Then the pair of them get together to cover the affair up, with Sejanus masterminding operations and the Wart providing the clout.'

'That would explain Aelius Lamia's appointment to Syria, too.'

'Right. On top of his official orders, being related to Sejanus Lamia would have a personal stake in making sure the shit at the Antioch end stayed buried. It kept things in the family, so to speak.'

'So how was it done?' Perilla rested her chin on her hand. 'The actual murder, I mean. Did Sejanus use Piso and Plancina after all?'

I shook my head. 'No. Maybe, but I don't think so. He wouldn't've had to, because being the emperor's accredited deputy he'd be able to use official channels of his own. Or semi-official. And he had his own agent on Germanicus's staff.'

Perilla frowned. 'Namely?'

'Your pal Acutia's husband. Publius Vitellius.'

She sat up. 'Marcus, Vitellius is impossible. He was one of Germanicus's closest friends, he drafted the case against Piso for the murder, and by implication he was one of the principals in Germanicus's own plot.'

'Yeah, I know. I haven't worked out the whys and wherefores myself yet, but I'd still bet my last copper penny Vitellius was the guy directly responsible.'

'Prove it,' Perilla said simply.

'Okay.' I took another swallow of wine before she woke up to the fact it wasn't medicinally correct. 'Remember Mancus?'

'Martina's mysterious contact. Yes, of course. But if you think . . .'

'Wait, lady. We knew Mancus was a pseudonym, right? And you suggested he chose the name after the old Etruscan death god.'

'Of course. And you said it tied in with . . .'

'With the guy who murdered Regulus. Right. Only I was wrong because we were being too clever. Vitellius didn't choose the pseudonym at all, Martina did. Even if she knew his real name she wouldn't've used it even to her sister, for obvious reasons. So she gave him a name herself. Because he was a Roman and she spoke Latin she chose a good Roman descriptive name, like Acutia means "sharp"; only being genuinely descriptive it fitted the guy perfectly.' I paused. 'So what does "mancus" mean in straight Latin?'

'"Maimed", of course. Is this supposed to prove something?'

'Yeah. "Maimed" in particular respect of what?'

'The hand.' Her startled eyes met mine. 'I'm a fool. Vitellius had a finger missing, or the top joint of one, rather. You're right, it fits.'

'Sure it does.' I took a smug mouthful of Falernian. 'Vitellius is our boy, sure as eggs is eggs, whether he claimed to be Germanicus's friend or not. And another thing. He was the only guy on the Syrian staff to be left over from the other team. The rest were either new like Lamia or they were Piso's appointees who the Wart would know were loyal.'

'Then you think Lamia knew that it was Vitellius who arranged Germanicus's death?'

'Sure he did. It explains the way Lamia held back from him at the party, for a start. He may've been Sejanus's cousin and involved in the cover-up, but he was basically a decent guy having to do a dirty job. He had to put personalities aside in the cause of duty but he still couldn't take Vitellius's smell. It explains why your pal Acutia wasn't flavour of the month with the wives, too. I'd bet a barrel of oysters to a button they all knew as well.'

'But that's dreadful!'

'It's politics, lady.' I emptied the last of the Falernian into my cup. Perilla didn't seem to notice. 'As games go they don't come any dirtier. There's not a lot we can do with the information now, except maybe pass it on to Martina's sister like we promised. I doubt if she'll be able to do anything but we'll've done our best.'

'But wasn't Vitellius taking a terrible risk? After all, if he was prosecuting Piso in Rome and Martina knew him then . . .' She stopped. 'Oh, yes. Yes, of course. That was why Martina had to die at Brindisi, wasn't it?'

'It was one of the reasons, sure. But she knew too much else anyway. And then Tiberius made sure the guy went straight back to Syria after Piso was safely dead. No wonder the trial went the way the Wart planned it, or Sejanus, rather. He had two of his own men on the prosecuting panel. It's a pity he couldn't've made absolutely certain by having . . .' I stopped. 'Shit. He did. Of course he did.'

'What's wrong, Marcus?' Perilla was staring at me.

'Sejanus didn't just have two lawyers in his pocket. He had three.'

'Who was the third? Another of Germanicus's friends?'

'Oh, no,' I said. 'That's the point. The third was Livineius Regulus.'

'But Regulus was . . . oh!'

I could see she'd got it too. 'Right. Regulus was on the other side. I wondered at the time why he should agree to defend Piso when the two weren't connected; not officially connected, anyway. The trial was sewn up from the start.'

'But what makes you think Regulus was an agent of Sejanus? Surely . . . ?'

'The way he died, Perilla. He was killed by Carillus who worked for Trio who worked for Sejanus. And he was killed as a traitor. I asked Trio two questions when I talked to him: who did Regulus betray, and what did he do? Maybe now I can answer them both myself.'

'The first's easy. He betrayed Sejanus.'

'Right. The hook and the Stairs are just the kind of brutal joke Sejanus would enjoy.'

'What about the second? What exactly did Regulus do?'

I took a swallow of wine, nearly the last. Doctor or not, it had done me good and I half considered yelling for Bathyllus to come out from wherever the hell he was hiding and bring another jug; but that would've been pushing things.

'He talked to someone,' I said. 'Or rather, he threatened to talk to them.'

'You mean Agrippina?'

'What would be the use in that, lady? If Sejanus was acting on orders from the Wart then Agrippina was stymied whether she knew the truth or not. And Regulus wouldn't dare cross the emperor, whatever inducements were offered.'

'So who, then?'

'Tiberius, of course.'

'But, Marcus, the emperor already knew the circumstances of Germanicus's death!'

'He thought he did, yeah. And he still thinks so. Sure, Sejanus was working for the Wart. But he had fish of his own to fry at the same time, very private fish. Regulus knew that and the Wart didn't.'

'Corvinus.' Perilla was being very patient. 'If Sejanus killed Germanicus for treason on Tiberius's instructions and they organised the trial and the cover-up together, then what information could Regulus have that would possibly interest the emperor?'

'That's what I don't know, lady. But I mean to find out.' Screw Cotta and his warnings: I was much too close to give the case up now, however dangerous it was. I'd have to go careful, sure, but if Sejanus was playing a game of his own then maybe there was a light at the end of the tunnel after all.

First things first. The hell with doctors. I yelled for Bathyllus. He came slinking out of the kitchen corridor with a smile that looked exactly like hair oil smelled.

'Hey, little guy,' I said. 'Go down to the cellar and bring us another belt of Falernian, okay?'

Perilla looked up but I gave her a look back and she didn't say a word. Sometimes we understand each other perfectly.

Maybe it was thanks to the Falernian, or maybe I'd just got fed up being treated like one of Lamia's Tyrian glasses, but I woke up the next morning feeling great. Sure, the hole in my ribs hadn't magically disappeared, but the pain was no worse now than the after-effects of a clout with a wooden sword at the gym. And not a patch on one of Scylax's famous massages.

We were out in the garden having breakfast when Bathyllus came through with what looked like a twelve-year-old kid in tow. I didn't recognise the guy at first. Then I did: Flavonius Lippillus of the Aventine Watch.

'So how're the ribs, Corvinus?' he said.

I tossed him an apple with my bad arm. Not a bad throw. Not good, mind, but it went the distance and he caught it without having to stretch. 'That answer your question, pal?'

'Just about.' He bit into the apple and sat down on the bench beside the hedge.

I introduced Perilla.

She smiled at him. 'Would you like some bread and olives?'

'I had breakfast long ago, ma'am. Thanks all the same.'

I dunked a scrap of my own bread in olive oil and speared a piece of cheese with my knife. That was another sign I was cured: I don't usually worry too much about breakfast but this morning I was starved. 'Who told you about my ribs, Lippillus? And what the hell are you doing here after we agreed to hang the plague sign up?'

He shrugged. 'The first question's simple. You're a purple-striper, Corvinus, and purple-stripers don't get knifed in German beer dens all that often.'

'It happened in the Subura, friend. That's not your district.'

'Maybe not. But word gets around. Even when big Illyrian blacksmiths don't bother to lodge a complaint.' Uhuh. Shit, the kid was smart, all right. It gave me a creepy feeling of being watched. You begin to wonder just how public your private affairs are. 'As far as being here's concerned, I just happened to be in the neighbourhood officially, so I thought I'd call in.'

'Yeah? Another murder?'

'Not quite.' He looked shamefaced. 'The lady down the road lost her pet monkey.'

'Oh, yes,' Perilla murmured. 'Fulvia Lucilla, Marcus. The City Watch commander's aunt.' She paused. 'His old, childless and very wealthy aunt.'

'You've got it, ma'am.' Lippillus's voice was expressionless. 'The boss put the entire force on full alert. We found the brute yesterday perched on the roof of the Queen Juno temple pelting the priests with loose tiles. I've just brought it back. Complete with Watch commander, all smiles and hair oil.'

I laughed. 'No kidding?'

'No kidding. The bastard pissed all over my tunic.' He glanced sideways at Perilla; now he was laughing too. 'The monkey, not my boss.'

'Hey, Bathyllus!' I shouted. The little guy was kicking his heels in the shelter of the portico. 'Bring our guest here a cup of wine. The special stuff we keep for monkey rescuers with pissed-on tunics.'

'You know, Corvinus, I was just hoping you'd say that.' Lippillus's grin widened. 'I'm parched. It's okay for you decadent purple-stripers who can get up when you like, but us workies have had a hard day already.'

Point taken. This was a man after my own heart. I called Bathyllus back. 'Scratch that last order, little guy. Make it a jug. And two cups.' I raised my eyebrows at Perilla, but she shook her head; she already had her chilled fruit juice. She was experimenting with new varieties, and her latest was a mixture of pear and seriously expensive banana. Ah, well. To each his own. I turned back to Lippillus. 'So, friend. What's the news?'

'Special offer. You get two for the price of one. First, you know the investigation into Regulus's death has been stopped?'

'Yeah. That message I got.'

'So now I've got the name you wanted. The guy responsible was Lucius Seius Tubero.' He paused for a reaction. 'You don't know him?'

'Not personally. He's one of the ex-consuls, isn't he?'

'Right. A half-brother of Aelius Sejanus's.' Lippillus kept his voice neutral, but I knew he'd made the jump himself. Like I say, the kid was smart. Still, this wasn't his quarrel, let alone his official business, so we both pretended he hadn't.

'Yeah,' I said. 'That fits. Thanks. So what's the freebie?'

'I didn't get that until earlier this morning. There's no case now anyway, at least I don't think there is. We fished your butcher pal out of the Tiber a few hours ago, just north of the Stairs.'

I'd been carving the rind off a lump of cheese, and I set it down carefully. How he'd made the Carillus link I didn't know, but it was academic now anyway.

'You don't say. Murdered?'

'Unless he managed to stab himself twice in the back, sure.'

Well, I wasn't sorry, although I'd've liked to nail the guy myself. No prizes for guessing who'd done it, either, or why. A one-way river trip was cheaper than a new start in Marseilles or Cologne. More permanent, too.

Bathyllus came back with the wine. He poured and Lippillus drank and wiped his lips with a napkin. 'It seems more of a coincidence than it is,' he went on. 'There's an old pier by the Stairs, and stuff floating downriver often snags there. The body's been in the water for days. Maybe it'd even come down the Drain, although with the dry weather that's unlikely. Still recognisable despite the rats. Just. We're not taking the matter any further, of course.' He turned to Perilla. 'Sorry, ma'am.'

'That's all right,' she said faintly. 'Marcus, I think I'll go inside for a little and leave you to talk. Nice to meet you, Flavonius Lippillus.'

He rose politely as she left and then sat down again. We drank for a while in silence and Lippillus nibbled at an olive.

'One more thing,' I said. 'You know anything about a guy named Publius Vitellius?'

He gave me a sharp look. 'Germanicus's pal? The one who helped prosecute Calpurnius Piso?'

'That's right.'

'Nothing official, no.' The eyes were still sharp. 'Nor unofficial either, if that's the sort of thing you're interested in. Just the usual background stuff.'

I topped up his wine cup. 'Anything you've got.'

'That's not much, Corvinus. He was on Germanicus's staff in Germany, involved in the campaign against the tribes. And of course he had a bad time coming back.'

'Yeah? Tell me.'

'If you're really interested you'd do better asking someone else. I'm no military expert.'

'You've just got the ordinary layman's knowledge. Sure, I'll bet.' I'd bet, too, that if I asked him about anything from domestic plumbing to the current state of trade with India he'd still claim to be an amateur and then give me exactly what I wanted to know. 'You're doing okay as far as I can see. What bad time?'

'Germanicus's fleet got caught by the low tides along the German coast. He lightened the ships by beaching two of his legions and ordering Vitellius to take them on by land. Trouble was, that meant crossing the mud flats. When the tide came in it was a shambles. A lot of the men were drowned before the fleet could pick them up again.'

'Uhuh.' I sipped my wine. If I was looking for a reason why Vitellius should betray Germanicus then I'd found it. Forget flash and histrionics, this was incompetence pure and simple. Generals've been wary of ocean tides since old Julius lost half his British fleet because he hadn't tied it up properly. That was seventy years ago, and there was no excuse nowadays for failing to take the local conditions into account. Two legions meant ten thousand men, plus the auxiliaries and baggage-handlers who would've contributed another couple of thousand at least; a major part of the Rhine force. Germanicus could've lost them all without a blow struck in anger, and through his own stupidity. Almost as bad as the Varus disaster in the Teutoburg. To a soldier like Vitellius a blunder like that would've been unforgivable . . .

Lippillus was getting to his feet. 'Corvinus, if you're going to drift off then I'll leave you to it, okay?'

'Hey, I'm sorry!' I brought my eyes back into focus. 'Sit down. There's still the best part of a jug here.'

'Yeah, I know. But I'm on duty, remember. I only called in while the boss is smarming his aunt, and if I report back legless he'll have my guts. Nice seeing you again, though.'

'Same here.' I stood up too. 'Thanks, Lippillus. You've been a great help.'

'Nothing. Sorry about leaving you with the wine. It's good stuff. Better than the Aventine gutrot Mother buys.'

'It's okay.' I made a mental note to send Bathyllus round to his flat with a jar or two. 'Hey. Come round for dinner tonight. We'll finish the jug properly.'

He hesitated. 'I'd like that. But Mother might be a problem.'

Jupiter! He didn't look like a mummy's boy to me, but then there might be family circumstances I didn't know about. Something like Perilla's, even. Still, I owed the guy far too much just to drop him. 'No hassle,' I said. 'Bring your mother with you.'

His face cleared. 'You sure?'

'Sure I'm sure.' I walked him to the gate in the wall. 'I'll even send a litter.'

'Okay. That would be great. Thanks.'

'You eat fish?'

'I eat anything. And so does Mother.'

'Good.' I opened the gate that gave out directly on to the street. 'See you later, then.'

When Lippillus had gone I settled down with my wine cup to think. So I'd been right, and Sejanus was behind this whole business: Tubero's involvement put that beyond doubt. The only question I still couldn't answer was why. Sure, he was following instructions and he had the Wart's backing, but what game was he playing for himself? Not power, that was sure. Sejanus was well enough connected through his mother's family, but he was still practically a nobody and he'd got as high as anyone outwith the imperial family itself could go. He was sole commander of the Praetorians, which was one of the empire's top jobs, and if the rumours in the Market Square were right he all but led the emperor by the nose already. And, as Cotta had said, he'd squirrelled a whole pack of his relatives into the government system. So power was out: he'd got it already, or as much as he could hope for. Money, too; that came naturally with power. Security? Tiberius was pretty constant in his likes and dislikes, and although they determined how he treated people he was fair, and he judged by the evidence. Despite his kinship with Germanicus the Wart hadn't liked the guy, and he positively loathed Agrippina. If either of them had tried to slag off Sejanus for some kind of double-dealing, real or imaginary, he'd've listened, sure, but he wouldn't've bent over backwards to believe them without firm proof. Unless, of course, that was it: Germanicus had had the proof, and he'd threatened to pull the carpet from under Sejanus while his own plots matured. And Regulus had somehow got hold of the secret. Whatever the hell it was.

I shook my head. No. As a theory it was too complicated, and I could never prove it anyway. Not now, not without a lot more digging, and after Tiberius's warning I couldn't risk that. I'd just have to wait and see if anything turned up. Or, of course, drop the whole thing down the nearest manhole and take up wood-turning . . .

Just then Perilla came out. She had my mother with her. Mother swept over in a cloud of perfume, kissed me, and planted a covered casserole on the table.

'Marcus, dear,' she said, 'I'm dreadfully sorry. We've been away and I've only just heard. How are you, darling?' I could see she'd noticed the wine. 'I've brought you some soup. Barley with rocket. Much better for you than that nonsense.'

Barley with rocket. Oh, hell. I tried a grin, but it didn't come off: mothers are all the same, and you never quite get rid of them.

Maybe Lippillus wasn't such a rarity after all.

42

Perilla was smiling all over her face – she has a sadistic streak a mile wide – but she didn't comment. Instead she said: 'Has Flavonius Lippillus gone, then, Marcus?'

'Yeah. I let him out the back. I think he had another monkey to deliver. Or maybe it was a tame snake this time. Anyway, he's coming to dinner tonight. With his mother.'

'Oh, really?' Nothing fazes Perilla. I could've said the guy was bringing six pigmy jugglers and a tame baboon and she would've said the same. I just hoped the baboon wasn't too near the truth, but from the sound of things it just might be. 'That's nice. I liked him.'

Bathyllus came out with an extra chair. Mother sat carefully and arranged her mantle in perfect folds. 'Perilla didn't explain what happened to you, Marcus,' she said. 'Not exactly. An accident with a kitchen knife, so I understand.'

'Uh, yeah.' Jupiter, I'd strangle that lady when I got her alone! Or maybe force-feed her the barley and rocket soup, which would come to the same thing. 'I was . . . uh . . . sharpening it.'

Mother stared at me. 'But what on earth were you doing that for, dear? I'm sure Meton is perfectly capable of sharpening a knife. Oh, Bathyllus.' The little guy was hovering. 'Yes. Some fruit juice, please. Apple, I think, with just a twist of wormwood.'

'And for me, Bathyllus,' Perilla said. She hadn't tried that one.

'Bring one for Marcus too.' Mother's voice was firm. 'And take that wine jug away.'

• David Wishart

Bathyllus gave me a look. I think one eyebrow was raised in sympathy but I wouldn't swear to it.

I sighed; I knew when I was beat. And I didn't actually have to drink the stuff, just glare at it until it went away. 'Okay, little guy. Do it. So, Mother, how are you?'

'*Terribly* well.' She looked it, but then she always did. 'We have a new chef who does things with colewort that you simply would not believe, Marcus.'

'Uh . . . yeah?' My stomach shifted. 'Is that right?'

'Titus is looking years younger.' She smoothed out a non-existent crease in the lambswool mantle. 'Acting it, too. We must have you both round to dinner again soon.'

'That would be lovely,' Perilla said brightly. 'As soon as Marcus is feeling better.'

I touched my ribs. 'Yeah. Give it a month or so, Mother, and we'll be back to normal.'

'Oh, it shouldn't take that long, dear! Unless there's something wrong with your diet. Send Meton round and we'll go through a few recipes together. Besides, I thought you said you had a friend coming round for dinner.'

'You mean Lippillus?' Jupiter! I didn't need this! 'Uh, Lippillus isn't a friend, Mother. At least not exactly a friend. He's . . . er . . . a doctor. He's coming round to check what I'm eating.'

'An animal doctor, presumably?'

'Sorry?'

'You said he was delivering a monkey, or possibly a snake. Delivering in the literal or the obstetrical sense? But I thought snakes laid eggs. Or is that crocodiles? Or perhaps they both do. Not the monkeys, of course, the other things. And why should he bring his mother with him?'

Shit! This was getting weird. Conversations with Mother in one of her freewheeling moods frequently did. The gods knew how Priscus survived them; they were probably the reason why he spent so much of his time grubbing around old Etruscan graveyards. 'Lippillus moonlights for his cousin,' I said firmly, trying not to look at Perilla. 'He runs an import agency. The monkey and the snake are customers' orders. And they're a very close family. So. What have you been up to?'

'Oh, nothing much,' Mother said. Bathyllus had arrived with

the wormwood twists and set them on the table. Mother picked hers up and sipped delicately; I had the distinct feeling from her expression that she knew damn well what was going on and the freewheeling was pure devilment. 'I'm trying to persuade Titus to take me to Baiae this summer, but I'm not having much luck. He wants us to go tomb-hunting around Lake Clusinus again, and it's so boring you wouldn't believe.'

'Why not go to Baiae by yourself?' Perilla suggested.

Mother looked at her wide-eyed. 'Oh, but I couldn't do that, my dear! Not for all summer. We may compromise, July and August tomb-bashing, September in Campania. Titus has a weakness for crayfish that I can exploit, and of course after that terrible business with the runaway column Lucia Philippa won't be needing her villa this year. Probably never again, for that matter, poor girl. But then perhaps Baiae wouldn't be the best choice either. It's bound to be more crowded than usual with the young Imperials being there. Bauli would be better. The problem is that I don't know anyone with a villa.'

'Which young Imperials?' Perilla sipped her own drink. I tried not to look.

Mother stared at her blankly, then shook her head. 'Oh, of course. You wouldn't know. You and Marcus were in Syria when the engagements were announced. Germanicus's eldest Nero and Drusus's daughter Livia. A lovely couple. Such a shame about the others, even although it was a mismatch from the beginning.'

'The others?'

'Poor mad Claudius's son and Sejanus's Aelia.'

I'd been wool-gathering, staring at a bee climbing the boxwood hedge. Now my head jerked round.

'*What?*'

'Marcus, dear, don't do that! You startled me.'

I'd done nothing of the kind. Not even Etna erupting six feet from her ear would startle my mother. 'Sorry. Uh, could you run that last bit past me again?'

'I was simply saying that the Drusus–Aelia match was a mistake, darling. Why don't you listen properly the first time?'

'You mean Sejanus's daughter's engaged to Claudius's son

Drusus? Claudius as in Claudius Caesar? The emperor's nephew?'

'Really, Marcus.' A sigh. 'I'm sorry but you are your own worst enemy. You simply will not listen. There *was* an engagement, dear, at the same time as Livia's and young Nero's. But the marriage won't take place for the simple reason that the poor boy is dead.'

I was staring at her. 'We're still talking about an Imperial, right? Engaged to Sejanus's daughter?' Jupiter! 'How did he die?'

'He choked on a pear, a few days after the ceremony. A pity for the boy, naturally, and for Aelia, of course, but politically . . .' She paused. 'Well, perhaps it was for the best.'

Perhaps it was for the best. Sure it was, but even so Fate had been given a little nudge along the way and I could bet whose elbow had done it. Brain churning, I picked up my cup and took a swallow . . .

Shit! The wormwood! Too late, and Bathyllus had taken away the wine jug!

'Marcus, will you stop making faces, please,' Perilla said. 'It's not as bad as all that.'

'It's worse, lady!'

'Then why did you drink it?'

I looked over at Mother. She was grinning. Freewheeling featherbrain, nothing. That was some clever cookie. She beats me every time.

So. Claudius's son and Sejanus's daughter. An alliance with the imperial family. That was it, the last piece. That was what Sejanus was angling for. It was power after all; not that there was a lot I could do about it. Face it, sunshine, I thought. There's nothing you can do. Nothing at all.

Except maybe have another word with Livia.

Lippillus came round to dinner that evening. I hardly recognised him, not because he still looked like a fresh-faced kid – I'd expected that – but because he was wearing a crisp new mantle instead of his usual grimy tunic. But the real surprise was our other guest. She was a real honey, dark-eyed and golden-skinned, probably African. And no more than twenty-five.

Lippillus was grinning at me. Probably because I was trying to lift my chin off the floor.

'Corvinus. Lady Perilla,' he said. 'This is Mother. Stepmother, rather. I'm sorry. Maybe I should've told you.'

Yeah, well, some guys have all the luck. I'd bet, though, that the bastard had strung me along on purpose.

43 ∫

Two days later, I was back in the palace. The appointment had been easy to arrange, suspiciously easy in fact; it was almost as though the old witch had been waiting for me to make it. Hermes the ape was wearing a new outfit, and he smelled of lilies. Maybe one of his bosses with sensitive nostrils had taken him in hand. Or maybe he was in love. In that case I just didn't want to know.

'Ah, Hermes.' The guy with the yellow tunic looked up when we arrived and gave us his full spread of teeth. 'Don't tell me. Valerius Curtinus to see Her Excellency. He's to go straight in.'

'That's Corvinus, you bastard. As if you didn't know.' I walked up to the double doors. 'Catch you later, Hermes. Enjoy your fruit.'

The ape shambled off with a parting grunt. I knocked and went in.

Camphor. I was getting used to the smell by now. The Egyptian chair was still there too, but no portable altar; I was expected to take her word for things this time, seemingly. Or not.

Livia looked even frailer than she had four months ago. I wondered how long she'd got left.

'Sit down, Valerius Corvinus,' she said. I sat; the Egyptian chair creaked. 'So. You've completed your investigations. Your conclusion?'

'Aelius Sejanus is plotting to be the next emperor, Excellency. Legitimately. If that isn't the wrong word.'

Her eyes narrowed, but I got the impression that I'd pleasantly surprised her. 'That wasn't your brief, young man,' she said. 'I commissioned you to find out who killed my grandson Germanicus.'

'Then the answer's the same. Aelius Sejanus, with your son's connivance and consent. But of course you knew that when you called me in in the first place.'

'Did I really?' The ghost of a smile. 'Now why should I ask you to tell me something I already know?'

'Because you wanted me to find out the whole thing for myself, Excellency, not just be handed it on a plate, because that way I might not have believed you.'

'Again, why should I do that?'

'So that someone who'd outlive you would know the truth, and remember it when you were gone.'

'Ah.' She was definitely smiling now: an odd smile, the kind you see on the faces of the old Etruscans lying on top of their tombs. 'I thought you were clever, Corvinus. I'm glad not to be disappointed.'

'Then I'm right?'

'Perhaps. Explain further, please.'

'About Sejanus? Or about Germanicus?'

'But you said they were the same thing.'

I shifted my weight; the wood and ivory struts of the chair creaked like old bones rubbing together.

'Germanicus was preparing treason,' I said. 'Him and Agrippina. Or the other way round, rather, because Agrippina was the driving force. Only neither of them would've used that word. Agrippina was righting what she considered to be a family wrong, while your idealistic grandson saw himself as heir to Mark Antony, championing the cause of civilisation against Tiberius's pedestrian Octavian; a more successful Antony, because he had the west in his pocket as well as the east.'

'Indeed? Go on.'

'He was almost ready to make his move. The Rhine legions were with him, maybe the Pannonian ones. He had the potential support of the Greek client-kingdoms and potential control of the Egyptian corn supply. Most important of all, he was the darling of Rome and Italy. In other words he had everything but Spain, Gaul and the African coast. And Syria. He needed Syria and its four legions to close the gap.'

'I'm impressed, Corvinus. Carry on, please.'

'The problem was that the emperor knew what the guy was up to all along; maybe he'd been suspicious ever since the Rhine mutiny when Germanicus had fouled things up for him personally while coming up smelling of roses himself. He couldn't take direct action, because Germanicus was too popular, but he could and did set a honey trap. He sent him east with full powers of deputy and sat back to see what would happen. Only he didn't just sit back, he appointed Calpurnius Piso as the Syrian governor, with secret instructions to keep his eyes open and report any signs of active or potential treason. And he passed over the conduct of the war against his son – we'll call it a war, because that's what it was – to the person most capable of dealing with it, Aelius Sejanus. Sejanus was given a free hand to do whatever was necessary to preserve the security of the empire. And of its current emperor.'

'And of its current emperor. Indeed.' Livia's mouth twisted. '"Let the consuls see to it that no harm befall the state."' The wording of the Senate's traditional Emergency Decree. 'Only for consuls read Sejanus. Very good, young man. Almost full marks, in fact.'

'Almost?'

She frowned. 'I'm afraid you rather underestimate Sejanus. He is not a man to – how shall I put it? – to wait for events to dictate his actions.'

Uhuh. Right. I hadn't thought of that angle, but it fitted. 'You mean Sejanus actively helped Germanicus's plot along? Gave the guy the occasional nudge in the right direction to make sure he stepped out of line?'

'I didn't say that.'

'No, but it's what you meant, Excellency. Publius Vitellius was Sejanus's agent. He was on Germanicus's staff, he was involved in the plot, and he would've offered advice and suggestions. Yeah. I should've spotted that.'

'Never mind.' The smile again. 'You've really done remarkably well otherwise. Remarkably well.'

'So.' I leaned back and the old bones whispered. 'Sejanus through his agent Vitellius has Germanicus poisoned. Up to now he's been following instructions, more or less, but from

here on in he starts playing his own game in tandem. Piso plays
into his hands, or maybe someone – Domitius Celer, say – gives
him one of Sejanus's nudges. Whatever the reason, relying on
his secret deal Piso tries to retake the province by force. The
guy's within his rights, because Germanicus is a traitor and most
of his senior staff are in on the scam. Only Piso's misread the
situation completely: Germanicus's treason is the one thing that
Tiberius can never admit publicly. Because no one would ever
believe him.'

Livia nodded. 'Unfortunate but true. My son has always had
a problem relating to people. Even – or especially – when he is
telling them the truth.'

I couldn't detect any sign of regret in her voice, despite the
words she'd used; but maybe that was just me. I suspect Livia
and Tiberius had never really liked each other, even in the
good days.

'Right,' I said. 'So now I'm guessing. Sejanus does his snake-
in-the-grass act. He begins to encourage the rumours that you
and the emperor were behind the death and that Germanicus
was sent east especially to make it easier to arrange. At the
same time he advises Tiberius to take a tough line with popular
feeling for Agrippina: her husband was a traitor, why should he
go through the hypocrisy of burying him like a hero? He sends a
company of Praetorians to escort the funeral party to Rome, but
he makes sure they give the impression of being there for crowd
control rather than to honour the guy's ashes. Little touches,
little nudges, but Rome and Italy are ready for them because
the emperor's not popular and Germanicus and Agrippina are.
The result is that by the time Piso gets back nine-tenths of Rome
believes that he and Plancina poisoned the blue-eyed boy on
Tiberius's instructions and they're howling for blood; Sejanus's
intention being, of course, to weaken the emperor's street cred
still further and so make him even more reliant on himself as
his one and only friend against the world. This is going to be
important later.' I paused. 'How am I doing, Excellency?'

'Remarkably well, Corvinus. I told you.'

'Good. So now we come to the trial, which Tiberius and
Sejanus have rigged together. Sejanus acts – or rather he says
he acts – as the emperor's go-between with Piso. Through

Fulcinius Trio he holds out the promise of a pardon to keep Piso's mouth shut.'

'Actually, that was my son's idea, Corvinus. Although you're right about Trio. Piso knew he was working with Sejanus, of course. And that Sejanus was my son's agent. What he didn't know was that the former was the predominant factor.'

'Uhuh. Anyway, Piso gets nervous. He decides he doesn't trust the emperor after all. He writes a letter to his lawyers giving the details of the deal and of Germanicus's treason, and he gives it to his freedman Carillus. Only Carillus is working for Trio, and he passes him the letter. Trio sees that Piso's on the verge of spilling the beans, and on Sejanus's instructions he has Carillus kill him, in a way that sheds more suspicion on the emperor.' I frowned. 'Lady, that's one thing I'm not clear on. Was it suicide – assisted suicide – or murder?'

'It was murder, young man. Quite definitely.'

'Yeah, but what about the suicide note Piso left? That sounded genuine as hell.'

'The note was forged. You don't believe me? It's true, I assure you.' I still must've looked pretty dubious because she smiled. 'A short digression, then, by way of proof. After Piso's "suicide" our obsequious Senate decreed that the imperial family, including myself, should be thanked for avenging Germanicus's death. This despite the fact that nine-tenths of them thought we had ordered it in the first place; but that, I'm afraid, is the natural stuff of politics. My grandson Claudius was omitted, for the excellent reason that he is mentally incapable of any coherent course of thought or action whatsoever. Sejanus, however, already had designs on him as his most likely link with our family and so to gain his goodwill arranged for the mistake to be rectified. He approached one of the "independent" senators with whom he already had secret dealings and had him make the relevant proposal on his behalf. I wonder if you know who that senator was?'

'You've got me there, lady.'

'Your friend Nonius Asprenas.' She smiled again. 'You remember him, Corvinus, don't you?'

I sat back. Sure, I remembered Asprenas. I wasn't likely to forget that bastard. And I knew now what Livia was driving at.

44 ∫

She'd surprised me, even so. It'd never crossed my mind that Asprenas might be involved with Sejanus, crook though he undoubtedly was, even although the Libo case had suggested that forgery was a distinct possibility. So now the guy was freelancing. Or maybe just riding on what he hoped was the next emperor's coat tails. That was good to know. 'You're sure, Excellency?' I said.

'I'm sure. And if Asprenas's fake suicide letter fooled you, then it must have been good. Very good indeed.'

'Gee thanks.' I couldn't help grinning.

'I mean it. But as I said that was a digression. Go on, young man.'

I'd noticed a tray of wine cups and a jug on a side table. It wasn't exactly etiquette, sure, but after all the old harpy had put me through these last few months I reckoned I deserved the right to a liberty or two. Besides, we were practically old friends by now. Or whatever. 'You mind if I have a cup of wine while I talk, Excellency?' I said. 'It greases the rollers.'

She smiled slightly. 'Ah, yes. I'd forgotten. It's only there for show. Help yourself, but none for me, I'm afraid. Doctor's orders.'

'Yeah. I know the feeling.' I got up and poured.

'Take the jug with you,' she said.

I sat down again in the chair and took a sip. Jupiter Best and Greatest! The wine was genuine five-star Caecuban, rich and smooth as velvet; probably, from the way it kissed the tongue, laid down when the Divine Augustus was plain ordinary Octavian and Actium was just a lump of rock sticking out from the Greek coast. Liquid poetry. It almost made coming to the palace worth the pain and anguish.

'Okay.' I held the cup carefully: this stuff you didn't even *shake* if you could help it. 'So Piso is out of the picture. Plancina too. That was a nice stroke of Sejanus's, because by getting the emperor to beg her off the charge he increased the suspicion that she'd been the one actually to arrange the poisoning.'

'Plancina was unfortunate,' Livia agreed. 'However, I had very little choice. I knew, of course, that in protecting her I was helping Sejanus, but she did have certain claims on me as a friend. And after all she was innocent. I saw no reason why she should die for nothing.'

'Very laudable, Excellency.'

She stiffened. 'Corvinus, I have never killed for no purpose, or for private gain. You should know that better than anyone. Nor has the emperor. Piso's death was a political necessity, but it would have been both criminal and immoral to extend punishment gratuitously to the other members of his family.'

'Hence the pardon for his son. Yeah, okay, I can see that. I'm sorry.' I was: sure, Livia might be a murderess ten times over but she had her own code of values. It wasn't fair to judge her by normal standards. 'So. Let's get back to Sejanus. He's got the emperor where he wants him. Sure, the empire's safe: Germanicus is dead, Agrippina's checkmated, the plot's cold. Only at a price, and that's been largely Sejanus's doing. Tiberius has come out of this thing smelling higher than a Raetan cheese in midsummer, he's in hock to his right-hand man and being Tiberius he takes it hard. Nobody likes him, everybody hates him. The only friend he's got left in the world is Sejanus. Am I right?'

Livia said nothing. She was doing her dead Etruscan act again. I went on.

'So. Sejanus begins to worm his way further in. The only wrinkle is a guy called Regulus, who's been in on the scam and knows Sejanus has been two-timing. He tries a bit of blackmail, which is stupid but then I suspect Regulus thought more of himself than was healthy. Naturally Sejanus has him chopped.' I took a sip of the Caecuban. Nectar! 'Sejanus has just about everything he needs, as much as a commoner can decently ask for. There's only one way now he can go, but he's created a situation where even that's possible. Tiberius owes him. He owes him a lot and, like I said, he's clinging on to him like he was a life raft. So Sejanus starts badgering. He's the partner of the old guy's labours, he's sweating his guts out for Rome just as much as Tiberius is. Why shouldn't he get his just recognition? Meaning, of course, a marriage alliance through his daughter with the imperial family. It's only Claudius's son, after all. No great deal, the guy's been kept under wraps for years. And Tiberius agrees.'

'Yes,' Livia said softly. 'My son agreed. It was silly of him. Very silly.'

'Only luckily' – I picked up the jug and casually refilled my cup, although it didn't need it – 'the marriage didn't come off. The poor kid died just after the engagement. An accident. He choked on a pear.'

'He choked' – the empress's voice was still soft – 'on a pear.'

I set the jug down. This time I looked at her directly. 'And he did it for the good of Rome. Right, Excellency?'

'For the good, as you say, of Rome.' Her chin came up. 'If it helps, Claudius's son Drusus always was a very disagreeable child.'

'Yeah.' I took a mouthful of wine, held it and swallowed. 'Yeah, well. So. End of Drusus, end of marriage hopes, end of story. At least as far as I know. But where does that leave us?'

'It leaves us with Sejanus. Still. That's a pity, but then it can't be helped.'

'Can't it?' I was still looking her in the eye.

She smiled and ducked her head. 'Unfortunately not. Corvinus, I am in my eightieth year. I can't expect to live much longer and I don't particularly want to. My son and I are for all practical purposes estranged, certainly I have no influence over him now except what a little . . . shared guilt can give. Sejanus is young, able, unscrupulous and extremely clever. Perhaps, and this is my one hope, too clever for his own good. Time will tell, but time is something I do not have very much of.' She paused. 'Nor, for that matter, does the emperor, who is no spring chicken himself and may not survive me by much in any case.'

I shifted in my chair. 'What you're saying, lady, is that Sejanus has got you beat. You may've won one battle but you'll lose the war.'

'Exactly. And that state of affairs is neither one that I am used to nor can I bring myself to tolerate it.'

'Hence me?'

'Hence' – she smiled again – 'you. Oh, there's nothing you can do immediately, and you'd be a fool to try. I know about my son's silly warning, and I also know that Sejanus will go from strength to strength because he's the only person now whom poor Tiberius trusts. As you said at the beginning, his eventual succession to the purple will be . . . legitimate. Soon he'll be emperor in all but name, and finally the name will come too.'

'So where do I come in?' Shit, this was depressing as hell. Worrying, too. I couldn't think of a worse fate for Rome than to have Sejanus emperor after the Wart.

'As I said, Corvinus, my one hope is that before my son dies Sejanus will become too self-confident and overreach himself so badly that even Tiberius will recognise him for what he is. I want someone to be there when that happens, and who is equipped to go to the emperor and present him with categorical proofs which he will have to accept. I've given you' – her mouth twisted – 'a small start with Germanicus. As you can appreciate.'

'And if Tiberius doesn't accept these categorical proofs of yours? Or if they aren't good enough?'

'Then you're dead, young man.'

'Hey, thanks, lady!'

She laughed: the sound like the dry rustle of winter leaves in a graveyard. 'You're a gambler, Corvinus. So am I. The difference is that I bet only on certainties. And I'm betting now on you. Tiberius may be a difficult person to convince, but his mind isn't completely closed. He is fair, even harshly fair, to himself as much as to others. Above all he feels he has a duty to Rome, however much she rejects him. If you can show him that Sejanus is a threat to the state then my son will squash him like a cockroach.'

'Unless by then the cockroach is powerful enough to do the squashing himself.'

'There is that danger, yes.' She nodded. 'But remember, the

emperor's no one's fool. He may raise Sejanus up, but it will be on his own terms and subject to his own safeguards. And if Sejanus doesn't realise that then he's the fool, not Tiberius.'

'Okay.' I set the wine cup down on the floor beside me. 'So that's the future taken care of. What about the present?'

'I told you. There isn't anything either of us can do about that. Forget it. For the moment.'

'That wasn't exactly what I had in mind, lady. Sejanus must be aware that I've been raking through the laundry basket and I've come up with a dirty set of smalls. What's to stop the guy sending me the same way as Carillus, down the Tiber with a knife in my back? Or maybe doing things more genteelly with a trumped-up treason rap?'

'Nothing. Nothing at all. It's a risk that both of us take.'

'Hey, that makes me feel a lot better.' I picked up the wine cup again and took a good swallow. 'And I like the *both*.'

Livia sighed. 'Corvinus, I told you. I bet on certainties. You're quite safe from Sejanus. At least if you keep out of his laundry basket from now on.'

'Is that right? And what makes you so sure, Excellency?'

'Because you don't matter,' she said gently. 'You're like my grandson Claudius, a useless, divine idiot who will never in a million years amount to anything.'

I stared at her with my jaw hanging. Jupiter! Not even my father had ever called me that! 'Hey, thanks, Excellency,' I said at last. 'Thanks a bunch.'

The tone didn't faze her. 'Oh, dear,' she said. 'Now I've insulted you, and I'm sorry. But I'm telling you how you appear to Sejanus, which is the important thing. You're not political, Corvinus, you pose no threat in yourself. You're not even especially rich. In fact, you're beneath his notice altogether, and killing you wouldn't be worth either the trouble or the risk. Stay as you are – and especially keep away from dirty laundry – and you'll stay alive.'

'Until the next time.'

'Until the next time. But then you'll have to choose your moment. You'll have to choose it very carefully indeed, because you won't have a second chance and I very much doubt if I'll be around to help you. I can do no more than wish you luck.'

There wasn't anything else to say. I stood up, drained the wine cup – even the Caecuban tasted sour – and set it on the desk. She could clear up after me for a change.

'Oh, and young man?'

I turned, on my way to the door. I felt used, like a pair of second-hand sandals. Worse, the bitch would still be using me long after she was dead.

'Yeah?' I said.

'Thank you. Thank you very much. In case we don't see each other again.'

I left without replying. Divine idiot. That had really hurt. Especially since it put me on a par with Claudius.

The lily-smelling Hermes was waiting to escort me back to the exit. Maybe I'd gone up a little in the world since my last visit, but I doubted it: the guy was probably going that way anyway. The street outside the palace gates was cold, despite the sunshine. I wrapped my cloak round me and set off for home.

Ah, well. At least this time I was ahead a cup of Caecuban.